Liberating Sky

Susan Spence

Liberating Sky

ISBN: 978-0-9851279-5-4

This book is also available as an ebook.

For my mom, Ellie Spence

Also by this author:

A Story of the West

Chapter 1

Light rain splattered the windshield in an uncertain rhythm, the drops becoming larger and more forceful as I drove into the storm. Within moments, the highway disappeared under a sheet of water and I could no longer see through the downpour. I pulled off onto a patch of dirt and waited, my journey delayed, as the rain pounded my car and water streamed across the windshield.

Unable to focus my attention on driving, it became an opportunity for contemplation, but I resisted. Instead, I fidgeted, searching for a distraction. I tried to keep my mind away from my mission because that was exactly what I didn't want, to sit and think about what I was doing. I opened the window slightly to stop the windshield from fogging and a huge drop of water blasted through and cracked my left ear. As I wiped the side of my face on my sleeve, my stomach provided a diversion. It grumbled with hunger. I wished I had thought of packing some food to eat on the road.

I glanced down at the gas gauge. It showed three quarters full and I intended to ignore my stomach and drive until the gas tank needed refilling. I picked up the map lying on the seat next to me. It didn't take much studying to realize that filling the tank and my stomach would both happen at the next distant town along this lonely stretch of road.

Once the cloudburst passed, continuing east, the road reappeared, running with water. Impatiently, I punched the gas pedal. Fresh mud sprayed out behind the rear tires and clumps thudded against the fenders as I spun back out onto the highway. Dark clouds continued to cover the sky and the tops of the surrounding hills. The Nevada desert I drove through showed the effects of the spring moisture by the sparse green covering the ground. I couldn't help but think how lucky I was, not having to run cattle in country with so little vegetation. Fortunately, I was just passing through.

My destination was Berkeley, California, a city I was only vaguely aware of. I had searched through maps at a filling station to find one of California and Nevada before I could figure out how to drive there. It was a little intimidating since I had spent little time in large cities, and never alone. All I had was an address torn from an envelope. The letter it originally contained hadn't been addressed to me, but that didn't stop me from taking off on what some probably considered a complete lack of sense on my part.

My family hadn't actually said much when I announced my intention, but I remembered the arched eyebrows. Imagined or not, I read relief on my mother's face. I wasn't planning on being gone long, as there was still a lot of work to be done at home that summer. My journey was part of my plan for the future.

Since I pulled off only long enough to sleep for a couple of hours when it became difficult to keep my eyes open, I made it to the coastal city in a couple of days. Berkeley was much bigger than I could have imagined and finding the address became complicated.

As I tried to make sense of the city streets, I couldn't help but stare at what I saw. With each passing block, I felt more uncomfortable and out of place, a real country bumpkin ogling the freaks. And there were a lot of them filling the streets, strange-looking people around my own age, dressed in colorful, and to me, odd-looking clothing. The few things I knew about hippies was what I'd heard, mainly that they crapped in their own yards and that they didn't wash. What I saw on the streets of Berkeley that June in 1968 were people who I would have sworn were living in a foreign country. I found myself in the midst of a bizarre freak show that I had only seen pictures of.

At least they spoke English. After asking for directions a third time, I finally pulled up to a large, blue Victorian on a quiet street. The paint peeling and overgrown yard matched others in the neighborhood.

I eased out of my car and tested my right ankle by moving it up and down a few times before attempting to put weight on it. A few days earlier I had landed awkwardly and twisted it when a horse I was riding dumped me. I felt nervous as I hobbled down the sidewalk and approached the steps. My ankle slowly loosened with each stride and I did my best to conceal the limp.

Spraining my ankle had settled the debate going on in my mind about whether or not to make this trip. Months before graduating from high school, I had started calculating. Driving to California hadn't been part of my original plan, but had lately become necessary for its success. I don't know if I would have had the guts to act on this latest glitch, but after the injury, there was no longer an excuse not to, since the alternative was to be trapped on the couch listening to my mother complain as I healed.

The front door of the Victorian stood open and rock music blasted from inside. Once I reached the porch, I peered inside, but saw no one, just a sticker across the door that read, *Make Love Not War*. My hesitant rapping on the door frame was covered up by a screaming electric guitar and pounding drums. I stood there for a few moments, fighting my apprehension. The guitar fell silent as the song ended. I knocked again, and this time, the loud rapping startled me.

After a moment I heard the faint slap of footsteps. I stared hopefully into the dim interior of the house, but was disappointed when, instead of a familiar face, a scrawny, pasty-faced guy came to the door. Our eyes met at the same level as he was barely taller than me. He smiled and studied my face for a long second. It was one of those looks that, even though brief, made me feel like I revealed more of myself to him than I intended. A ragged beard covered the lower half of his face. That, and his disheveled look, made me feel automatic disdain for him, even though his brown eyes were friendly.

"C'mon in." He tucked a tendril of loose hair behind his ear, raising his voice to be heard over the next song that blasted from the stereo. I followed him through the living room, past the booming speakers and back to the kitchen. My focus was on his bare feet and the pony tail that hung down his back.

"I'm Will. This is April and Fern." He stopped facing the table, where two girls sat. "Have a seat." Thankfully, the music wasn't nearly as loud back there.

"My name is Sky." I ignored the chair and tried not to stare, but it was hard. It was the first time I had seen anyone dressed in garish, hippy garb up close. The three of them smiled at me. Obviously there was nothing odd to them about a stranger showing up on their doorstep.

"That's a far out name… Sky." The girl named April spoke my name slowly, as if contemplating the meaning. The embroidered top and multi-colored print skirt she wore provided most of the color in the drab room. I decided to set her straight.

"It's short for Skylark."

"What's that?"

I shrugged my shoulders. "I'm not sure." The truth was, I don't know what my parents were thinking when they named me. And I had a hard time believing my father had agreed to such a curious label for his first born. But shortened, it fit me just fine.

They continued staring at me. I guess to them, I was the freak.

"Want some banana bread?" Will asked. I had first smelled and then spotted the half-eaten loaf, sitting on the worn, wooden table top. It had the slightly mangled look that came from being cut into before it had time to cool.

"Uh, sure." I accepted his hospitality. It would take a lot more than feeling out of place for me to turn down food. He sawed off a thick slice.

"Here."

"Thanks." The gesture made me feel more at ease and I dropped into the chair, much to the relief of my throbbing ankle. Although their nonchalance at sharing banana bread with a stranger helped me relax, I found it odd.

"This is good," I added and bit off another mouthful.

"Yeah, Will's a good cook," April chimed in. He took the compliment like his accomplishment was no big deal.

As the four of us sat around the table enjoying the snack, I was relieved that no one asked about why I was there and I desperately hoped the person I was looking for would suddenly appear.

"So, what's up?" Finally Fern thought to ask me the reason I had shown up at their door. I swallowed the last bite of bread and answered.

"I'm looking for Billy Marsh." I licked my fingertips before wiping my hands on my Levi's.

"Who?"

"I got this address from his mother. It was on a letter he sent her." Their quizzical looks caused me to squirm. "He came here from Montana last fall."

"Oh, Montana," Fern nodded. "Yeah, I remember. He gave me and my friend, Louann, a ride. Remember?" The other two nodded.

"Our car broke down and we ended up having to hitch. There's a lot of rednecks up that way." She looked at me as if to determine if I fit that category of humans. "Montana came by in his pickup, and drove us all the way out here. He even paid for gas."

I remembered the talk it created back home when Billy befriended the two women. They left the car sitting on the edge of the highway where it had died. I was pretty sure the abandoned auto still sat in the impound lot where it had been towed.

Billy's mother said he showed up at the family ranch long enough to grab a few things and to say he wouldn't be home for supper. That was the last they saw of him. Except for one letter to his mother, nobody had heard from him, including me.

That may have seemed strange since I was in love with him and considered him my boyfriend. But the fact that he had fled Montana wasn't about to deter me from The Plan. I just knew if I could convince him to come home, everything would be all right.

Fern expanded her story. "We were shit out of luck in the middle of nowhere." She shook her head. "Man, it was tense."

I imagined pickups with hard faced farmers and ranchers, glaring out from underneath their western hats. They would have grumbled something about the state of youth in this country while stomping on the gas pedal and speeding past. Most would have never even considered stopping to help the stranded hippies alongside the road. But Billy wasn't like that.

Fern continued. "We were trying to keep a good vibe, and along comes Montana. Our knight in shining armor." She gave an affectionate chuckle as she finished the story.

I felt a twinge of jealousy. "Where is he now? Does he live here?"

This time April answered. "I don't think Montana lives anywhere. He crashed here for a while, but he's into cruising."

I didn't know what she meant. "Do you know where he is?"

"We can probably find him," Will said. His voice sounded reassuring.

"Yeah, I think he's still around." April agreed.

After realizing it wasn't likely I was going to find him that day, I suddenly felt tired. I looked around and briefly wished I was back home where, even if life wasn't great, at least it was familiar. My trip had been hatched and acted on out of desperation because I didn't know what else to do. I had driven a long distance, so there was no way I could give up on my mission so quickly.

I had overlooked this aspect, figuring I would swoop in, grab Billy and leave. Now it seemed I might be staying a while. I never considered informing my family that I might be away longer than I had planned since I had been vague anyway and I doubted they cared how long I stayed. Meanwhile I began feeling even more self-conscious.

Once again I didn't fit in, not only my background, but also my appearance. My brown hair was cut short and I had noticed that California seemed to be short on barbers. My clothing didn't fit either, jeans and a long-sleeved, button down shirt. It was, with the exception of the sneakers on my feet, what I generally wore at home. I opted for sneakers over boots because of my sore ankle. Oh, I was self-conscious all right.

"Shit! I'm late." It was Fern who made the announcement.

"You work today?" April asked. "What time?"

"Ten. What time is it?" She still didn't leave her chair. I knew it was already past noon. Hippies were irresponsible. I also knew that about them. "Can you give me a ride?" She asked April.

"Space case," Will chuckled as the pair disappeared down the hallway. "So…" He looked back at me. "I have to go see a guy." He sounded slightly apologetic. "You can hang out here, if you want."

I took a better look around the kitchen. It was as sparsely furnished, as the living room had been. I couldn't imagine how sitting here all alone would help me find Billy.

"Why don't you come with me? It's a cool drive." He must have seen my look of disappointment.

"Okay, I guess I haven't done enough driving." I made no attempt at hiding my contempt for him and his friends with my sarcastic reply.

Back outside I felt better, but then I always felt better outdoors. I looked up into the trees, wondering what kind they were. Way beyond the tops, the breeze blew large fluffy clouds across the sky. Will and I climbed into a banged up, orange Volkswagen Beetle that was parked in the driveway.

"Come on, baby," he coaxed as he turned the key in the ignition. It took a few tries, and just before the battery ran out of juice, the engine sputtered to life. The vehicle seemed to give a slight jump with the effort. It continued vibrating as he forced the grinding gear-stick into reverse.

The bug chugged down the quiet avenue and we turned onto a busier street. After a few minutes we came to a highway. Will turned onto it, heading north.

"Where are we going?"

"Olompali."

"What's that?" Between the noise coming from the rear of the car and the wind blowing through the open windows, I had to shout. A new muffler wasn't the least of what the car needed, but it would have helped.

Will threw a quick glance my way. "It's a commune. I'm doing a story on organic gardening and I know a guy up there who grows vegetables."

I wasn't sure what a commune was, and had never heard of organic gardening, so I just nodded and turned to look out the side window, hiding my ignorance. It was too loud to hold a conversation anyway.

After crossing the bay on a bridge, that Will shouted to me, was over five miles long, we drove through a forested area and pulled up in front of a large, white house. I got out and looked around.

There seemed to be a lot of people just standing or sitting around. The only ones moving were children, and there seemed to be a lot of them, running naked and screaming as they played, with no supervision that I could see. I was shocked to see that quite a few of the adults were also buck naked. For a moment I wondered what I had gotten myself into, and not knowing where else to look, I glanced over at Will. The bare bodies didn't seem to bother him, but his expression showed puzzlement as he took in the scene.

"Over here." Notebook in hand, he started towards a sizeable vegetable garden. A tall, lanky man straightened up from where he'd been tending a row of plants. His face lit up into a broad smile as Will and I approached.

The man's jeans and shirt were old and faded, and covered with dirt. Uncombed hair hung in tangles around his face. To me he looked like a bum. But his appearance didn't faze Will.

"Hey, Will." The two of them hugged one another. I had never seen one guy hug another and decided it was one of the weirdest things I had ever witnessed.

"How's it going, Eric? This is Sky," he indicated me.

"Welcome to the Ranch, Sky." His warm smile never diminished.

"Yeah, nice to meet you," I answered, feeling so out of my element. I mean, I only occasionally saw anyone naked, and that was usually accidently. And to call the place a ranch. These people obviously didn't know much.

I looked at Will. He was studying his friend's face, so I did the same. Eric's smile had faded, replaced by a frown at some commotion behind me. I had positioned myself so the crowd was behind me and resisted turning to look.

"What's going on here?" Will asked.

Eric looked around at the milling people before answering. "Man, it's really changed since they started letting anyone in."

Will nodded. "Yeah, the vibe is way different." He also studied the spectacle.

"It's turned into a freak show. They cruise up from the city just to check out the naked chicks." Eric turned his attention back to the vegetables.

"The garden looks far out. It looks like you must be feeding quite a few people."

Eric's smile returned as the two of them focused on the cultivated plants at our feet. Will pulled a pen from his back pocket and opened his spiral notebook. He took notes as Eric discussed the growing practices he utilized. I stood there, still in disbelief at what I had gotten myself into.

Will continued asking questions, and since I had nothing better to do, I followed the conversation in silence. What I quickly realized was that Eric, despite his appearance, seemed quite intelligent as he articulated his responses. He spoke with passion about growing food to feed the inhabitants of the commune and I couldn't help but wonder why he obviously cared so little about his appearance. I imagined him sleeping in the dirt amongst the meticulously cared for vegetables and suppressed a smile at the thought.

He steered us to various spots and pointed out the different vegetables, while explaining the different needs of each variety. Most of them were unfamiliar to me, as in our household, vegetables were common ones that came from cans. For years I had obediently forced myself to eat the soggy and tasteless mounds on my plate just to avoid trouble.

Eric talked on and I became bored and frustrated. I glanced over at the loitering hippies. One thing I knew for sure. Billy would never be at a place like this. My visit to the commune was a waste of time.

Suddenly an arriving car backfired, a loud, startling bang. The three of us quickly turned in the direction of the noise to view the beater as it came to a stop nearby.

Eric was actually cringing, his face suddenly drained of color. I saw his hands shake as he pushed them deep into his pockets. He quickly turned and walked away.

"What's the matter with him?" I asked Will as we watched his retreating back.

"He just came back from Viet Nam." His voice sounded sad, and as if that was explanation enough.

I continued watching Eric walk away. He didn't look injured, at least not that I could tell. I turned back to Will with a puzzled look.

"He's messed up."

"What do you mean?"

"Something bad happened to him over there. Believe me, he's not the same guy he was before the army got a hold of him. He won't even talk about it."

I was still confused. "He seems to me to be one of the lucky ones. I mean, he made it back in one piece didn't he?"

Will shook his head. "He's broken in a lot worse ways." He looked at me. "You saw him." It seemed to be some sort of a challenge, but I didn't reply. The question that popped into my head was whether Will was a draft dodger.

The sun had sunk below the horizon a half hour ago. I noticed dishes of food being brought out from inside the house. People gravitated towards a long table and a young woman lit candles that had been placed amongst the bowls of food.

"Shouldn't we be going?" I was still feeling out of place.

"Aren't you hungry?"

"Yeah, but..."

"Well come on then." He led me over to the table where I took a bowl and hesitantly filled it with scoops of strange looking food from an odd assortment of serving dishes. Since I was used to eating at least three good-sized meals a day, I was starving. The problem was, I had no idea what most of the food was. There was no meat that I could see. The only thing I recognized for sure was rice, but it was mixed in with stuff I had never seen before. There were greens, from the garden I presumed, some cooked and some as salad. I carefully selected a few of them to go into my bowl.

Behind me, Will was greeted by a couple who acted like they were long lost friends. I faced forward, following others as I made my way down the line. To my relief, people had covered up as the evening air cooled.

Will paused at the end of the table and was talking to a man dressed in a long, purple shirt and billowy yellow pants, so I headed off by myself and found a spot to sit under a tree. It was almost dark by now, so it didn't matter if I recognized the food or not. I bravely dug in with a bent spoon. It had seemed the best choice remaining of the odd utensils that lay in a pile next to the bowls.

Will came over with a couple and introduced us once they settled down next to me. They greeted me warmly. We sat cross-legged, eating what I was told was Indian food, curried lentils and vegetables served over rice. It tasted surprisingly good.

Not long after we finished our meal, two men appeared with guitars. They sat and tuned the instruments in the candle light. One of them lit a hand rolled cigarette. He took a puff and passed it to the guy sitting next to him. I thought this was strange until I realized what it was they were smoking. That was another other thing I knew about hippies. They did drugs, illegal drugs. I looked around. From what I could tell, no one appeared concerned.

A bottle appeared. Will took a swig and passed it to me.

"What is it?" I had to ask because I couldn't read the label in the dim light.

"Peach brandy," he answered. Why not, I decided. I had never tasted brandy before, much less fruit flavored. It wasn't bad. I passed on the joint that came my way.

The musicians were strumming and harmonizing on a song I didn't recognize, which wasn't surprising. I was a long way from anything familiar. But, oddly enough, I suddenly felt comfortable sitting there in the dark amongst strange people, listening to the evening concert.

We drove home hours later with six people crowded into the bug. It would have been uncomfortable, but I felt sleepy not only from the brandy, but the effects of my marathon drive had also caught up with me. I found myself amused to be crammed into a small car with five other people. I had only just met them, but they all treated me like a friend.

Back at the Victorian, Will told me I could sleep on the couch and asked if I needed a blanket. I declined and hobbled out to my car for the bedroll I had put together for my trip. He said goodnight and disappeared towards the back of the house. No one else was around.

I arranged the sheet and blankets on the couch and crawled in. The images of happy faces mingled with my beliefs of the worthlessness of shiftless people crowded my brain briefly, but I quickly fell asleep.

Chapter 2

Gray light leaked through the windows, bringing the first chirping from the birds as they greeted the morning when I woke up. Being exhausted, I had slept dead to the world. Otherwise the lumpy couch might have been unbearable. I stretched and reflected for a moment about my situation.

It seemed I was going to have to get lucky if I was to find Billy. I missed him so much and knew he would come home with me if I could just talk to him. I imagined him lying next to me and enjoyed the thought for a minute before I got up.

I limped into the kitchen and snapped on the overhead light, wondering if it was all right to help myself to breakfast. After searching the cupboards for coffee and coming up empty handed, I opened the refrigerator. The little food it contained didn't look edible and I couldn't help wonder what the inhabitants of the household ate. The only evidence of the banana bread from yesterday was a few crumbs scattered across the table.

I remembered seeing a grocery store down the street and drove down to wait in the parking lot until I saw a light go on inside. When an older man came to the front of the store and unlocked the door, I went in and grabbed a cart. I quickly gathered up eggs, bacon, a loaf of bread, margarine, coffee and a can of frozen orange juice concentrate. I considered for a moment before adding a half gallon of milk.

Back at the house I rummaged for a coffee pot. I was thinking I was going to have to get creative in order to brew coffee when I checked under the sink and found one. It seemed a strange place to keep it, except it obviously hadn't been used in a while. At least all the parts were there. I washed it out before filling the bottom with water, then dumped coffee into the basket on top, replaced the lid and put it on the stove to boil. It became a challenging job figuring out how to cook a meal in the meagerly equipped kitchen.

Half an hour later I poured myself a second cup of coffee. I took a sip, wondering if I should wait before starting the eggs. I put the fried bacon strips in the oven to stay warm and leaned against the sink, still alone in the kitchen.

A girl I hadn't seen before appeared in the doorway. "Do I smell coffee?"

"Yeah, help yourself." She found a mug and poured herself a cup. Sitting at the table, she introduced herself.

"I'm Shawn."

"Sky." I decided to continue cooking and began beating the eggs with a fork.

"Do you go to school here?" She asked me.

"No, I'm just, uh, visiting." I didn't want to go into my mission with yet another stranger. "What about you?" I glanced up at her as my hand continued propelling the fork in a circular motion through the eggs. Her uncombed auburn hair framed a pretty face.

"I graduated this spring. Whoo hoo!" She gave herself a cheer and smiled.

I couldn't help but smile back. "What are you going to do now?"

She thought for a moment before answering. "Continue working on women's rights. I just have to decide how."

Will appeared in the doorway. "Whoa, dig this. You made breakfast." He smiled and gave Shawn's shoulder a squeeze as he headed for the coffee pot sitting on the stove.

"Don't look at me," Shawn laughed.

"Oh, I know your cooking skills all too well," he laughed back.

I didn't consider my cooking any kind of a feat. It was an easy meal. I had considered potatoes at the store, but decided against them since they take so long to fry.

I tended the eggs while Shawn spread margarine on bread toasted under the broiler in the oven. Will went through cupboards and drawers, collecting plates and eating utensils.

I was relieved he showed up when he did and the subject of women's rights dropped, as I knew little of the movement taking place at that time. Sure there were newspaper stories and the nightly news to spread information about what was going on in freak-filled California and other parts of the country. But newspapers didn't interest me, and I rarely watched the news on television. It seemed I mainly obtained information about events outside of our community from men my parent's age and older. Their loudest complaint seemed to be that communists were ruining the country. I never thought of disagreeing since I had learned in school about the evil attempting to take over the world. That was why we were fighting the war in Viet Nam, to keep the advancing socialist mobs at bay.

More people continued appearing in the kitchen, drawn to the smell of food. It had already become obvious that not a lot of cooking got done in the household, and I wondered if all the people gathering in the kitchen were inhabitants of the house. The coffee pot was quickly emptied and refilled. They dished food onto plates from the stove, filled the chairs around the table and dug in. The overflow went out and sat on the couch in the living room. I started thinking I should have bought more, but Shawn had only toast and orange juice.

"I'm a vegetarian," was her explanation. Once again I kept quiet so I wouldn't show my ignorance. The truth was, at that point in my life I had barely heard of such a thing. I mean, you just didn't come across people opposed to eating meat in ranching country.

Will filled the sink with water after everyone else had wandered off. "No, finish your coffee," he told me as I got up to help with the dishes. He searched under the sink and then disappeared into the bathroom. He came back holding a bottle of dish soap. He poured some into the sink and swirled it around. I thought it odd, but later realized it was the only soap in the house.

"What are you going to do today?" he asked over his shoulder.

"I need to find Billy."

Will turned and faced me. "I need to work on this article, but afterwards…"

"Do you know where he might be?" I hoped I didn't sound desperate.

He thought for a second. "There are a few places we could check out."

That afternoon, Will and I walked over to a nearby park. It was filled with more colorfully and outlandishly dressed, and to me exotic looking, young people. The talk was of revolution, and even I could feel the excitement in the air of the change they hoped to bring about.

Although I was fairly clueless about what was happening and why, I had heard about the recent assassination of Robert Kennedy. He had just won the Democratic presidential primary in California when he was shot. It had happened just before I left Montana. As usual, because it didn't directly concern me, the news meant little. Here in Berkeley however, it was a hot topic of conversation.

There was another assassination back in April that I had also heard about, Martin Luther King, Jr. I had overheard part of a conversation about an uppity colored man, and from the remark I overheard, it sounded like he had it coming. Of course I knew little of the reality. Back in Compton, Montana, my home town, people were more likely to speculate on the weather or gossip about their neighbors as discuss national events.

Now here I was inadvertently plunked down right in the middle of it all. In 1968, Berkeley was a center of social unrest. The free speech movement had begun on the college campus a few years earlier when students protested the college's bans on political activities. The city and the campus were still the site of frequent demonstrations as the self-proclaimed revolutionaries fought for social reforms. I hadn't known any of this when I arrived and didn't see how it affected me. There was no way I wanted to be a part of it.

What I saw were a bunch of degenerates flaunting their disregard for social order. There were laws specifically made to keep these sorts of things from happening. I didn't understand where the dissension was coming from. Instead of growing up and becoming adults, these young people seemed determined to avoid responsibility. Where I came from, if you wanted respect, you worked hard and made something of yourself. You didn't waste time sitting around in a park all afternoon plotting against the government.

Mainly I just didn't see anything to rebel against. The slogan that many were fond of quoting, "Never trust anyone over thirty," meant nothing to me. But, as I searched the crowd around me, hoping to glimpse a familiar face, I listened to their talk.

The main thing that struck me was their passion. It wasn't like a bunch of punks causing trouble. They seemed to really want to figure out how to improve society. The problem I had was with the way they were going about it. Their favorite method seemed to be protesting by drawing large crowds of demonstrators together to gain notice. I wondered who would take them seriously, acting the way they did.

I couldn't imagine the person I searched for would be in the crowd. There was no way Billy was anything like these people. I began to wonder if I was being played in some sort of way. As the afternoon wore on, my annoyance at the crowd grew.

Later, we walked back to the Victorian with some of Will's friends.

"Do you like the Grateful Dead?" Will directed the question at me.

"What's that?" I asked. There was a snicker from someone behind me.

"Hey, be cool!" Will sent out the reprimand. "They're a band from San Francisco."

"So?"

"They're giving a free concert over in Provo Park this evening."

He and his friends agreed to meet at what they referred to as the Taco Shack to get a bite to eat before the concert. I wasn't sure I wanted to go, but I relented when I realized that holing up alone wasn't going to find Billy. The others took off, planning to meet us in a couple of hours.

When the time came, I again listened to Will attempt to start his poor little bug. I stood beside the car, waiting to see if it came to life before climbing in the passenger side. Finally I couldn't stand the pathetic sounds as the starter continued its torture of the engine.

"Why don't we take my car," I suggested, grimacing at the latest grinding noise while studying the battered body. "That way maybe we'll get there." I just couldn't keep the disdain from my voice. Only derelicts would drive a heap like that and I didn't like being seen in it.

"Far out." Will got out. He sounded appreciative of the offer and ignored my tone.

My car was a nice one, a 1962 Chevy Impala, dark green, and I didn't mind showing it off. We climbed in and Will gave directions as I headed down the street. I wanted to think he was impressed, but as far as I could tell it was simply a ride to him. Then he asked me how I got it.

"I made the money selling calves."

"Selling calves?"

"Yeah, I raise a few bottle calves every year to sell." I explained that bottle calves were the bums, ones that were orphaned or the weaker of a set of twins. I told him about our family ranch and about raising cattle and how, when I got back it would be the start of haying season.

"Will your family need any help?" I was surprised that he showed any interest in working on a ranch.

"You can always find work picking up hay this time of year." I didn't go into the details of the back-breaking job. Secretly I was amused at the thought of him dragging around the field, trying to keep up with my brothers as they picked up bales.

We arrived at the Taco Shack. The name fit the description since the inside of the dilapidated building was as run-down as the outside. A crowd of people had gathered to eat with us, but, it seemed, these people always did everything in bunches. As we waited for our meal, I looked around.

A Negro woman sat at the table next to me. Her arrogant behavior made me want to dislike her. Her name was Gina and she had only glared when introduced to me. As we ate, she seemed to calm down somewhat. Everyone but me seemed to know what had upset her.

"Hey,Sky!" She suddenly barked at me. I jerked my head up. "What are you going to do with your life?" Her quick question confused me.

"I'm going to ranch."

"You own a ranch?" She sounded incredulous.

"No, but I could marry a rancher."

"What do you use for birth control?"

"What?" I looked around at the other faces watching me.

"That's what I thought. One more woman stuck in the kitchen, bare foot and pregnant." Her contempt for me appeared obvious. I was aware of the others closely watching me, but I kept my gaze on her, determined to defend myself.

"No, that's not how it would be. I'm a good hand. I can ride and work cattle, and…and work as hard as anybody."

"And what's gonna happen when the babies start coming? Who's going get stuck taking care of them?"

"No, it wouldn't be that way." I shook my head, as I had suddenly pictured my mother. I knew I was nothing like her.

"Mm hmm, we'll see."

That's not how it would be, I thought again. I didn't realize it, but I was also smack dab in the middle of the women's liberation movement.

What was suddenly obvious to me was that maybe I hadn't thought my plan through. It didn't deter me though. I intended to stick with it because I couldn't think of any other acceptable option for my life.

As we prepared to leave, Will looked around and counted. "Where'd Dave and Jim go?" We all looked around and soon realized that the two had skipped out without paying their share of the bill.

"Assholes," someone remarked. Everyone dug in their pockets, searching out every bit of change to help cover the bill. In the end they were still short, and I felt forced to cover it, as I was the only one who had more than the couple of dollars it took to buy a cheap meal in my pocket.

The night didn't get any better. Once at the park I became overwhelmed by thousands of people taking advantage of the free music. Even though I had never heard of the band, the Grateful Dead were a big deal in that part of the country. Since they had become popular, they rarely played for free, and thousands came that night to be a part of it.

I listened to the music, at least what I could hear of it and realized I might have enjoyed it under different circumstances. Instead, I felt lost amongst the sea of faces that I continuously searched, desperate to locate the one I would recognize.

After another night on the couch, interrupted by people coming and going at all hours, I once again awakened earlier than everyone else. I felt tired and frustrated. After I made coffee, I sat at the table trying to figure out what to do. Shawn entered the kitchen.

"Good morning." She smiled.

"Good morning." I answered back. I liked her, despite her strange beliefs.

By now I had figured out what a vegetarian was as there seemed to be quite a few of them around. One of them had felt the need to educate me. I had said nothing as I listened to self-righteous talk about cruelty to animals. I was outnumbered, so refused to argue and had simply walked away as the guy was in mid-sentence.

"Mmm, love that smell." Shawn poured coffee for herself. At least she didn't feel the need to preach about her food choices.

"If you guys like coffee, why don't you buy it?"

"We're all poor college students so it's a rare treat." She sat down and looked at me. "So, you want to find this dude, Montana."

I nodded, and before I knew it I was confiding in her, telling her about how Billy was my boyfriend, and how much I loved him. She sat and listened as I poured my heart out.

"Are you going to stay here after you find him?"

Hell no. But I didn't say that. "We're going back home."

"Are you sure that's what he's into?"

"Yes." I tried to sound convincing, but even I could see the flaws in my reasoning. I had stopped short of telling her The Plan. That was my secret, but I was sure that once I had Billy back in Compton, it would happen. It had to. My life depended on it.

"You know, you don't need a guy to realize your dreams." I heard the words, but they didn't reach me. The plan I had worked out in my mind was the only way I had any chance for a future. "You should come with me to the park this afternoon. Some women are going to talk about things you might dig on." I wasn't really interested, but agreed to tag along.

We walked over to a nearby park. Thankfully my ankle was feeling better because I was doing a lot more walking than I was used to. Once there, we headed towards a makeshift stage that had been erected. A couple of speakers were wired to a microphone for a sound system.

Another black woman, I had realized that Negro and colored weren't terms anyone there used, climbed up onto the stage to speak. She had a determined and grim look on her face as she faced the crowd. Her large, gold hoop earrings sparkled in the sunlight and her hair formed a dark halo above her that swayed with her movements.

I glanced around and noticed that the group was comprised mainly of women, although I saw Will off to the side, pen and notebook ready. My mind focused on two things. First was that I wouldn't find Billy here. Second, there seemed to be a lot of angry black people in California.

"Sisters," she began. "The time is…" a high pitched whine came from the speakers, obliterating her voice. She continued, but I only heard small bits of the speech.

"It's time to throw off the shackles of oppression… demand equality…take what is rightfully ours… Second class citizen is not an option for the newly liberated woman..."

Her words became stronger as she talked. The crowd cheered as she mapped out a future where women had the same career options as men, with equal pay. She went on and on as the cheers became louder. I have to admit, most of her speech was over my head, stuff I had never even considered before. My life was what it was and I saw little choice. Except for the changes that The Plan would create, I expected to be ranching my entire life. I listened more closely when she spoke of women being expected to stay home and raise children. I wasn't sure about becoming a mother, especially after having my own as an example. But that was the way it was. Ranching families needed children, especially sons, to help out.

Finally a chant united the cheering crowd. "Burn your bra! Burn your bra!" At the time I didn't understand what that action symbolized. Women began taking off their tops and removing their bras. Afterwards I realized many of them had donned the under garments especially for this demonstration of their liberation, as it had been obvious to me that most of the hippy chicks I had encountered didn't wear them. I envied their freedom, but was stuck on the belief knew that no decent woman would go without one.

There was a barrel below the stage. Women flocked to it and flung the bras into it, some of them didn't bother to put their tops back on. I stood there and watched, dumbfounded and definitely not joining in. Finally, a flammable liquid was dumped into the barrel and a lit match tossed on top. The whoosh of the flame brought an even louder cheer as bare-breasted women danced around the barrel.

I looked around for Will, but he had vanished. Suddenly I was aware of sirens. Shawn hurried over to me. "C'mon, let's split!" I followed her in the midst of the dispersing crowd of women, some struggling to get back into their blouses. I didn't know what was going to happen, as the sirens grew louder. But Shawn didn't seem too worried. I thought I heard a snicker from her and once we reached a side street, she paused and faced me as laughter overtook her. Suddenly I also saw the humor in what had just happened and joined in. We giggled as we continued our escape.

We hurried back to the safety of the house, getting through the doorway as a police car drove by. "Fucking pigs," Shawn remarked, but her look of amusement remained. We stayed inside, hiding out until the neighborhood was again quiet, discussing the woman's speech.

"My mother has spent her entire adult life taking care of my father and us kids. There's no way I'm doing that," Shawn was adamant.

I thought of my own mother, back home on the ranch. I thought about her for a second, but I couldn't relate to her life at all.

"Do you really think what happened today will change that?"

"All we can do is educate women, let them know there is more to life than becoming a housewife. What do you want to do with your life?" Her question was a challenge.

"I want to raise cattle." There was nothing that would make me change my mind about that.

We talked a while longer before Will came home.

"What happened to you?" Shawn asked him.

"I split before things got out of hand. I heard the pigs showed up." He laid his notebook on the table.

"Yea, but what were they gonna do? Stand around sneakin' peeks?" The two of them laughed, remembering the bold display from the crowd of girls running around with their boobs hanging out. "I bet you hung around for an eyeful," she accused Will, still laughing.

"What can I say? May as well stick around when there's an eyeful to be had," he teased back. I might have found the experience amusing except that I was getting nowhere with my search. By now I had expected to be back home with Billy.

A week later I had seen far more hippies than I could take. Besides being discouraged, I was fed up with hearing about the Viet Nam war and free speech and equal rights. And those idiotic beads. Almost all of them had the multi-colored strands wrapped around their heads, necks, waists, anywhere they could be attached, dripping symbols they were part of the hippy movement. There was no way I would ever fit in with these people, even if I wanted to.

"Sky?" I turned towards the unbelieving voice, not knowing what to expect. "What are you doin' here? My expression turned to puzzlement. The disheveled guy in front of me gave a faint smile before I recognized him.

"Billy?" But instead of joy at seeing me, I saw discomfort on a face that I should have instantly recognized. Between the overgrown hair on both his face and head were eyes that had a vacant look. I had to look hard before they became familiar. And despite the baggy clothing, or maybe because of it, he looked scrawny, way different from the guy I was in love with. Even his voice sounded different, kind of raspy. He was drunk. At least that was what I thought.

As he came closer I could smell him. It was obvious he hadn't bathed in a while. I glanced down at his grimy clothes, then back up to his gaunt face. It was a lot for me to take in.

"Billy." I repeated his name once I better recognized him, but I was too self-conscious to give him a hug. "I've been looking for you," I began, but noticed he wasn't really listening to me. I stopped talking, not knowing what to think. After a few seconds he looked at me again.

"So, what's up?" He looked confused as he scanned the room.

"Um," I looked around also. This wasn't a conversation I wanted to have shouting over music at a noisy party. He teetered a bit as he waited, but not for my answer. His eyes darted towards me, and then back out into the crowded room. I positioned myself directly in front of him. "I came to find you."

"Right on." He grinned, but his eyes never seemed to focus on me.

"When are you coming home?"

"Aww, Sky, I'm diggin' on the scene here." I noticed that he had learned some new words.

There was an uncomfortable silence. I stared at his face as his eyes darted around the room. Finally they fixed on a guy who had just come through the front door.

I couldn't explain the ominous feeling I had as I watched the shifty eyes scope out the room.

"I have to see…" Billy's words faded as he followed the man towards the back of the house. I was left standing all alone, feeling foolish. I looked around. No one was paying any attention, except for Will, my self-designated protector. His watchful eyes had witnessed the exchange. He couldn't have heard what was said, but it had to be obvious what had happened. He got up and walked over to me. His look of concern angered me as I realized there was something else going on.

"What's the matter with him?" I demanded. Someone had cranked the volume on the stereo so I had to shout even louder in order to be heard.

He put his face near mine and said as softly as he could against the noise. "He's on smack."

"What?"

"Heroin, has been the whole time he's been here."

"Why didn't you tell me?"

"What would you have done, split before you saw him?"

I really thought I could convince Billy to come home. I started down the hallway, but Will stood in my way. "Just wait until he comes out." He told me. I looked at the closed door and then back at him.

"Okay," I consented, when I saw the concern on his face.

I stood there staring at the door, resigned, but determined to snatch Billy if I had to, when he came out. Will sighed and walked off. I watched him out of the corner of my eye, since the alternative was to obsess about what might be happening in the back room.

It was close to an hour later when three people walked out of the bedroom, Billy, the scary looking guy and a woman. Here was my chance.

"Billy." He turned and smiled, but again looked confused. He slipped into his coat. Suddenly I knew I had to get him away from here, away from all these dangerous freaks who were obviously hurting him. "Come on, let's go home." I grabbed his arm.

His anger seemed to jump out of nowhere. Glaring at me, the only time he spoke clearly, his eyes momentarily focused, he told me, "There's no fuckin' way I'm going back to that shit hole." He pulled away as the girl caught up to him.

"You wanna split?" she asked him.

"C'mon." He put his arm around her and together they walked out the door.

I was devastated and humiliated, and just barely above begging. I stood there and watched the front door close behind them.

Not only was the guy I loved walking away with another girl, but in that instant the plan for my entire life was destroyed. I started to head outside, just wanting to get far away, but realized that I hadn't driven to the party.

I turned and found myself, once more, face to face with Will. Before he could speak, I said to him, "I need a ride back to your house." I managed to keep my voice level and calm. In fact I held in everything I was feeling, especially the fear radiating from the pit of my stomach. My life had suddenly become meaningless.

"Okay." He looked around. "I'll have to scrounge a ride, so hang on." I didn't watch where he went, but he quickly came back. "Come on." He led me out the door and across the street to the borrowed car. The damp night air cleared my head, but didn't help the feeling of loss that still threatened to overwhelm me.

We drove back to the old Victorian. Thankfully, it was a short drive and Will didn't say anything until we pulled into the driveway. "What are you going to do?" He looked over at me.

"Go home."

"Now?"

"Yes, now!" Suddenly I was fuming and completely fed up with California and hippies and all their idealism. I blamed them for what had happened to Billy. They got him hooked on drugs with their free way of living and corrupted him. In school we had been warned against this dangerous lifestyle, and now I had seen it firsthand. I just wanted to get back Montana, where my life was normal and predictable.

I slammed the car door as Will sat there silently. Inside the house I grabbed my few belongings and stomped back out to my car. I noticed Will still hadn't moved, but ignored him. I got in, started the engine and drove off into the night.

The plan I had for my life had derailed in a big way. There was simply no other way for me to live the life I wanted. In our family, as in many where I grew up, the first born son inherited the family ranch. It was how, first my Grandpa Mathew, and later my father, Garret, had gained control of the Daly ranch. No one else seemed to have any say in the matter. Billy Marsh was the first born son and so would inherit his family's ranch. I had fallen in love with him so he would marry me and I could help run his ranch. It was the only way I saw to live the life I wanted.

The city lights were far behind me when I pulled over and stopped. I bawled like a baby as I saw the life I had envisioned for myself collapsed in a heap before me, like a crumpled up piece of paper. I tried looking into my future, but there was none.

Chapter 3

Home appeared the same as when I left. Our two border collies, Jipper and Tag, ran out to greet me as I pulled up. After giving them each a quick pet, I walked through the kitchen door. I didn't know if, after making the long drive a second time, I was more exhausted or devastated. I just knew that facing my family was something I really wanted to avoid.

Ursula, my mother, stood at the stove preparing dinner. Her round body made her look almost as wide as she was tall. She turned when the screen door slammed, her expression its customary surly scowl of irritation and disgust. It didn't soften when she saw who was there.

"Where have you been? I could use some help around here." Her piercing eyes peered out from her blubbery face and tried to extract the answers to questions that she would never ask me.

I attempted to walk past, but she moved over to block my way, her bulk making an effective barrier. The familiar feeling of being trapped surfaced. I didn't want trouble with my mother. Why couldn't she just leave me alone?

"I need a shower."

Maybe she realized the wreck my trip had turned into, because after studying my face for a second, she moved back to the stove. I climbed the back stairs up to my bedroom, laid down on my bed, pulled the quilt up over my head and immediately fell asleep.

I didn't wake up until the following morning. I felt terrible and wished I could just sleep forever. Instead I pushed myself out of bed. My life was done, but I still had work to do. I went downstairs for breakfast, still dreading the prospect of facing the rest of my family.

Only when I was sick was I ever the last one down the stairs. This morning however, my parents and four siblings looked up at me from their seats at the breakfast table. I poured a cup of coffee and sat down, hoping to avoid their questions. I snuck a quick look around.

My father sat at the head of the table. At forty-five, his hair had a few flecks of gray, but otherwise he appeared as fit and strong as ever. My two brothers sat on either side of him. Adrian was seventeen, a year younger than me. He resembled my father and most of the Daly men with his blue eyes and square chin. Across from him sat Steve, who was another year younger. Steve took after my mother's side of the family and had brown eyes and lighter colored hair.

My sisters, Donna and Debbie were twins and also took after Ursula's side of the family. With their curly blond hair and fair complexions, they had always been cute. Now fourteen, they were attractive and popular teenagers. I would have been envious, if I cared about such things.

I mumbled a greeting and waited for the sarcastic remarks, knowing my brothers would have something to say about my chasing a boy all the way out to California. Thankfully, they spared me, and merely returned the greeting, showing little interest in my life. I couldn't blame their indifference. I was feeling more hostile towards them lately. Being sons, I had noticed long ago, gave their lives much more meaning than mine did. It hadn't mattered as much while I was still in school, but now with my life in limbo, the security sons seemed to have made it hard not to feel bitter towards them.

I was particularly resentful of Adrian. As the oldest son, he would inherit the ranch. All my life I wished I had been born a boy. Then, as the first born, the D would become mine. Instead I had been forced to figure out another way to do what I loved. That was how I came up with The Plan. By marrying the first born of another ranching family, I could continue ranching. I had never considered my chosen one leaving both me and his childhood home.

"What's it like out there?" Debbie asked me. Both she and Donna were much more interested in other places, especially cities, than the ranch.

"It's crazy, full of hippies." I meant to discourage them. The twins spent a lot of time in a world that included only the two of them. Their main goal in life was to escape to town. As far as I could tell, I had nothing in common with them.

My dad looked at me. "Did your car run all right?" He asked.

"Yeah, it ran fine." I answered. I purposely ignored Ursula, who sat at the end of the table closest to the stove.

"So what's Billy doing?" My dad continued.

"Not much." My tone suggested disgust, but I didn't go into details.

"Is he coming back?"

"He says he isn't."

"Well what's he going to do out there?"

"He didn't say." I saw the puzzled looks on everyone's faces. "That's all I know," I finished, hoping to put an end to their questions.

"Well, you can ride with Hawk and Jerry," my dad told me. "They're heading up the west basin." I knew what that meant, moving pairs to an upper pasture. It was time to think about putting up hay to feed our cattle next winter, but a few things needed to be done first. A horseback ride was just what I needed.

I got through breakfast and stepped outside, finally feeling like I could take a breath. As usual, I couldn't help but feel better. Despite my problems, I felt happy to be home. The ranch I had grown up on, the D Rocking D, or the D, as it was usually referred to, was my family's ranch. My great, great grandfather John Daly had homesteaded on this spot with his son Matt back in the 1880s and I was part of the fifth generation of Dalys to live here.

I knew the rough history of the ranch and the problems hanging onto the land my forefathers had claimed. Between the government with their laws and the homesteaders who had moved in and plowed up the prairie, the D had withstood it all. It was now roughly eighty thousand acres that we ran eighteen hundred pairs on.

The house I grew up in had been built around sixty years ago, but the original cabin and bunkhouse still stood. The big barn sitting down by the corrals had replaced the original one long before I was born. I crossed the driveway over to the corrals where the horses dozed in the early morning sun.

The next week I spent as much time horseback as possible. I rode out wearing a coat against the morning chill and returned in the late afternoon heat with the coat tied to the back of my saddle. With our two hired cowboys, I checked the pairs that had been turned out onto the range earlier in the month. The grass remained lush and green from the spring rains. The sleek red and white hides of the cattle dotted the landscape under blue skies. My disastrous trip faded somewhat in my mind as I spent the next week viewing life the way I liked it best, from the back of a horse.

Wilbur was by far, my prized possession, and sometimes, my best friend. He was a fifteen hand sorrel gelding with a blazed face and white stockings on both hind legs. I'd had him for six years and he knew the ranch as well as I did. Sometimes I thought he knew me better than I knew myself. I had competed on him at the county fair and in 4H shows all through high school.

We all had our own horses, of course, but lately mine was the only one that was ridden regularly. I frequently imagined what it would be like to have a string of horses, to need a string of horses, like in the days before there were fences and a lot of miles needed to be covered on horseback. As it was I used Wilbur as often as I could. When he needed a day off, I rode a sibling's horse. They didn't mind since otherwise their horses spent most of the time out in the pasture.

I couldn't understand their indifference to horseback riding. To them, moving cattle was just another chore and it was the only time they rode. Any more, it seemed even my father preferred sending others out when there was riding to be done. I was the only one in my family who saddled up because I loved being horseback.

In the days that followed my return, I had plenty of time for contemplation while out riding across our range. Of course my thoughts mainly revolved around The Plan, and how I could revive it. I just couldn't see any other option for my life. College was something I never considered. I had spent as many days as I intended to sitting at a desk while being forced to learn stuff I had no interest in.

I only wanted to ranch, and unless I found a big pile of money so could afford to buy one, I had to figure out how to acquire one another way. That left marrying into a ranching family. Billy seemed the perfect choice. Besides being good-looking and kind, he was competent and an excellent hand with a horse. His family's ranch, while not as large as the D, was still a nice spread and I imagined a good life as his wife.

I daydreamed that when we took over his parents' place we would have many horses and would spend our days riding every day. We could even breed them, something the D had done until my father took over. There was simply nothing else I could think of that I wanted to do.

By next week our lives would revolve around haying. While I spent my time riding, my brothers spent theirs in, around and underneath machinery, greasing gears, adjusting and tuning, and then testing the haying equipment. Those were the jobs that interested Adrian and Steve, anything mechanical. One by one the large pieces of machinery were driven or towed out of storage sheds. Soon tractors, mowers, balers and a rake lined the driveway, an army waiting to invade the hay ground.

One evening I rode into the yard and noticed a strange car parked next to mine. I was only slightly curious whose it was, and continued on to the barn to unsaddle my horse. The twins burst out of the kitchen and ran down to intercept me.

"Your boyfriend's here." Donna called out to me. They both giggled.

"Who?" I looked down at them from atop my horse and then back up to the car. Had Billy come back? I dared to get my hopes up.

"He says he's from California." Debbie threw out the hint. It seemed the twins were enjoying themselves way too much. An uneasy feeling overtook me.

The screen door slammed again and I looked over to see Will sauntering down the walk towards us. A broad smile covered his face. I just sat there, frozen and unbelieving. I almost expected the jolt of my shock to cause Wilbur to jump forward.

"Hi," he looked up at me, his expression showing that he was happy to see me. I imagine my expression was one of complete disbelief. There couldn't have been anything more oddly out of place than to see him standing there in the D's driveway. It was like an alien had suddenly plopped itself down in a bizarre clashing of two worlds and it was more than a little unsettling.

My hungry horse took a step towards the barn, anticipating his evening grain. I could just ride off and not look back, I thought. Instead I stopped him, focusing my attention on the movement as an excuse for not responding immediately.

Finally I swung my right leg over the back of the saddle and stepped down. I faced Will, feeling the twins' eyes studying my face.

"Where's the VW?" I looked towards the shiny blue car parked next to my Impala. I heard the contempt that hid my dread, but wasn't sorry for the rude greeting.

Will just chuckled. "It went to bug heaven." I said nothing, so he continued. "Remember Eric? The car's his. He decided he doesn't want it, so he gave it to me."

I remembered the grubby guy I had met and wondered aloud, "How'd he afford a new car?" The words were harsh and this time Will grimaced slightly at my tone.

"His parents bought it for him. I guess they felt guilty for tricking him into enlisting."

I turned to loosen the cinch on my saddle. It was unnecessary since I was on my way to the barn to unsaddle Wilbur. But it gave me a moment to avoid Will.

I was sure this situation would cause me nothing but embarrassment. He raised a tentative hand up to Wilbur and gently patted his face.

"Is this your horse?" Dumb question and I wanted nothing more than to prove his ignorance in any kind of way. I also wanted to tell him to leave my horse alone.

"Yep." I hoped my coldness was obvious.

"I came to see about a job." Since he was getting nowhere with small talk, he must have decided to state the reason he was standing in our driveway. I couldn't believe he had taken our talk in California seriously, yet here he was.

"You'll have to talk to my dad."

I couldn't stand the four extra eyes watching us. "What's your problem?" I glared at my sisters. They giggled again before starting back to the house.

Will looked around the yard and then down towards the corrals. He took in the new surroundings that I figured were as strange to him as California had been to me.

"I have to take care of my horse." I was wondering how I could escape, but knew it was almost dinner time. There was no way I was going to stand for the teasing that was sure to come from knowing a long haired hippy, especially one who had naively followed me from the city.

"Can I come?"

"Just stay out of the way." My reply was mean, but my life had suddenly been turned on end for a second time and I didn't like it. We went down to the barn where I led my horse into a tie stall. I pulled off his bridle and dumped a can of grain into the box built into one side of the manger. He stuck his nose in and ate hungrily while I pulled the saddle from his back.

As I walked between the stall and the tack room, carrying the saddle in and bringing a halter out, I pretended I was too busy to talk. Will wandered around and then uttered the annoying phrase he was so fond of.

"Far out."

After I turned Wilbur out into the pasture with the other horses, I paused, still stalling, to watch him lie down and roll, caking his sweaty back with dirt. Will chuckled at the horse's antics as he writhed on the ground. All four hooves jutting into the air as he scratched his back. After he heaved himself back onto his feet and gave a good shake, releasing a cloud of dirt, I reluctantly headed back.

We crossed the yard up to the house as my dread grew at having to face my family's curiosity. I figured I may as well have been walking through the door with an Eskimo. To my relief, only my mother was in the kitchen. Her agreeable behavior threw me until I realized that she and Will had already met. She actually appeared to enjoy his company. It was rare to see a smile on her face.

My dad and brothers walked in shortly after. They stopped and stared when they saw who, or rather what, stood in the kitchen.

"This is Sky's friend, Will." Ursula sounded down right pleasant. I wondered what she was up to.

"This is my dad, and my brothers, Adrian and Steve." I took over the introductions. At six feet tall, Steve was the shortest of the three Daly men. With their boots and hats they towered over Will.

"Nice to meet you." Undaunted, he shook their hands, and got right to the point. "I heard you could use some help putting up hay this summer."

"Well, yeah." I could tell my Dad didn't know what to think of the long hair standing in front of him. "Have you ever done ranch work before, son? You got to be strong to tackle it." I figured he would immediately dismiss Will.

" No, I haven't but I think I can handle it."

"You can show Will the bunkhouse after dinner," my mother cut in.

"What!?" The word shot out of my mouth. Somehow the decision had already been made. I gave her my best this can't be happening look, but her attention was on my dad. She seemed to be determined to get her way.

He simply shrugged and told Will, "Sure, I'll give you a shot."

"Right on." I cringed at Will's reply, his other favorite comment.

Dinner was some strange casserole my mother had thrown together with, it seemed, whatever ingredients her hands had first grabbed. I thought it a particularly poor effort on her part, but everyone dug in and ate. We knew better than to anger the cook.

Will seemed perfectly at ease, but I squirmed in my chair, keeping my head down as I hurriedly ate. Thankfully we weren't prone to family discussions at the dinner table. Talk was usually limited to "Pass the bread" or, "Did you doctor that sick heifer?" Tonight our guest provided a topic of conversation.

"That's a nice car you got." Steve addressed Will.

"Thanks."

"How's it drive?"

"It got me here." Will's humble reply amused my brothers.

"Mind if we take a look at it?"

"Go ahead. Take it for a drive if you want."

I still didn't know what the excitement was about. I had glanced at the car. It was obviously new, but I hadn't noticed much more than the blue color. It sure had my brothers excited though.

"Thank you for dinner, Mrs. Daly." Will stood up from the table and picked up his plate to carry it to the sink. My dad was already turning on the television in the next room, his plate sat on the table where he left it. Adrian and Steve headed out the door. Donna and Debbie were sticking around, no doubt because, as boy crazy fourteen year olds, they seized any opportunity to flirt.

"Uh, yeah, thanks." I felt a little ashamed, and not only by my own manners. But I guess having polite company agreed with Ursula because she was smiling in spite of our indifference to her cooking. She wouldn't let Will help with the dishes when he offered. None of the rest of us had made any effort.

She turned to me. "Take Will out to the bunkhouse."

He followed me out the door. In the driveway, his flashy car sat with the hood up, while Adrian and Steve studied the engine. I skirted the parked vehicles and followed a path through the overgrown grass. Once past the larger cabin, the path became fainter.

The neglected log building sat off by itself amongst the weeds. It was rarely used any longer since our full-time cowboys lived in D owned houses. I didn't know what shape it would be in. I pushed open the door and flipped the light switch. A bare, overhead bulb added little light to the single room and I smelled old wood and dust.

A few cobwebs hung from the ceiling and the two small windows needed washing, which I knew I wasn't going to do. I checked for signs of mice. There were a few droppings on the floor, but since there was nothing to nest in or eat, the rodents seemed to mainly pass through.

The small building was one of the two remaining original ranch cabins. A bathroom had been added, but other than that it was the same as when hired cowboys rolled their blankets out onto the bunks they called home when they worked for The D over the past eighty-five years.

"Far out," Will looked around before adding, "I can dig crashing here." I took his words to mean he was satisfied with his rustic sleeping quarters.

"You don't know if you can do the job yet." I just couldn't help my rudeness. He gave me an odd look. I guess it was another mean thing to say, but I really didn't want him here. It seemed his presence was threatening to upset some strange balance in our family. Then I remembered that Ursula had actually smiled that evening.

"We'll have to bring a mattress down from the house. We don't keep 'em in here because of the mice." I hoped my tone sounded a little friendlier.

I walked over to the house for the mattress while Will grabbed a box and a duffle bag from his car. Once he removed his belongings, Adrian and Steve closed the hood, got in and started the engine. The car disappeared down the drive as we unrolled the thin mattress across one of the bunks and Will got settled in.

"Where'd you find the weirdo?" I couldn't be sure if my dad was joking or serious. My brothers had returned from their test drive and all three waited for my answer.

"He's just a guy I met in California. We were talking one night and I told him we could always use an extra hand during haying. I didn't think he would come here." I looked at my brothers and then back to Dad, worried they would think I actually liked him.

"Well he's here. We may as well see what he can do." I understood my dad's thinking. It was a busy time of year and help just showing up simplified things for him.

Steve grinned. "A long hair. This could be fun."

I wasn't sure if Will needed to be worried. It seemed everyone had their stories about mistreating hippies, forcibly cutting their hair and worse. I had never actually seen any of this and suspected it was just talk, but I also knew that many in our tight-knit community didn't like outsiders. I never understood thinking the worst of others simply because they were different, but at the same time I didn't want Will here either. I was afraid he would get in the way.

Within a week we had descended onto the hay meadows. For the remainder of the summer our lives would revolve around the old saying, "Make hay while the sun shines." The only things that stopped us were darkness, rain or machinery breakdowns. My father and Jerry, one of our hired men, ran the mowers and my brothers each sat on a tractor pulling a baler. I usually pulled the rake around using the little tractor when the windrows needed flipping.

Otherwise I ran errands and helped pick up the thousands of sixty pound rectangular bales that had been spit out evenly spaced into long rows covering the meadows. Steve and Adrian were the logical choices to run the more complicated equipment since they knew more about mechanics. It was a small task for them to replace a busted shear pin on the baler out in the field, whereas I usually had to ask for help. That meant someone else had to stop what they were doing. Of course the guys were also more prone to clogging it with loose hay, as they pushed the machine to its limit. I was more cautious about feeding the windrows into the noisy machine. But I knew there was more to it. I felt I was designated the lesser tasks, more because of my sex than my lack of expertise.

Picking up bales from the field was the most physically demanding job. We used two teams of four. I worked with Adrian, Steve and Will, while another group of my dad and three hired men gathered the bales from another field. One drove the pickup pulling the wagon while two others walked along on either side picking up bales and one stayed on the wagon stacking the loaded bales. We all took turns, so everyone got to rest while steering the crawling pickup and wagon down through the rows. When the bales were stacked six high, everyone jumped in the bed of the pickup for the drive to the stack yard where every bale was handled again, as one by one they become part of tight stacks that would withstand the weather. The huge square mounds became monuments attesting to the fact that our livestock would be fed through the long winter.

The first morning of picking up bales, Will appeared in the kitchen wearing shorts, made by cutting the legs off a pair of corduroy pants, and a tee shirt. None of us could hold back a snicker at his attire.

"What're you going to a picnic?" Adrian asked him.

Ursula quickly turned from the stove and glared at us. Maybe she thought she finally had an ally. She sure was taking care of him.

"Sky…" I understood her undertone. Apparently it was my job to help him out. I decided to treat him like any other hired man.

"You better put on some jeans and a long sleeve shirt. I'll find you some gloves. Do you even have a hat?" As usual, Will didn't let what would have been for most people, an uncomfortable situation, bother him.

"Thanks," was all he said as he went to change. I rummaged through a pile of discarded gloves, looking for two that would make a fairly matched pair.

It was a demanding time of year. Once we started, we were hard at it all day and we didn't stop until there was no light to see by. Sometimes it seemed never ending when I looked around and all I saw was what seemed like mile after mile of windrows on one side and mile after mile of bales on the other, with the tractor pulling a baler chugging down through the middle.

The hot sun beat down, relentless in its attempts to slow us down. Tempers flared in an instant when inevitably something broke. Some parts could be replaced on the spot, but occasionally parts had to be gotten from town. This could mean the machine sat the better part of a day.

When it rained, we were shut down until it dried out. We all eyed clouds as they appeared on the horizon to the west. The thick cumulus ones caused us to move more quickly against a possible afternoon shower. High thin clouds meant some relief from the scorching sun.

One evening we all piled into a pickup to ride up to the house. As we crossed the field, I saw part of a windrow in a hard to reach corner. Steve had missed the small strip when he went through with the baler. Uh oh, I couldn't help thinking.

"What the hell were you doing out there?" My dad lit into Steve as soon as he sat down to dinner, acting as if he had missed an entire field, instead of, maybe twenty feet of the downed hay. "I oughta' make you get back out there to finish it."

"Go do it yourself." Steve lashed back.

"What did you say to me!?"

"If you don't like the way I do it, do it yourself!" That remark pushed my dad over the top. He pushed his chair back and jumped up. Steve did the same. They stood face to face.

"A girl could do a better job than you! Oh, look, your sister is a better hand than you'll ever be!" My dad was bigger, but Steve refused to back down. I was afraid that this time their fighting would come to blows. But Steve had had enough.

"Fuck you!" The screen door slammed shut after he shoved his way through, a loud, snapping exclamation to end the fight.

Dad sat back down and picked up his fork. I watched as he stabbed at the food in front of him, the thunk of his fork hitting the plate threatening to shatter it. The sounds of a racing motor and tires spinning in dirt came through the open door as Steve's pickup accelerated down the driveway. The rest of us passed bowls of food and ate in silence.

I was thoroughly embarrassed that an outsider had witnessed the fight. My dad and Steve just didn't get along. Sometimes my brother seemed to purposely antagonize him.

After supper I sat alone in the twilight on the porch of Great Grandpa Matt's cabin. I had begun sleeping in my great grandparent's original home during the warmer months when I was twelve. It had been reduced to a storage shed until I claimed it. Now it was my sanctuary, my private place where everyone left me alone. I imagined my ancestor sitting in the old, mouse-ridden recliner when it was new, keeping me company. Except I didn't see him as the broke-down old cowboy that he must have been at the end. Instead, in my mind he was still in his prime, working to make the D into the thriving ranch it had become.

Will appeared, carrying two bowls of ice cream. Silently he leaned over to offer me one of them. I took it while he stood there in the weeds just off the small porch.

"Come sit down." I relented. There was just no getting rid of him. He plopped down on the wooden boards next to me.

"So, what's so special about this cabin?" He had obviously noticed how protective I was of the original Daly home.

"I just like it." I didn't know how to explain the significance of it. Shortly after, I said goodnight and went inside to sleep.

The following morning my dad told me to take over Steve's baler, as he hadn't yet made it home. A couple hours later he drove out into the field and caught up with me where I continued the slow pace through the windrows. Neither of us said a word as he took my place on the tractor. He looked like he hadn't slept and I was sure he was hung over. I went back to raking.

Eventually it came down to picking up the remaining bales that lay on the ground, the rectangles laying in rows that disappeared into the distance across the final meadow. I walked beside the wagon, heaving the sixty pound bales up onto it. I'd like to be able to say that I could do the work of the guys, but the truth is there was no way I would ever be as strong as them. That didn't stop me from trying. I pushed myself, picking up and heaving each bale onto the wagon as I came to it. Rivers of sweat ran down my face and my clothing stuck to my skin, making it hard to move. Despite long pants and sleeves for protection, loose bits worked their way inward. I tried to ignore my scratched and itching skin and couldn't help but envy the hippy chicks without their bras, since it was one less piece of clothing to trap the chaff. The stuff also blew into my eyes, causing more irritation.

About the time I felt sure my arms were rubber and that there was no way I could lift another bale, Adrian opened the door of the pickup and jumped out. The vehicle never paused as we made a quick switch in the driver's seat. I turned in an arc and aimed the slow moving truck and wagon between the next two rows of bales. Glancing in the side mirror, I could see Will trailing along behind. Someone had found him an old pair of chaps to wear after he had scratched holes through his jeans where each bale brushed his legs as he lifted it. At the brief break he took the opportunity to pull his shirt off over his head and shake out the loose hay as he walked.

Dang, I couldn't help thinking, he doesn't look half bad. He had shaved the scraggly beard after a couple days of sweating in the hot sun. The muscles of his upper body had become well-defined from the daily workouts, while the sun had added a healthy tan to his skin. He barely resembled the pale city boy I had met six weeks earlier. He had also earned all of our respect. Despite his smaller size and inferior strength, he had kept going and never complained about the hard work.

He busted me checking him out and lifted his arm in a wave. I ignored the gesture and returned my attention to staying centered between the two rows. On the far side, Adrian slid his gloved fingers under the wires of the nearest bale and flung it up onto the wagon for Steve to stack.

Finally it was done. We had gotten lucky, with only a couple days of rain sprinkles to slow us down. We all stood and looked with satisfaction at the final completed stack in the last bit of light before heading to the house for a late supper.

Chapter 4

The following morning I walked into the kitchen as the sun rose over the hills. I had risen at first light and gone out to move the irrigation water that was again flowing over the newly mowed fields.

Ursula stood at the sink. "Peel those eggs," she ordered, barely looking up as the door opened. On the counter sat a pot containing hard boiled eggs sitting in cold water.

Today was the family picnic. Every year on the Saturday afternoon after first cutting was completed, the Daly family had a party. I had forgotten about it until I saw the steam rising above Ursula's head as she drained a pot of potatoes. The tradition had begun before I was born as a celebration of sorts. I suppose once they knew they had hay to feed their livestock over the winter, my relatives decided they had earned a day off. This year, since we finished on a Friday, the picnic had been planned for the following day.

Ursula was in no mood to celebrate just then because, besides her usual task of preparing breakfast for her family, she was also cooking for a crowd of relatives. I guess if I thought about it, there was justification to her crankiness. After spending the last month feeding the haying crew and on a day the rest of us had only light chores, she was again cooking for a crowd. I peeled the eggs and placed them on the counter, then retrieved pickles and mayonnaise from the refrigerator for the potato salad.

"Tell Will we'll be leaving around noon."

"This picnic is so stupid. He won't want to come," I protested, since I didn't want him to come.

"What should we do, make him stay home alone?"

"I was hoping he'd leave."

"He's welcome as long as he wants to stay." Her scowl dared me to voice another objection.

"Can I at least eat first?" I asked. She turned back to the stove and dumped a bowl of beaten eggs into a heated skillet. The yellow goo crackled and hissed as it hit the hot grease, echoing the hostility we felt towards one another.

Will was up for a family picnic, just like he was up for almost anything. I intended to drive my own car to the gathering, and I almost made him ride with my parents and sisters since I had a stop to make first. My brothers also drove together in Adrian's pickup. We all took advantage of the freedom a driver's license provided.

Will and I took off just after noon. The picnic was being held at my Aunt Lois' and Uncle Mason's place. Their ranch was off a road closer to town. I drove past it because I had to pick up my two best friends first. Darlynn Raeburn and Louise Martin weren't Dalys, but, as my friends, they were welcome. Normally our family picnic wouldn't have interested them, but they decided to come with me since we had barely seen each other since graduation. Our lives had already begun following different paths.

I immediately spied my two friends as we approached The Crossing, a restaurant and bar a couple miles north of town. Upon seeing my car, their expressions quickly turned to curiosity when they noticed who sat on the passenger side. They had heard about Will, of course, but hadn't met him. They slid into the back seat from opposite sides of the car.

"This is Will." I gave a look that dared them to tease me.

"Hello, Will, nice to meet you. I'm Darlynn. This is Louise." Her tone was amiable and polite, much to my relief. I turned the car around in the parking lot as Will turned in the front seat to face them.

Darlynn's name, we had decided came from her mother listening to too many country tunes where the singer went on about his darlun' while pregnant with her. Her long dark hair was pulled back in a ponytail. Louise had sandy colored hair cut short like mine.

"So what do you think of Sky, here? Is she a catch or what?" Louise reached up behind me and rubbed the top of my head as she spoke.

"Knock it off!" I glared at her in the rear view mirror as I reached one hand up to smooth my hair. She laughed, knowing there was nothing I could do to her just then. Will also chuckled, but, thankfully, he changed the subject.

By the time we arrived there were already quite a few people spread out on the lawn between the river and the house. More mingled in the shade that the trees provided. After climbing out of my car, the four of us paused for a moment and looked around. As usual, the men gravitated towards the beer as the women gathered around the food. Teenagers formed small groups, trying to see who could act the coolest, while the smaller kids just ran around making noise.

"Are you related to all these people?" Will asked.

"Pretty much." There were a few I wasn't sure of the connection, and certain individuals seemed to claim us as family only when there was free food involved. But since the Daly family had been around for close to a hundred years and was prone to raising large families, I was related to a lot of people in the county.

Aunt Lois hurried over to greet us. She was actually my great aunt, since she was married to my Grandpa Mathew's youngest brother. Her green and yellow print dress flapped around her legs. It was the style that most of the older, ranch women still wore with a short-sleeved, fitted bodice and full skirt that reached to mid-calf. Her legs were covered by thick stockings. I doubted she had ever owned a pair of pants. Sturdy black shoes with a low thick heel covered her feet. Her gray hair was pulled back into a tight, practical bun. It was the only look I could remember for her. She looked at Will.

"You must be the hippy," she said in her straightforward manner. There were snickers from Darlynn and Louise as they walked off. They knew about the interrogation about to take place.

"This is Will." I introduced him while she studied him carefully, as if determining for herself exactly who he was.

"What's your last name, son?"

"Daniels," he replied. I realized that up until now I hadn't known his last name.

"Where're you from?" Her eyes narrowed to see what the answer would reveal.

"Ohio." This answer also surprised me as I realized how little I knew about him.

"You're not a farmer are you?" Lois was the wife of a die-hard rancher, and she didn't tolerate sodbusters.

"No, I'm not a farmer." Will acted like he was enjoying the interrogation.

"Well, any friend of Sky's is welcome here." Her tone turned to a greeting. Apparently she was satisfied for now that Will posed no danger. "Go get yourself something to drink, but stick to soda pop," she warned and threw a glance in my direction. In her eyes we were still children. I smiled involuntarily as I knew there was enough secret alcohol to get any teenager who wanted to partake plastered. We may have to sneak back behind a shed, but it wouldn't stop us. Almost yearly there was a scene involving at least one kid staggering around as the grownups interrogated their own children, trying to figure out where the alcohol had come from.

Thank you," Will answered.

"We'll be eating shortly." Aunt Lois spied another car arriving and hurried off to greet the occupants.

"Congratulations. Apparently hippies rank above farmers to Aunt Lois." I glanced at the crowd. "One down, a hundred to go. Want a pop?" I looked in the direction Louise and Darlynn had gone.

"No, go ahead." He wandered off. I stood there alone for a moment. My worst fear had been that he wouldn't leave my side all afternoon and that we would be the attention of a lot of stares. Thankfully, it appeared that wasn't going to be the case.

"I thought you'd be gone by now." I caught up with my two friends at a water tank that had been filled with ice and was being used to chill cans of pop.

"Next week." Louise was on her way to Idaho. She had found a job through a cousin and would be the caretaker for a couple who lived there part-time and needed someone to look after their house, as well as their horses. I expected her to be upset as she had just broken up with her boyfriend. It was the reason she decided it was time to leave, but she acted like it was no big deal.

It was the end of our threesome as Darlynn was going to college over in Bozeman next month. It seemed everyone was moving on, except me. I might have felt left behind, but I had resurrected The Plan. I reached down and grabbed a Coke.

"C'mon, let's eat." A line was forming at the food table and I was hungry.

I loaded my plate with a hamburger, potato salad and baked beans, skipped the weird looking jello salads, and added a handful of potato chips. We found a spot at a picnic table under the trees and dug in.

There was silence as we chowed down, three hungry, hard-working girls filling our stomachs. No one mentioned diets or calories or weight, or felt guilty about what we ate. We stuffed our faces guilt free and boy did it taste good.

I saw Will scan the crowd, plate in hand, looking for a place to sit. He spied us and headed over.

"I think he's kinda' cute," Darlynn commented as she watched him move towards us, stepping around chairs and people in his way.

"What do you know? You used to like Petey McMann." Louise and I laughed, remembering a crush she had had on a cowboy who worked for her family years before. He had been a goofy character, but had paid attention to my preteen friend, so she had decided she was in love with him.

"Besides, you can have him." I wanted no pretense about how I felt about the guy walking towards us.

Will set his plate next to mine and sat down. I immediately stood up and headed back for desert. When I returned the three of them were laughing. I didn't know why it bothered me that he was enjoying himself with my friends, but it did. I sat down and dug into a slice of Aunt Lois' rhubarb pie.

A while later I leaned back against a tree, feeling bored. Out in the field a softball game had started up. I heard the smack of the ball against leather and an exaggerated "Stee-rike!" from the umpire, my cousin Simon. Darlynn and Louise had tried to drag me into it, but the game didn't interest me. The role of girls in these afternoon softball games was more for the boys to have someone to show off for and flirt with, than to exhibit any athletic skill. It always seemed we weren't actually supposed to know how to play.

A girly squeal from that direction proved my point, but I paid no attention. Out of the corner of my eye I saw Will. I turned my head and followed his movements as he walked over and plucked a soda out of the tank. Ursula walked up next to him holding a paper cup she had just filled from the beer keg. A cigarette waved from her right hand as she gestured in a flirtatious way. He spoke to her and she laughed as she replied. I felt disgusted looking at her. The floral print blouse she wore couldn't begin to hide the rolls of fat around her stomach. I knew she had a pretty good buzz going by now.

After a few minutes they went separate directions. My eyes stayed on Will. I watched as he approached Hawk, our hired hand.

The old cowboy sat under the shade of a cottonwood in a lawn chair, paper cup in one hand, cigarette in the other. His full name was Buchanan Franklin Buford, but instead of being called Buck or Frank, he had earned the nickname of Hawk because of his ability to distinguish objects way off in the distance. Apparently he had won many bets over the years because of his eyesight.

Most people at the party were dressed casually, like the shorts and sleeveless shirt I wore, but not Hawk. It didn't matter what the social event, he dressed for a party. His bright red shirt still showed the creases from where it had recently laid folded on a shelf in the Compton Emporium. Around his neck was a yellow scarf. His hat and boots were clean, and his Levi's also looked new. From the look on his face, he was enjoying himself.

He was an old time cowboy, one who hated fences and refused to string barb wire, or even repair it. I had heard that was what ruined many of the old timers. Being forced to get off their horses just broke their hearts. It wasn't only the manual labor they resented, but the loss of freedom from the fencing of the prairie.

Hawk got away with it because he was good with cattle and so proved his worth in other ways. He reluctantly helped with haying, probably because he had seen too many cattle starve to death during the long northern winters when they weren't provided for.

He and Will spoke and my interest grew, but in a wicked way. I couldn't help but think that this could get good as I imagined Hawk telling the long hair off before sending him on his way. Too bad I couldn't hear what he said.

A minute later Will pulled up an empty chair and sat as Hawk continued talking. Intrigued, I made my way towards the pair. I sidled up behind them to catch their words.

"You grew up near here, then." Will led the conversation.

"I was raised a couple counties over," Hawk affirmed. He looked off to the east, his face underneath the wide brim of his hat scrunched in thought. I thought he was remembering back to the days when he covered the distance on horseback.

"My pa homesteaded over there in that Twin Butte country when I was four or five years old. It was a fair spot to make a living, I guess, fertile soil 'n good water. There was just my brother and me until my sister came along. Only my pa was there to help when she was born. 'Course I didn't know what was happenin'."

I thought he was rambling, but Will let him talk. Neither of the men seemed to notice me standing behind them.

"We lived in a tent until the house had a roof on it. I remember the two of 'em up there, my ma and pa, nailing on shakes. My pa had set up a pulley to hoist the bundles up. I remember watching them. It looked like fun." A sad smile crossed his face.

"The wind came up all of a sudden like it does. It caught my ma's skirt and pitched her over the side. She landed flat on her back. I remember the cloud of dust and the sound she made as the air went out of her. I was probably thirty feet away is all. I thought she was dead." His voice was barely above a whisper.

I was fully captivated and leaned in a little to hear better. Everyone knew the story, so I had heard all this before, but never from Hawk himself. I didn't think he ever talked about it. He continued.

"I remember her laying there, gasping fer air. Pa got her onto the bed inside the tent and went back up onto the roof." His voice took on a tone of disbelief. He looked up to see what Will thought of his father's behavior. Will shook his head in sympathy, but remained silent.

"She lay there helpless while Pa finished the roof, plus did all the chores and cooking. It didn't make him none too happy, but he got us moved into the cabin. Then he got tired of playin' nurse maid and told my ma she was gonna have to start helping out because he had his fall plowing. He just hitched the mule and took off." I pictured Hawk's father walking off behind the one bottom plow, the long lines draped over one shoulder, as he tackled the back breaking task of busting sod, while the little boy watched him go.

"She drug herself around trying to cook and take care of us, but the pain..." He grimaced. "I pitched in the best I could, but I was too little to be much good. I could only carry half a pail of water at a time from the spring. Cut my finger tryin' to peel potatoes." He paused, still feeling the frustration at his incompetence after all these years. "She tried," he affirmed.

"One morning my pa took the rifle when he left. Said he'd seen a couple antelope the day before, and he hoped to get a shot at one. We didn't get much fresh meat. See, he usually left the rifle and took his pistol because it was easier to pack. After he was gone, Ma told me to take my brother and my little sister, she was just a baby, so I had to carry her, and git on over to the neighbor's. She said to wait there until our pa came for us. It made no sense to me, but I did what I was told. It was a fair distance. I could have made it fine by myself, but with the two young'uns, it took a while." He waved his hand to scatter the ash that had dropped onto it from his cigarette and then looked off into the distance again, recalling the incident from so long ago.

"We were up on the ridge just above their place. I remember looking down at the cabin, thinking we were about there, and then I heard a pop, like a gun shot off a ways. I looked back, but I didn't see nothing so we went on down. No one was around, so we sat on the step and waited. My brother and the baby fussed because they was tired and hungry. I was too, but I didn't let on. I just kept tellin' 'em that Pa would come soon.

"It was getting late before Mr. and Mrs. Cauley came back in their wagon. They had been to town that day. When I told them why we were there, they got real concerned. They tried not to scare us, but Mr. Cauley caught a fresh horse and headed over to our farm. Mrs. Cauley took us kids in and fed us." Hawk stopped, the part of the story he remembered finished, but I knew the rest.

After waiting until her children were gone, and I imagine, far enough away so they wouldn't hear, she picked up the pistol and shot herself. The rifle was too unwieldy for the injured woman, so when her husband left the pistol that day, she ended her misery once and for all.

The story was that Mr. Cauley arrived at his neighbor's homestead after sunset, and just after Hawk's father had found his wife. Together, with a lantern for light, the two men constructed a coffin, then went out, dug a hole and buried Hawk's mother.

"After she shot herself, he never spoke of her to us kids. I don't think he ever forgave her for leavin' her family," Hawk said of his father. He looked up and his face showed the anger he still felt towards him after all these years. "If only I could have helped more." The burnt-out cigarette dropped unnoticed from his fingers as he gestured helplessly. It was also obvious he had never forgiven himself for being unable to care for his mother.

Nor had Hawk had ever forgiven his father for not getting his wife to a doctor and seeing that she was taken care of. When he got older he took to cowboying, in part because his father was a farmer and disliked ranchers. He took off before he was grown and hired on at the first spread that would put an inexperienced boy to work.

I had heard tales of his adventures when he was younger. They involved working on ranches between Montana and Texas and I'd heard he'd spent time in the Owyhee country over in Oregon as well. He had settled down as much as was possible for him when he came to The D, working first for my grandfather and then for my dad. There were rumors of his having a girl in every town, and since he had never married, they were probably true.

He carried the sadness and bitterness from the loss of his mother around with him all those years and it showed. He was a hard drinker, which, as long as he wasn't drunk during the day, didn't concern his employers. He was a good hand and was always welcome at our table. I could recall quite a few mornings when he showed up at our house after a night of drinking. I never knew where he had slept, or if he had slept at all, but he'd look rough.

A soft tap on the kitchen door always announced his arrival. One of us would let him in, still reeking of whiskey, his eyes watery and red. Unless he volunteered information, we never found out where he had been because we never asked. Someone would pour him a cup of coffee as he settled himself into a chair at the kitchen table with a quiet thank you. As he ate breakfast his outgoing personality returned and he was soon ready for a day's work.

I didn't think of this though as he finished his story. Will had remained sitting on the edge of his chair, captivated as Hawk talked. Now I looked back and forth between the two of them in wonder.

Instead of not wanting anything to do with someone he would normally have ridiculed, Hawk opened up to the young man sitting next to him. The cowboy I knew could just as easily have called Will a commie pinko. Instead, at Will's quiet encouragement and rapt attention, his darkest memory had poured out.

My attitude towards Will changed in that instant. I saw him as a caring person and began to appreciate the trust and honesty he conveyed to people. He was a good conversationalist and interesting to talk to, but now I saw his gift. I still wouldn't have admitted to liking him, but suddenly he became more than just a thorn in my side.

Both men turned and looked, as if noticing me for the first time. Hawk took off his hat and scratched the pale forehead above his hat line before announcing, "I need a drink. It was good to meet you, Will." Once on his feet, he glanced at me. "Sky," he added and nodded before ambling off in search of a bottle.

Will looked at me and gave a slight smile. "Did you know about that?" His gaze had turned to Hawk's retreating back.

"Yeah, but I never heard him tell it."

"It's a sad story."

"He doesn't need you feeling sorry for him." My contempt for him had become habit.

"No, he doesn't." Will agreed.

The softball field had been abandoned and the crowd had thinned considerably as the last rays of the sun reflected orange off the river. The old folks, some of whom hadn't left their chairs all afternoon, rose and began shuffling around as cooler air circulated from the river with the setting sun.

"Come on. Let's go watch the sunset." Will was looking towards the river.

I hesitated, wanting to leave before the crowd gathered around the beer, which included my parents, became rowdy. One thing I avoided whenever possible was adult relatives after they had been drinking all afternoon. It was never a pretty sight. My brothers and most others my age were already gone, having more important social engagements than a family picnic. My friends had also caught a ride. The only reason I was still there was because I had gotten caught up listening to Hawk's story.

"I want to get going."

"Let's check it out, just for a couple of minutes."

I recognized a pickup line when I heard one, but Will was different than most guys. Curiosity got the best of me so I followed him down to the river's edge. I almost giggled at the thought of him trying anything since I was sure I could fend him off.

We stood on the shore and watched the glow deepen and then begin to darken. Once away from the noise of the party, I heard the quiet ripples as the water slipped smoothly past. Swallows silently skimmed the air above the water's surface, dive bombing mosquitoes in what seemed like a futile attempt to reduce the pesky insect's numbers. Downstream, a larger bird let out a squawk as it settled onto a tree limb for the night.

"Nice." Will turned towards me. "I'm ready to go when you are." The dusk had slowly advanced, but there was enough light to see as we made our way back through the trees. Apparently he had only wanted to watch the sunset. I felt confused by the disappointment I felt.

As we approached the last hangers-on, I increased my pace. "Don't we want to say good night?" Will asked as I skirted the crowd.

"No, it'll be ok," I assured him.

The laughter coming from the crowd encircling the beer was an indication of things to come. I could see my dad was in the thick of it, along with Ursula. The only young people left were the kids who had to rely on their parents to get them home.

We were silent on the drive home, but I could feel Will's contentment. He had had a good time. Talking to old people was something he obviously enjoyed. Go figure, I thought when I remembered the hostility towards adults from the college students in Berkeley. Once in the yard he headed off to the bunkhouse with a goodnight thrown over his shoulder, while I went to my great grandpa's cabin.

I once again walked into a flurry of activity when I returned from moving irrigation water the next morning. This time I was looking forward to it. My family was taking a vacation.

It might have seemed a bit strange, a rancher taking off in the middle of the summer, but my dad had no choice. Ursula had nagged him until he agreed to take the family out to the Oregon coast to visit her sister, my Aunt Myra, once first cutting was done.

The great thing was that, being eighteen, I didn't have to go. There was only one problem. Will was still here. He had noticed that the paint on the south side of the barn was peeling and convinced my dad to hire him to paint over the sun damaged portion. Although it bothered me that I couldn't seem to get rid of him, I was secretly a little relieved. It would be lonely on The D all by myself. Not that I was going to let on that I wanted his company.

"Come on," I called out. Will wasn't an early riser unless there was a good reason and he appeared from the bunkhouse as I went back outside after a quick breakfast. He followed along behind as I drove the old Chevy pickup down to the furthest shed. We loaded metal fence posts, a roll of barb wire, a post pounder and the wire stretcher into the back.

"Where are we going?" He finally asked me.

"To check fence." I had gotten my instructions also. I drove back up to the yard, letting him walk once more.

Final preparations were being made as Adrian and Steve tightened straps holding luggage to the top of the car. My mother bustled out the kitchen door carrying her purse and another bag. She barked out last minute commands as Will and I stood and watched.

"Donna, Debbie! Get that suitcase off the seat and in the back like I said." They obeyed and then got in the car.

My dad already sat behind the wheel with a stoic look on his face. Both brothers had the same look. One twin sat in between them while the other rode between Ursula and my dad. I smiled gaily, exaggerating a sarcastic grin as I waved goodbye. I knew it was going to be a long drive for them all.

The over-loaded station wagon bounced down the driveway and I went back to the house to scrounge a sack lunch. As I scraped the last of the grape jelly from the jar and spread it on a piece of bread, Will walked in. "You got some gloves?" I suddenly felt awkward being alone with the guy I had been doing little to hide my contempt for all summer.

"Yep." He answered.

"Let's go." I rolled down the open end of the paper bag holding our lunch and grabbed my hat on the way out.

I felt the morning air and tried to soak up as much of it as I could, wishing I could release it later to help cool me later during the hot afternoon. Will asked me questions about the country we drove through. I pointed out various homesteads that had become part of The D. Each section had at least a small home and a barn. Most of them hadn't been lived in for almost fifty years and were falling down, each representing the collapse of a family's dream. Earlier generations of Dalys had no interest in the buildings. The land was what held value for them.

I dared a quick look at the ruins of one such home, something I couldn't always do. The little bit of the burned house that remained was barely visible. Only the bottom half of the chimney jutted up through the weeds. The barn roof had fallen in years before. It hadn't always been neglected.

When I was six, my grandparents moved from the D headquarters into the smaller single story home where I spent the first part of my life. Grandpa Mathew had decided it was time for my dad to take over running the D. Their children were all grown up and gone and my parents needed more room for their family. Grandma

Rose claimed the smaller house suited them, especially since climbing the steps to reach their bedroom in the big house was becoming more difficult as they aged. In fact, the way I remembered Grandma Rose was with rounded shoulders and a limp, her body worn out from a life of hard work.

Only a couple months later the house caught fire while they slept. My dad, always on the alert for possible wildfires, had woken up when smoke from the burning building reached the D headquarters. Even though it was winter, he jumped up and went to find the source. But he was too late. Both my grandparents died in the flames that night. I never knew what caused the fire, as the horrible event was never discussed when I was present. It had given me nightmares, not only because my grandparents had died an awful death, but because it could have been me and my family. I still avoided looking at the burned remains where Grandma Rose and Grandpa Mathew died. Thankfully, Will didn't ask about it.

We followed a faint, two-track road through the hills, climbing higher until we reached the fence line on the western edge of the D. Driving along side of it, my gaze alternated between the fence and our route. I carefully maneuvered the pickup, avoiding sage brush, rocks and rough spots as I searched for broken wire and leaning posts. The three strands of barbed wire were minimal for a fence, so keeping the wire up and tight was important.

Most of the fence remained in good shape, but in the distance I could see a spot where several posts were leaning, pulling the wire inward with them. I drove as close to the lean as I could get and stopped. It was in a low spot that collected runoff and a couple of the old cedar posts had rotted and broken off at ground level. I directed Will to pull replacement metal posts and the post pounder out from the back of the pickup and then pulled the fencing pliers from my back pocket to yank out the staples holding the wire in place.

Once the old posts were free of wire, I slipped the heavy cylindrical pounder over a metal one. I then placed the post close to the broken off stub and grasped the handles of the pounder. I lifted it up over my head and crashed it down on the top of the post. I repeated the blows as the bottom of the post inched down into the soil. I let Will sink the next one. Luckily the wire remained taut. Tightening it would have complicated the repair process. I showed Will how to attach the wire to the new posts by wrapping clips around it and the post, using the fencing pliers. Once the job was completed, we climbed back into the pickup and continued on.

I hated admitting it to myself, but I was beginning to enjoy Will's company. His appreciation for the land was genuine. Plus he didn't rattle on telling stories to impress me. He was easy to be with.

"You getting hungry?"

"Yeah, I could eat."

"There's a good place up here." We continued in first gear to the top of the ridge. I had chosen this spot to eat lunch as I always did whenever I had the opportunity to come this way. Will got out of the pickup and looked around. I made sure the pickup was in gear and the parking brake on before stepping out. I placed a rock in front of one tire to block it as more insurance against a runaway, and then looked around myself.

"Far out," were Will's predictable words. And that described the view perfectly. The rolling hills covered with curing grass flattened out into the bright green of irrigated pastures below. A creek lined with cottonwoods flowed through the middle. On the far side, the hills began again, but this time they steepened and grew into craggy peaks. In other directions, the blue sky above seemed to go on forever.

We sat on a rock ledge in the shade of an ancient cedar. I had found this spot years before, when I tagged along with a fencing crew. It seemed made just for this purpose. I opened the paper bag and pulled out sandwiches. We studied the landscape in silence as we ate, sipping warm soda in between bites of peanut butter and jelly.

A hawk floated high above the valley floor, eye level where we sat. The slight breeze stirred enough air to keep the temperature in our shady spot bearable.

"I can see why you wouldn't want to leave here," Will commented. I remembered the restlessness of the young people in California and how odd I had felt around them. The hippies I met had left their homes, searching for change, something that I couldn't understand. I didn't want different. I wanted the security of the unchanging terrain of the D.

I pulled a bag of cookies from the sack and placed it between us. "Sometimes it seems like I'm the only one who wants to stay in one place." I wasn't only thinking about Billy, but about all the other people who had tried to live in this country and didn't make it. Will looked at me and nodded, but said nothing as his gaze returned to the scene before us.

"I don't know why anyone would want to leave here." I poured out the last bit of flat soda and we gathered up the remains of our lunch.

We loaded up into the pickup and continued driving. I followed the fence until we came to a steep ravine. There was no way around, and it was our turn around spot. The rest of the fence had to be checked by approaching from the opposite direction. That was a job for another day, though.

As we started back down, Will said something that I didn't understand at all. "It seems kind of strange, doesn't it, the amount of energy people use to keep their things separate from everyone else's?"

It was early evening when we returned home. I walked into the kitchen and past the dishes piled in the sink from breakfast. Opening first the refrigerator and then the cupboards, I checked out the food situation. Ursula must not have felt the need to see we were fed while she was gone.

"Well, there's string beans, corn." I hunted through the canned goods while Will carried out his own search of the fridge.

"Why don't we get something to eat in town, maybe check out a movie."

My first reaction was to say no, but I realized that being seen with the odd stranger no longer worried me. Besides, I had barely left the ranch in a month.

Again, I wondered about Will's intentions. It he didn't sound like he was asking me out on a date. He sounded no different than when he was with his friends in California. I looked over at him.

"You want a shower first?"

"Yeah, I'll be ready in fifteen minutes." He headed over to the bunkhouse while I started up the stairs.

Will offered to drive and it was the first time I had ridden in his flashy car, although I had heard all about it from Steve. It was a Pontiac GTO, and apparently one of the fastest vehicles on the road. All of this was lost on Will, and Steve and Adrian had both laughed about his nonchalance as they drooled over it. Most guys were overly possessive of their cars, and rarely let even close friends behind the wheel, but not Will. He was willing to share it with others, just like he shared any of his possessions with others and just like Eric had shared with him. Adrian and Steve had come home grinning after taking the GTO, which they called a Goat, for a fast trip down the highway.

Now, he sounded amused as he told me about the hidden headlights and concealed windshield wipers on the car. My brothers had pointed out why these features were special, that they were firsts for an automobile. Although cool, to the humble Will, they were just unusual curiosities.

A pickup approached from the opposite direction as we drove down the dirt road. Will acknowledged the driver with a friendly flip of his hand.

"Don't wave at him!" I raised my voice to issue the command. Normally we greeted all passing vehicles as most contained our friends and neighbors. Our closest neighbors were excluded however.

"Why not?" He asked and glanced over at me.

"Because they're water thieves." The venom in my voice turned his expression to surprise.

"What?"

"They stole our water and can't be trusted."

"What water?"

"Irrigation water, from the reservoir."

"Just drained it?" Of course Will didn't have a clue what I was talking about.

"No, they put it on their fields."

"When was that? You have enough now, don't you?"

"It happened a long time ago. I don't know exactly. It was before I was born."

"And you're mad at them?" He sounded incredulous, and obviously couldn't understand how I carried a grudge about something that happened before even my father was born.

"Of course I am. They stole from us."

Back in Great Grandpa Matt's time, the two families had constructed a dam above the hay meadows lining Turkey Creek to conserve water for irrigation during the dry summer months. The way I had heard the story was that, one day my grandfather, who was just a boy at the time, had caught a member of the Sheldon family diverting water off of our field and onto theirs. It was an unforgiveable offense and had created a feud. Unless you lived in our arid part of the country and relied on irrigation water for your livelihood, you wouldn't understand the implications of the theft. Without extra water, a ranch's survival was in jeopardy. There just wasn't enough rainfall to produce a substantial hay crop.

Water had started vicious fights all over the west. A man could steal another's wife and it was easier for the two of them to settle their differences. Murders happened over water rights and ranchers clung tightly to every drop like a prized possession that others coveted. Figuring out how to obtain more was an obsession for some.

I had never heard what the repercussions had been for the Sheldons when they were caught, but to this day, the families didn't speak. Our neighbors had been branded as water thieves, the lowest sort of person. It didn't matter that the family member who had done the diverting was long dead. In our eyes, the entire family was tainted.

The subject was dropped, as I didn't know how to explain the controversy. To me, it was an example of why sharing didn't work, as it had been instilled in me my entire life that there wasn't enough water to go around. It emphasized the difference between his lifestyle and mine.

"What do you feel like eating?" Will asked as we crossed the river at the edge of town.

I chuckled, as there weren't a lot of choices in restaurants in my home town. Then I remembered a new place had opened recently. I hadn't eaten there yet. "How about pizza?"

"Right on. How do we get there?"

"Take a right on main street. You can't miss it."

We had a good time sitting in the bright pizzeria with its red and white décor, sharing a meal. I even found myself laughing as we talked during dinner. He was so easy to talk to. I guess you could say he had grown on me.

After the movie, we started for home. As we crossed the river, I looked up ahead. In the distance I could already see the large sign that announced The Crossing.

The bar and restaurant were the closest spot for people on the north side of the river to gather and socialize. Families stopped off to give the wives a night off from cooking or to visit with their neighbors over a beer. It was standard food, steaks and burgers mostly, and lots of pies. Suddenly the pizza seemed like a distant memory.

"You hungry?" I asked as we approached the flashing neon sign.

"Sure." He slowed down and pulled into the parking lot.

Vehicles encircled the building on two sides and country music blared from the juke box through the open door as we pulled up. We entered and I led the way past the bar towards the restaurant.

"They don't serve long hairs here."

I whirled around and recognized the face. "What are you going to do about it?" I dared the speaker.

"I was just joking." The kid must not have seen me as his attention was on Will.

"Shut up, Chuckie, and go sit down." I glared at the trouble maker. He slumped down into a chair next to his brother, an equally ignorant kid in my opinion. My reaction had been automatic. Will and I sat down at an empty table.

"I do believe that's the first time I have ever had a chick protect me."

"I know how to handle those two." It was true. The brothers were a couple years younger than I was, and knew better than to cause trouble around me.

"What did you think was going to happen?"

"I don't know, but those two are trouble makers."

"What, are you some kind of a badass." I knew he was teasing me, but I didn't crack a smile.

"Why should you have to put up with their shit?" I asked him.

"I shouldn't, but there are other ways to deal with them." he replied as the waitress came over. I guess it did make him appear a wimp.

I decided on a chocolate milkshake and Will ordered a slice of peach pie and a cup of tea. Again, I enjoyed sitting across from him talking, just the two of us. For once, The Plan wasn't foremost on my mind.

It was late when we pulled into the yard. I was tired, but it was a good tired, the kind that comes from the end of a satisfying day. I got out of the car.

"Good night." I turned towards my great grandfather's cabin.

"Wait a sec." I turned back as he came towards me. "I just have to try this." Will cupped my face in his hands and kissed me.

I was a little bit surprised at what seemed for him a bold move, but I didn't pull away. It felt daring to be making out in the driveway, even knowing I wouldn't be caught. His lips tasted like peach pie.

"Do you want to come see my great grandpa's cabin?" It was the first time I had ever asked anyone into my private hideout.

"Yeah." It was too dark to see his face clearly, but I knew he was smiling with a tickled look he got when he was pleased.

He followed me through the heavy wooden door. I felt for matches and struck one to light a candle. The old cabin had never been wired for electricity.

Will stopped in the doorway and looked around the shadowy room. I wondered if he sensed the presence of my ancestors. Could he feel their lives as I did?

I turned to the wall to the left of the door and pointed out the shelf where Great Grandpa Matt had always kept a bottle of whiskey. An old can of coffee remained on the same shelf. He had been the last one to use it and it sat where he had placed it, a sort of memorial to him. I had been told that this is where he spent the last summers of his life, after my great grandmother died, his mind lost in memories of the past.

"My Great Grandpa was the last person to use that coffee."

But for once Will wasn't interested in history. I felt his lips on the back of my neck. When they moved around underneath my ear I gave up trying to talk. Like everything else about Will, it was easy to become his lover.

Chapter 5

Early the next morning I drove the old Chevy through the fields, moving dams in the irrigation ditches. I yanked a canvas tarp out from where I had placed it the day before and drug it lower down the ditch. Using clumps of sod and rocks around the edge, I anchored it in place. Once it successfully blocked the water from continuing down the ditch, I paused for a moment to watch the water, shining in the early light, as it spread across the dry soil.

The sun was barely above the horizon. It always seemed to me that the early light created optimism for each new day. Looking across the sky, I could see that the sunshine wouldn't last because, except for along the eastern edge, where they allowed a quick sunrise, dark clouds pushed across. Within fifteen minutes, the rays were lost behind the thick cover, leaving the morning gray and chilly as a breeze came up. It looked as if rain was settling in and it was a welcome sight to any rancher who had finished picking up hay.

Normally I enjoyed my ritual of walking out onto the fields to move water in the early morning peacefulness, but this morning I was bothered. It wasn't that I hadn't enjoyed my night with Will. It was that I had enjoyed it too much. I was afraid of what this distraction would do to The Plan. Since I returned I had convinced myself that Billy would come home eventually, once he got the rebellion, or whatever you'd call it, out of his system.

I felt uneasy as I drove the pickup back up to the yard and headed into the house to start breakfast. Will hadn't yet appeared and I was relieved. Maybe I still had time to make sense of my feelings.

Potatoes sizzled in the skillet while I washed yesterday's breakfast dishes, and were browned before he showed up. He came through the kitchen door with a pleased look on his face that I found annoying as he crossed over to me. He tried to kiss me, but I ducked.

"What's the matter?"

I shrugged, avoiding his eyes. It wasn't anything I could explain to him.

"Well, what's for breakfast?" He reached for a coffee cup.

"The usual." I knew he could see what was on the stove.

Rain drops began splattering softly on the roof as we ate in silence. Will got up and looked out the window as the rain came down harder. There would be no painting done that morning. He turned towards me.

"Hey, let me see your bedroom." There was a smile on his face and a bit of tease to his voice.

"Why?"

"I've never seen it." Apparently his curiosity had returned.

I led him up the creaky back steps and down the hall to my bedroom. Inside the doorway I looked around, wondering what he would think. It was sparsely decorated, and the theme was definitely horse. A collection of ribbons and trophies, won at local shows sat on a shelf.

A poster of Larry Mahan, the current world champion rodeo cowboy hung on one wall. It wasn't there because I was a fan of rodeo. I didn't even follow the sport. I just liked the photo that captured the concerned look on the cowboy's face as the bronc prepared to dislodge him.

The quilt that covered my bed had been made by Grandma Rose. Throughout my childhood I had spent hours studying the pieces of the elaborate star pattern, imagining the shirts and dresses sewn from the colorful fabrics. I wondered who each garment had been sewn for, as I couldn't recall ever seeing clothing that matched the small pieces of material. The quilt was my third most valuable possession, after Wilbur and my saddle, and still reminded me of my grandmother.

Will entered and looked around. I felt a really private part of me was being revealed to him and didn't know if it was a good thing or not. He studied the awards and pictures before turning to me. I braced for the words that would be his evaluation of me.

He had a sly look on his face. "Have you ever done it in here?"

"I should have figured that was your real motive for coming up here." I tried to keep my voice stern, but I cracked a smile for the first time that morning.

"Well, have you?" he teased.

"Yeah, right. I sneak guys past my parents' bedroom all the time."

"They're not here now." He tackled me and we landed in a heap on my bed. I could no longer hold it in and laughed out right.

"Right on." He sounded satisfied, as if my delight was an accomplishment.

He kissed me and once again the worry about my future dissolved, melting into the rain pouring down around us. At the same time, I knew he was just a temporary diversion.

The rain pounded the roof as we spent the morning underneath Grandma Rose's quilt. Part of the time we talked. "So you're not going to college?" He asked.

"I want to ranch."

"Still, if you have the chance… " His fingers softly stroked my skin as we lay next to one another.

I felt so comfortable with him at that moment that I nearly told him all about The Plan. Instead I kept it to myself, along with the desperation I felt about my life. I was afraid that if I left, it would be forever, that I could never come back. I turned the subject to his plans.

"What are you going to do when you graduate from college?"

"Be a reporter and get paid to cruise around the world. I've always wanted to check out what's over the next hill. And the next one after that."

"Sounds ambitious. I guess I'd rather ride a horse over every hill."

He laughed. "In some ways that's more ambitious." Suddenly his tone turned serious. "By the way, when did you have your last period?"

"What?" I rose up on my elbow to look at him in astonishment. Would the strange things coming out of his mouth never stop?

"Seriously, I mean you don't want to get pregnant, do you?

"Of course not." I couldn't believe I was having this conversation with a guy.

"Well what are you doing to prevent it?"

The truth was that the only thing I knew about preventing pregnancy was to cross my fingers and hope it didn't happen. Sex, and its possible repercussion, was generally discussed in the privacy of the school bathroom. The girls who were having sex often worried about it, but the threat of pregnancy didn't stop many. The two boys, Billy and one other before him, that I'd had sex with had never concerned themselves with the possibility.

"What do you know about it?"

"I know enough that I don't want to be a father."

"Then maybe you should have thought twice about what just happened."

He looked sheepish. "I know, I know, it was stupid. But we had better start being responsible."

"And how do we do that?" I was curious what he could possibly know about preventing pregnancy.

"I took a class," he began.

"On birth control?"

"No, not exactly. It was a macrobiotic cooking class."

"A what?"

"Macrobiotic cooking. It's Japanese, a way of eating, but it's also a lifestyle. Part of what we learned was about menstrual cycles and ovulation." I couldn't believe what he was telling me. He was using words that just weren't spoken out loud except maybe by a doctor. I remained silent, so he continued.

"What are your monthly cycles like."

"I don't know. What do you mean?" I felt embarrassed to be asked about something I rarely even discussed with my girlfriends and definitely not with Ursula. For me, it was a taboo subject and yet, he could have been asking about the weather.

"You don't keep track?"

"No, should I?"

"Women ovulate right in the middle of their monthly cycles, so if you know the length, you don't have sex on the day when you're fertile, plus a day or two on either side." This was all news to me. As far my friends and I believed, we were at the mercy of our bodies. I certainly didn't think I had any say over what happened. Now here was a guy telling me I did have control over getting pregnant, after taking a Japanese cooking class. I found it hard to believe.

I decided to play along and thought back. "Well, let's see..." I remembered roughly and, counting back, we decided we were safe.

"Good." Will gave me a devilish grin.

Just then the phone rang. I hurried out into the hallway to answer it. My mother's sister, Loretta, was on the other end. I knew my mother had asked her to check up on me.

"Yeah, it's raining out here too. Not much we can do today." I answered her question, realizing it must be noon, as that's the time she would call, when we would be up at the house for lunch.

"We? Who's there with you?" I guess Ursula had forgotten to mention that Will was helping paint the barn. I told her.

"He's still there?"

I stifled a laugh. "There's no need to worry, Aunt Loretta. The house is still standing."

"Well ok, let me know if you need anything."

"I will. Thanks for calling. Goodbye." Will and I dressed and went downstairs.

I debated calling Hawk and Jerry, the two hired men, and decided against it. They might resent being checked up on by a girl. Besides, they would call if it was necessary.

The rain let up to a drizzle. I glanced out the kitchen window. The puddles out in the driveway were a good gauge as to how much moisture had fallen. My guess was four tenths, maybe even half an inch had fallen that morning. It was soggy out.

Will had wandered into the living room. I found him standing in front of the book case, an open book in his hand. I felt bored and restless. "What do you want to do?"

He looked up and shrugged. "You're the boss."

I was tired of peanut butter. "We really need to get some food."

"Right on. Let's go."

Will eyed the ruins of the old town of Turkey Creek as we drove past. We were again in his car and he drove slowly past the fallen buildings. "Do you ever wonder about the people who lived there?"

I had zipped past so many times in my life that I no longer saw the dilapidated buildings. Of course the prairie was dotted with many such ruins. "It used to be the nearest town. My grandparents talked about picking up supplies at the general store when they were kids. It was a long way to Compton by wagon."

Will nodded as he pushed down on the accelerator. "I'll bet those buildings have some interesting stories to tell.

"Feel like driving to Billings?" There wasn't anything I particularly wanted to do there, but it was a way to fill a dreary afternoon.

"I'm in." We turned east at the main intersection in Compton and followed the highway out of town. As he drove, Will turned the tuning knob on the radio.

"Can't you get any good music around here?"

"Rarely."

Static-filled country music came in a couple of times as he fiddled with the knob, but it was hard to get reception until we got closer to Billings, the closest town with a radio station. I studied the landscape.

There was no activity in the fields as the rain had sent everyone inside. Cut hay lay in a few of the fields we passed, as well as some already baled, and I sympathized with the ranchers. Unless the wind picked up, it could be days before the wet windrows dried out enough to run through a baler and the bales picked up.

Will slowed the car as we entered the town of Cedar Junction. We drove down Main Street, stopping where it intersected First Street. I looked over at a corner building. The dirty windows had only empty space behind them, which is how the old store had looked as long as I could remember. The faded sign was no longer readable, but I knew what it used to say, Cedar Junction Mercantile.

"Relatives of mine used to own that general store." I told Will.

"Really?" His interest was instantly piqued. He stared out at the two-story building. "Where are they now?"

"Scattered I guess. They were my great grandmother's family." To me the building's past was simply a piece of family trivia.

A few blocks later we came to the town cemetery. Will turned the car and drove in through the gate. I looked over at him. "What are you doing?"

"You must have relatives buried here."

"It was a long time ago."

"Let's have a look. What was their last name?"

"Lavold."

"Maybe we can find out when they died." He stopped the car and got out. I did likewise.

The rain had almost stopped, with only the random drop hitting the two of us as we wandered the symmetrical rows. The cemetery wasn't large and it was easy to locate the oldest section, as many of the graves were neglected, the headstones partially hidden by tall grass. I went one direction and Will another as we read the names and inscriptions, searching for the resting places of my almost forgotten relatives. I had never met nor heard much about the Lavolds. Members of that branch of the family must have either moved away or died out.

In one section, I noticed something. There were a bunch of graves containing people who all died one spring within a week or two of one another. The year was 1887.

"Here they are." I went over and looked at the graves Will had found. Theodore and Elizabeth Lavold had been buried side by side a few years apart. They had barely lived into the 1900's. The granite headstones were large and ornate. They appeared to have been prosperous citizens of the town of Cedar Junction. On one side was the grave of Benjamin Lavold, a son I surmised since he was born in 1874 and died in 1943.

Glancing at the headstone on the other side, I read and then reread the inscription, confused as to what it said.

Here lie the Beloved children of
Mathew and Lavina Daly
John David April 3, 1885-May 4, 1887
Anne Elizabeth May 16, 1886-May 3, 1887

The children's deaths matched the epidemic dates. I stood and stared. "Look at this," I said.

"Who were they?" Will looked at me after studying the headstone.

"Well, Matt and Lavina were my great grandparents. I had no idea they had children who died. The son must have been named after my great, great grandfather who's buried on the D. I wonder why they weren't buried at home."

It was a mystery to me. I had never heard anyone talk of these two small children. Will read the inscriptions on nearby gravestones.

"Yeah, there was definitely an illness of some sort. Maybe they were visiting and the children caught whatever was going around. It wouldn't have been easy to take them back home to be buried."

"Maybe." I thought I knew my family's history. My grandparents, Mathew and Rose, had filled me in about my relatives, but it was obviously an incomplete history of the Daly family.

The rainfall increased so we got back in the car and continued to Billings. I wondered if my father knew about the two children and thought about who else I could ask. I was intrigued that there was more to my family history than I had been told.

The week flew past. Once the sun came back out and dried everything off, we started scraping the barn. With only one ladder, it was time consuming. It took both of us to jockey the rickety old contraption into a stable position. Then we took turns climbing it to reach the upper half of the tall barn while the other worked on the bottom. Once we started slapping on fresh red paint, we had a routine down and the job progressed more quickly. At the end of the day my arms ached from the endless back and forth strokes with the large brush.

Of course we did more than paint. We spent every night in Great Grandpa Matt's cabin. In fact we spent more time there than in the house. The rough-hewn log walls had always suited me better and Will also liked the feel of the old building.

I wouldn't say I was falling in love with him. Under the circumstances I couldn't let that happen. Not only was The Plan in my way, Will had already told me his philosophy on love.

It was while I was in California where the mentality of free love prevailed. He had explained to me about not wanting to be tied down to anyone or anything. He, like the other young people I met, wanted nothing to do with the lifestyle of preceding generations.

The girls I met there lived the same way. I remembered a daily parade of different people traipsing up and down the hallway of the blue Victorian. I never did figure out who lived there and who were casual guests.

One day I asked him about the attitudes of the chicks, as he called them, involved in the women's movement. I had thought about it and considered the different roles for men and women where I lived.

"Do you believe in equality for women?"

"Sure." He replied. But I knew from experience that, hard as I tried, I couldn't keep up with men working out in the field. I guess I didn't know where I belonged, because I also knew I didn't want to end up stuck inside being a cook and maid with a bunch of kids crawling around my feet.

"What about here?" I asked, meaning on a ranch.

"I hope women see it as a choice," he replied. It seemed a vague reply and I knew he had no answer as to how a ranch could run smoothly with any other arrangement.

"I don't think you'd ever catch my dad doing laundry." I thought about all the house wives I knew and wondered if they thought they had a choice. Most the women around Compton who had gone to college, like school teachers, went home and took care of their families after work. The couple I could think of who weren't married lived by themselves and were derisively referred to as old maids.

"That's what they're fighting for, to change that mentality. I don't mind doing my own laundry."

"I don't see how that's going to happen around here."

"Most of those chicks protesting are hoping for the opportunity to have the jobs men have. You're actually doing it." He spoke like I had accomplished something, but I felt no comfort from his words since I had no clear definition of my role.

I never allowed it to leave my mind that soon Will would be leaving the D. Once he was gone our relationship would be over, as I doubted I would ever see him again. I reassured myself with the belief that Billy would be coming home soon and that I would marry him and live happily ever after on a ranch that would become ours.

The day my family was to return came way too soon. That morning we sat finishing breakfast. "Damn," I declared as I looked around.

"What's the matter?" Will asked. It had suddenly dawned on me how this day would be spent. I had been told by Ursula that she expected the house clean when the family returned, including washing the huge pile of laundry she left me.

"I have to clean the house."

His gaze followed mine, making his own evaluation of the job. "It won't be that bad. I'll help."

Even after our talk, I was amazed at the non-assuming guy sitting across from me. If I were in his shoes, I'd bolt. Yet, he sat across from me with a straight face, offering to help. I decided the only way women were going to reach equality was if all men became like Will, and I couldn't see that happening.

"Do you realize what you're getting into?"

"Nothing I haven't done before," he replied as he carried his dishes to the sink and turned the water on. He reached for the bottle of dish soap, and then turned to me, smiling. "C'mon, we're burning daylight." It was a line from the Western we'd seen and I smiled back as my mood lifted.

That evening my family returned, looking tired, but happy to be back. They trudged into the kitchen hauling luggage. Looking at their faces I felt even more relieved that I hadn't had to sit crammed in a car with them all those miles. My brothers and sisters barely paused in the kitchen before continuing up the stairs.

My dad opened the refrigerator, pulled out a beer, and fished around in the top drawer for an opener. My mother looked around. I wondered what she would find to bitch about. The house was clean and every last piece of clothing laundered, folded and put away.

She gave me a sharp look. "Welcome home," I said dryly.

"It's good to be home," my dad slumped down into a chair.

"You could have at least tried to have a good time." Ursula charged in. I wondered for the umpteenth time what my dad could have seen in her and why he had married such a mean woman.

She turned to me. "I don't suppose you thought about supper."

"There's more food here than you left us." I defended myself. How could I be expected to have dinner made when I didn't know when they would arrive? Besides, I had done everything both parents had asked me to. Ursula was about to start in on me when Will walked through the door.

"You made it back. How was your trip?" His smile welcomed them back as he looked first at my mother then my father. The tension in the room eased immediately. Once again I was grateful for the buffer he provided.

"We enjoyed ourselves. It was nice to see the ocean again." Ursula's tone changed. I looked over at my dad. There was no enjoyment on his face.

"Far out. The ocean's a good place to be." As he asked questions about their trip, I was amazed at how easily Will could get my mother to relax.

What had turned into a fun vacation for me was also over. It was time to get back to work. I had lined up two outside horses to ride. That, along with whatever else my dad wanted me to do, would keep me busy until it was time to start haying again. The second cutting didn't take nearly as long as the dryland ground was cut just once. Only the irrigated land produced a second crop.

The next morning I watched as Will gathered up his typewriter and box of books and papers from the bunk house. I followed along behind with his bag of clothing as he loaded up his car. His stop-off at off at the D had been to earn money for the rest of his cross country trip. Now he was on his way to the Democratic National Convention in Chicago later in the month. After a visit with his parents, he would return to Berkeley and his final year of college.

As usual, his interest in politics was nothing I could relate to. I could think of nothing more boring than listening to a bunch of men wearing suits and ties ramble on. Besides, I had been taught to be wary of Democrats. Almost all the people around here were Republicans who ridiculed anyone affiliated with the liberals. According to gossip, most were secret communists.

Will had told me earlier that even though he was just a college student, he hoped to get lucky and find a story at the convention. He didn't even know if he could get in and was just going to hang around and see what happened.

Once he had his belongings stowed in the trunk, he turned to me. "So, did you like having me around, or was I just a little summer fun?"

"This has been the best summer of my life," Since he was leaving, I had nothing to lose by flattering him. Besides it was the truth. He got that tickled look on his face and we hugged goodbye.

Of course I still believed The Plan would work out, and told myself that this was goodbye forever, but at least I could have good memories of our time together. I watched him drive off in his fancy car and then turned towards the barn. I had horses to ride.

One day I stepped out of the hardware store onto the sidewalk and spied Billy's aunt coming towards me. Pearl Springer, like her sister, was a timid woman who kept mainly to herself. I knew her only by sight.

"Hello, Sky," she greeted me.

"Hello, Mrs. Springer." I intended to keep going, but she reached out with a thin hand and touched my arm. I stopped and faced her.

"I hear you saw Billy out in California. How's he doing?"

"He's doing all right." There was no way I was going to tell his aunt the truth.

"Good." She glanced down the sidewalk before she leaned in close and quietly confided to me, "I'm glad he got out of here."

"Why is that?"

"His daddy is awful hard on those kids of his." I heard fear in her voice.

"What do you mean?" I knew Billy's father was demanding, but from what I'd witnessed, no more so than most of the parents of other ranch kids, including my own.

She shook her head. "He beats 'em something awful." The way she talked, I thought she might be crazy. Billy had never said anything to me about being mistreated and I wasn't sure how to answer.

"I have to get going." Her hand was still on my arm.

"Wherever he is, it's got to be better than here." She took a step back. I couldn't tell her the condition Billy was in when I saw him last, but I was certain it wasn't worse than living on his family's ranch. It couldn't be, for my sake as well as his.

"Goodbye, Mrs. Springer." I continued on my way.

It was an odd encounter and I dismissed what she told me until I started thinking about it. Throughout our childhood, Billy seemed to have a lot of bruises. We even teased him about being clumsy. Most of us had the usual bumps and scratches that come from being kids, but he was accident prone. I couldn't ever remember anyone actually seeing any of his accidents, though.

A few nights later I was with Darlynn. We stopped off at The Crossing on our way home from seeing a movie.

"I think you like him. You just don't want to admit it." Darlynn paused a forkful of banana cream pie halfway to her mouth to accuse me.

"No, I don't," I shot back at her, although I had been feeling down since Will left. I had told her about my week with him when my family was gone, but insisted it was over and done. "I love Billy and I'm waiting for him to come back." I added.

She must have figured it was useless to state, yet again, what was obvious to everyone but me. Billy had been gone a year now, and except for the one letter to his mother, had not communicated with his family. Instead she rolled her eyes and said, "Well, let me know when he does get back."

"Hey, do you think his father beats him and his brothers?"

"What do you mean?" I told her about the conversation I'd had with his aunt.

"I know he was afraid of him. And he did seem to get banged up an awful lot, didn't he?"

"Yeah, he did," I agreed. I thought back to Billy's reply when I asked when he was coming home. But I still refused to believe there was a good reason for him to stay away.

"I still think you should forget Billy. You know Will likes you," she began again.

I denied to myself and to my friend that I was even a little bit attracted to the hippy from California. I enjoyed our time together, but I wasn't going to let him spoil The Plan. Besides, he had already told me he was a love the one you're with kind of guy. I figured he had already found another girl to share a bed with.

Meanwhile, I wished Billy would hurry up and get home. I just knew he would come back to run his family's ranch. I refused to believe it would happen any other way.

My dad spent less and less time with his family. Every chance he got, he'd take off. Sometimes I woke up when he returned late at night. Even though he cut the lights on his pickup before the glare hit the house and eased up next to the other vehicles that lined the drive in front of the house, I often heard him. His late night habits had become customary, but I figured he was simply getting away from Ursula. It was hard to catch him sleeping, but I knew he spent a lot of nights on the couch.

"You son of a bitch! Who do you think you are?" Ursula was tearing into my father one morning as I came in the door. Their fighting was becoming more intense as Ursula refused to leave him alone. I felt sorry for him, having to put up with her relentless attacks. Our whole family would be a lot better off if she just left.

"I'll do whatever I damn well please!"

"You can't treat me like this!"

"Just try and stop me."

I slipped past as both of them ignored me. Once the shouting stopped I came back down the stairs and into the kitchen. My dad was gone and Ursula sat at the table, her head down, sobbing. I sighed at her drama, feeling no sympathy for her. From my perspective, she brought it on herself.

She looked up. Usually she kept her mouth shut around me, but today she didn't keep it in. "He's got another one, a goddamned floozie down at The Crossing!"

"What?" I guess I was naïve, or maybe, because I idolized my father, I couldn't believe he would ever cheat on her.

"You think this is the first one? The bastard's been screwing around for years." She glared at me with her tear streaked face as if daring me to refute it.

I kept my mouth shut, knowing that if I defended my father, she would attack me. Besides there was no way I was going to listen to her. My father was an honorable man and I knew he would never do such a thing.

Not long after I drove with him to Billings. School had started the month before, and with my brothers and sisters gone five days a week, the house seemed empty. The weather had turned cold, and as the temperature dropped, the rain threatened to turn to snow. I asked him if I could make the trip with him since I didn't want to be stuck inside with Ursula.

He reluctantly agreed. I imagined he realized I was as anxious to get away as he was. He said little on the way over. We picked up the tractor part he needed and started back. I tried to get a conversation going.

"That cut on Sandy's fetlock is all healed." Adrian's horse had gotten into some wire a few weeks back.

"Mm hmm."

"That goop you got from Doc really worked." As usual I was the one who did the doctoring on the injured horse.

"Yeah? Good." His disinterested replies, consisting of a word or two, caused me to give up my attempts at conversation.

We crossed the Yellowstone and headed out the highway towards home. At The Crossing he slowed and turned into the parking lot.

"We may as well have a bite to eat." He pulled up to the building. I didn't object as I wasn't eager to get home and see Ursula either. Since their last argument, her mood had been even fouler.

We sat down and ordered and then my dad immediately got up and headed towards the back. I sat by myself and waited. He was still gone when our food arrived, so I went looking for him. I rounded the corner into the back and found him with the waitress. They weren't doing any talking, but instead were in the midst of what was obviously a sloppy kiss. I stood and stared, unable to believe what was right in front of me. Her arms were around his neck as he groped her ass.

I stood there staring for what seemed an eternity, unable to react. Finally she spotted me and pulled away. I didn't recognize her, but could see she wasn't much older than me. Since my dad was in his mid-forties, she had to have been about half his age. Her bleach blonde hair curled around her face in a style my friends and I sneeringly referred to as a rodeo queen look.

My dad followed her gaze and turned to see me standing there. I spun on my heel, walked out the door and got into the pickup. It couldn't be, I tried to convince myself, yet I had seen them. My mother had been right.

He came out a few minutes later, slowly climbed in and started the pickup. Before he put it in gear he turned and looked at me.

"Let's not tell your mother about this."

I literally wanted to spit on him. What he did was wrong, even if his wife was a bitter old hag. Instead I spat my answer.

"She knows all about her. And she knows about the others too."

My dad let his breath out in a long exhale, but remained silent. I sat next to him glowering in silence the rest of the way home. The thought I couldn't keep out of my head was that, even though what he did was wrong, if Ursula wasn't so mean to him, he wouldn't have to turn to other women.

After that I felt more isolated from my family than ever. I wondered if my brothers knew what was going on, but never brought up the subject with them. Maybe if his cheating remained hidden, it couldn't be real. The bond between my father and I had been weakening for years, ever since my brothers had gotten old enough to replace me as his helpers. Now it was completely broken. There was no place I fit in the only home I had ever known. I wanted to be out helping my dad, but he avoided me whenever he could after I caught him with the waitress. It became even more obvious that there was no place for me on the ranch I had grown up on.

Chapter 6

"Say, did that spotted calf of mine ever make it home?" My ears pricked up at the sound of my dad's voice on the phone as I entered the kitchen. He faced the living room so I saw only his back in the doorway as he leaned against the frame, conversing with Hank Henderson, a neighbor we shared a fence line with to the south.

We ran mainly pure-bred Herefords, but there were a few odd breed cows mixed in. One of them was a black and white spotted Shorthorn. Each spring we speculated on the coloring of her calf. Sometimes it came out resembling the red and white Herefords, and other years it looked like her. This year's bull calf had squeezed through the fence sometime the week before and was in with the neighbor's herd. His spotted hide stuck out amongst the solid colored Henderson cattle.

It was nearing weaning time, so the calf was no longer relying on his mother as his sole source of nourishment, but unless he found his way back through the barb wire, he needed to be cut out of the neighbor's herd and pushed through a gate back onto our place. I was hoping that meant a horseback ride for me.

"Uh huh…yeah," my dad listened as Hank chatted on. I poured coffee for myself and sat down. Ursula stirred potatoes on the stove, smoke rising off the cigarette that hung from the edge of the counter beneath her elbow. She also stood with her back to me.

My dad hung the phone back up on the wall. "Well, where's the calf?" I asked him as he refilled his coffee cup.

"Back home." He walked almost reluctantly over to the kitchen table and sunk down into his chair. The silence became awkward.

My brothers and sisters had left for school and the three of us didn't know what to do with one another. I felt like my parents were waiting for me to make a move about my life, but I had no idea what that move would be. And the two of them seemed barely able to stand one other's company. Each day the silent standoff between us created a wider rift.

But I was good help, and hoped my dad would keep me on because of it. Lately that seemed to matter more, not that I was his daughter, but that I could work.

That afternoon I sat on the bench in the mud room to remove my boots. I slumped back against the wall and looked into the kitchen. The well-worn table with its shiny, yellow top sat in the middle surrounded by scuffed, wooden chairs. The chair nearest the door had a rail broken off the back. As I stared at it I began to see the rails as prison bars. Even with the broken one there wasn't enough room to escape. I imagined myself struggling through the hole, trying to reach freedom, only to become hopelessly stuck.

Winter came and we began feeding. It was different this year. Instead of helping feed only on weekends and during school holidays, I was out seven days a week. It took most the day to scatter hay for the various herds and I was out every working side by side with my dad, while Hawk and Jerry fed their own route.

After shifting the John Deere into its lowest gear, so it just crawled along, my dad jumped down from the cab, came around to the back of the wagon and scrambled up onto the top next to me. I had already pulled wire cutters from my back pocket and snipped the wires holding the hay into a compacted bale. Holding onto one end of each of the two cut wires, I peeled off flakes in big chunks. Hungry cattle followed close behind and converged on each pile as it hit the ground. I quickly folded and crushed the wire before flipping it into a bucket and then reached for the next bale.

Once the wagon was empty for the last time, we headed back to the haystack to load it again so it was ready for the following morning. I tried to keep up with my dad, slinging bales from the stack to the wagon, but I always got behind and he had to help me stack it on the wagon. He was used to working with someone who was his equal physically and even though he never said anything, I imagined he didn't like that I slowed him down.

I held on tight as my horse struggled through a drift, pushing his way up the hillside. As we neared the crest, I urged him one last time and he scrambled out of the dense snow pack and up onto the top. The wind had blown the ridge clear of snow, and the bare, sandy soil made traveling much easier. I hunched my shoulders as the next gust caused Wilbur to turn his tail into the frigid northern air. Despite the wind chill, I patted his damp neck and let him stand and breathe a short minute before we continued on. Tag followed along at his heels, stopping periodically to glance back towards home, a forlorn look on his face.

According to the calendar, winter was two thirds gone, the end of February. The short gray days were taking their toll on me as except for the time feeding the cattle, I spent a lot of time trapped inside. Today I had an excuse to ride.

The better footing wasn't the only reason I wanted to reach the top, and as we paused I looked around from my vantage point. I still didn't see what I was looking for. Another gust caught us and we pushed on, following the ridgeline. The wind fought us every step of the way, as I continued scanning the countryside. It wasn't long before I was chilled to the bone, but there was no way I was returning home before finding what I searched for.

When the storm blew in, a small bunch of our cattle, separated from the main herd and drifted, letting the snow-filled wind push them until the fence stopped their progress. It didn't take long for the wooden posts to snap from the dozen or so thousand pound animals leaning against the barbed wire. Once the fence collapsed, the cows stepped over the wire and moved on, seeking a protected spot to wait out the storm.

We found the hole in the fence when we went out to feed that morning. I eagerly took on the job of looking for the missing cattle. Hawk had gone to the dentist that morning or I would have had company. I didn't mind braving the wind alone, as finding the lost bovines was a chance to go for a ride.

There was no telling how far they had gone. The blowing snow had quickly covered up any tracks. By now they would be hungry and looking for feed. My hands and feet became numb as I forced Wilbur to stay on top of the ridge instead of down below where the trees offered protection.

Even though the conditions weren't the most desirable, it was still where I preferred to be and I couldn't think of another job I would trade it for. At this point though, I wished I had another layer of clothing.

Eventually I spotted the red of the lost cows down amongst the trees in a deep ravine. I turned Wilbur and we plunged down off the ridge, again plowing through a drift, only this time it was downhill. Once down in the trees the air was calm and the snow only a few inches deep. Overhead the strong gale roared through the tree tops as I caught up with the cattle. They picked up their heads and watched us approach, their noses covered with snow where they'd been foraging for hidden grass.

I debated the best way to get the bunch home. Up and over the ridge was shortest, but forcing them through the drift by myself would be hard. I decided to take the longer route, around the base of the hill. The snow wasn't nearly as deep and it would be much easier traveling for the pregnant cows.

I circled around behind them. "Come on cows," I called out as I slapped my thigh. The sharp crack of my gloved hand hitting leather chaps stung my fingers, but it helped get the blood moving. The cows resisted, not wanting to leave the protection of the ponderosa and cedar trees.

"Get 'em up!" I ordered Tag and he charged in after the reluctant bovines, snapping at their heels, forcing them to move out into the wind. Every time one attempted to turn back, either Wilbur and I or the dog were there to halt the insurrection.

Once we were out into the open, we had to battle the wind as well as the unwilling cows. We were only a few miles from ranch headquarters, but it was a struggle almost the entire way. When the home pasture came into view they finally began a determined walk, realizing there would be feed waiting.

I was tired and cold when I finally closed the gate behind them. They didn't linger, but hurried off to find the hay that had been spread for them earlier that day. After I remounted, Wilbur and I plodded along behind. We crossed the pasture, passed through the gate on the other side and then up the driveway. The gray sky had turned to twilight by the time we reached the barn. I climbed down and stomped my feet to get the blood circulating before unsaddling Wilbur. Even in the barn it was freezing, but while I stood shivering, he leisurely licked up the last of his oats as his coat dried from where he had sweated underneath the wool saddle blanket. I turned him out with the other horses and made sure they had plenty of hay before hurrying up to the house.

I entered the kitchen and my parents immediately looked at me with solemn faces. My dad sat at the table, while Ursula stood in the doorway to the back hall.

"Did you find 'em?" My dad asked about the cattle.

"Yeah, they didn't get too far." I looked from him to Ursula. "What's going on?"

Ursula gestured at my dad, wanting him to speak.

"Sky, we heard some bad news."

"What is it?"

"Billy's dead."

"What are you talking about?" I thought I must have misunderstood him.

"Ahh," he shifted in his seat. "They found him in an alley. He was murdered." I sank down into a chair.

I learned the details of Billy's death, along with everyone else, as the news swept through town and beyond. The police in California concluded that he owed a drug dealer money and when he couldn't pay, was beaten to death. Of course everyone was shocked, disbelieving that a son of our community could have gotten himself involved in drugs on his own. It fed their beliefs about the weirdos out in California.

But I remembered when I had seen him last. It had been obvious something was very wrong back then, even if Will hadn't clued me in. I had no reason to disbelieve the assumption about why he died. What I couldn't understand is how he had come to be in that condition. He had known the damaging consequences of illegal drugs, so why had he begun taking them?

His death shattered me because it also killed The Plan. I felt ashamed as I questioned if I had really loved him or if I just wanted to use him. Maybe it was selfish of me to think that way, but without him I really could see nothing beyond my current existence. I thought of him lying in a dirty alley, smashed and broken, until I couldn't stand it and forced myself to remember him differently.

We had competed against one another on horseback in 4 H shows and at county fairs from the time we were old enough to sit a horse. I never really had a chance against him. He was just that much better. While the rest of us wrestled with our hard-headed ranch horses, manhandling them into behaving, Billy seemed to glide through horsemanship patterns.

When a judge had us switch horses, an obstinate mount suddenly acted like a well-trained show horse with Billy in the saddle. And it was the lucky kid who drew his horse to ride. I usually took second behind him in those classes. The other kids fought it out for third.

I lay on my bed and pictured him loping his big buckskin around the arena at the county fairgrounds. I always felt envious as I watched the gelding move, his rounded frame allowing him to use his hind end to easily power through maneuvers. I tried to copy him, but I struggled. Billy's horse seemed to naturally carry his head down, his neck arched, obedient and willing, moving on a loose rein like a seasoned bridle horse. Soft was the best word to describe how Billy rode, the way he sat in his saddle so casual looking.

In my mind, I focused my attention on his left hand steady above the saddle horn, his right relaxed at his side. The difference between a good horseman and a great one is the natural ability to communicate with a horse through the reins, to feel its mouth with the lightest touch. Billy was born with that talent. I had no doubt he could have gotten a horse to do anything he asked. Thinking of his hands caused me to finally cry over the loss of the guy I thought I loved.

A week after the funeral, Will called. "I just heard about Billy." I could hear traffic and imagined him leaning against a payphone on a street corner in Berkeley. "How are you doing?"

I heard the sincerity in his voice, but I took it as pity. "I'm okay."

"Man, I'm really bummed for you, Sky."

"Don't worry about me." I didn't want to have anything to do with anyone from California just then.

"I wish I could be there with you." Suddenly the genuineness of his words got through to me.

"I don't know what to do." My voice sounded feeble and whiny. I quickly looked around, but no one was there to hear my weakness.

"You have your family. They can help you get through this."

"Yeah, I guess." Apparently he didn't realize how alone I felt in the midst of my family.

We stayed on the phone for a few more minutes, but I had nothing more to say and I didn't feel like listening to someone else's life when I didn't have one.

Will continued writing me letters as he had done weekly since he left. Now, I set them on my dresser unopened. Even though I didn't care to know what he was doing, the growing stack allowed me to keep some kind of a connection to him.

It must have been having a set routine that kept me going the rest of the winter. Get up, go out to help feed, come in for lunch, go back out and load hay for the next morning. It had to be done every day regardless of the weather or how I felt. In freezing wind, heavy snowstorms and the gloomy days of late winter, I had to get my butt outside and up on the hay wagon.

I'm sure everyone thought my depression was from losing Billy, but truthfully, it was more about not knowing where I belonged. Once the hope that Billy would marry me was gone, I finally realized that I had been more in love with The Plan than with him. Maybe I had been fond of the Billy I grew up with, but I detested the version of him I had seen in California and that was the picture of him I now had in my mind.

Spring came and with it, calving season. We moved the cows up closer to ranch headquarters. During the day one of us rode through the herd regularly, pushing the ones closest to calving up to the sheds. I took my turn and spent cold nights bundled up, checking the heavies for signs of labor. Whenever I found one that seemed to be having difficulty, I had been told to immediately fetch my dad. He would decide if the cow needed assistance, plus he didn't think I was capable of pulling a calf by myself. That was fine with me as it was a brutal procedure which could result in tearing up the cow's uterus. That meant she would die and her calf, if it could be saved, would become a bottle fed orphan.

What I realized after I watched many labors in worried debate with myself whether to get help for the cow or give her a little time, was that oftentimes men were in too big of a hurry for the birth to happen. Even when she seemed to be struggling, I hung back, far enough away that she remained calm, just a quick look before moving back out of her sight. Unless the calf wasn't positioned right, it usually ended with a successful birth. Everybody soon realized that there were fewer problems when I was on watch. They thought it was luck, but I knew that patience, along with my quiet noninterference was the real reason.

Once the ground thawed and the mud dried up, I eagerly took on a couple more outside horses to train. All I really wanted to do was ride. One of my first memories was of sitting in front of my dad while we rode through a herd of cattle. I was probably only two or three, but I still remembered feeling secure in my father's arms while attempting to keep my tiny hands wrapped around his saddle horn. It was my first view of a horse's neck from up above and I enjoyed the movement the horse created as he walked. It became a craving that never went away.

Not only did I ride my own horse, but any other that I could get my saddle on. Even riding the other ranch horses wasn't enough. I needed more of a challenge. By the time I was fourteen I began training them for others when I had the time. I don't know how good I was, and most of what I knew I figured out on my own, but people seemed pleased with how their horses handled after I'd ridden them for a while. It wasn't long before people started paying me for my horse training services.

Chapter 7

Will showed up just before we began haying. This time we were expecting him. He called a couple weeks before and asked about helping out again. My dad told him we could use his help.

I have to admit I was looking forward to seeing him. With my family not getting along, I imagined we were all hoping his presence would create a truce. When the blue GTO pulled up to the house that evening, I was in the barn unsaddling a horse. I lingered for a couple minutes, so as not to appear over-eager, before I went to greet him.

He stood next to his car, talking to Adrian and Steve. I couldn't help notice that he looked good. His ponytail hung even further down his back, but his face remained clean shaven. He smiled when he saw me and I couldn't help but smile back. Despite the fact that I was waiting for him, I tried to act casual. That ended when he gave me a hug and I let loose with a laugh. It was the first real happiness I could remember feeling since he left the summer before.

By now, the twins had made their way down, so he gave each of them a hug also. They giggled and acted ditzy as usual. I looked up to see Ursula waving from the back door. I couldn't remember her smiling since he had left. Maybe home life would be a little less strained for the time Will stayed with us.

Of course the big question in my mind was if we would take up where we left off a year ago. I had spent a lonely year since I had last seen him. But first I had to take him in to see Ursula. It made me question if there might be something wrong with Will since Ursula liked him.

After dinner, I walked over to the bunkhouse with him as the sun set on a long Montana summer evening. He looked around, happy to be back on the D. Then he turned to me. He gave me a quick study in that way he had.

"I like your hair."

"Thanks." I had let it grow out over the winter. To me it looked like a shaggy mess that now covered my shoulders.

I felt awkward, not knowing what was going to happen. I felt like I had no say in the matter, like it was up to him to decide if, and how our relationship would continue.

I helped him haul a mattress down from the house to place on a bunk and saw that he was settled in. Behind us the sun reached the ridge to the west.

"It's good to be out of the city." He leaned against the log wall while holding his gaze on the sunset. "So quiet."

I glanced off to the west. The movement of the sun wasn't something I had been noticing much. My attention had mostly been concentrated on the worried thoughts that filled my head. I leaned against the warm logs next to him and waited, but he didn't even look at me. More doubts filled my mind.

"Good night." I finally said and walked off. Once I got to the other cabin I turned and looked back, but the twilight left little to be seen. I felt disappointed because it seemed he wanted nothing to do with me.

The next day Will got his first tractor driving lesson from Steve, as we waited for the fields to dry up. The water had been blocked from the irrigation ditches over a week before, but a soaking rain a couple days later delayed the start of our haying season.

He seemed to have fun helping my dad and brothers with the machinery and I felt jealous. He was my friend, I pouted to myself. Never mind that a year ago I had wanted nothing to do with him. Now I craved his company.

After dinner he set out for the bunkhouse. I could hear the tapping of his typewriter as I approached the cabin half an hour later.

"What are you writing?" I stood outside the open cabin door and called in to him. Part of me expected him to tell me to stop bothering him. He turned and looked at me.

"Nothing, much. Just some notes for a story I'm working on." He had just graduated from the university in Berkeley and I knew he was on his way to be a reporter for a newspaper down in Boulder, Colorado. Since he was replacing someone who was leaving in the fall, he had the summer to do as he wanted.

"I can't believe you want to do any more studying."

"I like to write. What's up?"

I didn't know what to say. "I guess I just want some company." I remained standing uncomfortably in the doorway.

He got up and walked out onto the porch and put his arms around me. "Is that all?"

"Well..." I didn't know how to tell him how lonely I was.

"You need to start telling people what you want," he coaxed me, but it wasn't something I knew how to do. I usually just waited for something to happen, for someone else to make a decision, since it seemed I was mainly ignored anyway.

"You could kiss me. I want that." I finally got the words out.

"Willingly." His lips tasted as delicious as I remembered.

He spent that night and every other with me in Great Grandpa Matt's cabin. I couldn't imagine my family didn't know what was going on, but nobody said a word. Maybe they decided it was my business, or maybe they figured I would marry Will and finally have a life. Maybe they just didn't care.

One evening we sat on the sofa in the living room. I had pulled out the photo album to show Will my family's history in pictures. He studied each photo as I flipped the pages and told him what I knew about each one, starting with my great grandfather Matt horseback. Next was a photo of him and my great grandmother Lavina sitting in a photographer's studio over in Miles City. Will shifted the album for a better look and a newspaper clipping fell out of the back and onto the floor. I picked it up and examined the photographs and accompanying story.

The first picture showed a smiling girl, her cheek pressed up close to a horse's head. The second photo showed the pair cutting a cow in competition. The photographer had caught the action as the mare held the cow, her haunches just inches from the ground, preventing it from returning to the herd. Her ears were cocked forward in eager anticipation. I looked at the rider and barely recognized Ursula, her face in total concentration on the animal in front of her, her body looking balanced and in sync as she sat the horse.

We read the story together. The clipping was from the Denver Post and the competition was the National Western Stock Show. The pair had come from nowhere and won a non pro class in cutting. I didn't know what to say as I studied one picture, then the other.

"That mare sure could squat." I jerked my head around at the sound of Ursula's voice. She stood behind the sofa, her eyes on the picture.

"When was this?" I asked.

"It was a long time ago," she replied. But I knew, as I had read the date on the clipping. It was from January, 1949, the year before I was born.

"What happened to the horse?"

"My father sold her that evening just after they took that picture, maybe before." She shrugged. "I don't know. The next morning she was gone. I never saw her again."

I had never heard my mother sound so sad. I was afraid to look at her, afraid that her anger would erupt after letting me see her so vulnerable. But she just walked off.

Will looked at me. "You never knew about this?"

"No." I was still incredulous. "She looks so happy," I continued, unable to believe the girl in the picture could be my mother. I had only seen Ursula ride a few times. It was obvious she knew how, but to win a class at one of the biggest cutting shows in the country when she was seventeen?

I looked in the direction she had gone. "How could she have let herself get like that?" I was referring not only to her weight, but also her slovenly appearance. It was like she simply didn't care.

"Why don't you ask her about it? She might dig having someone to talk to."

"She'd never talk to me."

"She just did."

I said no more as he didn't know Ursula like I did. My eyes went back to the picture of her smiling face. Her affection for the mare was obvious. I tried to imagine what it must have been like for her when she found the empty stall, how devastating it must have been. I knew there was a reason I never liked my Grandpa Gregory, and maybe I had just found out what it was.

Another day I made a comment about my mother to Will. We were all irritable from another long day out in the hot sun and I didn't think she had anything to complain about. Spending her days in the house, puttering around seemed to me a lot easier than working out in the field. It didn't prevent her from bitching at my father.

"Couldn't you at least brush off before coming into my kitchen?" She started in. His clothes, as well as his face were covered with chaff after cutting hay in the wind all day.

"Shut your mouth." My dad replied in an even voice, but the look on his face showed he was ready for a fight. Because our company wasn't present, she continued.

"What are you going to do if I don't?!" She shrieked. "If you want any dinner, you better go clean yourself off." It was a dare and I was afraid of the outcome. But he stomped out and brushed off his clothes before becoming back in and pouring a glass of whiskey. I couldn't believe he backed down. I wouldn't have. Later I told Will about it, still indignant at her nerve.

"Your mother works hard, Sky." It was one of his typical, neutral replies.

"We all work hard!" I snapped back, wishing he wouldn't defend her. If he only knew her better, he'd see, I thought to myself.

But at least for those few weeks, I was able to put much of my attention elsewhere. At night I escaped to Great Grandpa Matt's cabin and the comfort I got from Will's arms.

His last night on the D, Will and I talked about my future. We lay on the bed and watched the shadows made from the candles flutter against the wall. Outside, the crickets carried on loud and unrelenting with their mating calls.

"You know, there are other ways to make money." He chided me about my determination to remain on the D so I could ranch.

"I don't do it for the money."

"Is your dad even paying you?"

The truth was, women rarely drew wages on ranches. Most of them had the nonpaying jobs of being a wife or daughter. That they frequently went out and helped anytime an extra hand was needed didn't count. But I didn't mention that.

"I get the bottle calves and I earn money training horses."

"You work a lot of hours to not get paid," he pointed out. He didn't understand how it was, but I knew my place.

"What about you? What's your new job pay?"

"Not much," he admitted. Maybe we weren't that different. We both preferred doing what we liked, rather than having money as our main motivation.

"Why don't you come with me?" he suddenly asked. It was the first time he had suggested a future that could include me. Once again he was heading across country, this time to an outdoor rock concert back in New York, something he referred to as Woodstock. "It'll be fun, lotta great music."

"Why don't you stay here?" I asked back. I wasn't serious, but since he had expressed a desire to be with me longer than just these few weeks, I did the same.

"I could dig living here," but I knew his words were merely meant to appease since I had already seen a down-the-road look in his eyes and knew that tomorrow he'd be traveling on the far side of a cloud of dust, off on another adventure and out of my life again. I never even considered that I might be enough to keep him around.

The following morning I watched his car disappear down the driveway once again. I felt hurt and rejected. Blaming Will for abandoning me was much easier than taking any action to fix my own life.

Shortly after he left, I climbed in my car and drove to town. Once there I pulled into Connie's Cut and Curl. I took a seat in the chair and told Connie, "I need a haircut."

"What kind of style do you want?" Her eyes lit up as she eyed the ragged mess on my head.

"Just cut it short," I instructed her. With a dejected look on her face she picked up her scissors, resigning herself once more to another "usual," instead of having a chance to test her creativity. Realizing I wasn't in the mood for chitchat, she stayed silent as she snipped away. Finally she stepped out of the way to let me view her handiwork.

"Shorter," I told her as I glared at my reflection in the mirror.

By the time I allowed her to stop, there wasn't a lot of hair left on my head. The cut looked ugly and I thought it matched my hideous facial features. It also matched my mood perfectly.

I quickly stood up and paid the hairdresser, not wanting to look at my reflection any longer than necessary. Once outside, I walked down the block to the Yellowstone Diner for some lunch. It was the day of the annual Daly family picnic, but I didn't plan on attending. There was no one there I wanted to see and I didn't really care to socialize.

My mood didn't get any better throughout the remainder of the summer and into the fall. Adrian left for college over in Bozeman to study engineering. Steve left also. He was only sixteen and had two years of high school left, but he wasn't about to let it get in the way of his life, one that didn't include the D. He ended up over in Omaha, driving a semi for a cattle hauling outfit. I don't know if he lied about his age, but figured that anyone who talked to him about anything mechanical and then watched him drive any type of large machinery, including big rigs, would offer him a job. He seemed to have been born to it. The twins continued focusing on escaping to town any way possible.

Chapter 8

The call came in the early morning, like those types always seem to. The door to my parents' bedroom opened after six or seven rings. I heard Ursula's sleepy "Hello," followed by a short indistinct conversation. Then there was complete silence. Finally I got up and went out into the hallway. She stood holding the phone and I wondered why she didn't just hang it up.

"Who was that?" I asked.

"Your father's been in an accident. I have to go to the hospital. Stay here with your sisters." Her voice was calm and there was no urgency. She hung the phone up and went back into her bedroom, avoiding any questions.

In the morning the sheriff came out to check on the three of us and give us the news. He sat us down and told Debbie, Donna and I that our father was dead.

Later, I got the details. He and his latest girlfriend had driven to Billings the evening before. After spending most of the night in a bar, they started home. No one knew if he had fallen asleep, or if it was the alcohol, but the pickup missed a corner and rolled down a steep hill. Both of them were crushed and died before help arrived.

Aunt Loretta drove Ursula home that afternoon. My mother sat at the table looking around as if seeing her life for the first time. I blamed her for my dad's death. It was her fault he wasn't at home in bed. She drove him away with her meanness. I watched her detachment and used the fact that she didn't cry to fuel my hatred of her.

She seemed to take the next few days in stride, helping with the funeral arrangements while playing the grieving widow. I could only watch helplessly, waiting for my father's death to sink in, as I viewed Ursula's calm control.

If I thought I was lost before, it was nothing compared to how I felt as we buried my dad and then continued our lives without him. At least Ursula wasn't screaming. In fact she became rather quiet. Of course she had the entire county's sympathy. Her husband had died sinning, and I suppose that gave her some kind of moral stature and maybe rightly so. But even though I hated the scandal he brought upon our family, he was still my father.

Will called the evening after the funeral. I answered the phone and the familiar voice was like a lifeline on the other end.

"Do you want me to come up there?" He was in Boulder, just back from an assignment covering the trial of some guys he called the Chicago Seven. He had tried to explain it to me, something about these guys being arrested during a protest during the Democratic Convention the summer before. But, as usual, when something didn't affect me directly, I hadn't paid much attention when he tried to explain the significance of the event.

"Uh…" I hesitated, trying to think about what his being here would mean. But I just couldn't imagine how he could fit into my life since he was part of the problem. I was still angry from when he left the last time.

"No, don't you have a story to write." I suppose I wanted to feel sorry for myself, to prove that he put the politics of the day ahead of me.

"I could write it there and send it in. The paper would understand." He had once sent a story through the mail to be published when he was working at the D. "I could leave right now if you want me to."

I shifted my weight to my other foot and fiddled with the phone cord. The problem was, even though he might provide some comfort, he couldn't fix things. "No, that's ok." Suddenly I felt really tired. "I have to go."

"Well, keep in touch." I may have heard a little wanting in his voice, but I ignored it. It never occurred to me to wonder how he had found out about my father's death.

Adrian went back to school and Steve back to driving truck and it was only Ursula and her daughters who remained at the D. It was like the men had abandoned ship, or the ranch, in this case.

I carried on the best I could. The cows began dropping their calves and I tried to take charge, as there was no one else. Ursula seemed to have no interest in running the D. The twin's main concern returned to figuring out how to stay in town after school let out for the day. They begged and cajoled both my mother and whatever friends and relatives they decided to pounce on, until allowed to spend the night and even entire weekends away.

"Come on. You can pick us up in town. We'll meet you wherever you want." Donna was pleading with me so they didn't have to ride the bus home. Debbie looked on with what I assumed were supposed to be puppy dog eyes.

"I can't drop everything just to drive to town for you guys." It was two months after my father's death. Calving had barely begun, but I was already stressed out from lack of sleep. The other two herds were in capable hands, but the home cows were now my responsibility. I had asked Ursula if she would hire a couple men to help me out, but she refused. With my brothers home on weekends the previous year, I had some time off, but without them or my father, I didn't know how I was going to calve out seven hundred cows all by myself. The worst part was that my mother and sisters acted like this wasn't an important time on the D. They only ventured away from the house to get in the car and drive off.

And the truth was, I was getting no sleep other than a quick nap every once in a while. At least there were no heifers. The first time mothers were the ones who had to be watched carefully. The older cows usually birthed their calves easily. But Hawk had offered to take on the responsibility for the young cows and we moved them over to a pasture close to where he lived so he could watch them.

One morning I staggered into the house after being up all night. A cow was struggling with a breech birth. When I saw she was having problems I called Hawk and woke him. He hurried over to help. After struggling for hours to change the position of the calf, we had ended up losing both cow and calf.

When I got to the house I was not only tired, but upset over losing the pair. I was expecting a hot cup of coffee at least, but I closed the door on a dark and cold kitchen. I made coffee, wondering why Ursula hadn't yet drug her lazy ass out of bed. I knew the twins should be up and getting ready for school, but I refused to go up and wake them.

I scrounged in the refrigerator for some breakfast. I didn't have time to cook myself a meal, but I needed food before the growling beast in my stomach started taking bites out of me. I buttered a couple pieces of toast and dumped a can of fruit cocktail into a bowl. That, with coffee, temporarily stopped my hunger.

After pouring myself another cup, I sat at the table to rest for a few more minutes. Unable to keep my eyes open, I put my head in my arms and fell asleep.

"What are you doing!? Why didn't you get them up!?" Ursula's screeching startled me awake. I jerked my head up. "They missed the bus. You're going to have to take them to school." She slammed a cup on the counter to make her point.

"I have to go back out to check the cows again." At least, after the rude awakening, I was wide awake.

"No, you're driving your sisters to school."

"I can't do that." It was the first time I ever remembered defying a direct order from my mother. She glared at me, but said no more, even though her look told me I was responsible for creating more work for her.

I went back out into the chilly spring morning and over to the pasture we used for calving. In that short period of time, three more calves had hit the ground. I drove the old Chevy through the herd. It would have been easier to see each cow individually while riding Wilbur, but even the thought of saddling a horse seemed like too much work. Besides, I could take quick naps in the cab. Thankfully I found no more problems.

It was noon by the time I got back to the house. Once again the kitchen was cold and empty. Ursula and the twins were gone. I scrounged another cold meal before lying down on the couch in the living room for an hour before going back out.

That evening I was hoping to finally get a hot meal. Ursula was back, along with Donna and Debbie. The meal came, but not without a price. My mother couldn't really get on me for not driving my sisters to school, but she refused to let go of the fact that I hadn't woke them up that morning. I shoveled down my food, partly because I was ravenous, but also to more quickly get out of her sight. All I wanted to do at that point was go to sleep and never wake up.

I began avoiding the house when I spotted the station wagon in the driveway. Instead I snuck around, gathering up canned food and blankets. I made myself a nest down in the barn for my naps. Even though I felt like a degenerate of some type, it was preferable to tolerating Ursula. After a while, I even got used to being cold all the time.

Finally the number of calves born each day dwindled to only a few as the last cows birthed and I had the time to move on to other spring chores. The ditches needed cleaning before we could run water on the hay fields. I had never run the ditcher before, but had watched my father and brothers many times.

The hardest part was getting it hooking up to the tractor. I considered asking Hawk to come help me, but decided it would make me seem helpless. I finally got the heavy iron blades pinned to the draw bar after struggling with the alignment and the weight and headed out to the field. It took me days to complete the task of scraping out the silt that had collected, as well as ripping out the weeds that grew in the bottoms of the ditches. I may not have made the cleanest cuts, but I got it done. I was ready to run the irrigation water.

Not long after the last cow calved, Hawk appeared at the kitchen door, hat in hand. "It's time for me to be moving on," was his only explanation for leaving. Jerry quit shortly after. Ursula didn't seem concerned, but with haying season close, it added to my worries.

Adrian came home for the summer and became the D's logical choice for boss. He went through the haying machinery, preparing the equipment the same as usual, even though there were only the two of us. But he had a couple of college buddies looking for summer jobs, plus we found some high school kids, so we had a full, if inexperienced, crew when we rolled out onto the fields.

Everything proceeded better than I hoped. There were the expected small break downs like when a guard on the cutter bar broke after striking a rock, but nothing that couldn't be easily fixed with spare parts we already had on hand. I kept my fingers crossed as we progressed.

One day around noon we arrived at the house with the hired help, expecting lunch. I saw that the station wagon was gone and had a bad feeling. The twins had convinced Ursula to let them spend the entire summer in town with her sister, so I knew they wouldn't have lunch ready. It was the second time Ursula had taken off without a word. The six of us entered the empty kitchen.

I looked at Adrian. Disappointment showed on his face and he made no attempt to hide it. I felt the same way. Besides the fact that we were putting in long hours and expected to be fed accordingly, we were embarrassed. What ranch didn't feed their help? The pay might not be great for a ranch hand, but the food should be.

I didn't know what to say, at least not in front of the crew. Instead I opened cupboards and the refrigerator, rummaging for something to feed us all. We sat down to a meager lunch, one more fit for a bunch of old ladies.

"This can't keep happening." Adrian's urgent hiss came at me as the others trailed out the door ahead of us.

"What do you want me to do?"

"We need to eat."

"It's not my job." I felt I was being attacked

"You're gonna have to go to the grocery store," he persisted.

"Yeah, of course I am." I resigned myself to the fact that, being a girl, I was the one getting stuck with going shopping. I had never disliked Ursula more than right then.

The guys drove back out into the field while I went to town. I was angry at getting stuck doing women's work, but I'd gotten an idea. Instead of driving to the IGA, I went to my Aunt Dottie's house.

Dorothy was my father's younger sister. She was born when my grandparents were already in their forties and was only twelve years older than I was. I envied her because she knew Great Grandpa Matt, although she said she mainly remembered him as a crotchety old man.

She married Uncle Walter and moved to Livingston where he worked as a mechanic for the railroad. Only a couple months later a heavy piece of machinery fell on him at work, crushing bones and messing up his insides. They moved back to Compton with him a cripple, to live on a small pension he received from the railroad.

People said he was lucky to be alive, but I wasn't so sure. Ever since the accident, the past ten years or so, his life mainly consisted of sitting in his recliner in front of the television. I don't know how he did it, but in spite of the constant pain and difficulty getting around, he was always cheerful. I think I would have gone crazy a long time ago.

"Why, Sky, what a nice surprise. What brings you by?" Dottie glanced up at the sky as she greeted me, ever the rancher's daughter. The blue sky told her something was up because she knew I'd have been out with the haying crew unless it rained.

"Hi, Aunt Dorothy. I need to ask you something."

"Well come on in." She frowned slightly and I could see the wheels in her mind turning as she wondered what I had to ask. "Coffee?"

"No, thanks. I don't have time... well a quick cup." I could hear the television in the other room.

"Have a seat." She poured coffee and then sat opposite me.

"How would you like to cook for the D through haying?"

"Where's your momma, honey?"

"She hasn't been around much lately."

"What do you mean she's not around?"

"She takes off and is gone all day." I didn't mention she was gone most of the nights also.

"Well I did hear she was in The Leopard." The Leopard was a honky tonk over in Cedar Junction. My mother had never done such a thing before. I later found out that my aunt was actually trying to break it to me easy. It was all over town that Ursula had been seen in almost every bar between Compton and Billings. But that afternoon I needed a cook.

"The point is, she's not around. It'll be a paying job."

"Oh, but you wouldn't have to pay me." She sounded eager to help. "What about Walter?"

"Bring him with you. We have tv out there." I told her, feeling relieved. But then I knew she liked to keep busy.

"Well, ok, if you don't think your mother will mind."

I gave a snort. I couldn't imagine Ursula would get mad at anyone taking over her job. Besides, I didn't care.

"Meet me over at the IGA." I got up to go. Before I went out the door, I stuck my head into the living room.

"Hi Uncle Walter."

"Sky! What are you doing?"

"Had to talk to Aunt Dot. I'll see you soon." He was excited to have company, but I kept moving. Aunt Dot could fill him in, as I had work to do.

By the time Dot got to the grocery store, I had a shopping cart half full. Purposefully, we strode through the store, up and down each aisle, picking out food to feed the haying crew. After we lugged the bags of groceries out to my car and filled the trunk and back seat, we made final arrangements.

The next morning, I got up and started breakfast. I was in a much better mood. There was food in the house and Ursula wasn't around to fight with. Aunt Dot and I had made an arrangement. I would cook breakfast for Adrian and myself in the morning and then she would arrive in time to make lunch for the entire crew. Before driving home for the night, she made dinner and left it in the oven.

We had barely sat to eat when she came through the kitchen door, with Uncle Walter trailing painfully behind.

"Coffee's fresh." I jumped up to pour the two of them a cup, but she hurried over.

"I can get it. You sit and eat."

While I ate, she helped Uncle Walter get settled into a chair. When I finished, I carried my plate to the sink and began running water. I reached for the dish soap, but Dot told me, "I'll get that." I started thinking I was going to really like this arrangement.

When we came for lunch, there were pork chops with mashed potatoes and gravy waiting for us. Everyone smiled spontaneously at the smell as we came through the door. For desert there was a cherry pie baked fresh that morning. Another one waited for our dinner. Dottie may have left the ranch, but she hadn't forgotten how to cook for a crew. She didn't just throw something together. She prepared hearty meals for hard workers.

Our hired help started acting a lot happier. The food at the D was once again worth coming to work for. It made me proud.

Ursula's car was in the driveway the next morning. I hadn't heard her come in, even though, with the warm weather, I was sleeping out in the cabin. She clomped down the stairs as Adrian and I ate breakfast. She wore a bath robe and her uncombed hair stuck out in all directions. It had become her usual look for this time of day.

She didn't say a word as she reached for the coffee pot. Once her cup was full she turned and looked at us. We both turned our attention back to our plates.

"Good morning." Dottie burst through the door just then. She stopped dead in her tracks when she saw Ursula at the counter. The kitchen was the wife's domain, the one place she had control over. Dot had invaded my mother's space without being granted permission. I quickly saw her predicament.

"Aunt Dot is going to cook for us since you don't seem to want to." I kind of wanted to pick a fight, but Ursula shrugged as she sank into her chair.

"It's all yours." She yawned. Clearly she couldn't care less about her kitchen. In fact she barely resembled the angry house wife we all knew.

In the months since my father's death, she had gone through a transformation. She was losing a lot of weight and had grown her hair long enough that curls were beginning to appear. There was a glimpse of the girl in the newspaper clipping. She looked much younger than she had before my dad died, at least when she got enough sleep. This morning she looked rough.

When I came in at noon, she wasn't around. "Where's Ursula?" I had come in ahead of the others.

"Don't address your mother that way," Aunt Dot reprimanded me. "She said she didn't feel well, so she went upstairs to lie down." The television blared from the other room and I could see Uncle Walter's feet resting on a footstool through the doorway. That evening she was gone again.

The rumors about my mother's partying began to grow. I saw her little through the summer, which was fine by me. I heard she had first one boyfriend, then another. She never brought any of them to the D, and since I stuck pretty close to home, her social life affected me little.

Once the last bale was heaved onto the top row of the final stack of hay, Adrian laid off the haying crew and returned to school. My aunt and uncle went home for the last time. There was no one else to run the ranch, so I decided it was up to me to take charge and I intended to keep everything running smoothly.

I began riding out daily, checking cattle and feed. The calves were close to weaning age and I thought about how I was going to get the job done with no help. Meanwhile I waited to see if Ursula was going to take any interest in the operation. But she continued to come and go as if the ranch was simply a motel where she occasionally stayed.

One afternoon, I came up to the house after unsaddling my horse. I stopped in the doorway when I saw a strange man sitting at the table across from Ursula. She stopped what she was saying in mid-sentence when I appeared.

"This is Rad Johnson." She threw the name out. I looked at a man with dark hair, cut longer, as men who wanted to look cool wore their hair. It reached past his collar in the back. Thick side burns and a mustache gave him more of a sleazy look than the hip one he must have been after. His shirt, a loud print, was unbuttoned half way down his chest. I glanced down at his feet, the true evidence of who a person was, in my opinion. He was wearing boots, but not the kind made for working in.

"What kind of name is Rad?" I was instantly angry.

"Hello, Sky." He seemed to be appraising me.

"I've hired Mr. Johnson to manage the ranch." He and my mother smiled at one another.

"What? You can't be serious." I looked from one to another, doing nothing to hide my disdain. Surely this wasn't my father's replacement.

"You better just get used to it." Ursula took control of the situation.

I didn't know what to do. If I could have gotten my mother alone I might have pleaded with her, but I couldn't say anything in front of a stranger.

"Have you paid Aunt Dot yet?" I asked.

"I'm not paying her. What do you think, that just because family starts hanging around I should be giving them money?"

"I promised her."

"Forget it." As we bickered, Johnson closely watched the two of us.

"She cooked for us when you couldn't be bothered." I refused to give up, but Ursula wouldn't budge. "Well, we need to start weaning soon. And we need to get trucks lined up." I turned to Rad probing his knowledge of ranching.

"Actually we talked it over and decided to do things differently."

"What do you mean?"

"We don't see room for you here any longer." Ursula finally got out what she had obviously wanted to say all along.

I couldn't believe my ears. "You're kicking me out?"

"We feel it's better if you leave." Rad saw an opening and took over from my mother.

I went into shock, too stunned to continue talking. I looked at Ursula one last time. Her brown eyes resembled stone.

"Fine, I'll go." Suddenly I couldn't wait to get the hell out of there.

Within fifteen minutes I had gathered up a few belongings, including my saddle from the barn, and like the last time I was rejected, once more found myself driving into the night.

I stopped at The Crossing to use the pay phone outside. After shoving change into the slot, I heard Darlynn's voice on the other end of the line. She was still going to school in Bozeman.

"Can I come stay with you for a few days?" I asked her.

"Sure, what's up?"

"I need to get away for a while." I didn't have enough change to tell her the entire story over the phone. "I'll be there in a couple of hours." I got in my car and continued driving.

I arrived on her doorstep just after midnight. She met me in the doorway and handed me a beer. "Let's party!" she encouraged me and followed it with a whoop.

I took the beer. "Don't you have school tomorrow?"

"And the day after, and the day after that. It's not going anywhere. But how often does my best friend come visit?" I tried to smile, but couldn't.

"Ok, now what's going on?" she asked once we were inside the house and she had introduced me to her room mates.

"Ursula hired a manager for the D and they kicked me off."

"That's brutal. But you needed to get away from there."

Was it that obvious to everyone but me? Will had as much said the same thing before he left. But I had nowhere to go.

"No sympathy for me, huh?"

"Well sure, but what are you gonna do?"

"Well right now, I think I'll drink a beer."

The next couple of days revolved around Darlynn finding time in her schedule to spend time with me. She didn't seem very into school, even though she said she liked it fine. She said she just wanted to hang out with me for a couple days.

We sat in a diner on Main Street. Over dinner, we discussed my options.

"What's Will up to?"

I shrugged. "Nothing to do with me."

"You could get a job here. You already have a place to stay."

"I don't know." I just couldn't see a future in Bozeman.

"Oh, you know what? Louise is quitting that job over in Idaho. Maybe you could take over."

"Baby sitting other people's horses?" I was skeptical.

She's breaking colts for them too."

"Really?" Suddenly I was interested.

"Yeah, and it's a real sweet setup. She breaks a few colts and care takes the place for some rich people. I guess they're pretty nice."

"What's she going to do now?" I felt a little guilty at not keeping up on my friend's life.

"You haven't heard? She's going back home to marry Dave."

"She is?" I actually didn't find it surprising that she would marry her high school sweetheart. "Do you have her phone number over there?"

"Yeah, I think so." She rustled around in her bag and pulled out a piece of paper. "Here it is."

She handed the scrap of paper over and I didn't hesitate. I went over to the cashier and got change for a dollar before going to the pay phone in the back. Louise answered the phone and told me I had almost missed her, as she was leaving early the next morning. The couple she worked for hadn't found anyone to replace her yet and she said would put in a word for me.

A few days later, after stopping in Compton to withdraw money from my savings account, I was on my way to Idaho. At the bank I contemplated closing out my account, but I guess I wanted some tie to my childhood home, so I left fifty bucks. I figured it could collect interest for a while. I realized after I was gone that I would miss Louise's wedding and hoped she'd understand. Fleeing the D had become my main focus.

Paul and Rhonda Phillips owned fifty acres with a large, new house and barn near Sun Valley, Idaho. It was a gorgeous valley surrounded by mountains and with the ski area to the north. The couple only spent time there during the summer. By the time the snow came, they were long gone. I learned they had another home near Houston, plus they traveled a lot.

They had a half dozen cutting bred mares they raised foals from. My job was to break the two year olds and give them some basic training. The ones that seemed the most likely to have successful careers as cutters were then sent to a trainer down in Texas. The others were sold.

It was an easy job, as Louise had informed me. The youngsters were handled from birth, so putting a saddle and then a first ride on them was a lot different from breaking the half-wild range bred horses I was used to taking on.

That was what happened in the summer anyway. When I got there in the early fall, my job consisted mainly of caretaking. Since it snows a lot in that country during the winter, riding would have been difficult. I fed and cared for the mares and recently weaned foals, plus the yearlings. The two year olds were gone so there weren't even any horses to ride when I arrived.

The main house sat on a hill overlooking the valley and the mountain peaks beyond. Below was the barn, with a caretaker's apartment on one end. Not counting the bathroom, my new quarters were about the same size as my great grandpa's cabin, snug, but comfortable.

The Phillips' were a middle-aged couple. I arrived just in time to meet them before they left for the winter. I thought it a little odd that they left a stranger in charge of their magnificent house, not to mention close to twenty head of expensive horses.

They didn't seem worried though. Maybe because Louise knew what she was doing and since she recommended me, they figured I was also dependable. Before they drove off, Mrs. Phillips told me to go on up to the house and help myself to whatever was in the refrigerator, since it would go bad anyway.

It didn't take long for the snow to come. By Thanksgiving the ground was already covered for the winter. I noticed that ranches in the area had already begun feeding hay by then, and I couldn't help think that back on the D, the grass lasted until after Christmas.

The morning of the first snow, I heard the sound of an engine out in the driveway. It was before light and I had just made coffee. I looked out the window and realized it was a plow clearing off the snow. After the pickup pushed through to the cabin, the driver jumped out, came to the door and knocked. I opened it.

"Hi, my name is Troy Thomas. I live a few miles down the road." He jutted his chin in the direction. His hat told me that he must live on one of the neighboring ranches.

"I'm Sky Daly. It's nice to meet you."

"My wife sent these over, kind of a welcome gift I guess." He seemed slightly uncomfortable as he held out a paper bag. I tried to determine his age and couldn't get any closer than not a whole lot older than me.

"Thank you." I accepted the gift. "Do you have time for a cup of coffee?"

"Thanks, but no. I've got to finish plowing before I go out and feed." He turned to leave.

"Well, tell your wife thank you." I shut the door and opened the bag. Homemade cookies, just like I guessed.

The routine was easy. The horses were in three pastures, mares in one, yearlings in another and on the other side of the barn, the recently weaned foals. Each contained a run in-shed so the horses could get out of the weather. Once I tossed hay in to them and checked their water, there wasn't a lot to do. I drove up to the ski area to check it out since I had never seen skiers before. I watched people careening down the hill on thin wooden boards and couldn't decide if they were crazy. In the end I decided it looked like fun.

One morning the telephone rang. It didn't happen often and I figured it was Mrs. Phillips checking in.

"Hello, Sky?"

"Yes." It was a women's voice that I didn't recognize.

"This is Kate Thomas, from down the road."

"Oh, hi." I had waved to Troy when I passed him on the road, but hadn't spoken to him since he came by and introduced himself.

"I was wondering if you wanted to come over for dinner one night."

"Sure." I was definitely up for some socializing, along with a home cooked meal.

"How about tomorrow? I took a roast out to defrost, thought I'd cook it tomorrow."

"That sounds great. Do you want me to bring anything?"

"Just yourself. How's six o'clock?"

"I'll be there."

The Thomas' place was a beautiful ranch that was becoming surrounded by second homes owned by people who vacationed in Sun Valley. I arrived at their house right on the stroke of six. The front porch had a light on, but I could see from the trampled snow that most of the traffic went around back, so I followed the pathway to the back door. I walked through the mud room and knocked on the kitchen door.

Kate Thomas was short, not much over five feet, with sandy blonde hair that hung in a braid down her back. She was dressed in jeans and a flannel shirt, with slippers on her feet. She took one look at me and I could tell she recognized a ranch daughter just like herself.

"Don't mind the mess," she told me after greeting me and introducing herself.

I looked around. The house looked fine to me, especially since I knew that young children lived there. One of them, a girl, paused while setting the table to stare at me.

"This is Gabrielle, my oldest. You about finished there?" She glanced at the table. "Go get glasses." She turned back to me and smiled. I heard a shriek coming from down the hallway. Two more children came tearing around the corner and into view. They stopped short when they spied me. The toddler following behind also stopped and stared.

Kate introduced the rest of her children. "Scottie, Nicole and Ben, my baby." She pointed out each one in turn.

"Hi." They stood and stared at me without replying. I felt uncomfortable being the focal point of the little faces looking up at me. "This is a neat old house," I turned back to Kate and she showed me her living room. The house was made of huge, sturdy logs and I had admired it more than once from the road as I drove by.

The kitchen door opened and Troy came in. "Hello," he greeted us. He slipped a pair of slippers onto his stocking feet before opening the refrigerator door. "Beer?" he asked me. He seemed a man of few words.

"Sure, thanks." I took the cold can from him after he punctured two holes in the top with the opener hanging from the refrigerator door. Kate told me to sit and resumed her scurrying around the kitchen as Troy washed up.

We all crammed around the kitchen table as she dished out food and poured milk for the children before sitting down. It became instantly quiet as we all turned our attention to the food on our plates.

"So what brings you to this part of the country?" Kate could finally turn her attention to her company.

I explained that I had needed a job and that, when Louise quit, I had taken over horse training for the Phillips'.

"Where'd you learn to train horses?"

"Just by doing it."

"So you and Louise grew up together.

"We've been best friends since we were little. Her folks ranch a little bit east of where my…our place is." I looked down at my food. It was hard to talk about the D.

Kate continued chatting. I realized she probably didn't get a lot of company and it turned into a fun evening. I insisted on helping Troy with the dishes as she got the children ready for bed. It seemed she mainly chased after them and I found myself thankful it wasn't me. Once they were asleep, we settled into the living room for one last beer before I went home.

"There seem to be a lot of big houses around here," I commented.

"Yeah, land developers are buying up ranches, cutting them up, then selling off pieces to the rich people," Troy replied.

"Why are people selling?"

"It's not a hard decision when someone offers you the kind of money they're getting. After you've worked hard all your life and still don't have much to show for it and then suddenly you can move to town and retire in style, it's hard to resist." Troy's eyelids began drooping as he talked, which was small wonder. He was up long before dawn checking the weather and then going out to plow if it had snowed overnight.

"The worst part is that it's driving up property taxes," Kate added.

"That's what the extra job is for, paying the county," he explained.

Kate perched on the edge of the couch next to her husband. "Our hired man has a doctor's appointment in the morning. How would you like to come help Troy feed?"

"No, I can get along fine by myself."

"I can come help." I knew it was possible for one person feed off hay, but the job became a whole lot easier with two.

He reluctantly agreed, maybe because he sensed my eagerness. There was nothing I would like better than to be helping out on a ranch again.

"What's the matter with your hired man?"

"Oh, he got his nose busted in a fight last weekend at The Hole. It's all swelled up, looks awful. I told him to go to the doctor because I'm tired of looking at it."

"Sounds ugly. What time do you want me to be here in the morning?"

"First light, unless it snows. The forecast said it might."

"I'll be here." It had to be past their bedtime, so I thanked Kate for the wonderful meal

and said good night.

As usual, I woke up early the following morning. Since there was no new snow, I tossed hay to the horses and drove to the Thomas ranch. After a quick greeting to Kate in their warm, well-lit kitchen, Troy and I went back out the door. The tractor already sat idling, since the big, diesel engine needed time to warm up in the frigid air.

While Troy climbed up into the tractor seat, I hopped up onto the back of the hay wagon and found a spot to sit at the back of the carefully stacked bales of hay. We pulled out of the yard and headed out towards the pasture. I couldn't see, but when we stopped, I knew what it meant.

"I got it!" I yelled as I jumped down and hurried around to open the wire gate into the pasture.

"Leave it," Troy hollered as drove past me. I dropped the gate and quickly scrambled back up to my spot before he could stop. I stood up for a minute looking to see where we were headed, but the wind chill created by the movement quickly numbed my face. I hunkered back down amongst the bales again where it was warmer.

A few minutes later, the tractor slowed to a stop. I looked up to see cattle moving towards us, some at a walk, the more eager ones trotting to get to the hay.

"Now?" I called out.

"Come up here and steer."

"I can flake off."

In response, the tractor and wagon began moving forward at a slow crawl as Troy shifted into first gear. He jumped down off the moving tractor and came around to the back. I had already pulled wire cutters from my back pocket, cut the two wires from the top bale on the end and started peeling off flakes by the time he was up alongside of me.

I glanced in the direction we were slowly traveling and saw only the white expanse of a large pasture. We worked side by side, cutting wire and tossing off chunks of hay to the eager cattle. I carefully hung onto the wire, so as not to drop it on the ground. A lot of cattle had been killed through the years from ingesting pieces of it.

Occasionally Troy looked up to see that the driverless tractor tracked in a fairly straight line. The cattle had packed the snow enough that there was little danger of getting stuck and I couldn't yet see the back fence in the gray light.

We moved fast and after a few minutes the cold lost its effect on me. I unzipped my coat part way as I became warm from the exertion. Troy jumped down and went back to the tractor, quickly stepping up onto the lower step to miss the turning wheels. I guess it was a little bit dangerous, but it was the way ranchers had fed since they used horses. Of course, a good team pulling a sled needed less direction than the tractor did.

He gradually turned the wagon in a half circle until we were headed back towards the house. I continued flaking off bales in a line parallel to the first. The cattle converged on their breakfast, at first jostling one another for the best spots, then spreading out as the length of the line of hay grew.

I paused and looked around for stragglers. The sky turned blue as sunrise approached. This was the life and I couldn't help grinning at Troy as our breath escaped in clouds of vapor to disappear above us.

We arrived back at the house at noon and I couldn't hide my delight. Kate put lunch on the table and I again sat down to eat with the Thomas family.

Kate looked at me, then over at Troy. "How's everything?"

"Fine. Sky here is good help." It felt satisfying to once again put in a good morning's work.

"I'm happy to help out," I replied and thought I saw a hint of sadness on Kate's face. I wondered if she felt trapped in the house taking care of her young children while life went on around her.

Chapter 9

I started hanging out at a bar called The Watering Hole, or The Hole, as it was known locally, down in the small town of Hailey. Live bands played on weekends, usually country bands that played boot tapping dance tunes. An old barn on the edge of town had been renovated and it made a great dance hall. A stage had been added to one end, and even with a bar there was still plenty of room for dancing, not to mention the brawls that broke out and weren't uncommon.

Even though I was only twenty, I had no problem being admitted or ordering alcohol. I met a few people around my own age and became a regular on Friday and Saturday nights.

One evening I called over to the Thomas'. When Kate answered the phone, I told her about a band that was playing at the Hole that weekend. I'd heard them play before.

"You and Troy should check them out. They're pretty good," was my assessment of their talent. "Fun to dance to," I added for further enticement. I'd decided she needed a night out.

"I don't know. I'd have to find a sitter."

"I'll watch your kids." Suddenly it seemed important to get her out of the house for a night off.

"Really? They can be a handful."

"I'm pretty good at hog tying."

She laughed before replying. "Well, I'll think about it."

By Saturday it was all arranged. I went over to the Thomas house early so that Kate and Troy could make a night of it, dinner and then dancing.

The four children again stood and stared at me when I arrived. Kate flew around picking up toys and clothing, calling out instructions to all of us.

"They've all eaten, but they can have ice cream. The baby can be put down fairly soon, and the others can go in an hour." She turned to them. "Promise you'll mind Sky."

"I've got it." I attempted to divert her attention towards getting out the door. She seemed reluctant to go and I realized she didn't leave her children often.

Troy stood waiting, a happy look on his face at the prospect of a night out with his wife. "Come on, Kate. They're not going to hold the band for us."

She was still giving me advice in between telling her kids to behave. Finally the door closed and I turned to the four of them. They were already in pajamas, so there wasn't much for me to do. "Who wants ice cream?" I asked.

It was well after midnight when Kate and Troy blew through the door, tired but happy. I was pleased with myself that my plan had worked out for them. I walked out into the snow-covered driveway and drove home in the cold.

As spring came and the snow melted I geared up for the busier season. As usual, I turned my mind away from what would have been happening on The D. I hadn't had any contact with my family since I had left nearly seven months before and didn't intend to.

The Phillips' arrived just before their broodmares were due to foal. They had called regularly the last couple weeks, mainly to make sure I was closely watching the horses. The first thing they did after arriving was to call the vet, not because one was needed, but just to make sure there were no potential problems.

I kept a close eye on the pregnant mares. I had never seen one foal, but the signs of impending labor weren't much different than with cattle, so I was confident of my ability to help everything go smoothly.

Meanwhile the ground dried up and I began preparing the two year olds for riding. It took most of the day to handle all the horses individually. Once the mares foaled, the pairs were turned out into the pasture, while the yearlings and two year olds were put in corrals where, daily, I worked them one by one.

I'd never taught a young horse to lead before, so had to figure it out. Getting a halter on their heads was easy since they were already tame, but I quickly learned they would panic if I started tugging on the lead rope right away. After a couple of them reared up in an attempt to free themselves and almost went over backwards at the unfamiliar sensation of having their heads held, I realized I was going to have to try something different.

I started by giving gentle tugs on the halter, but let go if they got concerned. Gradually they became accustomed to being controlled.

Teaching them to lead took a little time. I knew that to get a stubborn horse to lead I had only to step to the side and pull. Once their heads were turned, it caused them to take a step sideways to regain their balance, which got their feet moving. I tried that on the yearlings and before long had them walking behind me after only a slight tug on the lead rope.

The two year olds were a different story. Louise was not nearly the rider I was and I had wondered how she had managed to successfully break horses to ride. I had no way of knowing how the ones she put first rides on turned out since they were gone, but I found out what kind of a job she did halter breaking the yearlings, now two year olds I became responsible for.

I realized that she used grain to get them to follow her around and as a result they had become spoiled. They expected a treat whenever I came near and became obstinate when they found I had nothing for them. After one quickly whirled around and attempted to kick me when I went to halter him, I realized they needed to be taught a lesson.

I made sure the Phillips' weren't around when I worked the bratty youngsters because I started carrying a long whip with me. They threatened to run me over looking for grain and I ended up having to crack them just to defend myself and also to teach them some respect.

Thankfully this went on for only a short while. Being young and impressionable, they learned good habits as quickly as they learned bad ones. When I got them to where I trusted them to behave when I was around, I began the saddling and riding process.

There was a small arena for putting first rides on the two year olds and I spent a lot of time there the next couple of weeks. Gradually, one by one, I accustomed them to the feel of a saddle. Then it was time to push my hat down tight, climb on and hope none of them took to bucking too hard. I had ridden quite a few bucking horses, and usually managed to stay on all but the most determined ones. Luckily, this batch of colts didn't give me too hard a time. A couple of them crow-hopped a few circles, but all in all they were agreeable to having a rider on their backs. Once they learned to respond to my cues, it was time to put some miles on them.

I spent the remainder of the summer taking the young horses out for rides down the country roads. Troy let me ride in his hay meadows just after they were cut. It was a great place to urge the youngsters up into a lope. Once he put the irrigation water back on, I went back to the roads.

It wasn't the most adventurous riding, but breaking horses was fun. In fact, I was beginning to think that maybe I could create another life for myself as a horse trainer.

Towards fall things slowed down again. Once the two year old horses were shipped off, either sold or sent down to Texas, I settled in for another long winter.

Besides the few chores in the mornings and evenings, the remainder of my day was free.

I still saw Kate and Troy occasionally, but I had attached myself to some of the regulars down at The Hole. We spent most Friday and Saturday nights down there as it was something to do that added a little excitement to my life. Other than that it was pretty dull.

I decided to look for another job to fill in the daytime hours. Besides the fact that I had free time on my hands, there was another reason to go to work. The Phillips' paid me very little in the winter time since I had fewer duties and all my living expenses were taken care of.

After looking around town for a couple of days, I was hired at the grocery store to stock shelves. It was a job that fit me, as it was physically demanding and I could work my own hours. I went in after I fed the Phillips' horses and left in time to get my chores done before dark. The job was nowhere near as satisfying as ranch work, but at least it left me feeling like I had accomplished something.

Winter time remained dreary though and my little home seemed to become smaller. I wondered if there was more I could do with my life and still occasionally fantasized that I might meet a single, young rancher looking for a wife, but as time went on that idea seemed more and more foolish.

I also gazed across snowy pastures whenever I drove down the road, and, out of habit, couldn't help checking the cattle within. When the snow melted, I took note as calving and haying seasons cycled through.

The second summer was much like the first. There was a new crop of foals and the others were a year older.

I looked forward to breaking the next set of two year olds. The Phillips came and went, leaving me to look after the place as they traveled.

One evening I rode down the lane towards the barn. It was unusually hot out, up in the nineties. Since I was on a filly that rarely slowed down, I was hoping the heat would help her to become a bit lethargic. It seemed to work as she relaxed into an easy walk, which she maintained even as we headed towards home. I finally began enjoying my ride.

As I passed the Phillips' I had to maneuver around all the cars that filled the driveway. Looking up, I saw a party in progress. I had been invited to the small gathering, but hoped to avoid it.

Voices, followed by laughter, drifted down towards me and I imagined the clink of ice in cocktail glasses like a scene out of a movie. One man caught my eye as I passed. He was younger than the other people mingling on the deck. Our eyes met for an instant, but then I quickly turned my attention back to the filly I rode as she wandered off the drive and down into the ditch. Using two-handed reining, I guided her back up onto the road, and continued on down to the barn.

After unsaddling the filly and turning her out, I put my saddle away and tidied up. I had barely gone inside when I heard a knock. I turned to see the guy from the deck standing at the screen door and pushed it open.

"Hi, I'm Pat Phillips. Mom said to come down and tell you to come up and have something to eat." He ran his fingers through his blond hair and studied me with more interest than just inviting me to a party.

"I'm Sky Daly." I took another look at him. His eyes crinkled at the corners as he smiled, just like his mother's did. "I'll be up in a minute."

"See you then," he turned and walked away.

I pulled on a clean pair of jeans and a fresh shirt before washing my face and combing my hair. I paused in front of the mirror, looking at my reflection and wondering if Pat had liked what he saw. My hair had again grown longer, mainly because I had never taken the time to find someone to cut it. It had gotten to the point that I would need more than a hat to restrain it. I pulled it back away from my face to see how it would look.

Looking into my eyes, I didn't see anything remarkable in them, or in any of my facial features. I turned away, dreading having to face the rich folks with their stylish clothing and confident attitudes. I pulled my boots back on before heading up the hill to the party at the big house.

Pat met me on the deck, grinning. "Here's the horse trainer." He said it loud enough to catch everyone's attention. The deck became quiet as the guests turned to look at me. I froze, caught in an awkward moment. Rhonda Phillips hurried over.

"Sky, hello. I see you met our son. Come get something to eat." Her hospitality helped relieve my awkwardness. As we made our way to the food and drinks, she introduced me to her guests.

"Hello, Sky," Paul Phillips greeted me from where he stood behind a makeshift bar. "What can I fix you to drink?" I hesitated, seeing all the bottles of alcohol and mixers. I didn't have a clue what most of them were.

"Can I have a beer?"

"Of course." He reached into an ice filled barrel and pulled out a bottle containing a dark-colored beer. He reached for an opener and popped the top. "Would you like a glass?"

"No, that's fine, thank you." I reached for the icy bottle he handed me and took a sip. The taste of the imported ale was a lot stronger than I was used to, but it wasn't bad. I took another sip before turning towards the buffet table.

"So, what's a pretty girl like you doing in a place like this?" I turned and faced Pat's question.

"Just ridin' horses." Even though I was flattered by his attention, I disliked stupid come-ons. Besides I didn't think he was interested in me.

He laughed, flashing white teeth. "Oh come on. There has to be more to it than that."

I tried to think of a snappy come back, but failed. I took another sip of beer and decided my best bet at conversation was to change the subject.

"Your folks have a nice place here." I glanced out at the view of the mountains that the deck was built to take advantage of.

"Yeah, it's quiet, but you can't beat the view."

"Hey, Pat, what was the name of that fellow with the airplane?" Paul Phillips paused the conversation he was having with two other men to catch his son's attention.

"Excuse me." Pat turned away from me.

I sat down in a vacant chair and turned my attention to my plate of food. After only a minute, a short, middle aged woman with bleach blonde hair approached me.

"Hi, I'm Missy Sears."

"Sky Daly."

"Is that your given name?" She sounded a little timid.

"My full name is Skylark," I told her.

"Oh. Where are you from?"

"Montana." I really didn't want to explain my life to her and thankfully she wanted to do the talking.

"I think it's wonderful that it's so much easier for young women to go out on their own these days. You know women's liberation." I couldn't help but stare, my eyes taking in her orange mini dress as she made the comment. It seemed a strange thing to tell me.

I didn't know how to reply either, since it wasn't by choice that I had left my childhood home. Instead I took a bite of food.

"I never had the choice. My parents pressured me into marrying Larry." She looked over at her husband and I followed her gaze. Larry turned out to be a short man with a large paunch. His eyes became slits as he opened his mouth and let loose a burst of laughter.

"My parents did what they thought was best for me." Missy Sears continued confiding in me. "He's not a bad man, not mean or anything." She seemed to be trying to convince herself she had a good marriage.

"Do you live around here?"

"Heavens no. We live down in Houston. Larry and Paul are business associates. We come here in the summer to get away from the heat."

"Yeah, I hear it gets hot down there." I really didn't care to hear about what business the two men were in together.

"It is. But how did you just leave and come here all by yourself?"

"I just did. A friend of mine told me that the Phillips' needed help, so I called them up and here I am." I figured my explanation was close enough to the truth. She didn't need to know I had been driven by desperation.

"I wish I had been brave enough to do that, years ago." I looked back over at her husband. They had a lot of money or they wouldn't be here, so I didn't feel sorry for Missy Sears. In fact I was puzzled that she felt so trapped.

"Can't you go where ever you want?"

"I guess I could." She sounded resigned, like she really couldn't do what she wanted. Didn't money give her the liberty to do what she pleased? I didn't understand how she could envy my life.

I had finished my dinner and now I got to my feet. I just couldn't feel sorry for the woman.

"It was nice meeting you." I looked down on her as she took a sip of her drink. She swallowed and gave me a weak smile.

I put my plate on top of a stack of dirty dishes and turned. Pat was again right next to me. I had already decided the attention from him was because I was the only single woman there. There was no one else for him to flirt with.

"Hey, want to go find some excitement. There's a decent band playing up in Ketchum."

"No thanks." It would have been too weird to taking off with him with his parents watching. Instead I gave him the excuse that I'd had a hard day and was tired.

The party was breaking up, even though it wasn't late. There was a classical music concert up in Sun Valley that some had tickets to attend.

"Well, let me walk you back down to the barn."

"You're not going to the concert?"

He cringed. "I had to sit through enough of that crap when I was little. It's as boring now as it was then."

I laughed. "It actually puts me to sleep,"

We walked down the driveway and over to the barn.

I glanced out into the pastures as we passed, counting the horses out of habit. It was pleasant and peaceful and I felt relaxed from the beer.

At the door I almost let him in when he asked. Sleeping with him would have been fun, but I didn't imagine it would go over too well with the Phillips' if I jumped in the sack with their son.

"Well then, have dinner with me Friday evening." Unable to resist his charming smile, I gave in and agreed to a date with him.

I thought the blue sundress I bought looked okay on me in the store. But later, as I prepared for my date, all I could see were the tan lines on my arms and neck that the dress revealed. Studying my face didn't help. I had not only the blue eyes and brown hair of my male relatives, I also had their strong features. It worked for them, as men, but the only word I could think of to describe my looks was coarse.

I felt self-conscious when Pat drove down to the barn to pick me up. He sounded sincere though, when he told me I looked nice and how the blue of my dress matched my eyes.

We drove up to Sun Valley and ate at an expensive restaurant. He was gracious as he held the door open for me and treated me like I was special. I found it odd when he ordered for me, but since I'm not picky when it comes to food, again I was flattered. It was a long, luxurious meal and Pat charmed me with stories about his recent trip to South America as he filled my wine glass.

Afterwards he seduced me in the barn apartment. I had noticed that his parents' car was gone from in front of their house, so let him come in. He was enchanting, as well as attractive, and I couldn't say no to his attentions.

We began seeing each other regularly whenever he was in town. Sometimes he stayed with me down at the barn and when his parents were away we slept together in their house. The Phillips' didn't say anything to me about it and treated me no differently. The fact that they acted indifferent probably should have clued me in, but I was falling in love with him and thought he felt the same way about me. I floated dreamily along, believing I was in a serious relationship and even started considering a future with him.

It only lasted a couple months, and then suddenly, one day he was gone. There was no goodbye, or any explanation. Mrs. Phillips simply told me in a vague kind of way that he was investigating business opportunities and that she didn't think he would be returning to Idaho anytime soon. I once again felt devastated after allowing myself to have feelings for a guy. There had been no reason to think he didn't feel the same way towards me and I thought back, trying to come up with a clue as to why he left me. I guess I should have realized I wasn't in his league.

Soon after, Paul Phillips came down to the barn and began a conversation. "Our trainer down in Texas was sure impressed with those last horses we sent down."

"That's good to hear."

"He's looking for an assistant trainer. I'll put in a word for you, if you're interested." Maybe it was his way of dismissing his son's old girlfriend and avoiding an uncomfortable situation, but I was thrilled at the thought of learning to train horses under a professional.

The trainer needed someone immediately. I accepted and within a week I was on my way to Texas, excited at the prospect of learning to work a horse on cattle in a cutting pen. I was happy to put my whole Idaho experience behind me. Since Pat dumped me the whole thing had soured anyway.

I followed the directions I was given and pulled up to the barn late in the afternoon. The training facility was north of Dallas, mainly flat farm land that was beginning to fill up with horse people. The twenty stall barn seemed large to me, but I soon learned that it was one of the more conservative ones in the area.

I was met by a tall good-looking guy not much older than me. "I'm Derek Payne." He gave a satisfied smile when he found out who I was. "Mr. Monroe is gone for the day, but I'll show you around." He led me down the center aisle. "Could you get this? We've been shorthanded." He explained the untidiness of the barn as he indicated a wheel barrow containing horse manure.

I realized that showing me around meant putting me to work, but I jumped right in. I pushed the cart down the aisle, picking up another pile as I went. He showed me where to dump it and then where the big push broom was kept so I could sweep the cement.

He disappeared into the office at the front end of the barn. When I finished, he reappeared and instructed me on the evening feeding procedure.

My main jobs were feeding the horses in training twice a day and saddling the ones to be ridden that day as they were needed. Derek showed me the tack room and the system they used to keep track of what tack was being used on which horse. It seemed easy enough.

Once the sun set, he seemed eager to leave. He pointed to a small, dilapidated travel trailer parked in one end of the hay shed and told me that was where I would be staying.

"Make sure to turn the gas off when you're done with it. There's a leak somewhere." He sounded a little vague as he rubbed his chin. "Well, I need to get going." He left as I went to check out my new home.

The tiny trailer was as rough on the inside as it was on the outside. There was barely room to move around in. It was hot and stuffy, not to mention dirty. There was a single working burner on the stove and it seemed it would take some maneuvering to use the shower. Most of the cupboard doors were missing. I sighed. It was a place to sleep and not much more.

I quickly learned the routine at the barn. Rising at four to haul hay and water to the stalled horses was easy enough and then I had my only break of the day. I was able to linger over my breakfast as the horses ate theirs.

By seven, I had the first one saddled and ready to ride for the head trainer, Mr. Monroe, when he showed up. I met him the first morning when he drove over from his house in the uncovered jeep that he used to get from his house to the barn. He, along with Derek, pushed through over a dozen young horses a day, so there was no time to waste. The horses came out of their stalls to be saddled, ridden, bathed and put back. I had to have the next one ready and down to the arena by the time he was done with the previous one. If I ever had a minute, Derek asked me to saddle one of his horses.

One or two pickups pulling horse trailers showed up about the same time as the trainers every morning. They unloaded their own horses and rode as turn back riders in the cutting pen. Some were clients who also took lessons or had horses in training.

It was a busy place and I ran to keep up. As soon as I had the first horse saddled, I went in and cleaned the empty stall. Then I saddled the next one. I led it down to the arena to exchange for the previous one. After handing me the reins of the heaving, lathered horse, Mr. Monroe would mount the fresh one I handed over.

I unsaddled and bathed the ridden horses before putting them on the hot walker where they finished cooling down. Meanwhile I mucked out an empty stall and saddled another horse. It was fast-paced and I rarely had time to pause.

One day the turn back riders were late. Derek had warmed up the first horse and Mr. Monroe was ready to start cutting. I hurried down to the arena to volunteer. I hadn't been on a horse since I left Idaho and was eager to show him what I could do.

As I neared the arena, he spotted me. "I could…" I began.

"Sky, could you go up and get that little grazing bit for this horse?" He interrupted me. I turned and hurried back up to the barn. By the time I got back, other riders had arrived and begun unloading their horses.

I was disappointed, but figured I just had to pay my dues and show that I was serious before he would let me get on a horse. Eventually I'd be in the arena alongside the others. Whenever I got a second, I'd watch through the rails as he put a young horse on a cow in an attempt to learn by catching brief glimpses of the action.

It was obvious to me that I rode better than most of his help. One day I paused for a moment and watched as two riders attempted to swap the used cows in the cutting pen for a fresh set from a back corral. As far as I could tell they knew nothing about sorting cattle. They quickly became excited with all the whooping and hollering going on. The simple task turned into a rodeo as the frantic animals literally began bouncing off the sides of the corral in an attempt to escape. By the time they got a bunch into the cutting pen, I was disgusted.

I continued watching as a rider entered to settle them. Instead of remaining in a group, they scattered as the man attempted to ride a circle around the small herd. It was obvious a lot of time was wasted since they needed to calm down before they would allow a horse and rider to enter the bunch and cut out just one. I knew I could do the job myself quietly and much more quickly. Feeling dejected, I went back to cleaning stalls.

I had now been away from the D for two years. My brother Adrian called me on Christmas when I was in Idaho He had gotten my number from Darlynn when he ran into her in the student union on campus. I didn't ask about Ursula and he didn't volunteer news about her or the D. Instead he told me about his life and that Steve was still driving for a trucking company out of Nebraska. We got caught up on local news and then said uneasy goodbyes as we promised one another to stay in touch.

Before long Derek and I began sleeping together. It happened for the first time after we went out for a beer together. As with Pat Phillips, it was hard to resist his charm or his good looks. It was convenient too as we both had a somewhat erratic schedule. After Mr. Monroe left for the day, it was easy for the two of us to sneak off to my trailer, or over to the small house he rented a few miles down the road.

Just before Christmas, Mr. Monroe told me to come on up to the house on Sunday afternoon. He was having a party for his help, just a little get together and there would be food and drinks. I arrived thinking I would get the chance to talk to him about when I could start riding and maybe brag myself up a little.

His wife, Pinky, let me in. "Go on in. They're watching the game."

I entered the living room to see Mr. Monroe, Derek and a few other men seated in front of the television. They barely turned their heads to call out a greeting before returning their attention to the football game. In a back corner sat a few other women.

"Have a beer." It was the wife of one of the turnback riders. I didn't know her, or the two others who sat perched on bar stools. She handed me a can when I walked over.

"Thank you." I looked over at the food table. A bowl of potato chips sat next to a mixture of dried onion soup mixed with sour cream, the old standby of dips. It had never appealed to me. Another bowl held store bought cookies.

During a commercial, Derek got up and came over. I smiled at him, but he barely nodded before he pulled four cans of beer out of the tub of ice He returned to the other side of the room and handed them out.

That was Cort Monroe's Christmas party. The men sat riveted to the television, cheering for the Dallas Cowboys, while the women sat in the back chatting about what I considered really boring topics. I sipped my beer, wondering if there was ever a more pathetic excuse of a party. It had become apparent that there was to be no meal, just cheap snacks. The afternoon gloom deepened into evening and I was hungry.

"You want to go get something to eat?" I finally spoke up as two of them wore out the subject of hair dryers.

"Well…" Pinky glanced over at the television.

"Come on, I'm dying for some barbeque." This came from a pretty girl with long blonde hair that I had just met named Bonnie.

We all agreed to go. Pinky told her husband we were leaving. I walked out and never even looked over in the direction of the television. The five of us piled into one car and drove towards Dallas to a restaurant that was known for its huge servings of ribs slathered in rich barbeque sauce.

Chapter 10

Winter went by with hardly any slowing down at the barn. On really cold days no one rode, which made my job easier, but I still did all the feeding, so had to be around in the mornings and evenings. The little trailer had no heat to speak of, and on those days it was a relief to go outside and get moving, warming up by hauling hay and grain to the blanketed horses before cleaning stalls.

It became a somewhat monotonous routine. The only variation was if a horse got sick or was injured and then a vet came out. I never thought I could get bored around horses, but this might just do it, I thought, plus the pay really sucked. It had now been six months since I had been on a horse and I wanted to ride.

Luckily winters are a lot shorter in Texas. As the weather warmed up, my optimism increased and I hoped

I would finally be given the chance to learn to train cutting horses. Instead, Derek and Mr. Monroe began preparing for the spring shows, which resulted in an increased workload. I ran myself ragged trying to keep up and nothing was said about me climbing on a horse. As usual, I watched from outside the pen while the men enjoyed the exhilarating sport of cutting cattle on horseback.

Derek and I became an official couple as we began going out together instead of just shacking up. For a while I had fun with him. He was a good dancer and on weekends we went to the local honky tonks where country western bands played, creating an energetic tempo for two step and swing dancing.

One spring afternoon we went to his house after a downpour had shut the barn down. Instead of immediately heading for his bedroom like we usually did whenever we had time to spend together, we sat on the couch reading. I wondered if Derek was getting as bored of me as I was of him.

I looked up from a *Western Horseman* magazine and glanced out the window. The sky had cleared off and it was almost time to head back for the evening chores. I decided it was time to bring up the subject that was most on my mind.

"How long's it going to take before Mr. Monroe lets me on a horse? I mean, he's never even seen me ride."

Derek's snort of laughter caught me off guard. "Cort aint gonna let a girl ride his horses." He continued chuckling, as if finding my question quite amusing.

"But I can ride better than most guys."

"Girls can't train horses."

"I hired on as a trainer, not a groom." I continued defending my position.

"It's not gonna happen." From the smirk on his face it was obvious the joke was on me. Anger replaced the confusion, as it suddenly became clear I was being used. I felt humiliated and didn't know what else to say. I got up from the couch.

"Oh, come on now, don't be mad. That's just the way it is." His tone only infuriated me further. I headed for the back door, hating his attitude of superiority.

"Get me a beer before you go," he called out as I stomped through the kitchen. I yanked open the refrigerator door and grabbed a can.

"Here!" I hurled it as hard as I could directly at his head. The swiftness of my movement caught him off guard. He put a hand up to deflect the projectile just in time and the can thudded against the wall.

"What the…? Fucking bitch!" he yelled. But I was out the door.

By the time I pulled up next to the wreck of a trailer I called home, my mind was made up. The horses looked up at me expectantly as I walked through the barn. A couple whinnied at me, anticipating their evening meal. I looked straight ahead, ignoring them, as I walked to the tack room and snatched my saddle.

I piled my few possessions into my car, started it up and then paused. Feeling sorry for the trapped horses, I got out and quickly threw hay into the stalls. As angry as I was, I couldn't take it out on them, knowing they wouldn't eat until the following morning when Derek and Mr. Monroe showed up to ride. That was my only satisfaction, knowing that their schedule would be messed up the next day. I climbed back into my car and once more made my escape from yet another unjust situation.

I glanced over at the Monroe's house as I drove off, but didn't see any activity, not that it would have stopped me. He owed me two week's pay, but he could have it. I was done being taken advantage of.

I had no idea where to go. For a minute I thought about The D and wondered how Ursula would react if I showed up at the ranch. I found myself heading north.

My mind churned as I remembered the derision on Derek's face. Once again I had fallen for someone who thought little of me, a temporary diversion to a guy with no qualms about hurting me. That, plus the fact I had been lied to fueled my anger. I pushed down harder on the accelerator, hoping that distance would relieve my hurt.

Near Oklahoma City I stopped to fill my gas tank. As much as I wished I could go home, with Ursula in charge, I knew it couldn't work. I turned onto the ramp leading to the newly built interstate going west.

Twelve hours later I stopped at a roadside diner on the outskirts of Albuquerque, New Mexico. My anger had turned into deep sadness, a bummer Will would have said. Since I was hungry I decided to use the opportunity to try and figure out what to do. The sign atop the roof of Bob's Hacienda displayed a billboard sized burger, which is just what I needed. As I pulled open the door, I noticed a help wanted sign amongst other notices taped to the glass.

The lone waitress hurried over, took my order and ran off again. I looked around. It seemed a big job for one person as there were quite a few tables, plus the seats at the counter.

My meal came and I dug in, a cheeseburger with fries and all the trimmings. Thankfully, the cook didn't skimp on the portions.

I glanced back behind the counter and watched him lift a basket of fries from the deep fryer before pulling plates from a tall stack. Bits of gray showed through his dark hair. His face seemed permanently scrunched into a scowl as he concentrated on his job.

The waitress scurried from table to table. She plunked plates down in front of a family seated at a table near the window and then made her way around with a pot of coffee. After refilling my cup, she caught my eye.

"How is everything?" She spoke with an accent.

"Really good, thank you."

"How about dessert?" The sound of a plate hitting the high counter top between the kitchen and dining room interrupted her. "Think about it." She scurried off to serve the waiting meals. The cook turned his frown on her as she hurried off carrying four plates at once.

A few minutes later she returned to where I sipped my coffee. "Piece of pie?"

"No, thank you." The burger had satisfied my hunger, and my attention again turned to the fact that I had no idea where I was going. I remembered the help wanted sign on the door.

"How is it working here?" Maybe I should find something to do while I came up with a plan.

"I'll be right back."

I waited a few minutes, but she was too busy to talk. Since it was obvious the cook was in charge, I got up and went to the door into the kitchen.

"It looks like you could use another waitress," I called over. The cook turned and gave me a hard look.

"You ever waited tables before?"

"No." I replied and then went on to explain how I knew how to work and that it seemed like something I could handle, the kinds of things you tell a potential boss to make yourself look good. He looked me up and down before flipping a row of burgers on the grill. His eyes went back to my feet. As usual I was wearing jeans and boots.

"What's your name?"

"Sky Daly."

"I'm Bob Ray and I'm the owner." He glared at me as if to gauge his effect on me.

"Nice to meet you." I held his gaze.

"Do you have a problem taking orders?"

"I've been taking them all my life."

"There are uniforms in the back." It seemed he had made a decision.

"You want me to change right now?" I asked. He looked at my feet again.

"Take those plates to that table over there and help Carla out." Part of his decision seemed to be that waitress uniforms didn't go well with cowboy boots.

I got busy. After delivering the food, Bob told me to take the coffee pot around once again. Then he had me remove dirty dishes before wiping down the tables where diners had left.

I assured myself that this was only temporary, until I figured out what to do, but felt my dreams of both ranching and training horses wither inside of me. I squashed it down further in an attempt to kill it once and for all. It was time to face reality

Carla seemed happy when I relieved her of part of the workload, but she didn't slow down. I tried to watch her as Bob barked orders at me.

I made it through the hectic lunch rush fairly easily. Even though I didn't have the time to be bored as I hurried around the restaurant, it was still an unspectacular beginning to my new life.

"Where do you live?" Bob asked me once the last customer had left.

"Um…" I didn't know what to tell him. Carla was watching me also.

"Come here." Bob apparently realized I had just gotten to town. Of course, he had seen the out of state plates on my car parked out front. He led me towards the back. He indicated a small room in the back containing a cot. "You can sleep here until you find a place."

"Thank you, but, are you sure?" He didn't answer me. Instead he walked out to the front and rustled through a newspaper a customer had left on the counter.

"Here." He thrust the section with the want ads at me. His terse manner made me cautious, but I took the paper from him.

"I'll help you find a place. Come over here." Carla led the way to a booth where we set down cups of coffee and slid into seats across from one another. I opened the newspaper to see what was available to rent as she lit a cigarette, took a drag and set it in an ash tray before putting her attention on her last task of the day. I studied the ads in the local newspaper, looking for a cheap rental while she counted the stack of bills from the cash register.

"Let me see what you've got there." I handed the paper to her. She read through the ads and marked a few of them. "Start with those. They're close by and the neighborhoods aren't bad." I listened to her Spanish accent and studied her face as she spoke. To me, she was exotic looking, with her thick black hair, dark eyes and full lips.

We could hear Bob moving around in the back. The back door slammed and it was quiet. After a couple minutes, I realized he had left.

"Is it ok to stay here if I don't find a place right away?"

"Oh, yeah, Bob's all right." Carla misinterpreted my meaning, but her comment gave me assurance.

She handed me part of the stack of money in front of her. "Your share of the tips. You can collect your own tomorrow."

I thanked her, and left shortly after. Besides finding a place to live, Carla advised me to buy a comfortable pair of shoes to work in.

Bob's Hacienda opened for breakfast at six am every day except Sunday. At eleven, lunch began and was served until two in the afternoon. After that Bob went home to "live his life" as he put it.

He wasn't really the hard-ass he appeared. And as grumpy as he always seemed, it was mainly for show. Besides giving me a job and a temporary place to stay, he was willing to help me any way he could. Carla and I were like his daughters, except that, outside of work, he couldn't tell us what to do.

It didn't take me long to find a place to live. After driving to a few mouse and bug infested crumbling adobe shacks, I reluctantly began studying the slightly pricier rentals. After calling a few phone numbers, I finally got ahold of a woman with an apartment to rent that sounded promising.

The house sat on the end of a row of adobe homes, almost identical and all matching the brown color of the earth. It was at the end of the street, surrounded by large trees. The elderly woman who answered my knock gave me a shrewd, but not unfriendly look.

"Ah, you called about the apartment. It is still available." I had talked to her only an hour before. "I am Mrs. Martinez." She also spoke with a Spanish accent and I got the impression that she was proud of her English speaking ability. I introduced myself and she invited me in.

"Where are you from?" She sat up straight in her chair.

"Up north."

"Where?"

"Montana, but I left a few years ago. I've been over in Texas."

"Why did you leave your home?" She gazed at me intently, very interested in why I would do such a thing.

"It was time to move on. I grew up on a ranch and I couldn't stay there forever."

"Why didn't you marry?"

"He died."

"Ohhh." She left it at that, which was good because I wasn't saying any more about it.

I moved into the apartment that evening. Her questioning had been non-judgmental, and I liked my new home. It was small, but seemed roomy after the trailer and it was furnished. It was also on the back side of her house, away from the street.

I settled into my new, easy and predictable life. I got up in the morning, dressed in an unattractive, gold, nylon uniform and white, nurses' shoes and drove to the diner to serve meals. Since I preferred to stay busy, I took as many shifts as I could get.

At night I began scouting out the local bars, looking for company my own age. As it turned out, the town was filled with people like Carla, of Spanish and Indian descent. Spanish seemed to be spoken as much as English, especially in some of the bars I checked out. I felt out of place and kept looking for white people my own age.

I also avoided places that catered to long hairs. Of course by now, the hippy phase was on its way out and a cowboy craze was taking over. Almost everyone it seemed was sporting a cowboy hat with boots and jeans, to keep up with the latest fad, just as I put mine away.

I still preferred the cowboy bars, even if the denim-clad patrons dressed mainly for show and eventually I found a group I fit in with. We all worked at various jobs and met at our hangouts after work and on weekends. None of us had a lot of ambition. The focus of our lives revolved mainly around who was sleeping with who and other trivial dramas.

One of the girls I met worked at a dinner club. She told me there was an opening for a waitress in the evenings and told me, "The tips are great. I make fifty bucks a night easy on weekends."

I decided what the heck. I got through at Bob's just before the evening shift at La Casa Grande started so I applied and then started working there. The second job kept me even busier. Waiting tables may not have been my first choice, but with tips, the pay was a lot better than working with horses.

On a rare day off, I drove out onto the mesa and stared out into the empty desert. I couldn't help but think I was glad that, like Nevada, I didn't have to make a living off that land. Even though I liked the dry desert air and the magnificent sunsets, spending much time alone was something I avoided because it gave me time to think. That might make me question the direction of my life even though I had already decided there were to be no more plans to set myself up for disappointment.

I turned the key in my car's ignition again and again. The engine turned over, but didn't start. I got out, lifted the hood and tried to make sense of the inside. Mechanics weren't my thing. Steve and Adrian had always kept my car running well, like they had with all the vehicles on the D.

I pulled off the air filter, hopped back in and turned the key again. Still nothing happened. I suspected the engine wasn't getting gas, since after pumping the accelerator repeatedly, I still couldn't smell anything.

Finally I went and knocked on Mrs. Martinez' door. "I will call my cousin. He's a good mechanic." She said when I told her my predicament.

"Can I use your phone to call work first? I'm going to be late."

Mrs. Martinez' cousin sent over his son, Roberto. I couldn't help but notice how cute he was with shiny black hair that curled over his collar. He pulled off the air filter again and had me turn the engine over while he studied the engine.

"It's not getting any gas." He peered around the raised hood to look at me sitting in the driver's seat and smiled.

I got out and walked around to where he leaned on his elbows on the front of the car. "Why not?"

He straightened up. "Could be the fuel pump, or the fuel line could be clogged. I'll have to take it apart to find out."

"Could you give Sky a ride? She's late for her job." Mrs. Martinez called out from her porch where she had been watching.

"Sure. Then I'll get your car to the garage." He looked back at me.

We climbed into his pickup and he drove me over to La Casa Grande. As he dropped me off, he asked, "Do you want me to come by and give you a lift home later?"

"I get off around eleven." This time I smiled back.

When my shift ended, Roberto was sitting at the bar waiting for me. "Your car's fixed. I had to replace the fuel pump." We had a couple drinks before heading back to my place.

"Want to come in?" I asked, knowing that he did.

In the morning he drove me to the garage. The two men already there smirked and winked when I climbed out of his pickup. I kept my eyes down while I paid the bill for replacing the fuel pump. I guess I should have seen it coming, but he could have warned me. I walked out the door and never saw Roberto again.

That became the extent of my love life, spending a night or two with strangers. I didn't try to see the men I slept with again, as I didn't care to get close to any of them. That way I couldn't be hurt. Love the one you're with finally had meaning for me.

Chapter 11

My eyes opened to bright daylight and I immediately closed them again. I still felt the alcohol I had consumed just a few hours before, but it was the down side of the buzz. I sat up and waited for the woozy feeling to subside before standing up. It was Sunday, my one day off and I would spend it my usual way, nursing a hangover. This one was going to be a killer. Once I dumped instant coffee into a mug, filled it with hot tap water and took a sip, I thought back to what I remembered of the night before. Someone had come up with a god awful drink, a bizarre combination of alcohols and mixers. The most I could remember was that they were red in color and how we laughed as we pounded down the "Gut Busters," one after another. I didn't remember coming home. Since I was alone, I must have driven myself.

It was pretty much the norm for me these days. Every friendship I had made revolved around hanging out in bars. I had been in Albuquerque for well over two years, and I didn't see any change in sight for my life. I was caught in a holding pattern that I didn't think I could change, even if I had the desire.

I pulled open the door and walked outside. Squinting up at the sun for the briefest instant, I determined that it was pushing noon. I looked up front to make sure my car was there, as I still remembered nothing about arriving home early that morning.

The fall sun still had plenty of warmth. Underneath the giant ash that dominated the back yard, I had placed an old, folding chair. I brushed a few yellow leaves off the seat before I eased down onto it. The rickety seat had a habit of dumping me quicker than a cold backed horse if I wasn't careful.

As I sipped my coffee, I heard a car pull up out front followed by voices as Mrs. Martinez answered her door. I paid no attention until she came around back, followed by two police officers.

"There." Mrs. Martinez indicated me after she led them through the gate to the back yard. They walked closer before stopping.

"Are you Skylark Daly?"

"Yeah." I tried to act unconcerned, but had begun to worry. The night before wasn't the first time I had had a black out while drinking. The younger cop consulted a piece of paper.

"Is your mother Ursula Daly?"

"Yes." I sat up in my chair.

"We regret to inform you," he continued in a monotone, "That your mother has passed away."

"What? How?" I barely made it to my feet as the chair collapsed, knocking the mug from my hand. There was a sharp crashing sound as it hit the ground and shattered.

"Uh... You need to contact Loretta Blackburn. I believe she's your aunt." He seemed confused as to how to continue and for an instant the only thing I could focus on was the thought that this must be his first next of kin contact.

"What happened to my mother?" I heard myself ask.

"I'm not sure." He seemed unsure as to how much information he should reveal.

"Nobody told you?" The shrillness of my voice surprised me.

"Ron Wallace, the sheriff in Dobbs County, Montana informed us she was shot." The older officer took over.

"Shot?!"

"Come use my telephone to call your family." Mrs. Martinez took control of the situation and grabbed my arm to guide me around to the front and into her house.

The phone rang and rang at Aunt Loretta's, but no one answered. I looked around, unsure what to do next.

"Try again in a minute." Mrs. Martinez seemed more worried than I was. Actually I was unable to think at all. The police officers had left, their work done.

"I have to get home." I headed towards the door. Action made more sense than waiting. Mrs. Martinez tried to persuade me to stay, but an overwhelming urge to return to Montana overtook me. I threw my clothes onto the back seat, and the rest of my things, including my dusty saddle, into the trunk of my car and I was ready to go.

Just before I drove off, I called Bob's Hacienda and La Casa Grande to quit my waitressing jobs. I was surprised, given the circumstances, how good it felt to break free from my stale life. I considered informing my party buddies I was leaving, but decided they would realize I was gone soon enough. Instead I thanked Mrs. Martinez, told her goodbye and hit the road. It was just over five years since I had left the D.

On the drive north my mind obsessed about what could have happened to Ursula. I couldn't imagine what she had gotten herself into. The only way I could picture her was with the satisfied look on her face when Rad Johnson had told me to leave. I felt no sadness. In fact my emotions seemed completely frozen because I couldn't believe she really was dead. Turning my thoughts to the D didn't help, as it was still really hard to think about my childhood home.

The wondering and worrying kept me awake as I drove through the night. I was finally forced to stop when the needle on the gas gauge hit the red line because there were no filling stations open late in the small town I was passing through. I slept in the back seat amongst my crumpled clothing.

I was jolted awake by the loud bellow of a horn as a train barreled through before light. I hadn't even realized there were tracks next to where I pulled off in the dark. The scare of the loud, unexpected blare left me wide awake with my heart pounding. I fueled up as soon as the solitary gas station opened and continued on my way.

The driveway in front of my aunt's house in Compton was full of vehicles when I pulled up just after noon the following day. A dog ran up to me. His barking turned into tail-wagging as he recognized me. It was Tag. He greeted me like a long lost friend and I shared his enthusiasm. I figured Jipper must be dead as he had been old when I left. My aunt Loretta greeted me with, "Oh my goodness!" She pulled me inside and hugged me.

"The funeral was yesterday. It took a while to contact you and we couldn't hold it off any longer." Her face showed what a tragedy she considered it, me not being there to see my mother buried.

I was relieved though. I had been to enough funerals and the thought of another one, especially Ursula's, had filled me with dread. I just didn't think I could have shown the appropriate mourning, given our relationship when she died.

I exchanged curious looks and subdued greetings with my brothers and sisters. They seemed not to know how to act any more than I did. The only one I had had any contact with was Adrian and that was only a phone call once or twice a year.

I looked from one to another. They all looked different. Adrian had grown his hair longer and replaced his jeans with khaki slacks.

"How have you been?" Steve asked. He sported a mustache to show off his maturity.

"Good. How about you?"

"Can't complain."

I turned to my twin sisters. "I can't believe you guys. You're all grown up." In fact I doubt I would have recognized Donna and Debbie if I had passed them on the street. Their features were disguised with makeup and they had definitely been spending money on clothing.

They smiled. "It has been awhile." Debbie answered for the both of them.

"You should have called and told us you were coming." My aunt still couldn't believe I had missed my mother's funeral. I felt like asking her if she knew what the situation was between us the past five years.

"I tried calling, a couple of times." I didn't know if this was the appropriate time to bring it up, but did anyway. "I still don't know what happened."

"Your mother was shot." My siblings watched me as Loretta began the story. The sorrow on her face made me finally start to feel some sadness, at least for my aunt losing her sister.

"That's what the cops said."

"We'll probably never know exactly what happened, but apparently she finally had a bellyful of Rad Johnson and kicked him out. She called me after he left. It was the best news I'd heard in a long time." Tears slid down Loretta's cheeks. A box of tissues sat on the table and she reached for one. I waited for her to continue.

"The next day, that was last Friday, he came back and shot her." She forced the words out. The story was completely unbelievable to me.

"Where is he now?"

"He took off in Mom's car. The cops are looking for him." It was Adrian who answered my question.

"Do they know for sure it was him?"

"Well, he just disappeared and the evidence points that way."

All eyes remained on me as I digested the information. I looked around to see how they were handling my mother's death. Only Loretta cried. The rest of us were silent. It was hard to feel openly sad about a woman who had been so nasty. I wondered if the best we could do was to wish things had been different growing up.

Loretta regained her composure as she wiped her eyes again. "We have to go see Jim Arnett." He was a lawyer in town and I couldn't imagine how Ursula's death concerned him.

"Why?"

"Apparently your mother made out a will recently. Jim said to come by as soon as you were all here. He said he'd make the time. I'll go call him." Having a mission helped her pull herself together. She blew her nose. "Have you eaten? There's food in the kitchen." But that was the farthest thought from my mind.

An hour later we drove over to his office. As soon as the word will was mentioned, I knew what was coming. My dread had grown to full size by the time we reached the law office.

It seemed to me Jim Arnett's condolences had the tone of someone who has practiced expressing sympathy for these occasions. But maybe I was being too hard on him since I didn't really know him. I knew my father had considered him a friend.

We sat in chairs he and his secretary hastily gathered around his desk and watched him shuffle papers. I knew what Ursula would have to say from beyond the grave. The D would continue to be passed down to the first born son and, if I stayed, I figured I would be kicked out on my butt again. I wondered why I had come back at all.

"The date of the document is the day before she died, October 16th, 1975, to be exact," he stated. I felt a chill run through me and wondered if she had already known her fate.

He began reading the opening formalities, but I wasn't listening. I didn't know why I had to be here for the passing of the crown. They could just as well have called me and told me that the D now belonged to Adrian.

"I leave the D Rocking D ranch and all its holdings to my daughter Skylark Daly." Arnett finished and looked up at me.

"Huh?" I stared at the lawyer. The D was mine? I looked around the room at my family's faces. They stared back at me. "What about everyone else?"

"That's what it says. That's all it says." He looked at me, repeating the contents of the document and answering my question by using simple words. "The D is yours."

The D was mine. All I could think was that it must be a trick. Why would Ursula, who had always disliked me, leave me the entire ranch? I looked around at my siblings again, and then held my gaze on Adrian. He quickly looked down, but his expression had been clear. Instead of any kind of resentment or jealousy, I saw relief on his face. In fact all four of my siblings' faces showed the same thing.

We drove the few blocks back to Loretta's house in silence. I held in my feelings, afraid to show any happiness, because everyone remained silent about

Ursula's final say. Suddenly I couldn't wait to get back to the ranch. But first I wanted to discuss the situation.

"We could all run it together." I sat with my brothers and sisters in a circle around Aunt Loretta's dining room table.

Adrian shook his head. "I don't want to fix fence the rest of my life." He was half way through a master's degree, his life way past ranching.

Steve sat back in his chair and lit a cigarette. "Sell it." His actions conveyed the confidence of a man much older than twenty-two. I would have felt indignant at my younger brother giving me advice, except I couldn't believe his words.

He had never completed high school and didn't seem to worry about getting a diploma. After spending a few years working for a trucking company, he had saved enough for a down payment on his own truck. Now he was set up to work for himself. He too had left the ranch life behind.

In a final attempt to include my family, I turned to the twins. Before I got a word out, they began shaking their heads.

"We like living in Seattle." Debbie answered for the two of them. I thought their haircuts and makeup made them resemble the mannequins modeling outfits in store windows. It was obvious they preferred city life.

None of my family had any intention of returning to The D. I don't know what surprised me more, their lack of envy that Ursula had left me the entire ranch, or how adamant they were about staying away. I also couldn't believe how far we had all scattered. None of us could be found anywhere near our childhood home. At least until now.

"Fine then. I'll run it myself."

Adrian sighed. "Just sell, get out from under it, like Steve said." Everyone, including my aunt nodded in agreement. None of them could see anything desirable about hanging onto the cattle ranch our ancestors had built over four generations.

"Never." I felt ready to fight anyone who stood in my way. I got to my feet.

"Where are you going?" Loretta asked.

"Home."

Her look showed that she thought my determined reply was foolish. "Stay here tonight. I'll drive out with you tomorrow."

"No, I'm going now." I was afraid they would use the time to work on me, to try and convince me the best thing to do was to put the ranch up for sale. Although I never questioned my resolve, I also didn't want to listen to their arguments.

"At least take the dog with you." I gladly loaded Tag up into my car and headed north across the river.

I drove the twenty miles from town feeling giddy. The D was mine. I still couldn't believe that what had started out as a really bad day had suddenly turned around completely. Mine all mine. I didn't want to be happy about Ursula's death, but without it, not only wouldn't the D belong to me, I would still be waiting tables. I flew down the highway as my mind spun around the conflicting thoughts.

As I came onto Daly land, I began seeing differences. It was probably nothing obvious to most, but when I spied a wire down on a fence and the pasture inside ungrazed, I began wondering what was going on. I was in for a bigger surprise as I came into sight of the hay meadows. Instead of being cut short this time of year, the grass was overgrown and uncared for. I began wondering where the cattle were and why the stack yards were empty.

I followed the driveway around to the kitchen. There wasn't a single vehicle parked back there, something I had never seen before. I guess I had expected the headquarters to look the same. Instead the buildings had begun showing their age. The yard was unkempt as well. What had my mother been doing the past five years? Obviously she hadn't been taking care of the place.

The oddest thing was the stillness. Nothing moved. The corrals were full of weeds instead of livestock. No dogs ran out to greet me. There wasn't even a cat to slink around the corner of the barn when I pulled in. Mine were the only fresh tracks in the driveway.

I got out and looked around. The house had an almost dejected appearance. I wondered again what had been going on. The screen door hung from the top hinge and the mesh was torn. I walked through the mudroom, opened the kitchen door and stepped inside. Tag stopped just short of the doorway. "Come on," I encouraged him. That was my first decision. Ursula had never let our pets in the house, but as far as I was concerned Tag was welcome inside. He sniffed suspiciously before entering.

At first glance, the kitchen appeared as when I left. I don't know why, but I felt relieved. Crossing over to the refrigerator, I pulled open the door and then immediately closed it again against the rotten smell it emitted. I looked around again and noticed that dust covered the counter tops and table and a gray film dulled the walls. It became obvious the kitchen hadn't been used for quite some time.

I headed for the living room, but stopped in the doorway as my jaw dropped. Looking around, it took me a moment to believe my eyes.

There was absolutely no trace of the furnishings I remembered. The couch and easy chairs had been replaced with shiny chrome-framed furniture upholstered in orange and yellow. Gold, shag carpeting with red and orange flowers covered the pine floor. Silvery wall paper shimmered in the background and abstract paintings hung from the walls. I stood and stared for a minute, wondering what had possessed Ursula. Gingerly, I crossed over to the stairs.

The worn boards let out the same old squeaks and groans as I climbed to the second floor. My first stop was my old bedroom. What appeared to be my parents' bed, the mattress, box springs and frame, filled the floor space, but my belongings looked untouched. I went down the hallway and examined each vacant room in turn. Except that, like mine, they were being used for storage, they also looked untouched from when we had all moved out.

Finally I had the courage to look into my parents' bedroom. A surprise waited me there also. Thick, plush burgundy carpet covered the floor. A new, larger bed sat in the middle of the floor. It looked like the room was in the middle of being redone.

Out of curiosity, I opened the closet door. It was stuffed full of clothing and shoes, many items unworn and still in bags. Ursula had done some shopping.

I couldn't take in anymore because the question I had when I saw the first downed fence wire hadn't been answered. Where were the cattle, my cattle?

I went down the back stairs to the kitchen and picked up the telephone, unsure of who to call to find what had been going on here. Ursula was closest to her sister, Loretta, but it seemed she hadn't told her much lately. Besides I was afraid my aunt would start in about selling the D. Finally I dialed the number of the closest neighbor.

"Hello, Mrs. Welch? This is Sky Daly."

"Sky, oh I'm so sorry about your mama. How are you doing?"

"I'm fine."

"I'm so sorry you missed the funeral. It was a lovely service." She began a sympathy speech, but I cut her off.

" Yeah, too bad, but do you know where our cattle are?"

"Oh, dear. I better let you talk to Marv. Let me go get him." I could hear her hollering for her husband as I held the phone in a death grip.

"Sky? That's just awful what happened to your mama." He started in with his own condolences, but I stopped him also.

"Where are The D's cattle?" There was a pause. I didn't think he would need to think about it. Finally he spoke.

"Why, your mama sold them all."

"What? All of them?"

"There haven't been any cattle on your place since, well, it was just after you left. We've been leasing those two sections next to us." I thanked Marvin Welch after he told me to call if I needed anything and hung up the phone.

The horses were gone too. I didn't want to think what might have happened to Wilbur. I felt guilty for abandoning him. Of course, on paper, he and the other geldings had all belonged to the D. They had been my mother's, to do with as she pleased.

I walked back outside and over to the barn and then to the other outbuildings. They used to contain the tractors and other ranch equipment. Except for the same worn out machinery that lined the back fence, some since before I was born, there was nothing left. Apparently Ursula had sold more than the livestock.

Discouraged, I crossed back over to the house. The empty driveway still looked odd to me. Even the ranch trucks were gone.

For the first time I understood what my family had told me. I was in over my head. I had thought I would just continue the same way. Taking over a well-managed ranch would have been easy, but all of a sudden that wasn't the case. Right now I had a more pressing concern though.

Except for candy bars I bought when I stopped for gas, I hadn't eaten since I left New Mexico. Suddenly I realized how hungry I was. My aunt had tried to feed me, and now I regretted turning her down.

Rummaging in the cupboards, I found mouse turds amongst a few cans of food, unidentifiable since the labels had been chewed off. Grossed out, I closed the doors and sat down. Why hadn't I thought of going to the grocery store before heading out here? My spirits sank as I contemplated my options.

Finally I drove back down to The Crossing. I still had a bad taste in my mouth for the restaurant since I had caught my father in the back with his girlfriend, but it was the closest spot to get a meal. I kept my head down going through the bar as I didn't want to have to endure sympathy from others. But of course almost everyone in the place knew me, so that was impossible. I ordered a meal and gave it my full attention.

By the time I paid the bill, everyone in the restaurant had stopped by the table where I sat, expressing both their condolences and offers of help. A couple of them simply squeezed my shoulder as they walked by. My replies sounded sincere and came with a weak smile. It was a good act and I felt a little comfort. If anyone wondered what I was doing there all by myself, they respected my privacy.

The truth was, I felt I had no one to confide in. My two best friends had scattered just like my family had. Darlynn graduated from MSU and got a job over in Spokane. As far as I knew, Louise was still married and living down in Wyoming. So far the only thing any family member had to say to me was what I didn't want to hear.

I decided to take a chance and go visit my Aunt Dottie. It was getting late, but I saw a light in the window as I drove down the street towards her house. She answered the door and looked surprised to see me standing there. I felt like an orphan standing on her porch. She stepped aside to allow me inside and shut the door.

"Did you hear?"

"Of course I heard about your mother, Sky." She gave me an odd look.

"Did you hear about the will?"

"Your mother had a will?"

"She left me the D." I looked at her, gauging her reaction.

"Are you sure?" Part of me wanted to feel resentment at her question, but I knew it was curious news to her as well.

"Jim Arnett read it this afternoon." I studied her face for another second before looking around. "Where's Uncle Walter?" His chair was empty and the television silent.

"He passed away just over a year ago."

"I'm sorry." I didn't know what else to say.

"He's in a better place now." She looked back at me. "I'm sorry you missed your mother's funeral."

I just nodded and tried to convey the appropriate amount of sadness. After a pause, I asked, "Do you know what she was doing for the last few years?"

"Well, I've heard rumors, but I hadn't seen her in quite a while."

"What did you hear?"

"Apparently she was spending a lot of time in Las Vegas with that boyfriend of hers."

"Did you know she sold all the cattle?"

"Well, I guess she had to be getting money from somewhere." She studied my face. "What are your plans?"

"To run the D."

"Oh, honey, how are you going to run a ranch all by yourself?" Her tone was as discouraging as everyone else's had been.

"I'll manage." I realized it was a mistake confiding in her. "Could you lend me some coffee until I can buy groceries?"

"Are you staying out there all by yourself?"

"Yes, I am." My tone dared her to question my decision. She became sympathetic instead.

"Of course I'll give you some coffee. What else do you need?"

"Um, well, maybe something for breakfast."

She rummaged through her refrigerator and pulled out a carton of eggs. "This is nearly full."

"No, I can't take that." I explained about the smell in the refrigerator and that I was going to have to clean and set traps before I could bring food into the house.

Dot's expression turned to concern. "Goodness, I had no idea..." She paused and then added, "I'll come out and help you tomorrow."

"You don't need to do that." My first reaction was to refuse. I still felt guilty because, after promising to pay her for cooking for the haying crew the last summer I was on the D, she had received nothing. Plus, I didn't really want her to see the condition of the ranch headquarters, and especially, my mother's redecorating.

"It's no bother and it's not like I have anything better to do." She looked around at her own immaculate house.

"Okay," I relented since I had seen a spark in her eye.

"What time should I come?"

"Whenever works for you," I replied, knowing she would be there early, ready to start scrubbing. I left her house with coffee and donuts for in the morning.

I drove back out to The D thinking about Great Grandpa Matt's cabin. I wondered if there was a possibility it was in any condition to sleep in. Given the state of the kitchen, I figured it would be full of rodents also.

I ended up on the front porch wrapped in blankets for the night. Between the rotting smell, the mice overrunning the house, and the redecorating job, I just didn't feel comfortable inside. I thought about the irony of the situation. The ranch was mine, but I was having difficulty finding a place to sleep. Still, I drifted off feeling content. I had come home and no one could make me leave.

Chapter 12

Aunt Dot showed up early, the back seat of her car full of groceries and cleaning supplies. She immediately headed for the refrigerator and bravely opened the door.

She wrinkled her nose before asking, "Does this thing still work?" She looked around the back for the cord.

"I don't know." It was plugged in, but I realized it wasn't running. "Maybe we better see if it works before we clean it out." Before I could warn her, Aunt Dot headed for the living room to further assess the condition of the house.

"What in the world?" She stared with amazement, as I had done upon seeing the modernized look to the room. She looked back at me.

"Kind of weird looking, don't you think?"

"Well it isn't what I expected that's for sure," she answered and entered the room to study the décor. I found it hideous and just wanted to tear it apart so I wouldn't have to look at it. I turned back to the refrigerator.

So the morning went. I had already realized the stove wasn't working and there was no hot water. It was disheartening. I couldn't believe how run down the house had become in only a few years. I realized Ursula's disdain for the kitchen when it became evident that she had been using the front door to come and go instead of our customary way of entering and exiting through the kitchen.

It was still early when the telephone rang. "Hello," I answered.

"Who am I speaking to please?"

"What? Who the hell is this?" Dot gave me a sharp look, but the voice was unfamiliar.

"This is Leroy Donner." The name meant nothing to me, so I didn't respond. "I'm a realtor, with New Homes Realty." He spoke like that would jog my memory.

"What do you want?"

"Is this Skylark Daly?"

"Yeah."

"I have a potential buyer for your ranch." He spoke like it was the best news I could have heard.

The first thing through my mind was that news sure travels fast. I could think of no intelligent answer because I suddenly became scared that someone was going to take The D away from me.

"Leave me alone!" I banged the phone back down onto the receiver.

"Who was that?" Dot stood looking at me. I eyed her suspiciously, doubting she was on my side.

"It was a realtor." I dared her with my eyes to say anything good about a phone call from a vulture. But Aunt Dot was smarter than that.

"Didn't I get some baking soda?" She rummaged around in a grocery bag and pulled out a box. "This will help with that smell in the refrigerator."

We finally figured out that breakers in the fuse box had been tripped and that was why the appliances and the hot water heater weren't working. We had no idea why it had happened, but Dottie advised me that I had better have it checked out.

I finished washing the inside of the refrigerator and left it open to air out. As we worked through the morning, scrubbing our way around the kitchen, Aunt Dot chatted away. Within a couple hours I was filled in on the latest happenings around Compton.

"These cupboards really need fresh paper. I'll bring some out with me tomorrow."

"You don't have to do that," I replied, but I was feeling a little more hopeful.

The sunny day had warmed up enough so the temperature was comfortable, so we took a break and sat outside on a blanket in the sun to eat the lunch Dottie had brought. Even with all the doors and windows open the stale and rotting smells inside lingered.

She seemed ready for a serious talk. "You know, your mother hasn't had the best reputation around here for the last few years."

"So? It doesn't concern me. She kicked me out, remember?" I was surprised my contempt for Ursula came to the surface so easily.

"You shouldn't be so hard on your mother."

"Why not? She left me a mess to clean up." I was referring to more than just the house.

"Maybe this wasn't her first choice for a life."

"What do you mean?" I always figured Ursula was lucky to have snagged my dad.

"You don't know why your parents got married?" She hesitated a second before asking the question.

"No."

Dottie paused again, considering whether what she was about to share might be better remaining buried in the past. "You should know the truth," she decided. "They had to. Your mother was pregnant with you."

"You mean a shotgun wedding?" I had heard of such a thing, but had never actually known it to happen.

"Oh, yes. When your grandpa, and your great grandpa Matt, he was still alive then, when they found out, they were furious. There was gonna be a wedding and there was no way your mother and father were going to get out of it. I was just a little girl, but I remember it well. They weren't going to allow the family reputation to be tarnished."

My dad and Ursula fooling around before they were married was news to me. Nobody had ever spoken of it in my presence. But I didn't see how it changed things. I still thought Ursula had been extremely lucky marrying my father and coming to The D. I would never understand why, instead of acting happy, she was so sour and angry all the time.

We went back in and finished giving the kitchen a thorough cleaning. Finally we sat at the table for a cup of coffee and to assess what we had accomplished. Despite the scrubbing, the room looked shabby.

"You'll need to paint soon."

I eyed the cracked linoleum. "It'll take more than paint. Tell me, what do you think about my mother leaving me the D?"

Aunt Dot hesitated. "Well, I don't think you can run it all by yourself." I knew it was her way of saying I was going to need a husband.

"But what about Urs…my mother leaving it to me instead of Adrian?"

"I really can't tell you what she was thinking." She evaded the question, but at least she didn't tell me it was the wrong thing to do. Of course, she didn't seem happy for me either.

"Well, I have to go. I've got my bridge club tonight." Dot got up and rinsed her cup out at the sink. "I'll be back tomorrow. Maybe we can tackle the upstairs." It seemed that in her own way she was supporting me.

"Sky? This is Bob Mullen. Can you stop by the next time you're in town? There's something I need to discuss with you." The banker's matter-of-fact voice came over the line the next morning.

"I can come by today." I decided it was better to get it over with as soon as possible. I would call Aunt Dot and tell her not to come out.

I showed up at the bank at our arranged time. A woman up front told me to go on back to his office. His face, as he greeted me, revealed nothing about the purpose of our meeting.

"It's awful, what happened to your mother."

"Uh huh." I answered, and sat in the chair he indicated as he sat also.

"What are your plans for The D?"

"I'm going to run it myself." I suddenly felt like a defiant child boasting about becoming an astronaut when I grew up.

The banker nodded solemnly. "You know, I've been friends with your family for a long time. And I've always handled the D's finances for your father." He studied my face way too carefully. I nodded, unsure if I wanted to hear what was coming next.

"I guess there's no easy way for me to tell you this. Your mother went a little wild with her spending while you were gone."

"Yes, I know." I had already seen Ursula's frivolous purchases.

"Sky, she bankrupted The D."

"What do you mean?"

"I mean you're broke."

"What about the land?"

"It's intact, but the bank accounts are drained and all other assets were sold off. The land is all that's left." He paused to let it sink in before continuing. "Your mother came to see me one last time not long before she died. She wanted to take out a mortgage."

"You mean borrow against the ranch?" I knew that was unheard of in our family. The Dalys would go hungry before they would jeopardize their land.

"I turned her down. Now you have to decide what's best." I understood the implication. A twenty-five year old girl had no business attempting to run a ranch.

"I'm figuring it out." I held his gaze and tried to sound confident, but I knew what was coming next.

"The best thing to do is sell out. You'd have to borrow heavily against the property to get going again, and you have no experience managing a ranch."

"But I worked on it most of my life.

"It's not the same as running it."

I wanted to argue with him, to convince him that I could do it, but I didn't. Instead, I slunk out of the bank, keeping my eyes fixed on the shiny hardwood floor, certain that everyone in the building was staring and whispering.

Over the next few days, I began receiving troubling phone calls. It seemed Ursula owed every business in the county money. I guess everyone worried that, with her death, they would never get paid.

I had saved most of what I made down in New Mexico and I could have stretched it out for quite a while, but it was nowhere near the amount I now needed. I didn't know what I was going to do, but was determined that somehow I would get every cent paid back because the Dalys never cheated anyone.

As more problems piled up, my return to the D became even less the happy homecoming I anticipated. Besides the bills, there was the fact that my mother's killer was still out there, and nobody knew where. Even though the sheriff tried to reassure me it was unlikely he'd return, no one could say for sure what he might do.

One evening I walked through the living room when twilight hid most of the gaudy effect. I avoided it as much as possible, but I was looking for the old photo album that had always sat on the bookshelf behind the couch. The bookcase was one of the pieces of furniture stuffed into Great Grandpa Matt's cabin, but the album wasn't there.

As I worried that Ursula had thrown it out, I reached for the light switch on the kitchen wall. It was just after six and with the shortening days, dusk was already setting in. Before my fingers found the switch, I saw headlights swoop around the corner and shine across the yard. Immediately I pulled my hand back, leaving the room dark. Tag barked, but I told him to be quiet. He remained by my side, emitting a low growl that put me even more on edge. My main thought was to find a weapon. I knew my dad's guns were gone, either sold by Ursula, or stolen by her boyfriend.

I crossed the kitchen, ducking as low as I could to peer out the window without being seen. The car pulled up next to mine and stopped. I felt in the drawer for a knife. The headlights disappeared, and as I watched through the window, the car door opened and a man stepped out. In the gray light, it was no one I immediately recognized. I watched the figure walk up to the back door, trying to remember what Rad Johnson looked like.

"Sky?" He paused on the steps to call out before knocking. Suddenly both he and the car became familiar. It was Will. I put the knife down and hurried over to greet him.

The screen door squeaked and swayed on the one hinge as I pushed it open and there he was with his wonderful smile. Without saying anything, he wrapped his arms around me. Tag bounced around us, obviously remembering Will as a friend.

"Man," he greeted me. "It's been a long time." The words were close to my ear.

"Ursula's dead."

"I know. I heard." He held me like he wasn't going to let go. "I've been trying to call you."

"I've been busy."

I had forgotten how good he felt and it was just what I needed, but finally I pulled away. I had meant to be angry at him if I ever saw him again.

I led the way inside, flipped the switch and turned to look at him in the light. He seemed to feel as uncertain of me as I did of him. In the few years since I saw him, he hadn't changed. He still looked handsome in a slightly scholarly way and I wondered if I looked the same to him.

"I missed you," he told me. I gave him another glance. His pony tail was gone, but I didn't comment on the change. I was wondering something.

"How did you know about Ursula?"

"Adrian told me."

"Adrian?"

"Yeah, we talk once in a while."

I didn't know whether to be flattered or annoyed with him. I didn't even have my brother's current phone number. Of course, I'd been living without a telephone for so long it was a wonder anyone had kept up with me.

"So you've been checking up on me?"

"You know that I care about you. Don't you?" For a moment I was afraid he would insist on an honest answer. The truth was I didn't know what to say. I had convinced myself long ago that I never even crossed his mind.

"Well I care about you too," I finally answered. It sounded like the lamest reply ever.

Will looked around. "The place looks the same."

"That's because you haven't seen it in the light." Besides the ugly decorating job in the living room, I had discovered something else. I walked over and flipped a switch on an electrical cord that ran down the wall along the front door frame. Instantly the room became a disco with colorful, spinning lights and sparkles dancing across the walls and floor.

Will did just as I had done. He stood in the doorway, slack jawed as he looked around. Since he didn't know what else to say, he lightened the mood.

"Far out. Where's the music?" I flipped the switch back to off since I couldn't stand the sight.

"It looks like your mom was keeping busy." He moved out of my way as I scurried back to the safety of the kitchen.

"Yeah, busy being crazy." It was the only explanation I could come up with. Will said nothing, so I changed the subject.

"What about you? What are you doing these days?" I asked him.

"Still living down in Boulder, but I've been working for a different newspaper. I tried calling a bunch of times," he said again. I realized he had been worried about me.

"I probably wasn't here."

"Oh." His answer was a statement, but he looked at me quizzically, sensing there was more to my answer.

I haven't been answering the phone."

"Why not?"

"Ursula quit paying the bills and I keep getting phone calls asking when I'm going to pay them."

"I have some money saved. You can have it if you want."

"No thanks, I'll manage." There was no way I was accepting charity. I just needed to figure some things out. I reached in the fridge and pulled out a couple beers. We sat down at the table and sipped from the cans while we caught each other up on the last few years of our lives. To my relief, he didn't ask about Ursula's death. Nor did he ask about my plans. Instead he told me about his life, which allowed me to just sit and listen.

"You look good," he finally said.

"So do you." My attitude always improved when he was around. As much as I hated to admit it, and as much as I wanted to hang onto my anger towards him, it seemed to have dissolved. Once again, he had come to my rescue. First he had saved me from my family and now he was saving me from my family's absence.

"Have you been sleeping out in the cabin?" He brought up a subject that needed to be addressed.

"No. You can barely get in the door. Ursula put the furniture from the living room over there. Besides it's too cold out." Aunt Dot had helped me push my parent's old bed out into the hall and I was again sleeping in my childhood bedroom.

"You can sleep in Steve's and Adrian's room." I looked down as I spoke, uncomfortable saying the words, but I was insistent we sleep in separate beds.

He just nodded. Maybe he understood and maybe he didn't, and even though sleeping with him was appealing in some ways, there was too much risk involved. Since my main objective was getting the D back on its feet, I didn't need the distraction of having to figure out how he fit into my life as well. That was what I told myself, but really I was already afraid of when he left again. Free love hadn't worked for me any more than attempting a steady relationship.

The following morning after breakfast we discussed my plan to run The D. Around the kitchen table was the site where, over the years, most decisions regarding the ranch had been made and this time was no different.

I explained the mess Ursula had left me. Once I finished, there was silence. Will carefully set his cup down before he spoke. I held my breath waiting, wondering whose side he would take regarding the future of the D.

"You need to come up with a plan," he said. I was relieved that he didn't automatically decide the best option was to sell out, as the others had.

"The plan is to keep ranching," I stated as a matter of fact. The reply was not only defensive, it was unkind. I quickly realized it was a dumb thing to say to someone wanting to help me.

Unfazed by my abrasive words, he brought up the obvious. "Well, how are you going to come up with the cash to restock?"

"I don't know."

He put his elbows on the table and leaned towards me. "There's only one way I can see." He was all seriousness. I felt my guard come up.

"What's that?"

"You're going to have to sell off part of the D."

"Absolutely not!"

"And you'll still have to take out a loan." He kept his eyes focused on me, despite my protest. But I refused to consider his suggestions.

"How much do you owe?"

"I don't know."

"How much will it take to restock?"

"I don't know." I began feeling really stupid.

"Well you're going to have to figure these things out and go from there."

I looked out the window. I could barely see the empty corrals and wished I had a horse to ride. I was sure that would help my situation. Planning and economics hadn't been part of my job description before.

"I could start training horses again." I thought of having to wait tables down at the Crossing and shuddered thinking of my father's waitress girlfriends. There was no way I was going to end up like them.

"You know you can't make nearly what you'll need that way."

Finally I agreed what I had to do, start figuring out finances. Will told me he'd help and together we went out and assessed the ranch headquarters. It was hard to believe how far it had fallen into disrepair in just a few years. Will had his ever-present notebook in hand and jotted down notes as we scrutinized the house and barn, plus the other outbuildings.

Then we went back inside, where I dug out the bills, including estate and property taxes. It was time consuming to come up with accurate dollar amounts for repairs, but we made rough estimates. Finally we began adding it all up.

It took days before we came up with some figures. I saw the amounts and knew for sure that I was in way over my head. Eventually I got up the nerve to call the sale barn and get current cattle prices. Even buying weanling heifers, the amount needed to restock the D was staggering.

"Don't forget upkeep on the place and fencing." I gave Will a dirty look as he found yet more expenses. Scattered in front of us, as we once again sat at the kitchen table, were papers filled with lists and columns of numbers. I was already depressed after reaching a total, and now he wanted to add on more.

"I'm going to have to redo the living room also," I gave a sigh of resignation.

After a week, I began wondering how long Will planned on staying. "Don't you have to get back to work?" I asked him.

"Nope, I quit."

"Oh." I immediately assumed that shortly he would be off on another adventure.

"I've decided to try free lancing."

"What's that?"

"Work on my own and sell my stories. I talked to editors at a couple of magazines and showed 'em my work. They sounded interested, so I decided, what the heck."

"Where are you going to live?"

He looked at me intently. "I don't know yet. I could stay in Boulder."

It was a hint, but I didn't get it. "Well, it was nice of you to stop by." Instead I used my same old sarcastic tone, used to show that I didn't care about him at all.

That afternoon we sat out on the porch. We had carried the old sofa over from the cabin and put it underneath the overhang. It had been full of mice nests and was basically ruined, but after cleaning it out and throwing an old bedspread over the top, it became an ideal place to lounge during the warm fall afternoons.

As we enjoyed the end of the day, Will was still going over the figures. The stack of lists sat on his lap. He lay them aside and turned to me.

"Wanna take a break?" He asked as he ran his fingers lightly over my arm. It would be so easy, I thought. Instead I looked directly into his eyes.

"Why do you keep coming back here?"

"Because I dig you." He slipped his arm around my shoulder. I felt his breath on my neck as he pulled me towards him. So easy.

But I couldn't do it. I just couldn't risk getting close to him only to have him leave me yet again. I was sure I had convinced myself long ago that I wasn't attracted to him. He was just another guy, I had repeatedly told myself. All that went through my mind again. I straightened up and pulled away.

"I just don't know if I can take being left again."

"You never asked me to stay."

"You never wanted to."

"Man, you sound like I ran out on you.

"Well, you did," I glowered, all the hurt I'd been carrying around refused to be ignored any longer. He could have pointed out that he had suggested I come with him, but he didn't. Instead he again put his arm around my shoulders and held me as the sun set, first filtering through the trees before sinking below the horizon.

Chapter 13

The lengthy discussion over the phone a couple days later worried me. I tried not to listen, but understood the gist of the conversation. Will hung up the phone and turned towards me.

"There's a story I want to cover out in San Francisco." Maybe I imagined it, but I thought he looked a little guilty. Apparently there had been a kidnapping with a political twist. I didn't really listen as he explained the details because all I could think was that my prophecy had come true. At least I hadn't let myself get close to him again. I felt my resolve strengthen.

"Well, you better go then." There was no way I was going to make even the slightest attempt to stop him.

He made a reservation to fly out to the west coast. When he asked me to drive him to the airport in Billings, you'd think I would finally have been clued in since he could have driven himself. I agreed to take him, but could only see that he was leaving. We said our goodbyes at the entrance to the airport.

"I'm coming back."

"Uh huh." I couldn't squelch the fear that I was being abandoned.

"I left all my stuff at your house." It was true. His car, and more importantly, his typewriter, remained at the D.

I managed a slight smile. "Well if you don't come get it, I'll throw it out." He laughed.

"I'll stay as long as you want me to."

"But you're leaving now."

"Only for a few days. Besides, I've been waiting."

"Waiting for what?"

"I fell for you the first time I saw you." He seemed to think that would help explain things. My mind flashed back to the blue Victorian, but I barely remembered our first meeting.

"Really?"

He put his bag down and put his hands on my shoulders. "Really."

"Well, why…" I didn't know what to say and wanted to continue feeling sorry for myself. But I couldn't. It was me who had been the flake.

"I have to go." He kissed my cheek, picked up his bag and opened the door. He looked over his shoulder and smiled. "See you next week." The door closed behind him and I wanted to panic.

While he was away, I poured over the expense lists we had made. The totals at the bottoms of the columns were huge, beyond my comprehension. The cost of equipment alone seemed enough to buy an entire ranch.

Even when I pared everything down to the bare minimum, I could see there was no way to come up with that kind of cash. And I knew that Bob Mullen, the banker, would never loan me that much, even if I did ask. As much as I hated the idea, the thought of losing the entire ranch caused me to consider Will's idea of selling off part of The D.

When it came time to pick him up my mind was pretty much made up. I drove to Billings knowing it would have to be done.

He approached me and gave me a hug. How could I doubt the intentions of a guy who greeted me so warmly every time he saw me? But I did. During the time he was gone, I had really tried to convince myself to think about saving the D and to keep thoughts of him away.

We drove home with two subjects to discuss. I figured he would want to talk about us, but I didn't give him the chance to begin that conversation.

"I decided to sell part of the D to get the money I need." I finally said the words aloud, finalizing my decision.

"Okay, then." Always the cool dude, Will didn't make a big deal out of my announcement. We were silent for a bit.

"So, did you get your story?"

"Yep."

I realized it was now time to talk about us, but I didn't know what to say. His admission the week before at the airport had made it clear how he felt towards me. But he didn't push me. Instead he told me about his trip as we drove home.

"You hungry?" I asked once we arrived back at the D. We had stopped at a supermarket in Billings for groceries. The paper bags sat on the kitchen table.

"I need a shower first."

He opened a bottle of wine, insisting it needed to sit there opened while he showered. I put the groceries away, still not knowing if he had decided to stay.

He poured the wine into glasses and we sat at the kitchen table. This was a new side to him, one of connoisseur, I thought, as we sampled the burgundy he had picked out.

"You know, you really have to redecorate your living room." He knew I was avoiding Ursula's creation by using only the kitchen.

"Yeah," I agreed and then added, "You know, if you're going to stick around, we'll need to change the sleeping arrangements around here." Will's face got that tickled look on it that I loved. He knew he had me. And I knew I had him.

We went upstairs to my parents' old bedroom. Even though I felt uncomfortable in Ursula's love nest, another name I used, I knew I would have to get over it. It was time I started assuming my place as head of the house, and that included taking over the bigger bedroom.

"I actually like the carpet." I couldn't believe I was admitting to liking anything that was her doing.

We finished evaluating the room and he turned towards me. "It works for me." He came close and reached out a hand to stroke my hair. "It really does look better long."

I had a brief thought of the irony of it. About the time others were cutting their hair, I had started growing mine out. It now hung in a braid down my back, which is how I generally wore it. My attention quickly returned to Will as he kissed me.

My doubts about him faded. Now if they would only stay gone, I briefly thought, but once again my mind wandered only for an instant. I kissed him back, feeling confidence building in myself that I had never felt before.

So we began sleeping together again. I enjoyed sex with him so much more without having to worry what anyone thought. Well, I still worried a little, but it mattered a lot less.

The thought of cleaning out Ursula's belongings was overwhelming. The closets were stuffed full of clothes and shoes from her shopping sprees. A lot of the clothing had never been worn. I wondered what her frame of mind had been as I examined designer labels with expensive price tags. I didn't know where to begin.

"What are you going to do with all this stuff?" It was the morning following Will's return and he stood looking over my shoulder as I studied the closet's contents.

"I don't know."

"Well I have a story to write. I'll help you when I'm done." He kissed my cheek and crossed the hall. He had made an office space for himself in Adrian's and Steve's old bedroom. Hand written notes lay scattered across the twin beds and his typewriter sat at the desk where Adrian had spent nights studying while in high school. I went to the hall phone and dialed a number.

"Do you want any of my mom's stuff?" I asked Aunt Loretta after greeting her on the other end of the line.

"Why are you getting rid of her belongings?" She seemed shocked that I would do that.

"Only clothes and stuff like that. I thought you might want to go through her closet with me."

"Well, all right. I suppose I could come over once I get the kids off to school tomorrow morning."

"That sounds good, Aunt Loretta. Goodbye."

Will remained upstairs. It was a beautiful fall day out, but I couldn't enjoy it. I knew I was postponing the inevitable.

We had collected topographical maps from the forest service to piece together the ranch. I could ride or drive to any of the disconnected pieces, but finding them on the maps and then determining fence lines wasn't easy. I spread the maps out and began studying them.

My parents must have had deeds with the legal descriptions of the D's boundaries. I searched for any official looking documents, but found nothing in the house. I even went out to Great Grandpa Matt's cabin and poked through abandoned mice nests looking for evidence of paper.

The only conclusion I could come up with was that Ursula threw everything out, important papers, the photo album, anything to do with my past. I didn't understand why she would do such a thing, and wondered if she did it after making out her will, for more spite.

Then I remembered the conversation with Aunt Dot about the forced marriage. For the first time I began to have a slight understanding of why my mother acted the way she did.

"Oh, my." Aunt Loretta could only stand and stare, one hand held to her chin as she took in the sight. "I had no idea." We peered into Ursula's closet, just as Will and I had the day before. I think it finally sunk in for both of us that no one had any idea what kind of life my mother had been living. It must be hard for her, I thought, as her sister had only been dead a month. I still felt very little about my mother's passing.

"What's that noise?" A tap, tap, tap sound came in through the open door.

"It's a typewriter."

"Excuse me?" Aunt Loretta looked at me as if there were no plausible explanation for the sound.

"It's Will. He's writing a story."

"Huh?" She leaned in a little closer.

"For a magazine."

"Oh." I realized that part of the reason for my aunt's visit was to find out about the hippy. Everyone knew he was back and shacking up with me, that foolish Daly girl.

I decided to keep up the intrigue and said no more. Aunt Louise glanced out into the hallway and then back at me. "Does he ever come out?"

I gave a slight laugh. "Of course he does."

"We better get to work here." My aunt realized how silly she was being and turned back to our task.

We hauled bags and stacks of clothing out of the closet, dumped them on the bed and began sorting. When we reached the floor underneath and revealed the old pink-flowered linoleum, Loretta burst out crying. I guess it must have somehow reminded her of my mother.

"Maybe we should stop for a while." I didn't know what to say to my aunt as she just stood there staring. All I could offer her was external comfort because I certainly couldn't relate to what she was feeling. She nodded.

"I'll go get Will," I told her. I needed the buffer he provided. He looked up as I peeked into the room.

"Wanna take a break?"

"Yeah."

"Coffee or tea?" He looked like he could use a boost.

"Coffee. Be down in a minute." His attention went back to the paper working its way through his typewriter.

Loretta and I trudged down the stairs into the kitchen. I glanced out the window. Thin clouds obscured the sun and the bare tree limbs shook in the brisk north wind. A storm was coming.

I put coffee on and waited by the stove. Loretta sat in a chair at the table. Her crying stopped, but she just sat there looking at the floor. I had no idea what to say and the silence became awkward.

Thankfully, Will clattered down the stairs as the coffee began percolating. He looked over at my aunt, then back at me, raised his eyebrows and gave me a look that plainly said, "Go comfort your aunt." I sat down opposite her.

"We don't have to keep working if you don't want to." I leaned across the table, the best effort I could make to get closer to her. Inwardly, I wondered if I shouldn't be feeling the same way she did.

"I'll be all right."

"Would you rather have tea?" I had meant to put water on to boil, but now Will was pouring coffee for us.

"No, this is fine," she assured me. But I doubt Aunt Loretta would have ever been so impolite as to make extra work for anyone.

"What are you writing about?" she asked as Will sat down with us.

"The Patty Hearst kidnapping. You probably heard about it."

"Yes, didn't they arrest her?" My aunt perked up. Part of me wanted to be irritated that Will could relate to people so easily. I decided to be relieved instead.

"Yeah, now they're preparing to go to trial. That's what I went to check out."

"Oh, that sounds like exciting work."

"It's pretty interesting." He nodded.

"And traveling, that must be fun."

"I enjoy seeing new places. How about you?"

"No, not really. I've only been out of Montana a few times." There was a little bit of the hardened tone in my aunt's voice that a person uses when they won't allow anyone else to question how they've spent their life.

I couldn't imagine how her life could have been much fun. Like my mother, she had married immediately out of high school. My grandfather had just sold the family ranch and was moving to town with his wife. She had been told there was no room for her, his youngest daughter, and marriage had become her best option.

Will helped bring the sorted clothing down the stairs and out to my aunt's car. Then he disappeared back upstairs. As Loretta and I stuffed her station wagon with

Ursula's belongings, I brought up the subject that I'd been pondering since my talk with Aunt Dottie.

"Did my dad marry my mom because she got pregnant?" I asked. We stood in the driveway without coats and the cold air cut through our clothing. As Loretta paused the wind caught the car door. I quickly closed it.

"Goodness, that was so long ago." Her tone told me it wasn't something she wanted to discuss. But I pressed on.

"What happened after the Denver Stock Show?" I was referring to the photograph of Ursula cutting a cow on the gray mare.

Loretta shrugged. "She came home, finished high school and started dating your father."

"She just quit riding horses?"

She looked at me, the reason my mother had to stop riding, remembering back to when Ursula graduated high school. "All your mother wanted to do was ride horses. But it's not like now. Women just didn't do that sort of thing back then." I didn't say anything about my experience in Texas.

"And then after Dad sold her horse…" She looked at me and I nodded that I knew about it. "She just quit trying after that. She pushed everyone away. Just out of high school, she started seeing your father, and then, well, you came along."

"Did he love her?"

"He liked her well enough, at first."

"Did she get pregnant on purpose?" I still wanted to blame the unhappy marriage on Ursula.

"Oh, no. They weren't even that serious. Your father was on to his next girlfriend before she even realized her condition."

"Then what happened?"

"She told our mother. And Mother told Dad." She frowned. "He was hoping he had struck gold, Ursula bagging a Daly. He couldn't wait to tell everyone."

I was amazed, as none of this had even been hinted about, at least not around me. Few people cared for my grandfather, including his own family, but I never really knew why. Apparently he had a habit of destroying his daughters' lives.

I began to see that my mother had been forced into marriage with a man who didn't love her, but I couldn't see how that was an excuse for the way she treated me. I wondered if she considered me the cause of her unhappy life. If she hadn't gotten pregnant with me, she wouldn't have been trapped into marriage with a man who didn't love her. But Loretta said she had given up before then.

"Did she ever love him?"

"At first, yes, and when he moved on, she was crushed. But by the time they got married, she realized what he was like."

"What do you mean?"

She shook her head. "He never changed. From before he ever knew who your mother was, until he died, he never could stick to one girl."

"Well she could have made the best of it," I was still not ready to forgive her for the way she treated me. Marriage to a prosperous rancher might have been the best she could have hoped for, and she had achieved that. Many, including her family, thought she had done very well for herself, and I tended to think the same way. Marrying my dad had to have been the best thing that could have happened to her. And I was the reason that happened.

Loretta gave me an uncomfortable look. "She told me your father never touched her after she became pregnant with your sisters." I knew that just bringing up the subject was difficult for my aunt, so she must have really wanted to make the point that Ursula was stuck in a miserable situation with my father. I did some math and realized that by age twenty-four, her husband was done with her. A year later, when she was my age, she had five children to care for.

After spending time with women active in the women's rights movement, my thinking had shifted. I realized that if I had married Billy Marsh, I could easily have ended up the same way. Stuck in the house with a bunch of kids seemed to be the reality for a lot of women around here. The best they hoped for was a husband who treated them well.

Of course neither of these conversations with my aunts helped answer the question I couldn't get out of my mind. Had Ursula left me The D because she wanted me to succeed, or had her motivation been to set me up to fail? I mean, she had left me the entire ranch, the thing I desired most in the world, but it was gutted, and if she'd had her way, it would have come to me with a mortgage. Remembering the way she treated me, I had to think she wanted me to fail.

It made me question myself. I wondered if I did have what it took to turn The D back into the prosperous operation it had been under my male relatives over the last four generations. If it was going to survive a fifth generation, I was going to have to start figuring some things out.

In the end my aunt Loretta hauled off most of Ursula's clothing. They wore the same size, unlike me who was taller. What she didn't want she could give away. I just wanted the closet cleaned out, and probably would have done it the old way, dug a hole and buried everything. Except Will insisted that everything be reused. As it was we had plenty of stuff to take to the second hand store in town.

A day later, I gave Will a quick kiss before heading to bed. Much later he came into the room. Plopping down on the bed, he said, "Done." I heaved a sigh of relief for him and went back to sleep as he crawled under the covers.

Once the story was in the mail, we finished emptying out the bedroom. I felt a little sad that I found absolutely no trace of my father in the room. Actually his presence seemed to have completely vanished from the entire house.

Will and I positioned the bed up against the west wall so it faced the rising sun, which seemed to signify new beginnings. I was back to my old sleeping schedule and was up before the sun came up, but I guess it was the thought that mattered. We decided that repainting would have to wait, but did everything else we could to make the room our own without spending much money.

Will scrounged two end tables and we lugged them up the stairs and placed them on either side of the bed. Ursula was almost gone from the room once I removed the curtains from the two windows. The room seemed stark, but I didn't mind.

"Absolutely not." I got up from where we were sitting at the kitchen table poring over maps. Will was free with his advice, but told me over and over that any final decisions were mine. And that was the problem. I was refusing to let any changes happen, especially selling off pieces of the D. He leaned back in his chair, ran his hands through his hair and looked at me, his annoyance with me plain to see.

We were discussing a particular piece of land. It was only two hundred acres, but it was next to the river with rich, black, soil. It seemed an insignificant little acreage, but it was prime agricultural land and produced a lot of hay. Will was proposing I sell it to a developer, but I just couldn't see myself doing it. I hated development of agricultural land anyway, and this was a fertile piece with excellent water rights coming from the Yellowstone River.

Of course, I wasn't looking at the down side of this particular piece of ground. Just the fact that it was located so far from the ranch headquarters should have been justification to let it go. The acreage was across the river from Compton, and the town was growing up around it. There were already houses built on one side. The last time The D had grazed cattle in the field, dogs from the subdivision had formed a pack and chased them.

I remembered my dad swearing when he received a phone call reporting the attack. We had brought the nervous cattle home and never ran livestock on it again.

From then on it was used strictly as a hay meadow. Just considering the fuel it took to haul the harvested hay home was justification to let it go.

Sitting with Will, my practical side said it had to be sacrificed, but my ranching background said no way was I going to allow development of an irrigated hay meadow.

"You're going to have to make some decisions." It was a challenge and I sat back down, determined to get what I saw as the butchering of the D, done once and for all.

"Okay, let's see."

"No, over here." Will jumped up and jerked the chair out from the end of the table, my father's chair. It had remained unoccupied since I returned, still reserved for the head of the household. "This is your ranch and you're in charge."

They were the strongest words I had ever heard him speak and he got my attention. Even though it was only a chair, what it represented had been ingrained in me from birth. The thought of sitting at the head of the table challenged my strongest beliefs. Except on rare occasions had anyone else sat in that spot, usually guests and they didn't count. The head of the table had remained reserved for my dad, the boss, even after he died. I stood up again, made the journey of a few steps to the head of the table and sat in the chair.

I looked around. Except that I now faced the stove, nothing had changed. I wasn't instantly transmuted into a queen or anything. Will sat down with a satisfied look on his face as I pulled the maps towards me and began studying them again.

A couple days later I had come no closer to making any decision about what parts of the D to sell off when Will made another suggestion. "You know, if you bypass the developer and subdivide and sell the pieces yourself, you could make a lot more on it."

I looked at Will like he was crazy, a look I'd been giving him a lot lately. "I'd have no idea how to go about doing it." It was the first excuse that popped into my mind.

"We could figure it out." There was also amazement in the looks I gave him. For someone who cared so little for money and material possessions, he seemed to have a head for business.

"I just want to get it done and start ranching again."

"You can't really do much until spring, can you?" He was right. The plan was to borrow only enough to meet expenses until I sold off the sacrificed acreage and then pay off the loan and buy cattle and equipment.

"Maybe you should consider it an option before you make a final decision."

"All right," I agreed. Selling off land put a sour taste in my mouth and I was all for avoiding it as long as possible.

Will started researching how to go about subdividing a piece of property, the approval process, and what would need to get done before it could happen. Of course there was money involved, and the amount would be added to the sum I intended to borrow from the bank.

The question raised by Ursula's final actions continued rattling around in my head. Did she anticipate me succeeding or failing?

Will drove us to town the morning of my meeting with the bank president. He had offered to cook breakfast before we left, but I was too nervous to eat. Inside the bank, he sat down on a bench in the lobby while I followed the receptionist back to Bob Mullen's office.

"Good morning, Sky," he put down his pen and stood up when she opened the door for me. "Sit down. What can I do for you?"

I quickly began explaining my plans. His face was expressionless as I went through the detailed lists and figures Will and I had spent weeks working on. He laid down his reading glasses and leaned back in his chair as I talked. I kept glancing at his face, trying to determine if I was wasting my time, or if I had a shot.

"Now, how do you expect to pay back a loan of this size?" I don't think he meant to be condescending. It seemed more like he was testing me.

I went into our plans for the subdivision, which had turned out to be an easy process. And when Will had figured the amount we could make as opposed to selling in one piece, the decision had become easier. I saw a slight involuntary lift of Mullen's brow as I explained this and knew he was impressed.

"Real estate's a risky market." He cautioned.

"We've already had people ask about it and a couple of realtors are interested." I wasn't sure if the last was right, but it sounded good. He realized we had done our homework and that's what mattered.

"Did you figure all this out by yourself?"

"I had some help." Actually Will had done most of it, but I had a banker to impress.

He looked at me, making slight up and down nods with his head as I answered his questions. I expected him to ask me the question I imagined everyone was wondering. Were Will and I going to get married, or rather, when was the wedding?

He didn't. Instead he took the folder I handed him, simultaneously picking up his glasses. He shuffled through the pages, giving each one a brief study. Will had typed them up and I thought the stack of papers looked very professional.

As he studied the lists adding up totals of our expected living expenses until the subdivision went through and lots began selling, I studied the Charlie Russell painting that hung above his head. It depicted a dicey situation involving a cowboy on horseback, a longhorn and a rope. I wondered how it all ended up, as it looked like the beginning of a bad wreck.

Mullen looked up, and from his expression, had apparently reached a decision he was satisfied with. The butterflies in my stomach lurched as I waited to hear what he had to say.

"I think we can come to an agreement on a loan to help you get back on your feet." His tone and expression were somber, but he again nodded his head at me. "We have more details to work out, but this is a start." He put the papers back in the folder.

I felt excited and tried to hold it in. "Thank you so much, Mr. Mullen." I got to my feet, unable to contain myself. He also stood up and walked around the desk. Once in front of me, he put out his hand and shaking mine, looked me straight in the eye.

"I'm glad to help out a Daly."

"Thank you," I repeated, not knowing what else to say.

"I'll let you know when I get the paperwork drawn up and you can look it over."

I walked out of the office feeling exuberant. I knew what a handshake meant to Bob Mullen. He had put me on even ground with himself and I knew I had an ally. I walked back out into the lobby and saw Will sitting on a bench, unassuming as always, watching the people around him. He smiled when he saw me, and I realized he would still like me regardless of the outcome of my meeting.

I smiled back. "Come on, let me buy you lunch."

The truth was, I felt a little uneasy at the amount that Will helped me. I wondered if I should be paying him. Maybe a little bit of professionalism between us would make me feel less like I was taking advantage of him. I finally brought it up one evening.

"Should I be paying you for all your help with this financial stuff?"

"No way. I have everything I need."

I guess living on the D really was the ideal situation for him. Since food and utilities went on the ranch accounts, it cost him little.

"Well, good. I just wanted to make sure."

He walked over to me and wrapped his arms around me. "The recompense is more than adequate." He kissed me, but my mind was still on his response.

"Jeez, I was just beginning to understand your hippy language. Now you're using these big words. I'm going to have to learn to understand you all over again."

"What do you mean?"

"Recompense?"

"Oh you mean polysyllabic words?" He teased me back.

"What?" But the conversation ended there as I lost my train of thought. I wondered briefly if I really was an airhead as Will's touch always seemed to cause my brain to shut down.

Chapter 14

Even though I didn't like some of the decisions I felt forced to make, my optimism grew. I averted my eyes from the subdivision as much as possible whenever I crossed the Yellowstone, but I couldn't help but notice the stakes tied with orange fluorescent tape that dotted the field once the surveyors showed up.

The sections of distant rangeland I put up for sale had been hard enough, but at least it would remain ranch land. I couldn't help but notice the situation was twisted. The fertile land was basically being destroyed, while the marginal land stayed in production. Actually, it was just plain backwards.

One morning, after Will left yet again, I drove to town on a mission. Thick clouds hid the sun, a raw day that felt colder than the thermometer read because of the wind. Once across the river, I turned onto a street that few ventured down. The dirt road crossed the railroad tracks and entered a small trailer park. Once past the mobile homes, it continued on for only another block.

Junked vehicles and broken appliances seemed to form peculiar monuments to this rundown section of town. Tiny, dilapidated houses showed the economic status of the people who resided there. Tar paper blew in the wind where siding and shingles were missing. The shacks were built originally by the railroad for their employees, but now the town derelicts had moved in.

I quickly spotted a familiar, old, Ford pickup. It belonged to Hawk and had the same crumpled right fender that it'd had for as long as I could remember. His story about what had happened was that the truck popped out of gear on a slight hill and plowed into a rock at the bottom. We suspected that he was drunk, but lacked proof. Not that we wanted to catch him because drinking while on the job would have gotten him fired.

He was just such a good guy that most overlooked his heavy alcohol consumption. Besides, he was also a good hand. He knew the D as well anyone as he had ridden over it for most of twenty years. An old time cowboy, he hated to walk, and only time and distance made driving an acceptable mode of transportation for him.

Hawk's favorite way of getting around was on horseback. When he had worked for us, my dad had given him his own horses to ride, just like outfits gave cowboys in years past.

He had kept them all ridden down through the summer months. In the winter he would simply saddle a horse and strike out on his own when cabin fever set in and the weather seemed it would hold long enough for him to clear the wood smoke from his lungs.

When I was little I wanted to be just like Hawk with a string of horses that no one else could ride. I wanted to be able to saddle a horse and head out across the prairie to check cattle every day. Even now I couldn't think of a better life.

I had heard he was now living in Dalton's Dump, as the neighborhood was called, named after a long ago railroad official. I pulled up next to the rusty old pickup. It was as good a day as any to pay him a visit. A gust of wind caught the door of my car and I hung on to it tightly as I climbed out.

I knocked on the door and it took a minute before the door opened a crack. "Sky?" Hawk's face broke into a grin as spied me. He yanked harder on the door knob. The door scraped across warped floor boards until the opening was wide enough for me to fit through. "Why, heck, it's good to see you. C'mon in."

Fumes from the oil stove hit me as I entered. I kept my gaze on his face so as not to see the conditions he was living in, but finally I had a quick look around. Rumpled blankets covered the narrow bunk. The kitchen consisted of a two foot counter with a sink on one end.

"I heard you were back. How you been?"

"Just fine."

He scratched the gray stubble covering his chin. "Here, have a seat." He indicated the single chair set next to a rickety table. "I was about to put on a fresh pot."

He acted like it wasn't the first pot of coffee he'd made that day, but I could tell that he had rolled out of bed only when he heard my knock. The sun poked through the clouds and briefly shone through the east window above the sink. As he stood there, filling the coffee pot from the tap, the light caught the age on his face. It had only been five years since I had seen him so it had come quickly. I wondered if this was where he had "moved on" to when he quit the D.

He placed the pot on the hot plate and turned back to me. "I'm sorry to hear about your momma." He looked down.

"Yeah, too bad," I replied and left it at that. I knew the old cowboy wouldn't be comfortable talking about Ursula's death.

I looked up at him again as he leaned against the sink. He had the puffy face and watery eyes of a hard drinker. Blotchy red patches covered his cheeks. It didn't appear Hawk had spent much time outdoors lately.

He tried to control the shaking of his hand as he poured coffee for us both, but it sloshed onto the peeling paint of the table top. I wanted to offer him the chair, but knew he wouldn't take it.

"What have you been up to?" I didn't want to put him on the spot, but couldn't think what else to ask.

"I've been around, doing a little bit of this and that." He sipped his coffee. I did the same as he changed the subject.

"Say, remember that time, you were just pint sized, but you insisted on riding with us all the way up to Grady's cabin. Your daddy tried to talk you out of it, but you wouldn't hear it." Hawk became enthusiastic as he took our attention into the past.

I remembered. Of course I did. My dad, Hawk and Grandpa Mathew were on their way to move pairs from one pasture to the next on a distant part of the ranch. Apparently they decided to turn it into a picnic and my mother and Grandma Rose made plans to drive around on the road with lunch.

I stubbornly refused to ride in the pickup bed with my younger siblings. They were just babies in my eyes while I had just gotten my first horse and considered myself quite capable, even though it was much further than I had ever ridden before. Finally my dad relented and told me I could come, but only if I kept up and didn't get in the way.

We started out at daybreak. I urged my little pony, Popper, into a trot, shivering in the early dawn. I still remembered the sting I felt every time my rear end slapped the cold leather of the saddle seat as I bounced along, but mainly I felt excited. No longer was I going to be stuck behind, helping load the picnic lunch. I was riding with the men.

They finally slowed their horses as the sun rose over the horizon. Gratefully I caught up and listened to their talk. It was their version of taking a break, rolling and smoking a cigarette as their horses moved forward in a fast, ground-covering walk. I still had to periodically jog my short-legged mount to keep up, but at least it wasn't a continuous hard-pounding trot.

When we arrived at the first pasture, my dad told me to stay on the trail we were following. The three men rode up and down the hills, searching the brush and trees. Any cattle they came across were pushed down towards me. I had the job of riding drag, meaning I stayed behind the increasingly larger herd, pushing the pairs up towards the higher meadow and fresh grass.

Most of the cows knew the way and moved along willingly, but occasionally one decided that her calf had been left behind and tried to go back to find it. I knew that wasn't so, as the calves were all accounted for.

It kept Pops and I on our toes. Being a kid's horse, he was a little bit lazy, but I was determined. Whenever a cow tried to make a break for it, I pounded his sides with my heels to hurry him up and get her turned back. Whenever I could I watched the men. Sometimes they moved as shadows through the trees on the hillsides.

We let the herd go in the meadow near the Grady cabin. I stood Popper next to my dad's horse, watching as intently as the men to see that each calf mothered up. The herd gradually quieted as they paired and the cows allowed their calves to nurse before going after the fresh grass. Slowly the brown and white cattle scattered across the pasture and I felt proud of myself. I had put in a good morning's work. We tied our horses in a corral next to the cabin and I reached up to tug the cinch loose on my saddle, rewarding my horse for a job well done.

Inside the cabin, the wood cook stove was blazing. Grandma Rose was an old time ranch wife. Instead of packing sandwiches and other picnic fare, she brought the makings for dinner, as she still called the midday meal. Building a fire in the cook stove and waiting for it to heat up before she could cook was no big deal to her. A pot of potatoes boiled on the stove and chicken sizzled in a skillet.

When it was ready I dug in and stuffed myself on the home cooking. After the meal, I felt sleepy. I slumped down near a cottonwood tree. The other men also lounged in the shade as Ursula and Grandma Rose cleaned up from our meal. Finally I couldn't keep my eyes open any longer and fell sleep. I woke to the sound of my mother and father discussing what to do with me.

"Let her sleep. You can lead her horse back."

"No, she wanted to come along. She needs to get her own horse home," my father answered.

I jumped to my feet, forcing myself awake. "I'm ready," I declared. Hawk and Grandpa Mathew had already mounted their horses and my dad stood next to his. Popper fretted over in the corral as he worried he was being left behind. I hurried over to him and tried to tighten the cinch. Every time I grabbed the latigo, he moved and pulled it from my hands. I struggled to hang on as he danced above me, threatening to knock me over and step on me.

Suddenly a pair of strong hands took over. I looked up and saw Hawk had dismounted and come over to help me. With one tug, he pulled the latigo tight, then pulled the slack through the knot, without looking at me. He picked me up, placed me in the saddle and handed me the reins. I felt a little bit ashamed as, not only had I held everyone up, I had relied on another's help.

But Hawk just smiled at me, his eyes twinkling at me from underneath the brim of his hat. He turned and mounted his horse and we caught up with my dad and grandfather.

"You shouldn't have helped her. If she wants to come, she's gonna have to learn to keep up."

"Aw, don't be so hard on her, Garrett. She's just a little girl," Hawk replied as we started off towards home.

The ride down was hard and I almost wished I could have ridden in the pickup. I was so tired and actually dozed off several times. My horse breaking into a trot to catch up woke me up each time my eyes shut. But I made it and after that I became determined to fit in by becoming as good a hand as the men.

Now, sitting in the dismal shack with Hawk grinning at me, I felt sure I had made the right decision in coming to see him. He had always treated me better than my own parents. I gave a wry smile as he finished the story and brought up the reason for my visit. "You know that Ursula left me the D and that I'm running it now?"

"I'd heard that, yeah." His face suddenly lost all expression. I continued.

"I'm buying more cattle, fixing the place up."

"Uh huh." He looked down. I was hoping to see some interest, but saw nothing to indicate that Hawk wanted anything other than to exist as a drunk in a one room hovel alongside the tracks. It puzzled me, but I kept talking.

"I'm going to need cowboys to ride for me, for the D. Since you know the country, I thought you might like to hire back on."

His tone turned so fast that I couldn't have seen it coming if I was expecting it. "I aint never workin' fer no damn woman!" He spat the words towards me with such force that I could smell the coffee mixed with last night's whiskey on his breath.

"Wha'...why?" I remained slammed up against the back of the chair as Hawk glared at me.

"Women just mess everything up. You got no right thinkin' you can run your daddy's ranch. Your momma didn't know what the hell she was doin' and neither do you."

My shock turned to indignation, then to anger. He looked down and went back to work on the same cigarette his stiff, unsteady fingers had been trying to roll for the past twenty minutes.

"Gimme that." I got to my feet and reached over to grab the tobacco and papers. I had never actually rolled a cigarette, but after studying the techniques of many cowboys during my childhood, and more recently, hippies rolling joints, I knew it had to be easier than Hawk was making it. I stuffed tobacco in a paper, worked it tight and licked the edge before sealing it.

"Here." I tossed the cigarette onto the table, a small proof of my competency. He didn't look up, just picked up the cigarette and put it to his lips. Suddenly my anger turned to pity as I saw a pathetic old man waiting for me to leave so he could have a morning drink without embarrassment.

"Goodbye, Hawk." I turned and left as he struck a match on the edge of the table, his eyes still refusing to meet mine.

I reminisced further during the drive home. Again I remembered when I was small, but this time I was younger than six.

Late one afternoon Hawk rode down off the ridge and into the yard, a handsome cowboy with a mustache and a tall hat. I saw him coming because I was waiting for him. He reached down, grabbed my arm and swung me up behind him. While I hugged him tight, we continued around the house and down to the barn. He let me pour oats into the manger to feed his horse after he pulled the saddle off.

Now he'd become a feeble old man, full of contempt and thinking he was better than me. I wanted to help him out, but all he could think was that I didn't know my place. I could still smell the rancid air from his shack on my clothes and hair. I pictured Gina, the woman I had met in California saying, "I told you so."

One place I hadn't been was down in the basement. Over the years it had become a cluttered storage room, filled with household junk and I hadn't had any desire to see what all was down there. Eventually I ventured down the steep, rickety steps.

A hundred, maybe more, empty canning jars sat on shelves lining the walls, glimmering in the dim light. They hadn't been touched since Grandma Rose washed them out after their last use and brought them down to store, expecting to fill them again the following year.

I poked around the discarded and broken household items, most of which should have been thrown out years ago. As I started back up the steps, I noticed a cardboard box back in a corner. Somehow, it seemed out of place as it sat perched on a top shelf, safe from mice or any other danger. I took it down and opened it up.

Inside were all the deeds and other valuable documents that I had searched for and been unable to find. At the bottom was the photo album. I carried the box up the steps, once again wondering what Ursula had been thinking. Did she sense something was going to happen to her and wanted to keep the papers safe? Maybe she simply dumped everything there to get it out of the way. No, the box had been too carefully placed. Had she purposely hidden everything from me?

I sat at the kitchen table and went through the old album, studying each familiar photograph and feeling like I had found my lost relatives. The empty pages in the back showed my parents' indifference to the Daly family. There were only a few more recent photos, most taken at the county fair by others and then given to Ursula. The most recent one of me was when I was fourteen.

I was standing next to Wilbur holding a ribbon and I remembered the day well. It was the only time, while competing against Billy Marsh, that I beat him. In a horsemanship class, his horse had stumbled. Since it had taken a few strides for him to recover, they made a mistake in the pattern. The blue ribbon wasn't what I most remembered about that day, however.

After I accepted my award, I went looking for Ursula. I found her sitting at a table near the concession stand, drinking coffee with a couple other women. She hadn't bothered to come watch me ride and I held up the ribbon to show what she missed. While the other mothers congratulated me, my own sat silent.

Exhaling smoke from her cigarette, she told me, "Take your sisters home and look after them until I get back." Then she got up and waddled off.

The devastation I felt when she ignored my accomplishment felt like a sliver that still festered after all these years. I had driven the pickup, towing the stock trailer containing Wilbur, back to the D, ten year old Donna and Debbie sitting next to me.

Maneuvering the outfit down the highway before I had a driver's license was no big deal, as I had been driving since I could reach the pedals. That was the easy part. Feeling Ursula's indifference was tough.

I closed the album and looked around. The kitchen cabinets had been upgraded to metal just before I was born. I thought the yellow theme of the kitchen ugly, and always had. Now, it seemed like a gaudy attempt at being cheerful in a room that had lost a family. I intended to remove all remnants of Ursula, even if I had to destroy the entire kitchen.

My gaze went out the window, beyond the corrals and over the empty horse pasture. I needed to be riding. But, with winter coming on and no income, it made no sense to spend money on a horse. Next year, I told myself.

Will came home and after some welcome home love making, he closed himself into his office. It became the routine when he returned from an assignment. He would disappear and except for brief breaks to eat and sleep, the only evidence of him being there was the sound of his typewriter as he tapped away. In order for him to live here with me, he was on a tight dead line. Sending his work through the mail added a week before the completed story reached the publication and he practically lived in his office as he turned his handwritten notes and tape recordings into a printable article.

Once the last page was pulled from his typewriter and the entire story proofed one more time, it was a matter of getting it to the post office and in the mail. When that was done, I had him back. It was something we both looked forward to and each return from the post office seemed cause for a mini celebration.

Sometimes we went out to dinner and then to hear a live band if one was playing nearby. Other times we stayed home and Will practiced his cooking skills. I teased him about a lot of the dishes he concocted, and sometimes the sarcastic remarks were deserved, but they were enjoyable evenings.

While he seemed content with his life, I was having a hard time with mine. Everywhere I looked seemed to remind me of things I would just as soon forget, but couldn't seem to get past. Will tried to console me.

"It's just memories."

"But how do I get rid of them?" I agreed with him, but I still needed them to go away.

"It may take time, or maybe you should forgive your mom."

There was an odd word to consider, forgiveness. I refused to let go of the resentment I felt towards her, even if, in the end I got what I wanted. I pictured her laughing at me, believing that, between my incompetence and the fact that I had little support as a woman ranch owner, I would fall on my face. It was easy to remember the last time I had seen her and I still cringed inside at the memory of the self-satisfied look on her face as Rad Johnson sided with her in forcing me to leave. Given the way she treated me, it seemed appropriate that it was the last time I saw or spoke to her.

"How can I ever forgive what she did to the D?"

"What if it means getting on with your life?"

That was the problem with Will, I thought. Instead of taking my side, he always jumped to my mother's defense. I wondered how long we could make it together with his attitude, probably not very. My mind still held a list of reasons why we wouldn't last as a couple.

A big one was that I just couldn't envision ranching with someone like Will as my partner. I wanted a strong, capable cowboy to swoop in and save me. Instead I ended up with a laid back, passive man who encouraged me to save myself.

There was another obstacle I couldn't get past. I had never heard the details of Ursula's death and I began obsessing about how it had happened. Everywhere I looked, I imagined blood. Splatters, smears and anything dark colored caused a stab of fear in the pit of my stomach. I scrutinized every speck, real or imagined, expecting it to be her blood. Was this the spot where my mother's life had ended? Will noticed my bizarre behavior, especially the increasing stress I was living in over it. I tried to explain my fixation to him and when I voiced it, I knew it sounded crazy. Still, I lived with a lot of anxiety.

One day a sheriff's deputy came by. It wasn't unusual. Well-meaning people occasionally stopped by to check on me. I wanted to be annoyed because I knew some just wanted to snoop, but I invited visitors into the house to satisfy their curiosity.

The deputy was a young guy named Ralph Henderson. He was a nephew of Hank Henderson, our neighbor. His family lived in Compton.

The coffee was still hot, so while Will pulled out cups and poured, I grabbed a bag of cookies from the cupboard and sat down with our guest, at the head of the table. He realized the significance of my spot, the same as others had and I couldn't help but wonder how everyone knew so well my family's positions around the kitchen table. We had a sip of coffee and a bite of cookie before Ralph looked across at me.

"How are you doing, Sky?" His question annoyed me, not only because I was sick of answering it, but also because of the big brother act he had adopted. I mean, come on.

"I'm fine." Will looked at me when he heard my terse answer. The truth was that I was frazzled and we both knew it.

"I hear you're gonna try and run the place yourself." He glanced quickly at Will while I set my chin, bracing for his disapproval.

"That's right." I answered. Ralph gave me a gentle look, like he might need to set me straight, but in a kindly way.

"With Will here?" The implication was that Will, as the man, would be in charge of the D. As everyone was aware, he knew nothing about running a ranch.

It suddenly occurred to me exactly how ridiculous the situation was. Ralph was a town kid. He had been one of the last of the greasers in Compton, with slicked back hair, a souped-up car and an attitude. He had barely graduated high school and had been kicked out of the army for reasons that were speculated about.

His mother's brother, the sheriff, had taken Ralph in under his wing. Somehow he had been turned loose in the county with a gun. He wasn't a bad guy really, just not very bright. And now here he was sitting in my home thinking he had some kind of authority to tell me what to do.

Will gave me another sharp look, wondering I'm sure, how I was going to answer. He disliked law enforcement of any kind and didn't understand why people here invited men he referred to as pigs into their homes. I didn't really care to have Ralph in my house either, but I had no real reason to exclude him. I also didn't want the speculation it would raise if I didn't ask him in.

"Pregnant and barefoot in the kitchen, huh Ralph?" I asked in reply.

"What?"

"Is that my place?"

Will saw where the conversation was heading and interjected. "You know what, there's something I want to ask you." The remark was directed at Ralph.

"What's that?" He asked.

Will looked at me. "We'll be right back," he assured me. I threw him an angry glare before they went outside.

Even though I was curious and couldn't imagine what Will could have to say to Ralph, I was relieved to have the deputy leave my table. That tragic expression on his face, as if he needed to chastise me, like I was the one being stupid, infuriated me. I sat smoldering for a few minutes about the unfairness of it all, but their discussion didn't take long. Will opened the kitchen door.

"Hey, Sky, come out here for a minute." His voice sounded serious. I followed him around the lilac bush and over to where Ralph stood at the edge of the front yard. His face had a frown as he faced me.

"Will says you never heard how your momma died." His voice sounded strained.

"Well, I know she was shot by Rad Johnson."

He nodded his head before glancing at Will, then back at me. "Do you really want to know?" I paused for a moment. No, I didn't, but I had to.

"Yeah," I answered and suddenly felt dizzy. Will watched me intently.

"I, um…," Ralph rubbed the top of his head. "I found her laying out here." He looked at his feet. His bowed head and hat in hand were apparently out of respect for Ursula. My eyes compulsively searched the ground around his feet. All I could see was dried-out lawn.

"She was dead, and Johnson was long gone before anyone realized what had happened. He took off in her car." I had already found out what had happened to Ursula's car.

"See, he stole Mrs. Lawler's car right out of her driveway. We found it parked out here. He came back with a hand gun. She must have run through the living room and out the front door trying to get away from him. He shot her in the back. From the porch. And this is where she fell." His voice had a catch in it. Carefully I examined the exact spot where my mother died, as much for Ralph's sake as for mine. Thankfully I saw no sign of her blood. I looked over at the porch.

Ralph and Will came closer to me. "We found shell casings, three of them. Every shot hit her. And any one of 'em could of killed her. Sky, I'm so sorry. I don't know if I should've been the one to tell you all this."

"It's all right," I assured him as I took in his words. The only lucid thought I could manage was that Johnson must have been a good shot to hit a moving target three times with a 38 revolver from that distance. The alternative was to think about my mother's terror as she fled and I couldn't allow my mind to go there.

"It looked like the bastard smoked a cigarette afterwards, crushed it out right there on the porch."

I shivered at the evilness of the man my mother had taken up with. I hoped she hadn't loved him, but why else would she have kept him around all that time? Suddenly I felt sorry for her.

"Any idea where he is?" I had forgotten Will was there.

"No, but we doubt he'll be back."

"Why did he kill her?" I asked the question I didn't know if anyone could answer.

Ralph shrugged, as clueless as everyone. The truth was, murders were rare around here. There were stories of men being killed for stealing livestock, water or another man's wife, but none during my life time and nothing like this. I imagined groups of people huddled together over coffee at cafés around town mulling over Johnson's actions and coming up with no clear explanation.

"Thank you for telling me." My voice seemed disconnected from me as I spoke.

Will came and stood in front of me, examining my face. "Are you okay?" There was that question again. I wanted to scream at him, but I didn't.

"Yeah." Instead, I just stared through him as I answered.

Ralph said goodbye, relieved to be leaving and looking slightly worried, like telling me these details might have been the wrong thing to do.

I searched the ground again. It must have rained recently. Or would somebody have hosed off the lawn to rinse the blood away? I glanced up at the porch, wanting to go examine it, to see if the cigarette butt remained, or maybe the ash where it had been ground into the wood.

I realized that I was acting crazy and turned back to see Will still watching me. Suddenly I began shivering in the cold air.

"Come on." He put his arm around me and pressed together we walked back around to the kitchen.

"Well, now I know." I told Will after I was sitting, elbows on the table, my head in my hands the only way I could keep it held up. Since everyone knew everyone else's business in our community, couldn't people see what was going on? I kept the question to myself since it was one he couldn't answer anyway.

I hadn't wanted to think about my mother's death in a concrete, real way, but now I was forced to. The vision of her lying on the lawn after being shot in the back threatened to become an unending nightmare. I worried that the way I had obtained the D was a curse, something that would hang over the ranch forever.

One gray, winter day, as Will and I lingered over lunch, he suggested we take a drive. I agreed since it was a good excuse to get out of the house. Ever since the visit from Deputy Ralph, I wasn't sleeping well. It bothered me that I was taking Ursula's death so hard.

"There's something I've been wanting to research," he told me.

"What's that?"

"Remember when we found the graves of your great grandparents' children? I want to look into it some more."

I had thought about our visit to the Cedar Junction graveyard occasionally. I didn't know why it interested Will, but given his fascination with history, plus his nose for a story, it could be the distraction I needed.

"Where do we start?" I asked twenty minutes later as we drove past the ruins of the town of Turkey Creek.

"Let's see what's in the Cedar Junction newspaper archives."

It was a short drive to the next town east of Compton along the Yellowstone River. We pulled up in front of a small, ramshackle building with a sign above the door that read

Cedar Junction Tribune
est. 1884

It was the original building and the weather-beaten boards showed their age. Will pushed open the warped door and we entered. Thick wood smoke engulfed us as the stove seemed to emit as much smoke as heat. A man practically leaped out of a chair behind the desk to greet us. Although his gray hair and stooped shoulders made him look old, his spry movements had the opposite effect.

"How can I help you? Do you want to place a want ad." His friendly attitude gave the impression he didn't get a lot of company in the dingy office.

"No." Will answered. "This is Sky Daly and I'm Will Daniels. I was wondering if we could look through your archives."

"Are you looking for anything particular?"

"Do they go back as far as 1887?"

"I got 'em all. They're down in the basement. What time of year."

Will looked at me. "Spring, wasn't it?" I nodded. "We were in the cemetery and noticed that a bunch of people died around the same time. There must have been an epidemic of some sort," he explained.

"Yep, Just after the hard winter of '86-'87. I don't know exactly what it was, but it took twelve people." The newspaper editor spoke as if he remembered the incident personally. "I've read all the back issues in the twenty-nine years I've owned the paper," he explained. "What's your interest?"

"Two of them, they were just children, were ancestors of mine," I spoke up. "I never knew about them, but they're buried in the cemetery."

"Well, I have a paper to put out, but I'll show you where to look. The only thing I ask is that you handle 'em carefully." He flipped a switch on the wall near the stairs and led us down into the clutter of the basement.

I looked around and wondered how he could find anything in the dim light. The newspaper owner never hesitated however, but went directly to a row of wooden crates overflowing with old newspapers.

"These boxes here are the first ten years. Like I said, be careful with them. By the way, my name's Joe Massey." He trotted back up the steps.

The shadowy room gave me the creeps, but Will was in his element. I could just make out the eager look on his face as he started through a stack of newspapers. He looked over at me.

"Come on. Let's see what we can find." He started checking the dates as I chose another box and did the same.

An hour later he called out. "Found it!" he exclaimed.

"Thank God" I replied. He walked over with the brittle paper in his hands. "Can we go upstairs?" By now the smoke was preferable to the chill of the basement.

"Sure," Will answered, his eyes glued to the paper.

We stood by the stove as he read the story out loud about the deaths from the epidemic. Joe Massey remained back at his desk and Will spoke softly so as not to disturb him. The illness after the devastating blizzards were blamed on all the rotting cattle carcasses that littered the prairie. The townspeople believed the disease was carried in on the wind. I knew better than to think that was the real cause of the illness, but the odor from that many dead animals had to have been revolting. The thought made me remember gagging one time when I found a dead cow down by the creek.

Will read down to the bottom where they listed the names of the victims. "This is odd."

"What?"

"Well it lists the two children, John and Anne Daly, but says they were living with their grandparents, Theodore and Elizabeth Lavold and their mother Mrs. Daly and that their father was deceased."

I practically tore the newspaper from his hands. I read the story for myself and still couldn't believe what it said. My great grandfather was buried at the D, where he had died just before I was born. I didn't know what to think.

"Could Lavina have been married twice…?" Will asked. "But the name is the same."

"I never heard anything about this." I was confused. I thought back to the stories Grandma Rose had told and didn't remember her ever mentioning this. "It has to be a mistake."

The editor looked up from his work as my voice became louder. "What's the matter?" He asked. I told him that the man the newspaper reported as dead was buried on my ranch.

"He's my great grandfather," I declared adamantly. The man listened and then thought a moment.

"The name Daly sounds familiar, but I don't remember why. You're welcome to go back down and look some more, see what you can find."

"Come on," Will urged, ready to keep searching. Although I didn't share his enthusiasm for research, I followed him back down the steps to learn more about the life of my great grandfather. He was my favorite relative, even if I had never met him.

We spent the rest of the afternoon digging through the old records. Finally the editor called down that he was going home. Will reluctantly returned the papers to the crate and followed me up the steps.

"We'll be back, if that's okay." Will said, as the editor put on his coat and walked us to the door.

"Sure, I'd like to see what you find."

I sat in silence on the ride home as Will hummed a tune. While my mind spun with possible explanations for what we had uncovered, his life had gained another purpose.

"Is there anyone you can ask about this?" He wondered.

"I still have relatives alive who knew him. You'd think they'd have talked about this if they knew about it, but someone must know something."

"We certainly have a mystery on our hands," Will stated gleefully.

The next morning he insisted on walking up to the old graveyard. I knew there was nothing new to discover on the headstones, but I hiked up the hill with him. I was due for a visit anyway as I hadn't been up there since I returned.

The five graves sat in a row, the headstones small and simple. Only the name and dates of birth and death had been chiseled into each rock. There had been no new ones added since the year before I was born, as first my grandparents and then my parents, had been buried in the cemetery at the edge of Compton. I supposed it was easier to bury people near town rather than transport the body and all the mourners to the top of the hill way out here, but it was the end of another family custom. I pulled dead grass from around the headstones of my long dead relatives while Will squatted down to study the inscriptions.

We had been up there together once before, the first summer Will had come to the D. Reading the markers, he had asked questions about the occupants. The only things I could tell him were what had been repeated to me.

John Daly was my great, great grandfather. He had been shot and killed outside the old cabin. Jesse Branson, a neighbor from across the creek, had been dipping water from the stream where the corrals now stand when he was picked off. The story was that the shooters were gunmen hired by a neighbor to kill them in order to gain control of their land. There was nothing to back up the account, and as far as I knew, it could have been just another tall tale about the Wild West. All I knew for sure was that they had died on the same day as that was what the inscriptions on their headstones read.

I knew little about the man buried in the middle. It was the only headstone that had no date of birth carved into it, only a name, Gray Eagle, and the date of his death in 1912. Apparently he had been a friend of my great grandfather's and had spent his last years on the D.

Continuing down the row was my great grandmother, Lavina. She had died well before my great grandfather. Grandma Rose was the only one I ever knew who remembered her. Apparently the two women had worked side by side for many years running the D household and had also been good friends. I wondered if Lavina's posture had been destroyed from hard work like Rose's had.

Great Grandpa Matt was buried at the end of the row. He died just before I was born. Ursula had stayed home when they buried him because of me.

Will studied the names and dates, as if he could get the granite to reveal more. "There has to be a lot more to the story. Why wasn't Matt killed that day? How did his wife and children come to be living with her parents? And why did they think he was dead?" He asked. I had no idea. The newspaper article was the first I had heard of it.

We started back down the hill. "I need to go down to the Compton newspaper. I bet I can find out more there." He trotted down the hill, energized at the prospect of spending long hours perusing old newspapers.

Chapter 15

We settled in for the winter. Except for working out details for the subdivision and a few other things, I thought it was going to be a quiet time. Then a carload of Will's friends showed up. Maybe they were looking for a place to winter where they would get fed or maybe they simply came for a visit as they passed through. The visitors didn't seem to know what their plans were any more than I did.

The car, a tan sedan, pulled into the driveway one gray midwinter day. Two couples emerged from the vehicle, seeming to spill out of the opened doors along with their belongings. I watched them take in their surroundings and felt a little possessive of the D.

The four of them were agreeable enough, and at first everything was fine. I didn't mind when they didn't pick up after themselves and left dirty dishes piled in the sink.

In some strange way it seemed payback to Ursula and the tyrannical way she had kept order in the house. The hippies believed in communal living and sharing everything they had and, at first, I had no problem with letting them stay at the ranch or even helping themselves to food.

Eventually things began to get out of hand. One of the women wasn't above going through my closet. I don't think she actually wore any of my clothes. Maybe nothing fit her, or maybe my boring wardrobe of work clothes didn't appeal to her, but she still managed to make a mess.

I began to wonder about their upbringings, although, maybe they were simply rebelling against their parents as I was against Ursula. I said nothing as I didn't want to offend anyone. After all they were Will's friends. Besides I had other things to think about. The loan had come through and I sold one section of the D to a neighbor.

My attitude changed the day I walked into the kitchen for some lunch and found the kitchen trashed. Dirty dishes and pots and pans filled the sink and covered the counters. I searched the refrigerator and cupboards, but found little food. I knew we needed to lay down some ground rules.

Will said he backed me, although I should have known that, since he avoided confrontation of any kind, I was on my own. I told our guests, that they had to clean up after themselves and leave some food for me.

"You need to relax, man," a disheveled man who went by the name of Ringer challenged me.

"No, I don't. I need you to clean up after yourselves."

"We'll get to it," Julia, his old lady, as he referred to her, attempted to appease me.

"That's not good enough." I insisted, my voice rising.

"It'll be ok, just mellow out." Will insisted.

"I will not," I snapped back. He walked over to the sink and ran dish water. Julia went over to help as the other three disappeared into the living room. I stomped out the door, climbed in my car and went to town to eat by myself.

That night when we were alone, I turned on Will. "Why didn't you back me? You told me you agreed with me about any guests pulling their weight."

"I do." Again he used that placating voice that drove me crazy.

"You told me to just mellow out. That's not being on my side. Those people need to help out if they want to stay here."

"You just get too upset about it. It's not that big of a deal."

"It is a big deal, and if you don't see it, then I don't want your friends here at all."

"I'm tired of talking about it. I'm going to bed." With that the discussion ended.

The following morning the four of them decided it was time to move on. I could imagine the things that were said about me, but I didn't care. I was just relieved they were gone and thought the problem was solved.

In March, another group showed up in a van that rattled up the driveway and rolled to a stop in what I was afraid might be its final resting place. The back door slid open and out spilled three more of Will's nonconformist friends. They reminded me of wandering gypsies.

He introduced me, and they acted nice enough. I was getting good at reading the signs though. I saw myself dismissed by the two men as simply Will's old lady.

They came into the house and looked around. "This is a far out place," one of them directed the comment at Will.

I decided right then to set them straight. "Actually it's my place." I answered. I got an odd look, but I continued. "You're welcome to stay here, but there are a few rules. You have to clean up after yourselves and it would be nice if you helped out with food." I think I lost them when I referred to rules. Will gave me an exasperated look.

"Fair enough," the one who seemed to be the leader of the group said, but he never made eye contact.

Of course, later, Will got on me about my behavior once again. "They're our guests," he insisted. "You need to treat them better."

"No, they need to treat me better. If they can't show some respect, I don't want them here."

"Why are you making such a big deal out of this?"

"Because it is a big deal. First you tell me I need to stand up for myself and when I do, you tell me to be quiet!" It was our second real argument; the first one was on the same subject a month earlier. I didn't understand why he couldn't see my point of view and realize what I said was the truth. He understood neither why I got so upset, nor why I treated company so poorly.

What bothered me the most was the way they acted like I was being a bitch, like I shouldn't have any say in my own home. I didn't like acting that way, but I wasn't about to give in. I was fed up with being disregarded.

It also seemed strange that even though I was setting up a subdivision and managing a ranch, at home I felt subservient. And this was from people who had supposedly supported equal rights for women. I can't say that I was in a position to observe the majority of them, but it seemed that some women were falling back into the traditional roles that only a few years earlier they had been so adamant about escaping.

The three guests showed no intention of moving on and we had what I considered an uneasy truce. The only one of them who tried to get along with me was the woman, Lucy. She cooked and cleaned up after the two men and kept a sunny disposition. The two men acted more like lords of the castle. So much for women's liberation, I thought.

One afternoon I returned from town. The early spring weather had turned pleasantly warm. I came around the final corner of the driveway and when I came into sight of the house, was startled by an unexpected sight. My three guests were sitting out in front of the house. Not only weren't they wearing a stitch of clothing, they were passing around a pipe. I jumped out of my car and hurried over to where they lounged on the lawn.

"You can't be doing that out here!" I was referring mainly to smoking pot, since the nudity, which wouldn't have gone over too well if a neighbor had come by, at least wasn't illegal.

Marijuana use had always caused a bit of contention between Will and me. He had brought some with him both summers he worked on the D. Of course he was ultra-secretive about smoking it, but I had known about it and he had urged me to try it. After what had happened to Billy, there was no way I would touch the stuff.

Some of my friends in New Mexico had spent a lot of time stoned. They laughed at me about my fear of what it could do to me. I didn't care. There was no way I was going to take a chance. I put up with it as long as people acted right. Now, in full view of the driveway, it had become a little too blatant.

"Man, you really need to chill out." Larry told me. Cal passed the pipe before exhaling in my direction.

"No, you don't understand. I don't mind what you're doing, but if a neighbor dropped by and saw you, they'd probably call the sheriff."

Larry ignored my warning. Taking the pipe, he glanced over at me. "We decided you're not in charge anymore."

"What?" His statement caught me off guard.

"We took a vote and decided we want to run things differently." The two men smirked at me, challenging me to defy them. Lucy became nervous. She stood up, clothing in hand.

Fury I didn't even know I was capable of surfaced. I turned and sprinted up to the house. As long as I could remember there had been a baseball bat in a corner of the mudroom. I grabbed it and raced back outside. Lifting the weapon, I charged the two men. I don't know if I really wanted to hurt Larry, but I did want to wipe the smirk off his face. And it worked.

A look of confusion, quickly followed by one of alarm, took over his face. Both men jumped up as I ran towards them, waving the wooden bat. I continued charging as they fled, staying out of reach. I chased after them, my rage in full control of me as we circled the yard.

"Get the fuck off my ranch! Nobody tells me what to do on my own place!" I swung the bat when I got close to either of the frightened men. Finally I held them at the edge of the lawn. I waited for either of them to make a move. I decided I was mad enough to land a blow if I got close enough.

"At least let us get our stuff." Larry pleaded. Lucy hurried out of the house carrying an armload of their possessions. She gave me a quick glance as she made a beeline for the van. I stood there panting and suddenly realized what the word berserk meant.

Will drove up shortly after they left. "What happened here?" He had a concerned look on his face.

"I had to evict your friends." My tone dared him to disapprove of my actions.

"Well you sure scared them. They were going down the road to beat hell. I had to turn around and chase them for a mile before they stopped. They told me to watch out, that you're nuts."

I let out a self-satisfied cackle. "What happened was that I finally found a friend to back me." I picked up the bat I had left leaning against the counter and pounded my free palm lightly with it to make my point.

"Seriously, you went after them with that?"

"Yep," I told him with new-found confidence. Standing in the driveway watching the van careen out of sight, I had finally felt head of my house.

Suddenly he laughed. "They were being assholes, weren't they?"

"I'm glad you finally see it my way."

I don't know if the word got out about what happened. Maybe Will just became more discriminating about who he invited to the D, but it ended our drop-in company.

We did have company one last time that spring. Unlike the previous visitors, Shawn, Will's old roommate, called first. After getting a master's degree in social work, she was working as a counselor at a women's shelter and was due some vacation time. Will and I both looked forward to seeing her. She brought Eric, the freaked out Viet Nam vet, with her.

As they appeared from yet another wreck of a car, I couldn't help wonder if Eric would want the GTO back from Will. Shawn gave us both hugs, while Eric hung back. He finally smiled when Will greeted him.

We couldn't help but stare. He had been thin before, but now his clothes seemed to hang on a skeleton beneath a pinched face. When I met him before he had looked tan and healthy; now worry lines crossed his pale face.

"Hey, Eric. Welcome to the D." I couldn't help but want to try and cheer him up. He managed another slight smile as he thanked me.

Shawn acted the opposite and her attitude was welcome. "Wow, this is a really cool place you have here," she told me. There was no envy in her voice, nor did she attempt to make me feel like I should be guilty for having so much. She seemed truly happy for me.

Will asked if I minded if he took the pickup to show Eric around. He didn't need to ask, but since I ran our previous visitors off, his attitude towards me had changed.

"Go ahead," I told him. I guess I was eager for a little girl talk.

"I am so happy you and Will finally got it together." Shawn said after they left.

"What do you mean?"

"When you split from Berkeley, he was pretty bummed out."

"Really?" I rarely thought about that brief period of my life, mainly because of the devastation I had felt when Billy told me to get lost.

"Oh, yeah. He really dug you. It's the only time I ever saw him hung up on a woman."

"I thought you two were sleeping together back then."

"We had a thing for a while. That's how he was, until you came along." Shawn was as amazed that I had realized none of this as I was at her words. I immediately felt guilty, because as much as I liked Will, I just refused to consider our situation long term. I wondered what the two men were talking about, what he was telling Eric about me.

We strolled around to the back of the house. The warm spring weather added to the agreeable nature of my guest made for a pleasurable day.

"Do you have a vegetable garden," Shawn asked me.

"Not since my grandmother died." I replied.

Grandma Rose had planted a huge garden every spring. Some of my best memories were of working beside her as she tended the garden. When my parents seemed to resent my company, she welcomed my help.

I glanced up at the root cellar. There used to be a path to the thick double door and I had a vague memory of trying to lug a basket of potatoes up from the garden. In the fall it was filled with root crops after they were harvested and stored there to feed our family during the winter.

She also put up hundreds of jars of pickled beets and cucumbers, as well as green beans and corn, whatever she managed to grow a bumper crop of in a harsh climate where many crops failed. I suppose Ursula had helped with the canning, but after my grandmother died, the plot of land went to weeds as my mother had no interest in growing food. Her idea of nutrition was heating up the contents of cans she brought home from the store. Now the entire back yard was overgrown with grass and littered with old machinery and showed no sign of ever having any other use.

Shawn also noticed the apple trees. "Do these still produce fruit?" she asked me.

"Rarely," I replied. I had another memory of picking apples in the late summer. Grandma Rose used to haul them up into the attic to dry for use in winter baking. We also ate homemade applesauce all winter. Now the orchard was full of dying trees with broken limbs littering the ground. I didn't remember how they looked when they were healthy and produced bushels of fruit.

"It's a shame," was Shawn's reply.

"Yes, it is," I answered. I pointed out the old chicken house with its collapsed roof and showed her, down in the barn, the milking stall. Both the chickens and the milk cow had disappeared after Grandma Rose died. With my parents in charge, the D had been fully modernized, with all food, except beef, bought at the store. It was no longer self-sufficient.

Not that there hadn't always been some reliance on the outside. The only plowing done on the D had been to grow oats to feed the draft horses. The big drafts were used to pull haying machinery, as well as wagons loaded with the cured grass as it was fed over the winter. After the horses were replaced by tractors, the oat fields had been reseeded to pasture. The Dalys never considered themselves farmers.

I enjoyed the visit as much as Will did. It was nice having Shawn around, partly because she didn't try and tell me what to do. Eric didn't hang around much. He preferred to be off by himself.

"I'm scared for him," Shawn told Will one morning after Eric disappeared outside. "He's been a basket case ever since he got kicked out of that commune over in Washington."

Will nodded. I hadn't heard what happened, but he obviously had. "I wish there was something I could do for him."

"Just being out of the city helps," she replied. He did seem a lot calmer after a few days on the D.

They spent a couple weeks with us, but as it turned warmer and the grass began greening up, they went on their way. It was time for me to get to work outside anyway.

When I started thinking about buying cattle that spring, planning for the future, the level-headed Will once again seemed determined to complicate things.

"Are you going to go with the same breed?" He was referring to the Herefords the Dalys had run ever since beef cattle had replaced the rangy longhorns, with most of the same bloodlines my forefathers had selected over the years.

"Yes. That's what worked for my dad and grandpa. Why?"

"Well, I was reading an article the other day and maybe you ought to check out different breeds, find out which would be best."

Here we go, I thought. Whenever he spent time in the library, he seemed to become an expert on any subject. I smiled at him. "I think I know what's best in this case."

"Didn't I hear that there were problems with the Herefords? Wasn't there a lot of pinkeye?"

"How do you know about that?"

"I was talking to your dad one time. Plus, he said their white bags can burn in the sun."

"Okay, what did the article say?"

"That Angus don't have those problems."

"No way." I told him. "Angus are mean and hard to handle."

"But if they're tougher, wouldn't it be worth it? Besides I read they aren't that bad. And they're good mothers."

"Ok, I'll look into it. Geez, sometimes you make everything harder than it needs to be."

"I'm just thorough." He grinned at me.

In the end I ended up changing my mind. After reading through the pamphlets Will brought home from the extension office, the Angus did seem a good choice. There was concern that the Herefords had been inbred to the point that they had lost some of their vitality. The information made sense to me.

The D wasn't ready for cattle though. As spring progressed, I began to get antsy. There was still a lot of work to do and I was attempting it all by myself.

One morning I ripped my arm open repairing a wire gate when a barb on the wire hooked my skin. I had to drive myself back up into the yard holding my arm out the window so I wouldn't bleed all over the inside of the pickup. Will was upstairs working when I burst into the kitchen. I hollered up to him as I rushed to the sink, still dripping blood.

He drove me to the doctor's office to get stitches, plus a tetanus shot. It didn't make him any too happy as he was trying to finish a story. On the way home he again brought up the subject of hired help.

"You can't do it all." That sentence had become like a mantra, but this time, trying to find a comfortable position for my arm as the anesthetic wore off, maybe I finally heard it.

"I just don't know where I'll find anyone to work for me." I still remembered Hawk, not to mention the unsolicited advice I had received from other men.

"You're going to have to get their respect."

"How?"

"By standing up for yourself and not taking any of their crap, just like you did with our company." The hardness in his voice was new.

"But..." I began the excuse that this was different.

"But what? Do you want this to work out or not?"

"Yes."

"Well then start acting like a boss. You are the boss."

We pulled up to the house and got out of the car. My arm throbbed with pain, but knowing I would get no sympathy, I said nothing as we walked inside.

"I have to finish this article." He still sounded cross. "I'll see you at dinner."

"Hey," I called out before he reached the stairs. He turned around. "Thanks for the pep talk." He laughed and headed up the steps.

A week later I was still wondering how to go about hiring some help. The day I went to town to get the stitches removed from my arm, I bumped into a guy I knew.

"Hey, Sky," he greeted me.

"Jake, I heard you were back in town."

I had gone to school with Jake Babcock. He grew up on a ranch on the south side of the river. When we were in high school, he got the rodeo bug and had spent the years since he graduated chasing the dream of being a bull rider. After realizing he was getting hurt a lot more than he was making rides, he finally quit and came back home.

When he arrived back in Compton, his father had just sold their ranch and his parents were preparing to move to Denver. I had already heard this bit of gossip when I bumped into him on the street.

"And I heard you took over your daddy's ranch." He was obviously caught up on the local goings on as well.

"That's right. What are you going to do now?"

"Find a job, I guess." He didn't sound too happy about it.

"You want to come to work for the D? All I've got right now is a lot of fence to mend, but once I restock I'll need riders."

"Yeah, okay." He nodded his head. "I got a buddy who could come out too."

"Bring him. I've got enough work for both of you."

"When do we start?"

"Tomorrow morning." We said goodbye and I drove home feeling like a weight had been lifted from my shoulders.

The next morning I drove with the pair out to a short stretch along the highway where the fence needed replacing. Jake and his friend, Fred Patterson, had showed up ready to work. They both jumped out and immediately began removing the wire from old posts. I was relieved that both of them knew what to do and didn't hesitate. Part of me thought I should stay and help them, but after assuring myself that they would do a good job, I left them there.

The first few days of having my new hired help went smoothly. I told them where I wanted them to work and the pair took off in an old Ford pickup I had recently bought at an auction. It was loaded with rolls of barb wire and other fencing supplies. At the end of the day they came back and reported their progress to me.

I was pleased since I had could now focus my attention on other matters. I hired Uncle George, Loretta's husband, to come out and work on the irrigation system. George was a building contractor and was waiting for a job to start, so had time to replace the old, wooden head gates in the ditches with cement ones.

One evening as Will and I were sitting on the back step enjoying the end of a beautiful spring day, the phone rang. I went in and answered it.

"Sky?"

"Yes."

"This is Bobbie Reynolds. Remember me?"

"Sure." Bobbie was another school mate, but we had never been friends. She had been a cheerleader, the type of girl I had no use for. I couldn't imagine why she would be calling me. "How have you been?" I asked.

"I'm fine, but I have a problem."

"What's that?"

"Well, I bought a horse, and I can't seem to get him to go where I want. He was fine when I bought him, but now…" She continued on about her struggles with her spoiled horse. It seemed a classic example of a savvy horse taking advantage of a novice rider. "I was wondering if you're still training horses."

I thought for a second. "Well, I'm kinda' busy right now."

"I just don't know what to do, and he seems to be getting worse. I can pay you." She sounded desperate.

My eagerness to ride again got the best of me. Also, it was an ideal situation, getting paid instead of having to buy a horse I didn't yet have a use for.

"Can you get him over here?" I asked her. A stock trailer was on the list of things the ranch would need at some point.

"Yes. When can I bring him?"

"Whenever you want."

"I'll be over tomorrow."

She must have been eager to get rid of the horse because she showed up in the morning. The gelding backed out of the trailer and I was impressed. Buster, as she called him, was a big stout gray. I admired his powerful build as I checked out his confirmation. Except for the fact that he had obviously been spending a lot of time standing around eating, and had the excess flesh to show for it, I saw little wrong with him. I looked into his eye as Bobbie led him towards me. It was calm and kind. She handed me the lead rope.

I don't know what I was expecting. Since Bobbie had grown up in town and never rode that I knew of, I would have guessed maybe a worthless reject someone had palmed off on her. When she told me he was only four years old, I saw a little more of the problem. He was probably just too young for an experienced rider.

I asked more about the difficulties she was having with him. It certainly wasn't his demeanor as he stood there quietly at the end of the lead rope, looking around at his new surroundings.

"Any time I try to ride him, he just turns around and runs home after we get a little ways out." I could tell she felt timid around the large animal.

"He's got a nice enough personality." I pet his face and looked into his friendly eyes.

"The people I bought him from told me he was well-broke, but he's not."

"Well, I'll have a go at him." I didn't explain to her that a horse his age just wasn't yet set enough in his ways to be considered well-broke.

She said good bye and drove off while I led Buster over to the barn to saddle him. Nothing like the present to find out what I was up against, I decided.

I found a long-shanked curb bit with a headstall that still had some life left to it. The stiff leather became slightly more supple once I took it out into the sunshine and worked it. I examined it for cracks and tears as I didn't need it falling apart in the middle of a shit storm, if it came to that. I also made a mental note to pick up a new headstall the next time I was in town.

Buster took the bit easily. I slipped the bridle over his ears and he didn't bat an eye as I adjusted the length to fit his head. I led him out to the driveway before tightening the cinch. There was still no reaction from him. He seemed perfectly agreeable. Tightening the near rein just in case he chose to act up when I was in a vulnerable position, I put a foot in the stirrup and mounted. He stood there quiet as a dude horse.

I urged him forward, but instead of stepping out, he showed his irritation at being asked to move by swishing his tail. I gave him a good kick and he reluctantly took a step before stopping. I slapped his butt with the end of the reins and he suddenly went into action. He whirled around and took off towards the corrals. He almost lost me as he spun around. I guess I was a little rusty since I hadn't been on a horse since breaking colts in Idaho.

I yanked hard on the reins and he stopped. Of course we were still within spitting distance of the barn, so he didn't have room to pick up any speed. I tried turning him around, but he resisted. I shortened the right rein, pulling his head around, and pounded his ribs with my heels at the same time. He spun again, doing a complete circle before coming to a stop once again facing the barn.

I tried again. And again. So far he was winning. I reversed directions, pulling his head to the left and got the same results. Buster was spoiled all right. Finally I got him to take a few steps away from the barn. By now I was sweating from the exertion. I was also determined that he was going to walk off.

I kept thumping his sides as I swatted his butt. This time he walked down the driveway. He went slowly, dragging his feet, but he walked. As we reached the first curve which would take us out of sight of the barn, he suddenly whirled again and took off running. By now I was cranky myself. I pulled back on the reins as hard as I could. The long shanks did their job and he stopped, but he wouldn't budge as I tried to turn him again.

This went on for over an hour. I finally got him to walk out of sight of the yard and wait until I initiated the turn back to the barn.

I dismounted, hot and tired. Buster nuzzled my arm, once again the agreeable horse he had started out as. I was still irritated with him even though I realized he was simply a sweet horse who had learned how to get out of work.

Will walked out into the driveway. He walked over to his car and I noticed he carried a notebook. "I'm going to town. I'll be home in a while," he called out.

I just waved and headed towards the barn. After I unsaddled Buster and turned him loose in the corral, he looked at me expectantly. I couldn't help but laugh.

"You think you deserve a treat, huh." I could no longer stay mad at him and stroked his face. After a minute, he wandered off. Not only did he not need extra feed, I had nothing to offer him anyway. I added oats to my mental shopping list. I would let him stand in the corral all day and turn him out into the pasture in the evening.

Will returned home that evening excited. "Guess what I found?" he called out as he burst through the door.

"No idea."

"Well, I went to the newspaper office and did some digging."

"And…?" I asked, as he must have been looking at old newspapers as we had done in Cedar Junction.

I found the obituaries of John Daly and Jesse Branson. They died as you said."

"So, that doesn't tell us anything."

"Yeah, but I looked further back to see if I could find out what started the whole thing." He referred to his notes. "Did you know they called him Big John?" He looked up at me.

"No."

"Guess what else?"

"I have no idea."

"Another man was shot and killed nearby that fall. Apparently he was a big cattle rancher in the area and he made some enemies. I don't know if they ever discovered who did it because some of the newspapers were missing."

"What was his name?" I asked, wondering if I would recognize the name of a family who still lived in the area.

Will looked at his notes once more before replying. "His name was Wilford Buehler, but they called him Bully. Doesn't sound like a very nice character, does he?"

"No, he doesn't and I've never heard the name before." I read the story as Will had copied it all down and we speculated on his findings, but didn't have enough to go on to solve the mystery of why my great grandfather was thought to have died way before the date on his headstone.

"I need to get back over to Cedar Junction," Will concluded.

I had thought about who might know more of the story and came up with a possibility. I called Aunt Dot to make sure the old man was still alive and then told Will.

"Shouldn't we call first?" Will asked as we planned the drive.

"I doubt they have a phone and chances are, he's home," I replied.

Saturday morning we made the drive east to a ranch whose owners had been friends with my family since way before I was born. We pulled up to the house and amongst a pack of barking dogs, a middle aged man made his way down the driveway.

His name was Ed Hedge. I always thought it was a strange sounding name, said aloud. I introduced him to Will, but before we could explain the reason for our visit, he spoke to me.

"My wife's not here. Her mother is sick and she went to take care of her." He acted like the only possible reason I would show up on his ranch would be to visit with his wife. I had never noticed this when I was younger, but now the behavior seemed odd. Visits consisted of the men attending to their business while the women visited amongst themselves, a segregation of the sexes.

"We're sorry we missed her." Will answered.

"We were wondering if Grandpa Hedge is up for a visit." I had found out the old man, Ed's father wasn't in good health. "I want to ask him about my great grandpa."

"He's inside and I'm sure he'd enjoy visiting with you." He led the way back up to the house.

Inside the kitchen, the old man sat at the table, his head on his chest as he dozed. I wondered why he didn't fall to the floor, as he slouched to one side in the straight-back chair.

"Dad. Hey, Dad," Ed called out. Grandpa Hedge picked his head up.

"What do you want?" He blinked his eyes, looking confused as he tried to focus.

"Sit down," Ed told us.

"Hello, Mr. Hedge. My name is Will Daniels. I'm doing some research on the Daly family and wondered if we could ask you some questions since you've known them a long time." Will explained after we sat.

He looked from Will over to me. "I know you. You're a Daly."

I resisted the urge to squirm as he stared at me. "That's right. You knew my great grandpa, Matt, didn't you?"

"Yeah, I knew him."

"Did you know about his two children who died over in Cedar Junction?"

He shook his head. "No, I never knew anything about that. 'Course I was quite a bit younger than him."

"The newspaper reported him dead in 1888, but his head stone says he died in 1950, just before I was born."

"That's right. I was at his funeral."

"Did you know him well?" Will asked.

"I remember my grandfather used to sell him a horse from time to time when I was a kid."

I thought that was all we would learn. We sipped coffee and discussed the weather with Ed for a few minutes. At first, Grandpa Hedge sat in silence, but then he spoke up.

"They used to talk about Matt Daly being an outlaw in his younger days. Some claimed he was a gun fighter. It was all before I was born though and maybe it was just stories. I remember everyone liked him, so I don't know." The old man's voice trailed off again.

We drove home a little bit disappointed that we hadn't found out more about my great grandfather's past, but Grandpa Hedge's words did add to the intrigue. Will seemed deep in thought, probably planning his next move.

Chapter 16

Each day I rode Buster he behaved better. He had no buck or any kind of meanness in him. He had simply learned to take advantage of his owner. I took him further and further away from the ranch headquarters and began enjoying our rides. I still had to pay attention though, because when he decided it was time to head home, he'd do a one-eighty without notice.

He was also looking better as he became fit from regular riding. In fact his whole attitude began to change from a barn sour nag to a willing horse. Since there were no other horses on the D, I became his best friend. He greeted me when I went out to catch him and enjoyed the attention he received from me.

I wish I could have said the same thing about other things that were happening. Jake and Fred, the two guys I hired, quickly began getting on my nerves. The two of them showed up late almost every morning and each time their excuse became sketchier. Worse, when I gave my orders for the day, it seemed as if they were mocking me.

I also suspected that they weren't doing what I told them to. The rolls of wire in the back of the pickup remained unused. When I asked them about it, they told me the existing wire was still in good shape, and didn't need replacing. I had more to do than baby sit two grown men, so I let it go.

Will offered them lunch their first day of work and after that they came to expect it. I had purposely not mentioned meals as part the deal when I hired them because there was no way I was going to get stuck cooking for them.

The three men had a great time during their lunch break, telling stories and laughing. As the boss, I felt left out since they didn't share the jokes with me. Or maybe, it was because I was a girl.

Will didn't understand the problem. To him the two were simply good natured. But I saw their looks and the way they shut up when I was within earshot. When he left to cover a news story in Los Angeles, their behavior became even more disrespectful. The day after he left, the two of them didn't show up until late morning.

"Fred's pickup wouldn't start. We tried to figure out what was wrong, guess we'll have to take it to a mechanic." Jake looked at me, his woebegone expression asking for sympathy.

"You could have called." I retorted.

"We didn't want to take the time. We were really trying to get here on time." This time Fred voiced the explanation. I let it drop.

"Did you get that fence line going up the back side done?"

"Yes ma'am," Jake told me. He spit a stream of tobacco juice in my direction.

I hated it when they called me ma'am. Their tone seemed disrespectful, a taunt. Added to the tobacco juice that stirred the dust near my boot, I felt like it had become a game to them, one that I felt on the verge of losing.

"Well go on up and get started on that cross fence that takes off from the corner."

"We're on it," Jake replied. More tobacco juice hit the dirt as they turned towards the Ford.

I went to catch and saddle Buster. After I mounted, I steered him around back of the house, following the two-track that wound around up the hill, first passing the old cemetery before climbing north. My mood improved as I looked around at the green grass. Next year there would be cattle to graze it. As usual, I also watched Buster for any indication that he might decide it was time to turn back.

We neared the fence, as I intended to go through the corner gate and continue on. It appeared the top wire was missing. As I got closer I could see the broken strand lying on the ground. It was the same fence Jake and Fred just told me they had finished repairing.

I stared at the wire on the ground, realizing their blatant lie and didn't immediately know what to do. I had never had to discipline grown men before and didn't know if I could. No longer in the mood for a ride, I turned back as my anger grew.

By the time I had my horse unsaddled, I was seething inside, but outwardly I remained cool. When Jake and Fred drove up at noon expecting lunch, I was ready. I met them in the driveway, my decision made.

"Come up to the house and draw your pay." I felt Great Grandpa Matt's voice come through me. At least that's what it seemed like because I didn't know where else the words could have come from.

The two stared at me in disbelief. I didn't wait for a reaction, but turned and strode up to the house. When they showed up a minute later I stood in the kitchen waiting, check book in hand. They rapped lightly on the door frame before entering and took their hats off once inside, things they had never done before.

"We didn't mean to disrespect you." Jake started in on another excuse for their behavior, but I'd had enough.

"I figure I owe you each eight and a half days." I glared at them, daring an argument. They were silent as I made out two checks.

I handed them their pay and Fred decided to challenge me. "You can't just fire us. You're never going to find anyone else to work here, you know."

"Just leave." My voice was unyielding, a tone I didn't know I was capable of. They realized they would get nowhere with me and turned towards the door.

"Come on, we can do better than this bitch," Fred said. Jake kicked a chair before the door slammed behind them.

I quickly sat down. My words may have sounded confident, but inside I was shaking. I didn't know what I was going to do. There was no way I was going to put up with that behavior, but how could I find anyone different?

I went outside and wandered around. If only Will were here to talk to, but that thought worried me also. I couldn't keep relying on him for solutions to my problems. I thought I knew about being alone, but was finding out that being a female boss in a male dominated occupation really isolated me. As usual I sought comfort the best place I knew. I went down to the corral to visit Buster.

Will returned the next day. He was concerned when I told him I had fired the two men, not only because I again had no one to help me, but also because he didn't think it was a good idea for me to be all alone on the ranch.

"I mean, what if something happened?"

"I'm not worried about that." I replied. "I just don't know how I'm going to find anyone who won't try to take advantage of me."

He was serious as he nodded at my predicament, but then his tone lightened. "So, what was it like to sack them?"

I laughed. "It felt really good actually. I just wanted them gone when I realized they weren't doing any work."

"How'd they take it?"

"They didn't like it."

"I'll bet, but it's your place so it doesn't matter."

"Yeah, but I still don't have any help and obviously I have to start being more careful about who I hire."

"You know what you could do," Will began cautiously. I was immediately suspicious.

"What?"

"Hire a manager."

"Uh uh. Nope." Again, I automatically dismissed his idea. "The D has never needed a manger before." I was already feeling incompetent, and I viewed hiring one as simply proving I couldn't do the job.

"Hasn't your family always worked together? Now you're trying to do it alone."

It was true. My father had my grandfather to help him. He only took over completely after my Grandpa Mathew died. I never had the advantage of learning the management end from a parent.

"But how can I ever find a manager if I can't even hire decent help?"

"You'll figure something out." He gave me a look of encouragement. I appreciated his faith in me, something I couldn't always seem to find in myself.

I mulled the idea over in my mind for the next few days, but kept coming to a dead end. I thought about my many, male relatives and dismissed them all as potential help on the D. Most of them would never accept me as their boss, and others were uninterested in ranch work. I still didn't like the idea of hiring a manager.

One night I dreamed about being back in Idaho training horses. As I rode down the road, I looked over and saw Troy Thomas out in the field amongst his cattle. Over at the house, Kate waved at me from the back steps as their children played in the yard.

In the morning I awoke and, remembering the dream, instantly had my answer. I had kept in loose contact with the Thomas' since I left Idaho as Kate and I exchanged Christmas cards every year. She always enclosed a letter to keep me up to date on her family. The winter before the card contained depressing news. Troy's mother had died that spring. In order to settle her estate, and since none of his siblings were interested in continuing the tradition, the family ranch had been sold. It was another case where circumstances had forced a fourth generation family off the land homesteaded by their great grandparents.

Troy and Kate moved their children over to Boise, and even though they had gotten a good price for the ranch, the sum had been divided amongst five siblings. The card explained that they had bought a house in town and that Troy was now driving truck. It sounded like he was none too happy about it.

I thought he might make a good manager, if he wanted the job. I decided to contact them and see if he would be interested in working for me. I called information in Boise and got the number listed for them. That evening I dialed it. Kate answered the phone.

"Hello?"

"Kate? This is Sky Daly."

"Sky, what on earth? How are you doing? Where are you? Are you still down in New Mexico?" She sounded relieved to hear from me.

" No, I'm back in Montana." I realized the last card I received had been forwarded. I told her about Ursula's death and that I was running the D.

"Oh, I'm so sorry about your mother."

"Yeah, it's too bad. Say, is Troy still driving truck?"

"Yes, but he hates it." She sounded sad. At this point most would have asked to speak to the man of the house, but there was no way I was going to leave his wife in the cold about the purpose of my call since it involved her just as much.

"Does he still want to ranch?"

"Oh yeah, it's all he wants to do."

Well, I'm looking for a manager. Do you think you might want to move over here so Troy can work for me?"

There was a slight hesitation before Kate replied. "Let me go get him and you can ask him yourself." I thought I heard a hint of excitement in her voice. After a minute, during which I could hear muffled talk, Troy's voice came over the phone.

"Hello, Sky?"

"Hey, I hear you could use a new job."

We discussed my proposition for a few minutes. I imagined Kate standing at her husband's elbow as we talked. In the background I heard children's voices and once a sharp "Shh!" from her.

"I'd like to come see your place," he concluded.

"You're welcome any time."

We left it at that, but only a week later, Kate called to tell me that they had made plans to make the trip over to Montana. Instantly I became nervous. The Thomas' ranch had been a well-run operation and I didn't know if the D, in its present state, would measure up in Troy's eyes.

Will was with me in the kitchen as I waited their arrival just days later. It was a long drive from Boise, so I knew not to expect them early.

"Will you chill out," he scolded. "I'm sure they'll love the D." He opened the oven door to check the contents. When he had volunteered to cook dinner, I had at first been reluctant to accept his offer. He had come up with some exotic meals recently and I agreed to let him cook only after he assured me he would prepare a wholesome meal simple country people would enjoy.

"If only we could have slapped some paint on the barn." The ranch looked ramshackle to me, an operation mismanaged by an incompetent. I was ashamed of its appearance. Again I doubted my ability to turn the D around.

Will remained calm. "Either it'll work out or it won't." I tried not to let his nonchalance bother me.

Finally I went out to putter around in an attempt at checking my nervousness. Amongst the dusty old saddles and harness in the tack room I thought about long ago days. I tugged at the curling skirts and fenders on Great Grandpa Matt's saddle, as if that could undo all the years of neglect, and wondered what he would think of the changes that were happening on the D.

An old broom sat in a corner. I picked it up and jabbed at the cobwebs up in the corners, pulling the worst of them down and then swept the floor. Outside, Tag barked, but I swept up the pile of debris before going out to greet my guests.

Will was already out in the driveway and I watched him shake Troy's hand as I walked up from the barn. Kate spotted me and called out.

"Sky! Dang it's good to see you." She hurried over and gave me a hug. Will and Troy waited by their station wagon.

"I see you met Will." I said to them. That was actually another concern. I knew they hadn't liked the types of people moving into the area in Idaho where they lived and liberals were high on the list of undesirables.

We chatted for a few minutes. They had left their children with relatives, so if nothing else, it was a short vacation. "Come up to the house and have a beer." Will invited them.

"You know, we've been sitting all day. Maybe we could stretch our legs and take a look around first." Troy answered. I detected eagerness in his voice.

"Well I can show you the barn and corrals," I told him.

"I have food on the stove." Will started back up to the house. Kate watched him go for a second before following Troy and me. I imagine it was their first realization that the way I was running the D was not a traditional ranch setup. I led the way to the barn.

Troy gave what I perceived as a critical eye to the old structure and I expected criticism for the repairs that needed attention. "This is a great barn," he commented as we entered.

I felt a huge relief at his compliment. We went all the way through and out the other end to visit Buster. He stood waiting patiently to be let out into the pasture to graze for the night. He nickered quietly to remind me in case I had forgotten about him. I slipped through the rails into the corral and gave him a pat.

"Nice looking horse," Kate commented.

"He's not mine. I'm just riding him for someone," I explained, before walking to the far side to open the gate to the pasture. Buster followed along and then passed me as he continued through, nose to the ground, ready to bite the first blade of grass he came to. I paused for a minute, watching him. I had spied Troy speaking to his wife and turned my back so they could have their discussion in private.

We strolled back up to the house. It was a pleasant evening as the heat of summer hadn't yet hit in full force. It was the perfect time to show off the D, when it was covered in the new green of spring that seemed bright with optimism. We went inside and enjoyed a cold beer as Will put the finishing touches on dinner. Kate again watched him, delight showing on her face.

The meal turned out to be roast chicken with all the trimmings. Troy politely thanked us for the meal, but Kate gushed on and on about how delicious it was. Clearly she was impressed by Will's talent in the kitchen.

"Where did you learn to cook?" she finally asked.

"From my mom and just by doing it mostly," Will answered. His humble reply made me remember when I complemented him on the banana bread he had fed me the day we met.

"You are a lucky girl," she told me.

"You don't have to tell me," I answered. "Tomorrow we can take a drive and I'll show you more of the ranch."

"That'd be great." Troy replied.

"Here, let me help with that." Kate jumped up, unable to sit still any longer as Will began clearing the table after we finished.

"Not a chance," I told her as I got up to help.

"I guess I'm not used to not having anything to do." She sat back down. "And it's so quiet without the kids."

"Just relax and enjoy yourself." Troy advised. "You'll still have plenty of time to chase them around."

"Come on. I'll show you where you'll be sleeping." They followed me up the stairs to our bedroom. With the warmer weather, Will and I were once again sleeping out in Great Grandpa Matt's cabin.

It was an enjoyable evening. They got along fine with Will, but then who didn't. I realized my fears had been irrational and wondered to myself when I would quit worrying about what people thought of him. We talked late into the night. If nothing else, the Thomas' were enjoying their time away.

The next morning Kate, Troy and I drove off in the pickup. Will stayed behind as there wasn't room for four in the cab. I packed sandwiches to take along so we could take our time and cover some country.

First I wanted to take a look at the Hubbard house to see what it would take to make it livable. It was the only dwelling large enough to house the Thomas' and where I intended to put them up if Troy decided to hire on. Hawk had the place to himself when he worked for the D. With three small bedrooms, it would barely be adequate for a family with four children, but it was the best I could do.

Like every other building on the place, it needed a new roof and fresh paint. Inside, the mice and pack rats had been into everything, but it was structurally intact. We searched, but found only minor water damage from leaks in the roof.

Most of the old plaster walls were intact. I flipped the breaker in the fuse box and the lights came on. Rusty colored water flowed when I turned the faucet on.

Once outside again, we looked around the yard. Willows and cottonwoods surrounded the old homestead, offering protection from the sun in the summer, as well as from the ferocious winds that howled relentlessly at times.

"What do you think? Could you live here?"

Kate looked out over the prairie before answering her husband. "It would definitely beat living in town."

We climbed back in the pickup and continued on. I pointed out other homesteads that had become part of the D over the years. Eventually we began climbing. I followed the faint road as it wound through the hills. Troy got out and opened gates as we progressed from one pasture to the next.

Finally we reached one of my favorite places on the ranch, the spot that had impressed Will the first summer he was at the D. We piled out of the pickup and admired the view.

"We're definitely not in Idaho." Troy remarked.

We sat and ate our lunch on the rock ledge in the awed silence that the scene inspired. The three of us gazed out, attempting to take in every detail of the vast expanse before us. I hadn't been up the ridge in quite a while, but it hadn't changed. Daly land, my land, stretched before us with the snow covered peaks beneath the blue sky accenting the grasslands below us.

One thing I noticed that I should have expected was that the vegetation on that distant and neglected part of the D had been eaten down to dirt the previous year. We saw a couple of places where the fence was down, possibly pulled down intentionally. It was a habit that went back as far as there had been cattle grazing in this country. Ranchers, always as hungry for more grass as their cattle, took advantage of any area that wasn't being used. The open range law was in effect in Montana, which meant that if I didn't want the neighbors' cattle on my land, I had to fence them out. Since wire fences needed maintenance, it was impossible to determine if the downed wires had human help or not.

Still, it pissed me off. What made matters worse was that, not being their land, the neighbors thought nothing of overusing it. I wasn't real worried though. The piece could have a couple years to rest as I slowly rebuilt the D.

"It looks like you have some work to do," Troy commented. He realized what had happened.

Late in the afternoon we arrived back at the D headquarters. Will came down from his office and joined us. We planned to go to town that evening for dinner, but first I wanted to find out if it would be as a celebration or simply as friends having an evening out. I leaned against the sink as the others sat at the kitchen table.

"Well, what do you think?" Addressing both Kate and Troy, I tried to be bold with my question, but had to force the words past the catch in my throat.

Troy and Kate looked at one another before he answered. "We're interested." A typical cowboy, he guarded his thoughts. What's he think, this is a card game? I couldn't help wondering to myself. I glanced over at Kate. She was smiling, but then I think she would have agreed to anything he decided.

We talked it over some more. I again went over my plan to fix up the Hubbard house for them and their children. I also explained what I expected from him as my manager. Troy in turn voiced his expectations if he agreed to manage the D.

"There's one thing I need to know for sure." I looked directly at Troy. It was time to find out if this arrangement could work. "I need to know that you won't have a problem working for me, and that you can accept my word as final."

There was a pause as he thought for a moment. Kate looked expectantly into his face as if she might learn something new about her husband.

"I think I'm ok with that." He spoke his answer slowly and sincerely while his head bobbed, as if to finalize his decision.

I realized I was holding my breath and let it go with relief. "Well let's go to town and I'll buy you a steak…if you're sure you've made your minds up." I looked at Kate.

Troy looked at his wife also. "What do you think? Do you want to move to Montana."

"I've wanted to come ever since Sky first called and you hung up the phone with a smile on your face." She beamed at him and I couldn't help but feel a little envious of the couple.

I looked over at Will. He had stayed silent during our negotiations. Now he too smiled, his grin directed at me.

Chapter 17

I watched the Thomas children escape from the station wagon, while Tag bounced around the car, yipping his excitement at their arrival. Kate emerged last, looking frazzled. I imagine the trip from Idaho couldn't have been easy with four kids to drive her crazy. She headed towards me, looking over her shoulder at them as they scattered.

"Stay on the lawn!" she hollered. They had caravanned over, with Troy driving their pickup pulling the stock trailer packed with as many of their belongings as they could stuff in. He had gone directly to their new home, while Kate stopped off to let me know they had arrived. When she got close, I noticed a dark stain down the front of her shirt.

"You made it," I greeted her.

"The trip from hell." She sounded tired, and noticing my gaze, explained. "Ben spilled his milkshake."

It was now late August. Six weeks, most of the summer, had passed since the couple visited. The weather remained hot and dry, typical for the time of year. Will had left the day before, this time up to Canada. Since he enjoyed traveling, he had decided to try his hand at writing a travel article. I didn't expect him back for another week.

I invited the family up to the house and passed out cans of pop to the kids. They, of course, had grown a lot and I never would have recognized any of them. Gabrielle, the oldest was twelve, and Ben, the baby, had just turned seven.

"What do you say?" Kate asked them. I received a dutiful thank you from each child.

"What do you want? I can make coffee…"

"Oh no, it's way too hot. A coke would be great."

We went out and sat on the old couch and chatted for a few minutes while the kids tore around the lawn like wild animals finally freed from their cage.

"Don't you get lonesome here all by yourself?" Kate was referring to Will's absences.

"Sometimes, but now I have permanent company."

"Oh, you'll get sick of us soon enough," Kate replied wryly before yelling at her two sons. "Cut it out!"

"He started it," Scottie, whined at being caught shaking his can of pop and spraying his little brother with the sticky fizz.

"Well, I guess we better go help Troy unpack." She collected the pop cans before herding her kids back down to the car.

"When are we going to get there?" One complained at having to get back in the car.

"It's just up the road," she assured them as she turned and waved.

"Let me know if you need anything. The phone's hooked up," I called out. "And check the mouse traps."

The family drove off to their new home, which I hoped they liked. I had hired my uncle George to remodel it and thought it looked really nice once the walls were repaired and painted. Outside, a new roof and fresh paint restored the homestead house to its original red color. It actually looked quite charming, I decided. The plumbing and electricity had been updated as well, so I knew it would be comfortable for my new manager and his family. I couldn't help but think that I would have done the same for Hawk if he had returned to the D.

Will thought it was over-kill, but I had also stocked the cupboards and refrigerator with food for their arrival. The one thing I did know about running a ranch was that you kept your help fed. I turned and went inside to scrounge some supper for myself, feeling satisfied. For the first time I could see my time away from the D as more than a dark, hopeless time in my life. If I hadn't gone to Idaho, I never would have met Kate and Troy Thomas.

Will drove back over to Cedar Junction to continue searching old newspapers for information about Great Grandpa Matt. I wasn't sure if he was bored or if he just couldn't let it go that there were unanswered questions about my ancestor's life. I was curious, of course, but had work to do at home.

That evening he filled me in on what he found. Once again, he had copied the entire story and he read from his notebook as I cooked dinner.

Apparently, Matt Daly returned to Cedar Junction after it was thought he was dead, just showed up and in rough shape a year after his children died. Even his wife, Lavina, didn't recognize him at first. The newspaper reporter had written the story to sound very dramatic. The sudden reappearance of my great grandfather must have created quite a stir in the small town.

I tried to imagine what had happened to cause the separation from his family, but all either of us could do was speculate. Then we found out in an unexpected way.

While searching through the recovered box of papers from the basement, I found an unopened piece of mail from the state brand office. I opened the five year old piece of mail and found a notice about renewing the D Rocking D brand. Brands need to be registered every ten years and I realized Ursula had never re-registered the Daly family brand in 1971. My stomach jumped when I saw the unreturned form, as it meant that anyone could now claim the D's brand. It might not even belong to the ranch anymore. In that case, I would have to select a different one.

I immediately planned a trip to Helena, the state capitol. I could have completed the process through the mail, but I was way too anxious to wait that long. Will, of course, was up for a road trip. We took off early one bright fall day and planned to spend the night. My only goal was to reclaim the D Rocking D mark and I desperately hoped no one else had taken it.

The livestock department was stuck in a small, cluttered office at the back of a state office building. I quickly got the list of unclaimed brands from the clerk and began searching. To my relief, the D Rocking D was still available and I quickly filled out the paper work and wrote a check to make it legally mine again.

"Is there any history of brands in the state?" Will asked the clerk once I finished.

"Not yet," the woman said. "I've been attempting to compile one, but I don't have a lot of time to work on it and the records are really disorganized."

"Can I take a look?"

"Access is allowed only for government business," she informed us as she pushed her glasses up her nose. That didn't deter Will.

"I'm a journalist and I'm working on the history of Sky's family ranch. They started it back in the 1880s. There are some gaps in the history that we're trying to fill in."

Apparently she was satisfied that it was for a good reason, or maybe she decided it added some value to her paper shuffling job, but she let us into the back room. She showed us the general area to search and cleared a spot on a table where we could sort through the mess.

Will acted like a kid at Christmas as side by side, we plunged in. We pulled stacks of files out of the boxes and examined hundreds of papers, some mere scraps with the handwriting faded to become unreadable.

I didn't know what he expected to find, but what did come to light was that the D Rocking D brand had been re-registered by my great grandfather in 1891. Before that, a man named Hubert Bailey owned it. It made no sense to me, as I had been told that my dead relatives had been marking cattle with it for almost ten years by then.

We spent the entire afternoon in the store room and emerged as the city lights came on at twilight. Over dinner, we wondered why there was a lapse in the brand registration. It must have been sold, but we had no idea if it was before or after Great Grandpa Matt disappeared. Will made another suggestion.

"Tomorrow morning let's go over to the historical society and do some digging."

"What do you think you'll find there?"

"You never know what you'll find. It'll be fun to poke around."

"You have a strange idea of fun."

We arrived at the historical society just as it opened in the morning. Will wasn't even sure if they'd let us in to look through the archives, but knew it was worth a try. More than once I had witnessed his ability to talk his way into places most people weren't allowed.

He explained what he was researching and the clerk behind the desk seemed to welcome interest in a topic many consider boring. When he mentioned the name Matt Daly, the man got a strange look on his face.

"There's something I need to show you," he said. He led us over to where a battered, cardboard box sat. "I can't believe the coincidence. We just received this yesterday." He picked up the box and set it on a table. On top was a folder made of heavy, brown paper. He carefully untied the string holding it closed.

"What is it?" Will asked.

"These papers belonged to a newspaper reporter named Charles Becker. He died in 1928. He never had children and his papers have been sitting in his nephew's house over in Great Falls all this time. The house just sold and he was cleaning it out. He was going to throw it all away, but his wife convinced him they might have some value, so he donated everything to the historical society.

"I've been going through his notes. He was documenting Montana in the late 1800s and he found an interesting story just before he died." The clerk carefully shuffled through the contents of the folder as he spoke, searching for something he had recently read. "Here it is." He handed the pages over to Will.

We stood side by side, eagerly peering at the paper. While I had a hard time deciphering the scribbled words, Will, having had more practice, quickly skimmed the page. He found the name Daly and I could feel his excitement.

"I think it's all here, the entire story!"

"What's it say?" I demanded impatiently.

"Give me a sec." He pulled up a chair and sat down, so I did the same.

"I have to get back to work…" the clerk began, but walked off when he saw we weren't paying any attention.

Charles Becker's interesting story turned out to be an interview with my great grandfather and he told quite a tale that day. The account began the day Bully Beuhler, his neighbor, was killed. Matt claimed to have shot him in self-defense and then, believing he was wanted for taking a life, he fled down into Wyoming. The gunman who had been hired to kill him apparently followed him and Matt took care of him also. After he made it down to Texas, he killed again after another man shot at him while he slept.

That day, I found out that my great grandfather had killed three men. He claimed self-defense, but I no longer knew exactly what to think of my favorite relative, except it seemed he stopped at nothing to protect his family and home.

According to his story, his days as a gunfighter ended the day he found himself on the slow side of a gunfight in a town down in Wyoming. He had almost died and afterwards returned to find his wife was alive, but that his young children and father were not.

We sat there for hours examining the papers. At first I didn't believe it could be my ancestor, but the names were the same and the dates matched what we had found. I couldn't believe my great grandpa had really been an outlaw. Of course it started when he was defending the D.

Taking turns reading and writing, we copied down every word of the account and it kept us at the historical society all day. As we drove home that night, our excitement kept us wide awake and we marveled at our timing. "I need to get to Wyoming and verify this." Will stated. I don't know what he intended to do with the information, but the reporter in him knew he had found something big, at least to the two of us.

What I realized was that when Ursula sold the D's cattle, it was the second time the ranch had been abandoned. The first time was when my great grandmother, Lavina, thinking her husband dead, had taken her children over to Cedar Junction to live with her parents. I thought about the hopelessness she must have felt at having no way of knowing for sure what had happened to him. Then, to lose her children, it was heartbreaking.

I wanted to read the story again when we returned home, but it was late, so I decided to wait until the next day. Instead, I fell asleep wondering if Great Grandpa Matt really had been defending himself, or if there was a side to him nobody knew about.

As late summer turned into fall, my enthusiasm grew. Troy immediately got to work after he arrived and began preparing for the arrival of six hundred bred, black, Angus heifers. It was now his job to hire more help and he found a couple of men to again work at repairing the aging fences encircling the D's pastures.

I couldn't disagree with what Adrian had said about not wanting to fix fence the rest of his life. Ranchers humorously describe the never ending task as job security, but it got old after a while.

The three men started in the corrals, nailing up rails that had fallen down and replacing ones that were broken or rotting. The loading chute also needed weathered boards replaced to ensure that the young cows came off the trucks safely.

Then the crew moved on to the hay meadows where we would winter the cattle. Unless it was a heavy snow year and I was forced to buy hay, there would be plenty of feed to get them through to next spring. I hoped for a mild winter.

The morning the trucks rolled in felt like a day of celebration. The dust the heavy trailers stirred up deepened the orange of the early morning sunshine and the crisp air of the changing season added to the excitement.

Within minutes the first trailer was backed up to the loading dock and with a loud clanging the doors opened. The thunderous clumping of hundreds of hooves across wood began and continued on and on as a stream of cattle clamored down the wooden ramp.

"Heyaww. Hup, hup." The voices of the drivers urged the black bodies on. The continuous deep "mmuuwawws" as the heifers called out added to the din.

I sat on the top rail counting each one as she hit solid ground. Soon the corral was a churning sea of black backs. The men opened a gate and pushed the first bunch into a back corral next to the creek to let them drink as another truck backed up to the ramp.

I watched as the heifers reached the creek and plunged in. The fresh water was quickly churned to mud from so many animals trying to drink at once, but it couldn't be helped. We had to burn the D Rocking D brand into their hides before turning them out.

Once the last heifer was unloaded and I was satisfied the count was correct, I went over to the head driver, a tall burly man wearing a baseball cap. He held a clipboard with a stack of papers attached.

"I'll need someone to sign these," he said as he looked around.

"I'll sign." I told him. He looked at me skeptically. It was a look I had grown accustomed to. "No, really, I'm a big girl." At my sarcastic tone he handed over the clipboard.

"Well, okay," he replied, as if something didn't seem right.

But I had better things to think about, mainly that the D was once again running cattle. While Troy and the other men prepared to brand, I watched the milling heifers, looking for any sign of sickness or injury. Once satisfied they were all healthy, I went over to the end of the alley where the new squeeze chute had been placed. Troy practiced working the handles.

"These things have certainly improved over the ones I used," he commented.

"Well, for what I paid for it, it should be able to do the whole job itself."

Troy smiled. "It'll be a lot easier than those old head catches." He was referring to the older models where, once in the chute, even with their heads caught, there was still a lot of room for the cow to thrash around. This one had a mechanism to squeeze the near side inward, as well a head catch, so the cow was pinned and could barely wiggle within its confines.

Branding was one task I always disliked, and although I felt a little guilty, I was also relieved that as boss, I could leave it to the men. I went back up to the house for a quick break.

Kate was acting as cook. She told me she didn't mind, but with homeschooling her kids, I knew she had her hands full.

As I entered, a pot on the stove boiled over, spilling its contents onto the hot burner. I rushed over, turned off the heat and picked up the pot in one quick motion. Kate was a step behind. She had turned her back to help Gabrielle with her lesson. All four children sat at the table, books open, as Kate attempted to cook lunch at the same time.

The odor of the burned food filled my nose and made me nauseous. I had become light headed sitting atop the fence watching the sea of cattle below me and had escaped to the house to sit down for a moment. Now my discomfort increased.

"I'm so sorry." Kate opened the door before grabbing a dish cloth to clean up the mess.

"This is just too much for you to do by yourself." I felt bad asking her to cook. So far, Will and I were taking turns at kitchen duty and this was the first time I had asked Kate to fill in.

She looked dejected. I was about to ask if she and her kids wanted to take a break and go see the new heifers, when she spoke.

"Oh, Bob Mullen called."

"What did he want?" I pushed aside my discomfort.

"He said he needs to talk to you."

I dialed the number to the bank. As I waited for him to come on the line, I worried. I couldn't imagine what he could want. I had begun making payments on the loan, so that subject seemed unlikely.

"Sky, how are you" His deep voice came over the line.

"I'm fine. We had six hundred heifers delivered this morning."

"Good for you." Instead of sounding happy, his voice was serious. "The reason I called is to ask if you cashed a large check recently? I don't mean to pry, it's your money and all, but it raised a red flag with me."

"How much money?"

"Eight hundred dollars."

"I never withdrew that kind of money."

"Uh, what about anyone else?" He sounded hesitant, and I understood what he was getting at.

"I'm the only one with access to that account. Will has his own money." Part of me wanted to be irritated that he was checking up on me, but more importantly, who had taken the money?

"That's what I thought. I think you better come take a look at it and see if we can't figure this out."

"I can be there in an hour."

"That'll be fine."

I hung up the phone and turned to Kate. "I have to run to town."

"Is everything all right?"

"I don't know." I headed out the door and down to the corrals, my stomach threatening to forcefully release its contents with the anxiety added to my discomfort. The acrid smell of singed hair and flesh stung my nose, but I refused to give in to the stench and vomit.

The three men worked as a team, moving quickly and efficiently. One kept a bunch pushed down the alley while the other urged the heifers into the chute one at a time. Troy worked the control levers and then laid the hot brand on their hips when he had them situated.

Each one gave a bellow and tried to struggle as she felt the hot iron on her hip, but the chute did its job, and held her in place. Once released, the freshly branded young cow ran off to the opposite side of the corral as the next one, attempting to follow, entered the trap. I felt bad for them, but branding was the only sure way to prevent cattle rustling since it produced a permanent mark.

"It looks like it's working well," I called out as I approached Troy.

"Yeah, it makes the job a lot easier," he agreed.

"I have to run to town." We talked loudly over the roar of the propane torch rigged to heat the brand.

He simply nodded and turned his attention back to his task. The timing had to be precise as he released the head catch to enclose the neck. Too early and he'd miss. Then, with her forward movement blocked, the heifer would quickly back out and realizing it was a trap, it was much harder to get her to enter the chute again. If he was too late releasing the catch, he'd miss her entirely and she'd simply run through. In that case they'd have to cut her out of the already branded cattle and bring her back around.

Normally, there would be a couple of horses tied off to the side for that purpose. This time they would have to do any sorting on foot, all the more reason to pay attention. I hurried over to my car, relieved to be away from the smoke.

Once in town, I parked in front of the bank and hurried in. During the drive, my anxiety increased. The first and obvious thought of who would have access to the D's bank account was Rad Johnson, my mother's killer. Although the police had found Ursula's car abandoned over in South Dakota, her purse was never found and he had never been caught.

The banker greeted me and pointed to a chair. I sat down and he slid the cashed check across his desk towards me. I picked it up and studied it. It was made out to cash and my name was signed. I knew immediately I didn't recognize the handwriting.

I looked up. "I have no idea who filled this out."

"I had one of the girls dig out a cancelled check." He handed it over to me. It was made out to Rad Johnson and signed by my mother. I easily recognized the flowery loops and swirls of her handwriting.

"Look at the back," Mullen instructed. I turned it over and a chill ran down my spine as I read the endorser's name. The signature resembled the handwriting of the recent check. All the assurances that he would never come back suddenly seemed meaningless. I looked up at the banker.

"What's he stupid?"

"Or desperate."

"So what do we do?"

"I think we better inform the sheriff."

I spent the next hour at the sheriff's office. It seemed like a waste of time, especially since, in the end, I was told there was nothing they could do unless they caught him in the act. Since Bob Mullen assured me that the bank wouldn't cash checks from the D without first verifying they were legitimate, busting him seemed doubtful.

I said nothing about what happened when I returned home and instead focused on finishing up branding so we could turn the heifers out into the pasture. That evening, after their children were asleep, I drove up to the Thomas' home to speak to Troy and Kate.

"What's the matter?" Kate asked me.

"I never told you about how my mother died, did I?" They shook their heads. I proceeded to relate the whole story about how Rad Johnson had bled her dry financially and then killed her. Kate looked at me, horrified.

"I'm so sorry. We didn't know."

"The reason I'm telling you is because we believe he's come back to the area. He cashed a check from Ursula's old check book."

Troy frowned. "What can I do?"

"Nothing. I just wanted to let you know about it." After a pause, I added, "If you want to leave I understand. I mean you have your family to think about."

The couple looked at one another. "What do you think he's going to do?" Troy asked me.

"I don't know. Everybody seemed to think he was gone for good."

We discussed the situation and they reached a decision. "We're here for you, Sky," Troy assured me. "Just let me know what I can do to help."

"Thank you," I replied, much relieved.

"Are you sure you want to be in your house all by yourself tonight?" Kate asked.

"I'll be fine," I answered, but I intended to bring Tag in. If only Will were here, I thought yet one more time, even though his presence would probably be more for comfort than protection.

One morning Troy and I stood and looked out into the pasture where the herd grazed contentedly. He turned towards me.

"You know," he began a little tentatively. "It'd really help to have a horse to ride." I had seen his wistful look when I rode Buster and of course, I had been thinking the same thing. I wanted a reliable string of horses on the ranch more than anything, but still wanted to wait until spring

"Go take Buster for a ride," I suggested.

"You sure?"

"Yeah, I'm sure." I knew he wanted to be careful about stepping on toes and I felt the same way. I had purposely not ridden out amongst the heifers when all he could do was watch. "Go ahead," I encouraged him.

He immediately went and caught the gelding and tossed his saddle up on the dappled gray back. I could see he was excited. It had been a while since he had seen the world from the back of a horse.

"Be careful. Sometimes he decides on his own when it's time to turn back." I knew the caution was unnecessary, but called out anyway as he sent Buster off at a trot. The two entered the pasture and I continued to watch. I wanted to see how he acted around cattle. The horse and rider appeared to be getting along just fine as they became specks in the distance. I turned away, once more feeling pleased about my choice of manager for the D.

Late fall turned to winter. Will had decided not to go after any more news stories until spring. I looked forward to having him around for months at a time. Except for the occasional squabble, I couldn't complain, because we got along really well. I still didn't think we had the spark needed to really be in love though.

With the Thomas' up at the Hubbard place, and Troy doing a good job of looking after things, we figured we were ready for winter. Will wanted to keep digging to learn more of the story about my great grandfather that we had found over in Helena. He suggested we take a trip down into Wyoming to see if we could find anything to back it up. I was a little reluctant to leave, but finally agreed to take off for a couple of days, as after all, I would be leaving the D in capable hands.

We took off one morning with the names of two towns I had never heard of, one where Great Grandpa Matt told the reporter he had killed a man and the other where he had been shot himself. Only one of them appeared, as a tiny dot, on the map we studied. I didn't even know the route Great Grandpa Matt would have travelled as he fled Montana on horseback.

The first time we stopped for gas across the state line, Will asked the kid who came out to fill our tank if he knew where Sandy Flat was.

He shook his head, and then said, "Let me go ask Pop." When the young attendant returned with our change, he had learned nothing about the location of the town.

We continued south to Kincaid, the place where Great Grandpa Matt said he had lost his last gunfight. I studied the main street of the small town as we slowly drove through. Even though newer buildings sat amongst the older, abandoned ones with their false fronts, it was easy to visualize, with the help of scenes from movies I'd watched, a shootout in the street. I imagined townspeople running for cover as the two men faced one another, each determined to have the quickest draw.

Our first stop was to find out if there was a newspaper in town, or if there had been one at the end of the last century. We pulled into an empty parking spot on the block that seemed to have the most business activity.

"Well, the new office is down on the other end." The man behind the counter in the hardware store jutted his chin in the opposite direction we had come in. "The first one burned a few years back."

We thanked him and continued through town. The Kincaid Journal building didn't appear new and I wondered what the clerk had meant when he spoke of the new office.

"Everything was lost in the fire." The editor shook his head at our request after Will explained that we wanted to look through newspapers from the last century. We learned that when the original building burned almost fifty years ago, nothing had survived.

After exiting the building, we stood out on the street. Will, the investigator, seemed at a loss as to our next move. Since it was getting late, we decided to get a room at the lone motel. Sleeping in the town where Great Grandpa Matt had almost died seemed a little bizarre, but also intriguing. I planned to wander the streets and look around.

After checking into the motel, our final stop that evening was the steak house we had seen on the way in. Since dark was settling in at the end of the short winter day, any exploring would have to wait until morning.

Not a whole lot of people travel through Kincaid, Wyoming. I could tell because when Will and I entered the restaurant, the few locals in the bar studied us. Not in a bad way, but like we were something new to look at and wonder about.

Most of them were friendly, though. We sat at the bar to have a beer before dinner and struck up a conversation with the bartender.

When he asked our purpose for visiting the remote town, Will told him about researching my great grandfather's account of being shot out on the main street and the man became more interested. He looked at me as he finished wiping the counter.

"That outlaw was a relative of yours, was he?"

"Yes."

"What do you know, everyone figured he died. What was his name?"

"Matt Daly.

"Yeah, Daly, that sounds right."

You know about it?" I doubted anyone alive now could have been around back then.

"Heck, yeah. It's part of Kincaid's history, the best story we've got. In fact, there's someone you ought to meet." He went to the phone and made a call. "He'll be right over."

In only a few minutes a grizzled, old man came through the door. He spotted us and shuffled over.

"This is Cliff Young." The bartender introduced us.

"You that feller Daly's granddaughter?" He carefully studied my face as he asked. Despite his age, his eyes were bright with curiosity.

"Great granddaughter," I corrected.

"Do you know what happened?" Will asked.

"Sure I do. My daddy saw the whole thing and he told me all about it. But he never knew the fellow's first name or that he lived." He seemed pleased to have learned two facts his father had never known.

"Can we buy you a drink?" Will asked.

"Sure you can." Apparently he was the self-designated Kincaid tour guide and Will had just paid the fee to learn the local history.

As Cliff sipped his beer, he hinted at what he had to tell. Since he wanted to show, as well as recite, the incident from long ago, he merely dropped hints that evening to arouse our curiosity.

When word got around, I found myself some kind of a celebrity. It seemed everyone wanted to meet a descendent of one of the participants in the gunfight that had taken place in their town. A ring of people gathered around us as we ate and I was questioned about my family and where we lived. We finally made plans to meet in the daylight and left.

After we finished breakfast the next morning, we met Cliff and followed him as he slowly made his way down the street. A small crowd tagged along. Even though they had heard the tale before, probably many times, the town's people played along with the mystery and excitement. Plus a new twist had been added, that the slain outlaw had survived the gunshot.

In the next block, Cliff slipped between two decrepit buildings. We trailed behind, single file. In the back sat a tiny cabin. He paused in front of it.

"This is where Daly sat, waiting for the other."

"Wha..." I was impatient to hear the rest of the story, but Will quickly put his hand on my arm to stop my question.

Cliff went up to the door and pushed it open. We peered inside. Except for trash and broken bottles littering the floor, it was empty.

"See, there was a chair by the window. My pa said he sat there all night, drinking out of a bottle and smokin'. He watched out the window, but Pa said he never saw him hiding down in the trees. He had to get home, but the next morning, he came back and your granddaddy was in the same spot.

"Then, another man came around. He was real ugly, had part of an ear gone." Cliff pinched his own ear between his thumb and finger, as if he had seen the incident himself and wasn't merely repeating what he'd been told. "But he stayed back behind the corner where he couldn't be seen. I guess he didn't trust your granddaddy." The old man grinned at me.

"Anyway, he hollered out, 'Hey, Daly, there's someone here to see you.'" Cliff raised his voice in imitation.

"Your grandpa went out into the street and a faced a big, mean-looking man, had a devilish grin, my pa said. They called him Red 'cause of his hair." He led us back out to the main street and pointed out where each man had stood.

I looked at the spot where another relative had fallen after being gunned down. It was easy to imagine the scene from so long ago, but I had a hard time believing it was the ancestor I had idolized all my life.

"Then what happened?"

"My pa and one of his friends went over to look at him after he fell. They'd never seen a dead body before. But he wasn't dead. They loaded him up in the back of a wagon and hauled him off. There was an old Indian lived down the creek a ways. He used to take care of sick and hurt people and that's where they left him. That was the last anyone heard about him. He was in rough shape and they thought he died.

"What was the Indian's name?" I asked, wondering if it was the same man buried at the D.

"That I don't know." Cliff came closer and his voice became the conspiratorial whisper of a practiced story teller. "They say your grandpa's blood stained the ground in the shape of the devil and that it stayed there for years. Horses shied at this spot and it caused more than one accident. My pappy swore it was still there after he was all grown up." He beamed. We had made his day, as not only did he have fresh ears to hear his story, he got to tell it to a relative of the man his father had seen gunned down.

"Great grandfather," I automatically corrected him one more time. I studied the setting in the cold morning light. A wind stirred the winter air and added a chill to the spooky tale. The part about the blood stain seemed too incredible to be true, but the details about the shooting seemed too coincidental to be made up.

After saying goodbye, we started for home. When we stopped for gas a hundred miles north, Will again struck up a conversation with the attendant who came out to fill the tank.

"Is there a town by the name of Sandy Flat around here?"

"Sandy Flats," the man corrected as he leaned against the pump.

"I didn't see it on the map."

"Nobody lives there anymore. What's your interest?"

"We're trying to trace the route an ancestor of mine travelled." I walked around the car to join the conversation. The man studied us for as second.

"There's not much left."

"That's all right," Will assured him.

"Well, go on back the way you came. In about ten miles or so, you'll come to a dirt road that takes off to the east. Follow it until you come to a fork in the road."

The man continued talking as the directions became more complicated. I glanced at Will, hoping he was getting it all. He just listened, nodding occasionally as the man rambled on. We paid for the gas and left, heading south again.

There was no way we would have found Sandy Flats on our own as it was at the end of a little-used dirt road. The ruins of buildings, uninhabited since the railroad laid a spur line forty miles to the east, slumped in the middle of the desolate prairie. Once again, I stood in the place where Great Grandpa Matt had faced another man with the intention of killing him. This, the first time, he had been successful. I wondered how he felt afterwards.

Early one morning not long after we returned from Wyoming, we sat at the breakfast table. The sky was just beginning to show gray in the east when the telephone rang.

"Hello," I answered.

"You better get down here!" I recognized the voice as Ron Wallace, the sheriff, hollered at me. I jerked the receiver away from my ear at the loudness of his voice.

"What's the matter?"

"You got cattle all over the highway down here by Turkey Creek. It's a big mess."

"You sure they're mine?" I asked. The heifers shouldn't have been that far away.

"Yeah, they're yours," he answered, his anger added force to the disgust he was obviously feeling.

"I'm coming." I put the phone down and Will and I grabbed our coats and headed out the door. "Shit, I better call Troy." I quickly dialed the number while Will went out and started the pickup.

After I made the call, I ran out the door, jumped in beside him and we sped down the driveway. Troy was going to meet us out on the highway since I wasn't waiting for him. How could the cattle have possibly gotten all the way down there, we wondered.

At the end of the Turkey Creek Road, I looked out onto the highway. The lights from a highway patrol car flashed, signaling oncoming traffic to slow down. When I saw what was causing the holdup, I felt sick. Black mounds, the dead bodies of my cattle, lay sprawled across the asphalt, while others ran up and down the ditch, searching for a way to get through the fence and away from the danger. A deputy and a highway patrolman tried their best to keep them contained in a bunch.

Forcing myself not to puke as nausea once again overcame me, I told Will to drive up next to the sheriff where he stood directing traffic. I got out and when he saw me, he let me have it.

"What the hell were you thinking!? You're lucky no one was killed!" My immediate reaction was to lash back.

"You think I put my cattle out on the highway!?"

He glared at me. "We have to get this mess cleaned up fast." He turned and surveyed the scene again.

"Do you know where they got out?"

"No, but you better get them rounded up quick." He turned back, a hard look on his face that made me want to cringe. I steeled myself to deal with the situation.

Using people and vehicles, we were able to make enough of a barrier to contain the panicked young cows. It wasn't easy, as they scattered under the slightest pressure. A couple minutes later Troy pulled up. He had hauled Buster in his trailer and quickly unloaded the horse.

As he prepared to mount, I hurried over and told him, "No, let me." He handed over the reins without a word. I mounted and since the gelding wore Troy's saddle, the stirrups were too long for me. I did without and urged the horse across the highway. Luckily there was little traffic, but persuading the heifers to cross the pavement proved difficult. Another pickup stopped and the occupants jumped out to help. Soon there was a barricade of people on either side, creating a corridor that forced the jittery animals out onto the pavement. I pushed from behind and tried not to look at the carcasses scattered across the road.

Apparently a semi had come along as the bunch stood confused on the highway, frozen in place by the headlights coming at them. Luckily the trucker had kept his rig on the road, but he couldn't avoid plowing through them.

Once on the dirt road, my job became easier. Although still jumpy, I was able to keep the animals moving towards home with a fence on either side to guide them. Will drove ahead to alert any oncoming traffic, while Troy brought up the rear.

Dark clouds covered the early morning sun and the wind picked up as I rode. I had grabbed only a light coat on my way out the door and the wind easily cut through my clothing. Without gloves and a hat, my hands and ears had gone numb about the time the sheriff finished yelling at me. I ignored my discomfort and kept my attention on the rumps of the cattle in front of me.

As I neared the pasture the heifers escaped from, I spied what we had been unable to see earlier as we hurried down the road in the dim light. There was a spot in the corner of the pasture, where not only had the wire been cut, but the strands pulled aside to make a gaping hole.

I let the cattle pause and watched them momentarily as I rode over to examine the gap. They immediately put their heads down and began biting the roadside grass. Troy stopped his pickup, got out and followed me over. He had also seen the break.

Instead of speaking, he gave me a hard, questioning stare. Without saying anything, I looked down to study the ground. What could I say? I had no explanation for what had happened. I just knew that I was really scared.

We could see tire tracks amongst those of the cattle going through the cut. And we knew that, somehow, the cattle had made it all the way down to the highway.

"Well, let's get them home." I really tried to keep my voice steady, but anxiety mixed with nausea sent my stomach into a fit. Will had begun to back up to see why Troy and I had stopped, but I waved him forward.

By the time we had the heifers back on the ranch and situated in another pasture away from the road, it was almost noon. I went inside and called the sheriff's office.

"Sky, we can't have this kind of thing happening. If..."

"You better come out here and take a look," I cut him off before he could continue his lecture.

"What do you mean?"

"I mean you better come out and look at the fence." It took all my self-control to keep my voice beneath a shout. The fact that he automatically blamed me made it hard.

"I'll be right out." He answered. Thankfully he was level-headed and probably realized that he better do his job and get the facts before blaming me.

I grabbed a heavier coat, a wool hat and gloves before going out. In the barn, I re-saddled Buster with my saddle. Only around fifty of the herd had gone through the fence and I decided it was up to me to find the rest. I told Troy to go home and have some lunch.

"I'll be back in twenty minutes." I knew he wanted to check on his family and I didn't blame him.

Then I turned to Will. "You don't have to come," I told him.

"Yeah, I think I better." He replied. I shrugged and turned to mount Buster.

"I'll meet you down there." I called back over my shoulder as I rode off.

It didn't take long before I caught glimpses of the remainder of the herd down in the trees along the creek. I would come for them after I met with the sheriff.

Will and I waited for Wallace at the cut in the fence. He pulled up, took one look at the blatant vandalism and became very concerned. I was sure the same person came to our mind as the probable culprit, but I had a couple more suspects in mind as well.

He went out into the field and examined the tire tracks that had spun into the dirt, leaving circular skid marks. Horseback, I could survey the damage from a higher viewpoint.

"There's two sets of tracks," I called out. From my perspective atop Buster, the trespassers' moves became more obvious. The three of us converged back at the break in the fence.

"How many were killed?" I had been too determined to get the rest to safety to fully assess the massacre.

"Three out right. We shot two others. Jack Marsh went out and cleaned up the highway." I nodded. The man mentioned was a relative of Billy's. Since he lived nearby, I imagine he went over in his tractor and dragged the dead animals off. I would call him and offer payment for his time.

"What do we do now?" Will asked the sheriff.

"We'll keep our eyes out, spread the word to look for anything suspicious. Hopefully if they make any more attempts, we'll catch 'em." He looked up at me. "Come by the office tomorrow morning and we'll do the paperwork." He got in his pickup and drove off.

I told Will I'd see him back home and set off to round up the other heifers. He met Troy on the road and stopped to fill him in on what we had found. I tried to keep my chin pushed down inside my coat against the cold as I trotted off to where I had seen the rest of the herd.

My thoughts were on who would have wanted revenge on the D. I kept seeing the mocking faces of the two cowboys I had fired, but I also wondered if Rad Johnson was to blame. Then I thought about my great grandpa Matt and wondered how he would have dealt with this situation. After what I had learned about him, I doubted he would have relied on the law to take care of it. I decided anyone caught messing with his cattle would have been hung from the nearest tree.

The two men sat in the pickup waiting for me an hour later. Troy got out and swung the gate open as I guided the bunch towards it. He counted them as they went through. Once I got through on Buster, he pushed it shut again.

"What's the count?" My anxiety hadn't lessened as I worried that some might still be missing, maybe stolen.

"It adds up." I nodded to him as he hesitated a second. "Do you want me to take over?" I knew both men were probably feeling a little guilty, sitting in the warm pickup while I rode out in the cold, but I needed the feel of a horse beneath me and the harshness of the elements just then.

"I got it," I answered and rode on.

When Will and I entered the kitchen at dusk, breakfast sat on the table where we had dropped our forks early that morning. I sat down and picked up a piece of cold toast.

"Don't eat that," Will told me. I looked up at him, numb not only from the cold, but also from the events of the day. I had felt hungry, but now looking at the congealed fat covering the limp bread, I lost my appetite. Suddenly the whole day was summed up as I sprinted for the toilet, unable to hold back the retching any longer.

Will put me to bed just like I was a little kid. If I hadn't felt so weak and exhausted I would have been amused at his fussing over me. But I was touched by his concern. As he carefully crawled into bed beside me, I felt closer to him than I ever had. I whispered a feeble thank you as he snuggled up close to me.

That night I dreamed about dead cattle scattered across a dark highway. When I went over for a closer look, an eerie light revealed Ursula's face on each of them. I jerked awake and lay there for hours worrying about what had happened.

The next morning started way too early. Even though I felt tired, I got out of bed in the dark. My stomach still didn't feel right and I rummaged in the cupboard for tea. As soon as there was light enough to see, I went out and fed Buster. The cold air revived me and I leaned on the fence rail to watch him eat for a few minutes.

During the ride home the day before, I had made a decision. At the first opportunity I would take Troy and go horse shopping. It just wasn't right that we had only one horse between us. Bobbie hadn't called about her horse and it seemed she had lost interest in him. The first thing would be to call her and see if she wanted to sell Buster. I had watched Troy throw a rope from his back and he had taken the loop snaking out from above in stride. He was on the verge of becoming a reliable ranch horse. But we needed at least one other horse. Two riders would have made trailing the heifers home the day before much easier.

I walked back up to the house. When I entered, the smell of coffee hit me. Normally I loved the aroma in the morning, but not today. Will wanted to make me breakfast, but I declined. The stress of the day before was again causing my stomach all kinds of distress.

"I have to get to town." It was a poor excuse not to eat.

"Well, I'm coming too."

"No, just stay here. I can take care of it."

"Right. You think I didn't feel you tossing and turning all night? Come on, I'll drive."

I didn't mind being a passenger on our trip to town. I had only objected to his coming because I didn't want to drag him into my mess. He steered one handed, holding my left hand with his free one, sometimes a little too tightly, as we drove to town. It seemed like there was something on his mind, but I didn't ask about it. We both remained silent as we stared straight ahead.

That evening, back home, he cooked me soup and brewed something called chamomile tea. I sniffed the strange smelling stuff and pushed it away.

"No thanks."

"What if it helps you feel better?" he reasoned with me, and pushed the cup back over. Reluctantly I drank the bland brew. I didn't like it, but it wasn't awful either. And it did seem to ease the ache in my stomach. I was so exhausted that, not long after I ate, I went up to bed.

The next morning I woke up, feeling groggy from a sound night's sleep. I wasn't yet fully awake when I became aware of Will sitting on the bed next to me. His look of concern didn't lessen when he saw my eyes were open.

"Are you pregnant?" He quietly asked.

Chapter 18

I shot up into a seated position, as seemingly out of the blue, for some reason, was the possibility that my greatest fear had become real. Suddenly the loss of D cattle paled in comparison to this bigger threat.

Will's eyes never left mine. I got all the way out of bed and stood in front of him before I spoke.

"That's impossible. Isn't it? Why would you say that?"

"You know, the nausea you've been feeling…morning sickness?"

"No. It can't be." The bad feeling in the pit of my stomach had turned to pure terror. I never would have considered that to be the cause of my discomfort. I figured I had caught a bug somewhere. Actually, I wasn't even sure what the symptoms of pregnancy were. It just wasn't something I ever thought about. Now, it seemed

Will, once again, knew more about the female body than I did. He continued studying me.

"You wouldn't think so." He answered me. I also watched him carefully, trying to determine what he was thinking, but not saying. That he seemed at a loss for words worried me further.

"What are we going to do?"

"I guess we better find out." He paused for my reaction, but I didn't know what to say either. This couldn't be happening on top of the fact that someone had it out for me. After a moment, he asked, "Do you want to talk about this now, or wait until we know?" He was so level-headed; it drove me crazy. I squashed the feeling of panic deep into my gut and refused to consider the possibility.

"It'll have to wait. I have to deal with this other stuff first." Putting off finding out if I was pregnant seemed by far the best option.

We decided to find a doctor over in Billings. That way, there was no possibility of gossip around town. When we received the news that, yes, I had gotten myself knocked up, I thought I must be cursed. I wanted to blame Will, but the fact was, neither of us had been paying attention to when we had sex. The thing I wanted least to happen was as much my fault as his. Still, I couldn't help thinking, so much for the Japanese diet form of birth control.

We drove home from Billings pretty much in silence. My worst fear had materialized and was now replaced by the redundant fear that Will would take off again, only this time I would be stuck with a baby to raise by myself. My mind churned with worry. Will was my best friend, at least he had been, but I had no idea how to talk to him about this. I felt distance growing between us and by the time we reached the D, the gap seemed too wide to cross.

"Hey, we'll get through this." He grabbed my arm as I turned away from him once we were in the house.

"How? I don't want a child and neither do you."

"I could get used to the idea of being a father."

"What about me?"

He got a concerned look on his face. "You're not thinking about having an abortion, are you?"

I didn't admit to him that the thought had crossed my mind. "What do you care?" As afraid as I was of his answer, I had to find out where he stood.

"Well, I don't think that's the answer."

"Why not? Then you wouldn't have to feel bad about leaving." The words just slipped out as I had never intended to tell him about the fear I couldn't seem to shake.

"You think I'm going to split on you?" His incredulous tone was only slightly reassuring.

"Well, what are you going to do?"

He sat down in a chair, pulled me onto his lap and wrapped me in his arms. "Shouldn't it be what are we going to do?"

The relief I felt was quickly replaced by the realization that he and I were going to have a baby together. I pulled away, sizing him up. Then I asked something I had been wondering for a long time.

"What do you see in me?"

"I see a beautiful, strong woman." He never hesitated with his reply.

They were alien words to me as I had never considered myself attractive and I was always wishing I was stronger. I didn't know what to say. I looked away, but first caught his expression as it turned to worry.

"No, I'm not having an abortion." As much as I really would have liked the problem to just go away, the thought of killing the fetus inside of me was too repulsive.

The look of relief on his face surprised me. I never thought he would want to get stuck with a kid. It was something I thought protected me from becoming like Ursula. He pulled me closer and I leaned against him, my head resting on his shoulder. I couldn't begin to describe what I felt. We sat silent for a couple minutes and then he spoke again.

"I love you. You know that, don't you?" He had never spoken the words to me and hearing them also took me by surprise.

I sat up. "Um, yeah, I guess." I stammered. The look of disappointment on his face made me realize just how into our relationship he was. He loosened his grip and I stood up.

"Why do you think I'm living here in the middle of a bunch of rednecks?"

"Well, I figured you like me."

"Is that all? What about you? Do you want to keep going with this, or should we just quit?" Now he had made himself vulnerable.

Maybe this is what love was, I thought. Not intense feelings, but just feeling comfortable and getting along well. Maybe I had watched too many movies and was waiting for something that didn't really exist. I looked him square in the eye, knowing I had to be honest.

"I really don't know." I was letting my best friend down, but it was the truth. I immediately became afraid of his reaction.

"Really? You don't know how you feel about me after all this time?"

"I guess I always figured this was temporary, that you would get tired of living here, or of me and move on."

He stood up and came over to where I leaned on the counter, once again lessening the distance I had put between us. "I can't think of anything I would rather do than stay here and raise a child with you. But I'll leave if you want me to."

"I don't want you to go, but I don't want to end up like Ursula."

"You're not your mother and I'm not your father. If you want, I'll cook and change shitty diapers and you can ride every day."

I had to smile at the image of Will in the reverse role, wearing an apron and waving to me from the door, a dish towel in his hand, as I rode out to move cattle. "That would get old in a hurry, I bet."

He smiled too. "Yeah, it would. But we'll figure things out as we go." Our talk made me feel slightly better, but I still had a long ways to go before I was ready to become a mother.

For the next few days, I didn't know how to direct my mind. I went from worrying about the stampeded cattle to the fear that, being pregnant, I was going to become Ursula, back and forth, back and forth. Added to that was the nausea I now felt daily. I didn't know how my life could have taken such a wrong turn. Just a few days earlier everything seemed to be going along so well, and then suddenly things completely fell apart.

"I want to call Shawn," Will told me one evening.

"What for?" I had asked him to wait before telling anyone about my pregnancy, to give me a little time to let it sink in.

"Because she has a friend who could help you."

"What do you mean?"

"She's into herbs. She knows what would make you feel better." I had stopped listening, but he kept pushing. "Come on, isn't it worth a shot. It can't hurt." The only herbs I had ever seen were the strange teas that Will bought and I was suddenly fed up with what seemed like voodoo and potions that he and his California friends were into.

"Just leave me alone."

My cranky reply didn't stop him. He dialed the number and spoke into the phone. I tried to slip past him through the doorway, but he shoved it towards me.

"Here, Shawn wants to talk to you." With my escape blocked, I reluctantly took the handset and said hello.

"Congratulations!" Shawn's enthusiastic voice came over the line. I glared at Will for blabbing the news.

I knew the correct response should be to say thank you, but I couldn't do it. She didn't wait, but gushed on.

"This is so cool. "When are you due?"

"Not until next summer." I finally forced some words out.

"Have you told Will's parents yet? His mom's a trip, don't you think?"

Will's parents, I groaned inwardly. I hadn't even thought about that aspect of my pregnancy. "I've never met them and we haven't told anyone yet."

"What's going on?" She finally realized I didn't share her happiness. I glanced around and noticed Will had gone upstairs.

"I'm just not ready for this," I confided, realizing the real reason he had called his old friend. He knew I needed someone to talk to, besides him, about this major change in our lives.

There was a pause. "But you're going to have the baby?

"Yes," I told her, although, part of me felt weak for not being able to take care of the problem once and for all.

"You know what, I have more vacation time coming. I think it's time to take a trip and I would love to see you and Will. And you should meet my herbalist friend. She's also a midwife. I'll see if she wants to come along."

We left it at that. Shawn told me she'd let me know when they were coming, probably in a month or so. Meanwhile she would have the midwife send me some herbs I could brew as tea to help with the morning sickness. I hung up the phone, knowing there was no reason to bring a midwife. I would have the baby in the hospital where I was born.

A couple weeks later Shawn called us back. I supposed it was to let us know her plans, but the conversation quickly become serious. Will turned to me.

"Shawn wants to know if it's all right to bring Eric along. Apparently he's in some kind of trouble."

I didn't mind and we both wondered what he could have gotten himself into. When they showed up less than a week later, we got the story. His parents had tried to commit him to a mental institution because his anti-social behavior was getting even worse and he refused to do anything about it. Apparently they had already made the arrangements, but then he disappeared. His mother called Shawn looking for him and explained that they simply didn't know what else to do with him.

When he showed up at her house, she called the D before helping him escape to Montana. The three of them, Shawn, Eric and Joanie, the midwife, arrived at the ranch a few days later. Once more I welcomed the unhappy war veteran into my home.

"They were just going to lock him up." Shawn's voice sounded indignant as she told us what happened.

"Man, I wish there was something I could do," Will replied.

We were discussing Eric, while he wandered around outside. Despite the cold weather, it was where he preferred to be.

"He can stay here." The words came out of my mouth before I even thought. All three looked at me. "I mean, if he wants to."

"Are you sure?" The hope in Shawn's voice sounded like I was tossing her, or more likely Eric, a lifeline.

"Where would he stay?" Will asked, testing my offer.

"There are enough old houses on the D. We ought to be able to make one livable for him."

Will smiled at me like he was proud of me for offering to help his friend, but I just couldn't see Eric surviving being locked up. And maybe the generous sharing nature of Will's friends was rubbing off on me. Plus, it wasn't like I didn't have room for him.

"I'll see what Eric thinks of the idea." Will went out to find him.

He not only liked the idea, he became excited about it. He and Will set off the next morning in a light snow storm to check out possible homes.

"I guess I better tell Troy and Kate there's gonna be a wild man living here." I got up from the table. "Do you want another piece of toast?" I asked.

"No, thank you. Yeah, it'd be quite the surprise if they came across him unexpectedly." Shawn replied as Joanie shook her head at my question. We all chuckled at the thought of such an encounter.

"You know, you don't look so good." It was Joanie expressing her concern. I looked over at her, automatically wondering what business it was of hers, but I knew what she meant. Looking in the mirror was a little scary lately. The pallor of my complexion, along with the dark circles under my eyes made a ghastly combination.

She continued studying my face as I studied hers. I saw nothing but compassion in her expression and as much as I wanted to find fault with her, I couldn't. In fact, except for the fact that she wanted to tell me how to handle my pregnancy, I liked her. Her face, with its cute little nose and delicate features seemed to always have an agreeable expression. She appeared to be a genuinely happy person.

I had noticed her quietly watching me since she arrived, but she had said nothing. By now both she and

Shawn both must have realized I was avoiding talking about my pregnancy.

"There's just been so much going on," I suddenly began. And then my voice just kept going. I told them everything that had been going on lately, as the expressions on their faces turned from amazement to shock.

Shawn shook her head as I finished. "You must have some kind of weird karma."

I didn't know what she meant, but I accepted her sympathy. "I just don't know why I had to get pregnant now." The whine in my voice was becoming unbearable to me.

"Have you been making tea with the herbs I sent you?" Joanie asked me. Will had tried to get me to, but I refused.

"I haven't really had time."

"You need to start taking care of yourself." Just like Will's lectures on nutrition, her words went unheard by me. I guess my disinterest in my own or the baby's health prompted a lecture about the importance of eating right and taking care of myself. I listened, but couldn't relate to her words as I still couldn't picture myself as a mother.

Will and Eric came back a few hours later. They had found what Eric considered the perfect home. Up at the head of a short draw was an abandoned cabin. There was no longer even a road up to it, but Eric had spied it off in the distance, so they went to look at it.

Although most of the old buildings on the D were named after their previous owners, I had no idea who had built this one. It was only a single room, maybe twenty by twenty feet, with an outhouse in the back.

"What kind of shape is it in?" I couldn't imagine it could be made habitable after all this time.

"The walls are sturdy." Eric told me.

We all loaded up in my car to go have a look. I viewed the cracks between the weathered logs that showed daylight where the chinking had fallen out. The building looked beyond repair to me, but Eric was enthusiastic, so I listened to his and Will's ideas.

"We could cut a window here." Will indicated the east side of the tiny log house. "And we'd need to put in a woodstove." He watched my face as he spoke since any money spent would be mine. But I wasn't worried about the expense as I knew Will's knack for pinching pennies and for finding deals.

Once outside again, I looked around. The cabin was in a great spot. Because there was underground water, a small forest of cottonwood and willow surrounded the cabin.

The spring had been developed up above and the water piped down to the house. There was no electricity, which Eric said he didn't need. He'd have to use the outhouse, but that didn't bother him either. And I supposed he could come down to the headquarters to shower.

I made a deal with him. In exchange for repair work around the D, he had a place to live and a salary. He told me he didn't need any pay, but I insisted. I had already seen how handy he was with a hammer and that was just what I needed.

The next day there was a break in the weather. The wind died down and the sky cleared. With the still air and the sunshine, the cold hardly mattered, so Will and Eric went right to work restoring the cabin.

I spent the next week mainly in the company of other women. It was the most female companionship I had had for quite a while. I felt lazy hanging around the house, but it also felt good to just lounge. Joanie encouraged me to take naps and I actually took her suggestion.

One evening I called Kate and she arranged to spend the next afternoon with us. Troy dropped her off on his way to town with their children.

Shawn and Joanie had decided to have a tea party to celebrate my pregnancy. They baked treats and served tea with little cut-up sandwiches. I helped them dig out a table cloth and the old china and the four of us sat around the decorated table. It was fun acting goofy and giggling and I found myself feeling better than I had in a long time. We also discussed serious subjects.

"How can you stand being around that kind of thing all the time?" I asked Shawn. She had been describing her job to me. Basically, she did what she could to help women trying to escape abusive situations.

"Every time I see a light go back on in their eyes when they see someone is on their side, it makes it all worthwhile." It was just one of the conversations that helped me expand my thoughts beyond the D for a while.

A couple days later, Shawn and Joanie left to go back to California. As we said goodbye, both of them again urged me to use a midwife for the delivery. I told them I'd think about it, but knew I wouldn't.

"Shawn likes Eric," I told Will after they left.

"What ? You're crazy. She's just helping him out."

"It's more than that." I had seen her wistful look in his direction when I encouraged her to come back.

"We'll see," she had said.

The sunny weather remained and one afternoon I ventured out on horseback for a couple of hours. I rode over to the cabin to see the progress Eric and Will were making. The short distance made it a perfect winter ride, as I'd easily be home before dark.

On my way back, as I rounded the last turn and the back side of the ranch headquarters came into view, I heard the sound of tires spinning in the driveway. Buster raised his head, also startled by the sharp scratching in the dirt. I kicked him up into a lope to see what was going on.

By the time I reached the house, the vehicle was gone. It caused me to again worry about, not only the safety of my cattle, but whether somebody might cause trouble for the D out of spite.

The week before, while in town shopping, I had received what seemed an ominous warning. The surly cashier at the local IGA, a middle aged woman who had stood behind the counter for as long as I could remember had said to me, "You think you're somebody, stealing your daddy's ranch. Well, you'll get yours!"

I stared at her for a moment, shocked at her words. Without even attempting a reply, I gathered up the grocery bags and left the store. Once outside I paused and looked around, feeling alienated in my home town. I knew there had been gossip going around about the D. Some of it had been repeated to me, about how uppity I was to have fired the two men I had just hired. Since I knew the cashier only from the store, it seemed uncalled for. I tried to ignore her bitter words.

The way people in the community reacted to my taking over the D was hard to believe. Many of them weren't the least bit shy about voicing their opinions. I was developing a thick skin because I never knew who would lash out at me, or when, and I usually didn't see it coming.

"I heard you let your cattle out on the highway. Don't you have enough land, you want to take over the highway too?" The comment came from an old rancher and it was not only ignorant, it was mean. Once again, I was too shocked to become angry and I struggled to see his point of view. A twenty-five year girl old running a cattle ranch not only stretched his belief system, it seemed to threaten the basis of his life.

I left the feed store that day thinking that I was no different than the hippies fighting what they referred to as the establishment, wanting to destroy the social structures that were in place and open people's minds to a different, hopefully better way of doing things. Except I didn't have the support of millions of others who wanted the same thing.

Equally ignorant was a remark made to me about the subdivision. "Following along in your mother's footsteps, are you? Pretty soon you won't have anything left to sell. Then what'll you do?" Once again I just stood there staring at the man, dumbfounded by the remark.

"I just can't believe I never saw this before. I never realized people around here are so opposed to women controlling land. What's wrong with it? Why are women so against it?" I asked Will that evening.

He shook his head. "I guess they're just jealous. You have something they'll never have."

"Well, it's not like I stole the D. No one else wanted it. And it's not like running it has been a piece of cake."

"I know, I know," he used a quieting tone that had the opposite effect on me.

One night I was home completely alone for the first time in a while. It was about a month after Eric had come and he had just moved into his remote new home. Will was away and even the Thomas' had left for the weekend. I was thinking about heading up to bed and wondered where Tag could be. He had become good friends with Eric and occasionally followed him home.

I saw movement outside the kitchen window and thought it must be Eric bringing the dog back. I turned to open the door, but it burst open before I got there. Quickly Fred Patterson, one of the cowboys I had fired, stepped through.

"Hello, Sky." He shut the door behind him and his smirk told me he was up to no good. I didn't know whether to stand my ground or run. There was a noise behind me. I turned and Jake Blackburn, the other low-life I had run off, entered through the living room.

"Well, it looks like we have ourselves a party now, doesn't it?"

"Get out of here!" I tried to sound tough, but there was fear in my voice. The two men just laughed.

"No, we didn't like the way we were treated the last time we were here. This time we expect something different."

I wasn't sure what they intended, and I was trapped. They inched closer, enjoying their game.

"I hear you let your cattle out on the highway. We don't know nothing about that, do we Jake?"

"Not a thing."

I knew it was their way of gloating without admitting they had run my cattle out onto the highway. What a couple of idiots, I thought, because now I knew for sure who had caused the death of D cattle. Meanwhile, they continued coming towards me.

I could see there was a little hesitation on their part and waited for my chance. The latch on the kitchen door needed adjusting, which made it difficult to close tight. I dared a quick peek and could see the door was just barely open.

As Fred turned slightly, I made my move. I darted towards the door, trying to get past him. He reached out to grab me, but was suddenly slammed to the floor. By the time I realized what had happened, Eric had rolled against the sink and was back on his feet. Fred got up more slowly, but Eric didn't pause. Before Fred fully had his balance, he kicked out and landed a side shot to Fred's knee. With a cry of pain, he went down again.

Jake was next and he tried to defend himself, but Eric was too quick. He got between Jake's fists and had him on the ground before he could connect. I turned my attention back to Fred. He was getting to his feet. I looked for a weapon, but he headed for the door, hopping on his good leg. Jake made a hasty exit out the front door, his nose bloodied from hitting the floor face down with his arms pinned.

Eric and I just stood there and let them get away. I was in shock. It had all happened so quickly. I imagined my eyes were as round as his as we stared at one another.

He looked out the window to make sure the two were leaving. The sound of a racing motor told me they were.

"I guess some of that shit they taught me did come in handy," he said in a matter-of-fact voice, as his breathing returned to normal. We stared at one another again.

"Thank you." They were the only words I could get out.

He just nodded. I knew Eric considered himself a pacifist and did his best to avoid any kind of conflict. Luckily he hadn't hesitated to take action when it was needed.

"I don't think we should tell anyone about this." I added.

"No, no one," he agreed. I knew I couldn't get the sheriff involved because Eric didn't want the attention. Except for a short telephone call to his parents to let them know he was all right, he had had no communication with them. He hadn't told them where he was because he thought they might be looking for him.

I also didn't want Will worrying about me. It was time to take care of my own problems. And I didn't want to worry the Thomas' either. They were loyal to the D, but I didn't want to find out how far it went.

"I better go get Tag. I put him in your car when I saw who was here. I didn't want him to get hurt." I couldn't suppress a slight smile. How many people would have worried about a dog? He went to release Tag while I closed the bathroom window he had snuck through.

My mind refused to focus on the implication of what had just happened. The two men obviously still held a grudge and I don't know what they would have done to me. The thought that finally stuck was that my main motivation for preventing anything from happening to myself was because of the little life growing inside of me. It was the first time I felt the instinct of wanting to protect my child. I finally acknowledged to myself that I was going to be a mother.

After that I felt a lot closer to Eric. Will, who never missed a thing, noticed that I went out of my way to fix him a meal whenever he appeared at the house. After fighting off the two revenge seeking ex-employees, I was willing to do anything for him.

"What happened here when I was gone?" He asked me one night as we prepared for bed.

"What do you mean?"

"You and Eric sure seem tight all of a sudden."

I shrugged. "He's a nice guy. I want him to feel comfortable here." Will studied my face. He didn't look convinced, but said nothing more. I had the brief thought that I hoped he didn't think we had cheated on him.

There was an obvious change in Eric that winter. It was as if his life began making a little sense. Although he still mainly did his own thing, when he did come around, he talked more and began smiling again. Whenever he came to visit, he walked the mile and a half down to the ranch headquarters. In fact he walked all over the place. Sometimes we didn't see him for days, and some days we only saw him from far away. He really was the wild man living on the D. And I was grateful to have him.

Of course I didn't know what Fred and Jake might try next. I also didn't know what I could do to prevent them from trying. I became more aware and made sure Tag stayed around at all times. What worried me was that they seemed to know I was alone that night. I wondered if they had been watching the place and if they still were. But with Will, plus the Thomas' nearby, not to mention Eric, I felt fairly safe.

The incident increased my anger towards them. I wanted revenge and thought about ways of going about it. Each plan ended with images of them lying slaughtered and bleeding, just like my cattle had been out on the highway.

Chapter 19

The windshield intensified the sun and I felt hot enough to bake in the solar oven it created. I shifted on the seat in an attempt to get comfortable as I looked out the side window. Off in the distance Will was moving a canvas dam further down a ditch. I grew more irritated as I watched his pathetic attempts. I knew I was being hard on him, but I just wanted him to get the dam set so we could get going to my doctor's appointment. I moved again, but there wasn't a whole lot I could do to ease my discomfort as my big belly was in the way.

Will and I were on our way to my weekly checkup. Since I was over eight months pregnant, I wasn't allowed to work. Troy and my other hired help had taken over the job of irrigating, but today Will offered to move the water in this spot as it was on our way to town.

I thought the attempts at keeping me sedentary were ridiculous. Staring out at him, I knew that even in my so-called delicate condition, I could have had the water running onto the field and been half way to town by now. He struggled as the ditch water took the dam every time he attempted to place it.

It seemed he had imposed ridiculous restrictions on me throughout the pregnancy. I accused him of being a drill sergeant, someone I knew he would hate being compared to. But he promised Shawn and Joanie to take care of me and didn't relent. Since they left he had convinced me to give up coffee and what he considered unhealthy eating practices. I had always considered that food was food. My only standards for what I ate were what tasted good.

As usual, he had other ideas. Since he did a lot of the cooking, he also did most of the grocery shopping. That meant the food he stocked the kitchen with changed as he managed to come home without many of my staples. Apparently, somewhere along the way, he had become an expert on nutrition.

A lot of the new foods I enjoyed, like whole wheat bread, but the disappearance of some things irritated me. He refused to bring home bacon. When he attempted to explain the dangers of things called nitrates that were added to cured meats to preserve them, my eyes glazed over. I had always thought that if it sat on a grocery shelf, it must be nutritious.

Reluctantly I agreed to the changes since I had learned long ago not to anger the cook, but I disliked being told what to do. Of course the doctor was doing the same and that was another reason for my annoyance.

Their attitudes made me want to dig in my heels in protest.

"Jeez, where'd you learn to irrigate?" I couldn't resist a sarcastic comment after he finally got the dam to hold and trekked back over the field to the road. He opened the rear door of the car.

"It's harder than it looks," he admitted as he replaced rubber boots for the sneakers stashed in the back. Of course he had never learned the tricks.

Once the car was in motion I felt a little better from the cool breeze it created. I was only a couple weeks away from giving birth and I felt almost as unprepared for adding a child to my life as when I had first found out I was pregnant the winter before.

I dreaded the weekly visits to the doctor. The cold, institution feel to the exam room made me uncomfortable, plus it seemed like a waste of time. After each quick exam, the doctor said everything was fine and sent me home.

This week he had Will and I come to his office afterwards. He started in about the delivery and the procedure for being admitted to the hospital when the time came and the conversation immediately became uncomfortable.

"Umm...," I didn't know how to bring up our plans.

"We decided to have the baby at home." Will finished.

"That's not a good idea." The doctor, a young man, barely out of medical school cautioned. He had recently replaced Dr. Carey, the ancient old doctor who had delivered me and most of the babies in Compton for the last forty years. "There are all kinds of things that can go wrong. You need to be in a hospital where you can receive expert care."

"We have a midwife who has helped deliver over a hundred babies." I replied. I couldn't believe that this man had overseen a tenth that number.

"Midwives are not trained professionals. They have neither the expertise nor the equipment to respond to complications. We're no longer in the Middle Ages, you know." He gave a condescending chuckle at our ignorance.

"You tell me every week I couldn't be healthier and now you expect complications?" I felt cranky enough to start an argument. Will darted me a look.

"I can't believe you would even consider such a dangerous practice."

Will stood up. He took my arm, helped me up out of the chair and urged me towards the door. The doctor's scare tactics were intended to put doubt in our minds, but he knew that the attempts at intimidation would only bring out belligerence in me.

I ducked down into the car as Will held the door open. After sliding in behind the steering wheel on the opposite side, he looked over at me.

"Are you sure you want to stay at home for this?"

"After the way that idiot treated me?"

"That's what I figured."

I had considered a home birth for the first time in the spring. Once the heifers had calved and I saw the young mothers with their small calves out on the new grass, I thought again about what Joanie, the midwife, had told me.

When she visited the winter before, she had explained that giving birth involved more than having a baby, that it also kept the land alive. The concept had been way over my head. But now, maybe I was turning into a weirdo myself, because after watching the mothering instincts of the young cows kick in, my perception shifted.

There had also been a conversation about women taking control of their own bodies instead of relying on medical doctors who seemed to know little about the natural birthing process. Both women had insisted that I could have a much better experience at home. In the end I agreed to have the birth in a more natural setting.

We had already been in touch with Joanie. She had questioned me to make sure my decision was final. I knew it for sure when Will and I moved back into the cabin for the summer, as that gave me the best plan yet. I decided I wanted my baby born in the same place my great grandmother had hers.

Joanie also asked about my health and eating habits before she agreed to make the trip back out to Montana. She wasn't going to take on a birth if she thought there was the possibility of complications. She also warned us that the doctor would attempt to convince us that a hospital birth was the only safe way to have a child. I decided it was one more thing I could prove others wrong about.

Everybody knew Will and I weren't married and that we didn't intend to. I received additional unsolicited comments, mainly warnings, about this next big mistake I was making. The words were almost comical, about how a man who wouldn't put a ring on my finger was unreliable and how stupid I was not to see that he would quickly abandon me once the baby came. In their eyes, apparently, trapping him was the only way to keep him around.

It was another thing we discussed. Will asked me if I wanted to get married. It wasn't a proposal, just an inquiry on how I felt about it. I knew by then that he wasn't going anywhere and I had heard enough gossip about us to get my hackles up.

I decided that having a child out of wedlock would really give them something to talk about. We were already living in sin, may as well add some spice to it. Besides, I knew that if marriage was important to me, Will would go through with it. That was enough for me.

All my worries about our compatibility had vanished. I was beginning to see that, despite our different upbringings, we turned out to be a lot alike. From the first summer I knew him, we had continued to grow closer and even when we were apart he had maintained that closeness the best he could. I could no longer imagine my life without him.

Of course, all that had happened during the spring when the weather was still cool, and before I had gotten so big and uncomfortable. Now it was midsummer and hot. I just wanted the pregnancy over with so I could go back to my regular routine and start riding again. The two horses I had bought, Buster and another one from the same outfit, were only being ridden by Troy. I didn't know if it seemed my main objective for wanting the birth to happen was so that I could ride again, but it was high on the list.

The trouble I had with the two men I fired faded as this new change to my life loomed. Once the word about my pregnancy got around, I figured I was safe anyway, as I couldn't imagine anyone wanting to hurt an innocent baby. Part of me still wanted a chance for revenge, though.

I paced the kitchen floor, once again nervous about impending company. This time it was Will's parents we were expecting. They left Ohio a few days before and had just called from town, so would be arriving at any time.

I guess there were still old-fashioned beliefs imbedded in my mind because the thought of having to face the parents of the man who I was not married to, but whose child I carried, made me uneasy. Will had told me over and over not to worry, but I feared their judgment of me.

The commotion on the back staircase as he clumped down the steps momentarily interrupted my thoughts. He entered the kitchen and the happiness at his parents arriving for the birth showed on his face. He came over and gave me a hug.

"Want to drive down to the highway with me to make sure they don't miss the turn?"

"No, go ahead. I want to try and relax for a minute." He took off and I continued my pacing, while examining the kitchen with a critical eye.

With Eric doing most of the work, we had redone the room, replacing the metal cabinets with wooden ones, stained to show the grain of the wood. The yellow walls were repainted pale green and the old counter tops replaced with off-white formica. I even splurged and had a larger window put in. It seemed like a brand new room.

I entered the living room and gave it the same scrutiny. All remnants of Ursula were gone from there as well. The shag carpeting had been pulled up to again reveal the pine floor. After stripping the paper, the plaster walls were back to the original white and the old bookcase once again occupied its place behind a new sofa. Tag barked and I went out to meet my latest company.

Will's parents stepped out of their car and looked around as I lumbered down the sidewalk. Upon seeing me, they hurried over to greet me with huge grins on their faces. Will was close behind.

"You must be Sky. It's so nice to finally meet you!" His mom gushed as she patted my protruding belly.

"This is a beautiful place you have here, Sky." His dad seemed equally enthusiastic about meeting me. I invited them inside.

The four of us sat around the kitchen table sipping lemonade as we talked. Bert and Kitty, as they wanted to me to call them, were impressed with the D and especially with the fact that I was running the ranch by myself.

It soon became obvious that Will got his good nature from his dad and his unique perspective from his mom. Like Shawn had said, she was a trip, from her oversized sunglasses to her bright-colored clothing.

Will couldn't contain his happiness and I couldn't help but notice the difference between his family and mine. Where the Dalys usually sat in restrained silence, the Daniels' were outgoing almost to the point of being obnoxious. Their cheerful laughter enlivened the entire house. And once again, my fears about being judged turned out to be unfounded.

The birth happened just like we planned. Well, just like everyone else planned. Shawn came back to the D with Joanie so we had a houseful for the event. I felt like the main attraction in the middle of a three ring circus, a place where I wasn't comfortable.

Both of Will's parents supported our decision of a home birth, although Bert insisted on being prepared for a speedy trip to town just in case. I didn't disagree as I had a few last minute jitters.

Kitty was behind a home birth because she had no use for doctors. There was anger in her voice when she spoke about them. She told us about an experimental drug that had been prescribed to her when she was pregnant with Will. It had messed up her reproductive system and she had never been able to conceive again. That was why Will was an only child. Shawn and Joanie shook their heads in sympathy as she described how believing that the doctor knew best had not only destroyed her fertility, but had also greatly increased the chances her son would be born with birth defects. Thankfully that hadn't happened.

So, yeah, the place was a little crazy. I was uncomfortable being the center of attention until the labor began and the contractions got so bad I didn't care anymore. Of course Joanie then shut the door to the bedroom so it was only her, me and Will inside. I briefly thought about my great grandmother, Lavina, and wondered how her birthing had gone. I hoped easier than mine because it was far worse than I ever imagined. I was finally happy about the birth just because the pain stopped.

I had agonized over the sex of the baby and thought about the implications of having one over the other. Will was happy either way. In the end, I decided I preferred a girl, for obvious reasons, and that's what we got.

We had thought about different names and he had even suggested Ursula if it was a girl. There was no way I was hanging that label on her, though. There were still too many bad memories associated with the word.

We decided on Jesse Rose. It was a just different enough sounding first name and I hoped it would help prevent her from being labeled or categorized. Rose was, of course, for my grandmother. Will even insisted I use Daly as her last name. Family names meant a lot more to me than to him.

At first she seemed an odd little creature, but like her dad, she began growing on me. I surprised myself at how I immediately became protective of her. I had worried that my fear of her disrupting my life would keep me indifferent towards her and that caring for her would become a chore that filled me with resentment.

For the first couple of weeks that certainly wasn't the case. She was fussed over by all our company to the point that I didn't see enough of her.

Of course, I was comparing myself to Ursula. When I looked down at her tiny face and felt my love for her, I wondered if Ursula had ever felt that way towards me. She had to have, didn't she? Maybe that was why, in the end, at least in part, she had left me the D, because she remembered that feeling.

Jesse was three months old when strange things started happening. It was after we weaned the first crop of calves and sold them. Besides being a new mother, I had just received my first paycheck as owner of the D.

One afternoon I returned from town and heard Tag howling. I went and released him from the barn. I couldn't imagine how he had come to be locked in there. When I got up to the house, I noticed the cupboard doors were wide open. I found it odd, but I was accustomed to having people around. Maybe one of the Thomas kids had been looking for something.

When I found the medicine cabinet in the upstairs bathroom emptied, with my toothbrush and other items sitting on the counter, I got chills. I called Kate and asked if she had been over while I was in town.

"No, I haven't left here all day. Why?"

"It's nothing." I said goodbye and hung up the phone. I knew I should have found a way to take care of those two worthless cowboys.

The moved items unnerved me, but I kept my mouth shut about the incident. Then it happened again a few days later. This time I had been away from the house for barely an hour. I walked into the house holding Jesse and immediately noticed something was wrong.

Tag had been outside when I left, but he wasn't around when I returned. I finally found him laid out on the bathroom floor with the door shut. I thought he was dead until I saw him breathing. A while later he woke up and seemed confused, I had to think he had been drugged. I figured the motive was robbery and had my main suspects, but could find nothing missing. The only differences I could detect were where, once again things were rearranged. I became angry at the game that was obviously being played to intimidate me.

I realized I had some unfinished business. It was easy not to involve others since the intrusions into the house happened when I was the only one around. I never even told Will, as I was determined to deal with the problem on my own. He had never had much to say when the heifers were chased out onto the highway and I realized it stretched his beliefs that others would do such a thing. I decided he wouldn't be much help handling the situation.

I thought about Great Grandpa Matt and how determined he was to rid the D of any threats. It had caused a lot of bloodshed and he had almost lost his life, but he had never backed down. I decided I would do the same if forced to.

I also remembered what I had found out about my ancestor. I tried to imagine how he felt after losing most of his family and his friend and wondered about events we hadn't uncovered. He had never given the name of the town down in Texas where he said he had been ambushed, so I doubted I would ever discover why certain events in his life happened as they did.

We had both been driven out of Montana and comparing his flight to my own I wondered if he had felt as lost as I had. Had he forgotten about the D as he attempted a new life? In the end he had returned to successfully run the ranch. Now it was my job to do the same and ensure its survival. I had run away for the last time.

Will left for Denver to research a story. He decided to drive and took Eric with him. He had been reluctant to take the assignment, as it would be the first time away from his daughter. I had encouraged him to go because I wanted them both gone. Being alone might bring my two taunters' entertainment to a head.

Troy left on horseback that morning and I knew he wouldn't be back until later. I wished I was with him, but when I looked into my daughter's sleeping face, decided I had plenty of time to ride when she was older and could come along. I had of course been on Buster since she was born, but only for short rides.

That night I thought I saw movement outside in the bushes. Tag barked, but I saw no one. The phone rang and I jumped.

"Hello?"

"Sky?" I heard Troy's voice.

"Yeah."

"My uncle just died. Do you think it would be all right if we went over to Idaho for the funeral? We'd come right back."

"Sure." I expressed my condolences and hung up the phone. I felt myself become cold and calculating. Maybe I should have been scared at the thought of being all alone with my daughter. Instead I saw an opportunity I hoped whoever was watching me would take advantage of.

The next morning I dressed Jesse and prepared for a trip to town. I had never locked the doors before. In fact I didn't know if the doors had ever been locked, but I rummaged around in the catch-all drawer and found a key to the kitchen door. I checked the windows to make sure they were latched before I left.

I also loaded Tag into the car. Not only was I afraid of him being poisoned, but since I had found him in the bathroom he had been acting strangely. At the slightest sound he cowered at my feet. He had become worthless as a guard dog.

Outside the hardware store, I ran into an old classmate, Julie Webber. She had gone out with Jake Babcock in high school and they had resumed their relationship when he returned to Compton. She waited tables at one of the diners in town, where she had worked first summers, then full-time since graduating from high school. At the sight of a baby, she hurried over to ooh and awe.

"So, what's Jake up to?" I didn't know how to be subtle and my voice dripped with the contempt I had for him.

"That bastard. I hope I never see him again."

"What'd he do?"

"You didn't hear? Him and that Fred took off for Arizona. He talked me into lending him some money. He said it was to fix his pickup and then he just left."

"When was that?"

"A couple weeks ago. And then I find out he was getting into trouble here, stealing and stuff."

"And they haven't been back?"

"No, the sheriff was about to run them off. They're not coming back." She returned her attention to Jesse as I went numb. If they hadn't been the ones coming into my house, the suspect list was reduced to one. I said goodbye and entered the store to make a purchase.

I returned to the D, afraid of what I might find. The kitchen door stood open and a chill ran through me. I was reluctant to enter the house, but after watching Tag sniff around, I determined the intruder was gone.

Inside, a bowl lay shattered in the center of the floor. The broken pieces of china, along with the open door, were an obvious message. It unnerved me enough that I considered calling the sheriff, but I was done filling out reports. It had to be Rad Johnson playing some sick, perverted game with me and I didn't want to scare him away. I decided I was the only one who could permanently remove the threat. I didn't understand his motivation, but he must have thought he had unfinished business with the Daly family. It didn't matter. I was ready.

That evening I put Jessie to bed and went back down to fix some dinner. I didn't know for sure anything would happen that night, but thought, that with the Thomas' gone, this would be his best chance at whatever he intended.

I sat and ate, at least I went through the motions, my nerves on end. I continued sitting at the table pretending to read a book as minutes and then hours crept by. I began thinking that nothing was going to happen and that I should just go up to bed, when I heard a faint scratching sound. Tag growled, but I quickly shushed him.

The sound continued and I determined it was coming from the front door. I listened and realized the son of a bitch had a key. There was a click as the lock popped open and then the barely perceptible sound of the door knob slowly turning.

Silently I got up and eased over to poke my head around and look into the living room. Tag cowered beside me. The door was open and a man stood in the doorway. It was no one I recognized. The disheveled look with his beard and uncombed hair, plus the grimy, ragged clothing made me think it was a bum breaking into my house. He saw me and spoke.

"Hello, Sky." His attempt at a smile was more of an evil grimace that threatened to crack his face. I never would have recognized him, but the voice made me want to cringe. It was Rad Johnson. I stood my ground as I thought to myself, just one more step. It seemed like an eternity, but then he probably figured there was no hurry, as he had me trapped.

"I like what you've done to the place." His smirk seemed to become even more wicked. Finally he took a step forward. Part of me wanted to turn and run, but my child sleeping upstairs forced me to stand my ground. It was time to end this.

In one motion I stepped sideways into the doorway while raising the shot gun I held hidden at my side. Without hesitating, I aimed at his chest and fired. I watched his look turn to disbelief as the blast slammed him back against the open door. A pistol flew from his hand as he tried to pull it from his belt. He was dead by the time he hit the floor, his chest torn apart from a spray of buck shot at close range.

There was a cry of terror. The gunshot had woken Jesse. I sprinted up the stairs to her crib. Setting the gun down, I picked her up and hugged her to me.

"It's okay, everything's okay now." I went out to the hall phone and dialed.

"Sheriff's office," the sleepy dispatcher on the other end answered.

"This is Sky Daly. I just shot someone in my house."

"Will you repeat that?"

"You better send someone out here." I pushed the button down and waited for her to hang up while I reached into my pocket and pulled out a piece of paper. It was the number to the hotel where Will was staying with Eric. After a couple minutes, I got him on the line.

"I just shot Rad Johnson. You better get home."

"What? What are you talking about?" His voice became instantly frantic.

"Jessie is fine, we're both fine, but I have to go now." I disconnected the call, dropped the receiver and let it hang. Then, I sunk to the floor, clutching my daughter.

I sat there looking into her face, my tiny anchor to reality. Without her holding me there I think I would have just drifted away into nothingness. Looking into the trusting eyes that studied my own, my reality shrunk to just the two of us.

I don't know how long I sat there holding her. I just knew I never wanted to move and disrupt the peace I had finally found. I heard sirens, and then saw lights go on downstairs. My name was called, but I ignored it. Finally there were heavy footsteps as someone charged up the stairs.

"Shh, It's all right," I said to the dog that crouched beside me, as well as to my baby.

"Here she is!" Ralph Henderson reached the top and spotted me. My peaceful interlude was over. It didn't matter. I had finally realized my place in this world, protecting my daughter and my land and I now knew I was fully capable, no matter what happened. I imagined Great Grandpa Matt smiling at me and knew he had my back, two desperados protecting what was theirs. Still clinging to my daughter, I got to my feet and prepared to deal with the aftermath of my actions.

Epilogue

After Rad Johnson's death a lot of questions were answered. A grimy piece of paper was found in his pocket. It was handwritten and stated that my mother was handing the D over to him. When I was shown the paper, I examined Ursula's signature at the bottom. The handwriting looked shaky and we could only wonder if she had been forced to sign the document. It was dated just days before her will. It hadn't been notarized and so was unofficial, but obviously he thought he could take the D away from her.

From his appearance, it was obvious Johnson had been living as a vagrant, but we didn't know where until Eric and Will decided to stop at the old town of Turkey Creek to check out the ruins a month or after his death…after I killed him. That's the first time I have been able to get those words out since the night it happened.

Anyway, inside the lone intact building they found a sleeping bag and other camping gear. Outside were the remains of a campfire as well as empty cans and other garbage. Will said it looked like he had been holed up there for a while and that by using a pair of binoculars, he could easily watch the road without being seen. He knew exactly who was coming and going from the D.

The sheriff had found a stolen car hidden in a grove of trees near the creek. From there a faint trail, made by his going back and forth, cut through the trees. It ended below the barn. From there he could hunker down and watch the house and driveway unseen.

He had to have been completely crazy, as he seemed to believe that once he took care of me, he could claim the D. It would have been laughable, except that he came close to succeeding with the first part.

Hopefully, I removed the last big threat to the ranch. There will always be smaller ones, of course, since I can't control the economy or the weather. Those are persistent, but minor compared to what Great Grandpa Matt and I dealt with.

As for Jake Babcock and Fred Patterson, we recently received word of their deaths. A drunk drove head on into their pickup just after they held up a liquor store outside of Phoenix. Good riddance to bad rubbish, as the saying goes. Maybe that's being bitter, but I sure sleep better at night.

I now have to live with the fact that I took a life. Even though Rad Johnson had it coming, it's still something I regret and can never take back. I wonder how Great Grandpa Matt accepted what he did and if it changed him. I know it's changed me. It's like a heaviness on my soul that I can only hope eases somewhat as time goes on. I doubt it will ever completely go away.

I think it changed all of us. Will was so freaked about it that it became my turn to comfort him. He was angry, and rightly so, that I didn't tell him what was going on and he could barely speak to me for weeks. He seems to have gotten over it, but I doubt he will ever really understand that not only did I have to protect the D, I had to avenge my mother's death. I willingly promised there would be no more lies.

Eric didn't handle it too well either, but other than that, he's doing a lot better. Of course, he now has Shawn living with him, as she quit her job and moved here to be with him. I don't know if they'll stay on the D, but I'd like them to.

She's talked about starting a battered women's shelter in Compton. I didn't think there would be a need around here, but Shawn told me I'd be surprised at the prevalence of violence against women.

The three of them talk about the end of the hippy movement. Will says the same thing has happened throughout history when people revolt. The leaders have a vision, in this case bringing social equality to the world, while dissolving outdated hierarchies and bringing greater freedom. It started out strong. Then people who have no real passion for the cause latch on and pull it down. I have to think Billy Marsh was someone who contributed to the collapse. In attempting to escape his past, he was unable to change the circumstances that caused his unhappiness.

Once most of the communes that had sprung up around the country were abandoned, the back to the earth movement also stalled. On the D it's gaining momentum. One thing I have been able to find amusing lately is the unintentional community I started here.

Eric is determined to grow food and has turned over the soil in the old garden plot. It's going to be a learning experience for him because he'll have to adjust to the harsh growing conditions here. But my ancestors were able to feed their families, so he ought to be able to contribute food to ours.

There's been a discussion about getting chickens and even a milk cow. I have no objection, as long as it doesn't get in the way of returning the D once again to a prosperous ranch.

I don't think any of them know what to think of what I did. They were all peaceful protesters, against war and other violence and this was an eye opener for them. I think they are all a little naïve. All I can say is, I agree with Will that it's wrong to send young men over to invade other countries and kill the inhabitants, but if someone comes here and threatens me, I see nothing wrong with protecting myself and my ranch. I know my ancestors would back me.

I've thought back to my time in California and the different kind of people I met out there. I remember the shaggy looking hippies with their strange attire to match their beliefs.

But when I looked into their eyes, what I saw were people no different than the rest of us, except in the way they chose to express their outer appearance. They have souls and everything that comes with being alive. It always puzzles me that so few people are able to really see others, and instead, stop at outer appearances. Of course I discovered first-hand what it's like to be a rebel and shunned for standing up for myself.

Will and I have been through some challenging times together, going all the way back to when we first met. In fact, thinking back, I realize just how much he has stuck with me, through a lot of deaths, that's for sure. I wake up every day grateful he's in my life.

Thinking about people's comments about him becoming the boss on the D is a little bit amusing, as he still has little interest in ranching. He pitches in and helps out when needed, and has even been on Buster for a short ride or two. But his passion lies elsewhere. Maybe one day he'll write a history of the D. It would make quite a story.

It's taken a while, but gradually I'm changing my feelings towards Ursula. I doubt I will ever understand why she treated me, her own daughter, so poorly, but at least I have developed some compassion. She was trapped in her role as my mother. These days she could have freed herself by divorcing my father, an option few women had before. I doubt I will ever stop wishing my childhood was different. Will finally convinced me to visit her grave, something I had never done. I brought her granddaughter along.

I now think she wanted me to succeed when she left me the D. Maybe she did blame me for her wretched marriage, but in the end she wanted what every mother wants for her children, a happy life. Not only does that make the most sense of her actions, but for my own sake, that's what I have to believe.

There's something else I found out, something Bob Mullen, the banker, told me. He spilled his guts one evening in the spring before Jesse's birth when I stopped at The Crossing on my way home from town. Will and the Thomas family were meeting me there for dinner. I was early and went in to wait for them. The banker sat by himself at the bar. He saw me and invited me to sit next to him.

"Can I buy you a drink?"

"Can't do it," I replied.

"That's right." He glanced down at my belly, then back up at my face. "How are you getting along out there?" He looked at me intently and I realized he was wondering about more than my financial situation.

"Just fine."

"That's good." He nodded. I said nothing, as it seemed there was something on his mind. I don't know how long he had sat there, but had evidently consumed enough alcohol to divulge a secret.

"You know when your dad and I were kids, we used to talk about what we wanted to be when we grew up. He wanted to fly airplanes."

"You mean before he took over the D." Mullen let out a snort of laughter at my statement.

"No, instead of taking it over."

"You mean he never wanted to ranch?"

"No more than I wanted to be a banker." He evicted the last word from his mouth like he couldn't stand the taste of it.

"Well…" I began, but had no idea how to reply.

"He even joined the army to get away, but as soon as they found out he had come off a ranch, he was assigned to a base down in Texas. He spent the war cleaning stalls in a general's stable."

I had heard the story before and thought, like others, that my dad had been lucky avoiding combat. Afterwards he had returned to the D. I couldn't believe he had actually been trying to escape.

"So, he never wanted the D?"

"Nope, he was a victim of circumstances, the first born son and all." He looked at me to see how I took the news. "I suggested he sell the ranch so he could go off and do what he wanted, but even after your grandpa died, he couldn't do it. He felt like he would be letting your family down, even if the ones it mattered to were dead." I heard bitterness in the laugh he let out.

I sat there in shock, not believing that my dad, whom I had idolized and always wanted to be like, had been trapped, just like my mother. It explained his anger, I guess, and the fact that he never wanted to stay home. I thought about my brother Adrian, and his refusal to take over the family ranch. What would have happened if my dad had done the same thing years before. He never would have married Ursula and I don't know what I would be, if I even existed.

I often think about what was revealed to me that evening. I have to believe that neither of my parents' lives were lived in vain, that even though it wasn't their first choice, they still found purpose to their lives on the D.

I have planned a family Thanksgiving on the ranch. My brothers and sisters all agreed to come back to meet their niece. I hope they will be able to find some kind of appreciation for their childhood home. I also hope they realize that selling the ranch was never a good idea.

There's no way of knowing what's going to happen to the D in the future. All I know is that I will run it as long as I can, but eventually it's going to become someone else's responsibility. Jesse may want to run it or maybe not. After realizing that neither my father nor my mother wanted the job of preserving it and how unhappy they were at being forced into their roles, there's no way I could try and do the same to my daughter if she didn't want to stay. I tell myself to believe the future will work out for the best, whatever that may be.

I think about The Plan and how it came about in an unexpected way even after I gave up on it. I never could envision any other way of living. Even though I was forced to do things that I'll always wish I didn't, my life is working out just like I planned.

Read about the beginning of the D Rocking D ranch and the lives of Sky's great grandparents, Matt and Lavina Daly, as they helped settle the Western Frontier, in ***A Story of the West.***

To learn about me and my books, visit my website:
SusanSpenceauthor.com